Cara Lockwood is author of more than *I Do (But I Don't)*, Original movie. Sh series for young adults and has had translated into several languages around the world. Born and raised in Dallas, Cara now lives near Chicago with her husband and their blended family. Find out more about her at caralockwood.com, friend her on Facebook: Facebook.com/authorcaralockwood, or follow her on Twitter: @caralockwood, or Instagram: Instagram.com/cara_lockwood.

USA TODAY bestselling author **Jamie K. Schmidt** is known for her erotically charged romances. Jamie's books have been called 'hot and sexy, with just the right amount of emotional punch' and 'turbo-paced, gritty, highly sexual thrill rides'. A Number One Amazon bestseller, and a 2018 Romance Writers of America RITA® Award finalist in erotica, Jamie writes daily, drinks lots of tea and sneaks away to play *World of Warcraft* whenever she makes her deadlines. Along with her husband, who lets her stick magnetic signs on his car about her books, and her twelve-year-old son, who wants to be her cover model, Jamie lives in Connecticut with her rescue pup Romeo, who is cool with her writing schedule as long as he can cuddle up in a blanket next to her. You can find Jamie on Twitter: @jamiekswriter, and on Facebook at jamie.k.schmidt.1, where she'll be chatting about her latest book and wishing desperately for a kitten to be her new writing buddy and some carbs—not necessarily in that order.

CUFFS

CARA LOCKWOOD

HOLIDAY HOOKUP

JAMIE K. SCHMIDT

MILLS & BOON

First Published in Great Britain 2020
by Mills & Boon, an imprint of HarperCollins*Publishers*
1 London Bridge Street, London, SE1 9GF

Cuffs © 2020 Cara Lockwood

Holiday Hookup © 2020 Jamie K. Schmidt

ISBN: 978-0-263-27766-1

MIX
Paper from
responsible sources
FSC™ C007454

This book is produced from independently certified FSC™ paper
to ensure responsible forest management.
For more information visit www.harpercollins.co.uk/green.

Printed and bound in Spain
by CPI, Barcelona

CUFFS

CARA LOCKWOOD

MILLS & BOON

For P.J. Benoit, husband, partner,
best friend and the love of my life.

I'll happily be cuffed to you in this life and the next.

CHAPTER ONE

Mags McHenry might not believe in true love, but she sure as hell believed in hate at first sight. It was a cool autumn afternoon on the near west side of Chicago, when she saw the corporate suit who walked into her tattoo parlor and instantly fell into serious, heated hate. Sure, the man was good-looking: dark, wavy hair rolling back from his forehead, a chiseled chin that could cut glass and those vigilant green eyes. But him winning the genetic lottery only made her hate him more. Privilege and entitlement rolled off him from his expensive, custom-made suit and designer silk tie to his Italian leather lace-ups. His clothes screamed money made by soft hands.

She watched him from the corner of her eye as she paused in her work, tattoo needle in midair above the shoulder of Angus, a big, beefy bar bouncer who lay reclined on the leather client chair, arm out, patiently waiting to have the outline of his eagle tattoo finished. Angus had his eyes closed and earbuds in, listening to whatever death metal he was following this week, and hadn't noticed they had company.

The suit meandered around the lobby of her joint as if he were measuring it for new carpet. She didn't like the way he studied the wall of her tattoo art—her creations—and frowned at the line of skulls flanked with roses near the bottom row. He glanced at the expensive smart watch on his wrist, which irked. If he was going to judge her work and find it wanting, he ought to at least give it his full attention. Not that she cared for the skulls in particular, anyway. She far preferred to tattoo birds. Birds were her specialty: eagles, hawks, falcons—even sparrows. She'd been told more than once that her detail in the artwork made it look as if the bird were real, caught frozen in midflight.

The suit's pocket jangled an obnoxious ringtone, and he reached in for the brand-new, too-expensive-for-most-mortals phone and pressed it to his ear.

"Quinn," he said, briskly, all business. He listened a beat. "Look, you know we can handle seven figures," the suit said, far too loudly, as if he wanted *everyone* to hear how important he was. "We can handle eight. Or nine, for that matter."

What the hell was nine figures, anyway? Mags hadn't ever been more than a thousandaire. Money made people assholes, though. That was a fact she'd learned in her twenty-eight years on this planet. "We're not your normal bank."

Bank, one of Mags's trigger words. If possible, she

fell into deeper hate. Figured he'd work for a bank. He looked like the type who didn't mind foreclosing on single moms or wounded vets. Mags glanced around the front of the shop, ready to yell for her counter guy, John, to escort this guy out, but John was nowhere to be found. This was the second time her new hire had ducked out for a smoking break, and it was barely two in the afternoon. Good help was hard to find.

Ignore the suit and he'll go away, Mags thought as she refocused on the eagle tattoo in front of her, her attention entirely on the artwork she was creating on Angus's shoulder. Angus lay on the leather recliner in the small alcove near the lobby of her shop, complete with a sink, fresh needles, and three walls for privacy with mirrors on each one, which came in handy now that she could keep an eye on the suit without turning. A wave of her own blue hair fell into her face, and she flipped it away with a twitch of her head. She needed to pay attention to Angus, one of her best customers. She'd covered his right arm in ink and now was busy working on making the left look the same.

She heard the suit end his call and could feel his sharp gaze on her back. She wasn't going to look up. She was going to ignore him. Except that he languidly paced the lobby of her shop, like a tiger in a cage, barely restrained power in each step. Why did he feel so predatory? She wondered. It couldn't just be the tie. And why did she care? She was tracking him out of the corner of her eye, telling herself it was because she didn't trust him. Not because she was just a little bit curious about why he'd come.

Also, it seemed the suit was taking an interest in her. *Staring*, even, watching her closely. Why? Did he get off on watching tattoo artists work? She couldn't imagine why else he seemed to be locked onto her. *Ignore those intelligent green eyes*, she told herself. *Ignore that jawline so strong and chiseled it could probably whittle wood.*

"Excuse me?" The suit was talking. To her.

Ignore him. She focused on the wing of the eagle as she saw him move behind her, his reflection in the mirror in front of her.

"Excuse me?" His voice was rich, like chocolate—smooth, too. She felt the baritone in her toes. Also, since when were suits so...*tall. Broad. Intimidating.* "Sorry to bother you."

You'll be sorrier if you keep trying.

"I'm looking for Mags McHenry?"

She let out a frustrated breath. He was just like the other strangers who came looking for her by name alone, surprised to find a blue-haired Asian woman named McHenry. It was her adopted name. She'd been taken in by a sweet old Scottish couple who'd been truer parents than her own, whom she'd never known.

"I'm Mags." She raised her rotary tattoo tool and glanced back at him just in time to see the bloom of surprise on his face that he quickly hid behind a brilliant white smile, perfect even teeth. Lord, she ought to just change her name to Chan or Ling. Then she wouldn't have to explain. Of course, she kind of liked throwing people off. Liked it when they stumbled over themselves to apologize—or even better, when they argued with her. As if she wouldn't know her own legal name.

She inwardly dared the suit to start something. She almost wanted him to.

But he didn't argue. Didn't push back. His sharp green eyes held something...dangerous. Intelligence? He wasn't some empty suit. She got that impression right away. She ignored the warming sensation in her belly. So the man was good-looking. So he was tall and broad in the shoulders, but with a tapered waist that told her he was probably no stranger to the gym. Hell, he looked like he belonged on the cover of some damn men's health magazine. She didn't care. He wasn't her type. Her type was bad boys in leather jackets covered in tattoos, with or without hair, and fists crisscrossed with the scars they bore from their share of scrapes. She preferred men who didn't own a tie, much less know how to knot one.

"Gael Quinn." He grinned, a half smile, all too confident in the crease of the dimple in his cheek. Well, the Irish name suited him. No one likely challenged his Kelly-green eyes and jet-black hair, told him *no, really, what's your real name?* Or looked past him when calling his name from a restaurant wait list. She couldn't imagine anyone looking past

him, really. Looking like a romance hero brought
to life, a McDreamy and McSteamy rolled into one.
Look at that damn high-voltage smile. He no doubt
used it to get those status-seeking Lincoln Park Trix-
ies to fall into his bed. Well, he was a helluva long
way from Lincoln Park. She wasn't an empty-headed
single looking for a rich man to buy her things. She
found his striking good looks just annoyed her.

"Is that supposed to mean something to me?"
Mags swiped at the slight sheen of blood on Angus's shoulder and returned to her work.

"I called. About the Shaded Moon album tattoo?
Talked to John about it? He said I could come in
today for a consultation. I hope that's all right."

No, it wasn't all right. John hadn't bothered to tell
her someone had called. But then again, how could
he? He was never here, she thought bitterly.

"He should've told you I don't do the Shaded
Moon album." Not anymore. For a while, everybody
had wanted one of those. The album had been a hit
a year ago, showcasing the falcon, midflight, she'd
created for the band. The lead singer's favorite bird.
Mags had done the work and sold the rights to it for
cheap because she thought the musicians had been
her friends, but then she learned they were making money hand over fist by putting her image on
T-shirts, hats and everything but bumper stickers.
Mags didn't like that she'd had no say in how her art
was replicated, that they'd not even bothered to ask
her permission. Because they'd intended to do that

all along, even though at the time she'd drawn it, they promised they wouldn't. The betrayal still burned.

"You don't?" Gael seemed surprised. But more than that, taken aback that she was telling him no. Clearly, he was used to getting what he wanted. Not this time. "You don't do this art?" The suit actually pulled up a picture of the cover art on his phone. As if she didn't already know what it looked like: peregrine falcon, midflight, its belly dotted with gray and brown, its dark wings expanded, yellow talons poised to snatch up its prey. Why did he care so much about it? The bass-heavy, borderline metal band didn't seem his speed.

"No, I don't." She sighed, feeling bone weary all of a sudden.

"I have to have this tattoo. Money is no object." He reached for his back pocket, ready to pull out his wallet. Of course, a man like him would think money solves everything. Mags finished the very last line of the eagle tattoo on Angus and sat back to admire her work. Nice job, if she did say so herself.

"Keep your money," she said, and his hand froze, midway to pulling out the expensive leather bifold, which somehow looked miniature in his big hands. The man had the build of a lumberjack, not a businessman. Not that Mags noticed, she told herself. "Like I said, I don't do that tattoo. Go to another shop. They'll help you with your midlife crisis."

He didn't rise to her bait. "I don't want another artist. I want you."

The sound of his voice, the confident, deep bass, plucked a string that vibrated through the center of her chest.

"I'm confident we could reach a *mutually beneficial* agreement." Was he talking about tattoos or sex? It was hard to tell with the man whose sensual mouth seemed to tease her. Who cared if the suit was sexy? He was still a suit.

Mags tried to dig into her basket of witty retorts to shut the man down but found it strangely empty.

"Are you?" she managed, hoping for heavy sarcasm, but instead, she sounded uncertain.

Her stomach growled instead, a little too loudly. She'd skipped breakfast, and her stomach was telling her lunch should've been an hour ago, now that it was close to one o'clock. But when she got in the zone, like she did with Angus, she didn't think about anything else but the job at hand. Now that she'd finished Angus's tattoo, her stomach told her it was time to focus on the important things, like food.

She pulled her attention from the man and his *mutual benefits* and tapped Angus on the shoulder to let him know their time was done. Angus's eyes flicked open then, and he pulled out his earbuds and saw the suit for the first time. He glanced at Mags. One nod from her and Angus would see the man out. Not gently, either. It'd be a shame if the man's good looks were marred by a one-way trip to the concrete. Angus slowly wound up the cord of his earbuds and sat up. He sneaked a glance at his shoulder.

"Damn, Mags. You outdid yourself."

"Glad you like it." She gave Angus a genuine smile and could feel Gael studying her as she leaned back on her stool, unlocking its wheel with her left foot and kicking backward as she whipped off her surgical glove with a snap. She tossed them in the nearby trash can. She stood and stretched herself, her back and upper shoulders stiff, all the while aware of Gael's unblinking gaze. "You know what to do to take care of it, yeah?"

He nodded. With all the tattoos he had, he could probably write a book on new-tattoo care. Then he refocused his attention on the suit. To the suit's credit, he met the man's stare and didn't look away as Angus walked into the expanse of the lobby and into the sunlight that warred with the fluorescent lights. Not easily intimidated, then. Interesting. She would've thought he'd run scared when Angus stood and stretched his beefy shoulders. Angus was six feet four, weighing in at over three hundred pounds, pretty much the opposite of svelte. He worked as a bouncer at the biker bar on the wrong side of town. Yet, now that Angus straightened to his full height, she saw that he only had an inch, maybe, on Gael. Angus was broader, but that was mostly fat, Mags had to admit. Gael had more muscle on his lean frame. Angus pulled out a money clip and rolled off four $100 bills. Mags didn't ask where he got that kind of cash. She didn't care. Mags took it with a nod of thanks.

"Uh… Mags." Angus rubbed the back of his massive neck as he lingered on the black tile of the lobby of her shop. "There's something else, too." The big man wasn't looking her in the eye. He seemed almost to squirm. "I'm supposed to pass on a message. From Clint."

Clint was Mags's on-again, off-again friends-with-benefits partner. He was a bartender at the bar where Angus worked, and the two men were friends. Clint and Mags had most recently been *on again* in the summer. A casual, no-questions-asked relationship. The perfect kind, in Mags's opinion. Except now she had a feeling that bad news was coming.

"Clint's, uh… Well…" Angus really did not want to get to the point. Mags felt the suit lean in, attention piqued. Great. Now she was *his* entertainment, too.

"Just spit it out, Angus. It's okay."

Angus took a deep breath, his brow furrowed. "He's cuffed. He wanted me to tell you."

Mags felt surprise at the disappointment that poked her belly. She was kind of expecting this, but still. The news didn't land well. Cuffed meant going monogamous. It was that time of year again. Everybody did it. Fall setting in, winter coming fast. Nobody wanted their Chicago beds cold and empty for the polar vortex months.

Angus was still talking. "It's that blonde waitress. Elena." Angus's shoulder slumped. "They've been seeing each other, and…"

Mags held up her hand. "I don't need to know the

details." They weren't any of her business. She and Clint had never been exclusive. Never were going to be exclusive. What he did with his time away from her bed was his business. Still, she was going to miss the way he fucked. Hard, fast and unapologetic, just like he rode his Harley. She knew they'd eventually go their separate ways, so why did his decision to move on sting? Because it did.

It was probably because up until now, Clint had done everything she asked him to. She'd kind of felt like she had the upper hand in the relationship. Now she felt blindsided. Especially since it was November. She hated November. For a lot of reasons. None of which she wanted to think about right now.

She tried hard to press down the hurt that threatened to bubble up to the surface. What the hell did she care if Clint jumped into bed with Elena or anyone else? She wasn't going to marry him. She wasn't going to marry anyone. She'd promised herself that a long time ago.

"He's a damn coward for not telling you himself," Angus said. "But I think he's a little afraid of you."

Mags threw back her head and laughed. "Good," she said, thankful for small favors. She knew he didn't have the courage to tell her himself. Because she would've ordered him to quit being stupid, and he probably would've listened. The fact that he'd sent a lackey to deliver the bad news just told her that he was really serious about it. That he didn't even want to give Mags the chance to change his mind.

Angus glanced over at Gael and then back at Mags. "If it's anything, I'd never treat you like that. If, you know…" Angus stared at his feet, color rising in his cheeks. Mags suspected the big man had a little crush on her. For his sake, she ignored it. Mags would never go for Angus. He might be a big bruiser on the outside, but he was a giant teddy bear on the inside. He'd fall in love with her in two weeks flat, and then she'd have to live with breaking his heart. No way. She wasn't going to do it.

She gave him a gentle pat on his forearm. "Thanks, Angus."

Angus hung for a second. "You need anything else before I go?" Angus gave a slight head nod toward Gael, his offer clear.

"Nah. I got it." She stood and moved to the glass counter at the front of the store. She could take Gael. There was the folding knife in her back pocket, the baseball bat beneath the front counter and the industrial-size bottle of Mace near the register. Not that a banker would ever give her that kind of trouble. They only robbed people blind if it was technically legal. Cowards, the lot of them. She'd never forget the look on the banker's face as he'd delivered the news to her father that there was nothing he could do—the bank owned their house now, and they had twenty-four hours to get out.

"Okay, then. See you around," Angus said.

"'Bye, big guy," Mags called as Angus slid on out, bumping the suit's shoulder as he went, and Mags had to hide a smile. Angus hated suits as much as she did. The suit said nothing, but he stared at Angus's retreating back, probably working out whether or not he could sue him in civil court for the bump.

Mags went to the register and dumped the cash inside. She was ignoring Gael, even though she was well aware of his presence. How could she not be? He was like a bright neon light, a chiseled, muscled, manly neon light.

"I need this tattoo." His voice rumbled in her belly. There was power in that voice. He moved closer to the register, and she got a whiff of something sweet and spicy—cologne? Of course a suit would wear cologne. But she kind of liked it, despite herself.

"Why? Midlife crisis?" She didn't bother to keep the disdain from her voice.

"No. I made a promise." His green eyes never left hers, and for the briefest of seconds, she imagined what that voice would be like talking about naughty things. How his gravelly bass would sound whispering naughty things in her ear. Then she shook herself. Why was she imagining the suit talking dirty? Clint had been cuffed for five minutes, and she was acting sex depraved.

"Look, I don't want to hear it. I'm not doing that tattoo." Even thinking about Shaded Moon made her feel vulnerable. And she was no victim. She hated the feeling. Hated feeling like she wasn't in control. It was her life, her rules. It had been that way since she was seventeen. She'd been on her own for a whole lifetime. She'd learned to take care of herself.

So why did the suit make her feel uncertain?

"But…" His smile wavered.

"I said no." Her stomach growled again. All she wanted was some food, preferably the greasy kind, and for the suit to leave her in peace. If that made her the bad guy, then she'd be the bad guy. She wasn't in the mood to be generous. The sting from Clint's rejection didn't help, either. She told herself she didn't care he'd latched himself on to a barmaid, but still, part of her did. She could feel a lot of feelings swirling around the murky pit of her stomach, and that made her grumpy. She didn't like the feels. She preferred to keep her emotions stuffed into a lockbox she kept deep inside her. They didn't need to come out. When they came out, bad things happened.

"Surely there's some way we can negotiate this. I'll double your hourly rate." The man was actually reaching for his damn wallet again. He pulled it out this time and grabbed some sleek black metal card. He actually put it down on her glass counter, and it landed with a resounding plink of metal against glass. Nothing written on it. Mags had seen one only once before. She knew it was one of those limitless cards. She'd heard that was the kind of card you could buy a car with. Or, hell, even a house.

"No. All I want is a double cheeseburger and some peace and quiet."

Genuine shock bloomed on Gael's face, and Mags liked it. *How do you like feeling off-kilter, Mr. Suit?*

"Come on. Let's talk about this. *Please.*" That bass voice, and that smile again. Full wattage this time.

"Get out." She crossed her arms across her chest, liking the power she was wielding over him. A bit too much. Still, she wouldn't take a sleek metal card. She wasn't for sale.

"I'll give you twenty times your rate. And that's my final offer." He was serious. She did a quick calculation. He was talking about $10,000. His single tattoo would pay her rent, her salary and her clerk's salary for the month. She considered it for exactly half a second. Then she cursed herself for even doing that. She wasn't for sale. Period. "You should leave," she told him.

He blinked fast, still baffled and desperately trying to get handle on her. He wasn't used to being kicked out of places, clearly. He was used to talking his way into anything. Well, not this time. If this *one* time she could hand a suit a loss, she would.

"I—"

"I told you to leave." Mags's voice left no room for argument. She pointed to the door. "That means *get out.*"

CHAPTER TWO

GAEL STOOD ON the sidewalk outside Mags's tattoo parlor, stunned. He'd never in a million years expected she'd *turn him down*. He'd offered *twenty times* her rate! It made no sense. The cold November air whipped fallen brown leaves at his feet, and he felt the chill all the way to his bones. He watched Mags through the window of her shop, trying to calculate which of his dealing-with-Quinn-sisters strategies he was going to employ. Bribery? Flattery? Flat-out begging? He hadn't survived as the only son in a house of three sisters without honing a few lifesaving skills.

Mags was a tough one, though. Full of surprises. Like for the fact that she was Asian, not Scottish or Irish, for starters. But this was Chicago. Big city, diverse population. Not the first time he'd run into someone with a name that didn't match expectations. She was beautiful, he had to admit, even though she tried hard to hide it. Her hair, a riot of two different shades of blue highlights running through her natural dark brown, ran straight down her back. And her big brown eyes had flashed fire at him when she'd kicked him out. She had flawless, poreless skin, though, and wore a single silver ring through her delicate nose. She had on a black concert tee over black leggings, which clung to her impressively toned butt, and her feet were clad in Doc Martens. Her dark black eyeliner and intensely smoky eye added to the vibe that screamed, *Don't mess with me or I'll mess with you back.* She was trying hard to look tough, even though her delicate cheekbones and the curve of her rosebud lips suggested she was fragile somehow. Then, of course, there was the ornate tattoo on her forearm, the one with two robins flying in tandem, their wings spread. It was a beautifully drawn and colored masterpiece that seemed as if it belonged in an old book illustration, not on her thin, pale arm. She was a walking enigma. A very rude, very hostile, walking enigma.

One that seemed determined to cut off her own nose to spite her face. Who turned down that kind of cash out of...what? Stubbornness? Maybe she was just like his older sister, Kathleen, who'd rather walk off a cliff than admit she was wrong.

Gael stood on the sidewalk, frozen, watching Mags tidy up the register at her tattoo place, thinking this wasn't the first time a woman had made his life hell. Most of his sisters had frozen him out at some time or another, for offenses as large as forgotten birthdays to as small as taking the last serving of cereal. He had to think. He needed this tattoo. He'd *promised* his youngest sister, Ava, he'd do this. And he never broke a promise. Not to her. Plus, if he didn't get this done, he'd have to deal with the criticism from the other two, who also knew about the promise and would hold him to it.

Gael shook his head. He'd was about to close a $1 billion investment deal that would bring thousands of good-paying jobs to Chicago, and he'd had to run the gauntlet of nervous bank board members, hardball city officials and a state government where four of the last seven governors were in jail, and he'd managed to get all the skittish antelope and bloodthirsty hyenas to the table, but *this* was what was going to trip up his day? One grumpy tattoo artist? Seriously? He almost wanted to laugh out loud. He wrangled more dangerous prey than this in every boardroom and conference room across the city, but he couldn't get a simple five-figure tattoo deal done?

He shook his head. No. He wasn't going to be thwarted. He paced the sidewalk, thinking.

Then his phone rang. His older sister by three years, Kathleen, was calling.

"You get it yet?" she asked him, in the all-business tone she usually saved for city council meetings. She hadn't been elected mayor of the city of big shoulders for being soft.

"I'm working on it." The last thing he needed was for the bossiest of the Quinn sisters to be on his back.

"Better work faster. Ava's surgery is Friday."

As if he didn't already know that.

"I'll get it done. I just have to work around one little problem."

Kathleen hesitated on the line. "What's that?"

"The tattoo artist kicked me out."

"What did you do *now*?" Kathleen's disapproval was thick in her voice. But then again, with his older sister, it nearly always was.

"Nothing. She just didn't like the look of me."

"She?" Kathleen snorted. "Since when do *you* have trouble with women, Mr. King of Tinder?" Kathleen cackled, and Gael almost took it personally. Sure, he dated around. What was wrong with that?

"I think, technically, the term is prime minister of Tinder."

"Ha-ha. Maybe she doesn't fancy guys?"

"She has an ex named Clint. So you tell me?"

"Then you're just losing a step. Getting lazy. Might need new pickup lines that aren't from 2005."

"Enough, Kathleen Kelly O'Brien Quinn."

"Stop it with the full name. Only Dad could get away with that." She let out a frustrated breath. "I could send down a few Chicago police patrols. Or city inspectors. They'd lean on her. If you want."

Just like Kathleen to think pure muscle would fix things. She was the one who used to twist his skin in opposite directions until it burned, refusing to let up until he'd let her have the last bite of his dessert. This happened until he got big enough to stop her, around seventh grade.

"No. That's okay. I don't need help." Taking help from Kathleen would mean admitting defeat, and he'd rather pick up a pot of ink and a needle and tattoo himself. Besides, he already knew bullying wouldn't get him anywhere with Mags. He could tell the woman was fiercely independent. He kind of admired that. Even if it meant she'd kicked him out on his ass.

But Mags wasn't as tough as she let on, either. He'd seen her face when Angus had delivered the news her boyfriend (or maybe just friend with benefits?) had moved on. He'd seen the sheen of hurt in her brown eyes, the rejection that she quickly hid behind a steel reserve of forced indifference. The ice queen had a heart, and that gave him hope.

"Are you sure you don't need help? I can—"

"No. I'm fine. I'll get it done. 'Bye, Kathleen." He hung up before she could promise to send cop cars to his rescue. No need to encourage her to overstep her bounds as mayor. He was sure she was already plotting to do that all on her own.

He shoved his phone into his coat pocket and braced himself against the autumn chill. He glanced to the busy street as a city bus blew by, trying to think. He needed to figure out a way in. He wasn't the kind to give up easily. If he gave up every time somebody disliked him, he would never have made that first investment with his parents' insurance money, which he'd parlayed into equity he used to invest in his first business, ten long years ago, and then he'd turned that into another deal and another, with an uncanny ability to get investors to say yes, even to the most impossible deals. Sweet-talking had helped him when he'd been looking after his sisters, pretty much from the age of twenty-one. He'd learned how to get things they needed using no more than the right words. And he could be persuasive. Very damn persuasive.

He glanced down the street and saw the neon lights of a local burger joint. Then he thought of younger sister Maeve, who was the sweetest, most helpful woman on earth—unless she was hungry. Maybe words weren't what he needed. Maybe, he thought, struck with inspiration, what he needed was a double cheeseburger.

He glanced back through the pane-glass window at Mags, who was now on the phone, working the counter. He buttoned up his jacket and hurried down the street. With any luck, he could be back in ten minutes with a peace offering.

CHAPTER THREE

THE TATTOO SHOP BELL dinged as the front door swung open and Gael walked in—once more like he owned the place. There he was: Mr. Tall, Dark and Arrogant. Mags shook her head in disbelief. Hadn't she *just* kicked this suit out ten minutes ago? But then, what did she expect? Bankers were worse than cockroaches. Always showing up no matter how much they weren't invited.

"Look, man. I don't want to call the cops, but I will." The last thing Mags wanted to do was call the police. That was a headache she just didn't want. But she would, if pressed. And Gael seemed determined to press.

"No need for that." The suit smiled, his cheeks pink from the whipping autumn wind outside. He held up two greasy bags of burgers and fries from Romer's Burgers down the street. Her stomach instantly growled its want. Romer's double cheeseburgers beat any she'd ever had, and normally, she only saved them for a special treat. They ran five dollars more per meal than the fast food place around the corner, and, sometimes, business was tight. "I know you're hungry. I just…thought you might want lunch."

He set the greasy bags down on her counter, and the amazing aroma of freshly grilled patties and deep-fried waffle fries hit her nose. Her mouth instantly watered. She wanted it all. And she wanted it *now*.

Except he was a suit. And she wasn't for sale. And if she wanted a damn burger so bad, she could walk down and get one herself.

"You think a lousy cheeseburger is going to make me change my mind?"

Gael laughed a little, his green eyes sparkling. "No. I think a cheeseburger is going to make your stomach stop yowling." As if on cue, her stomach growled again, a high-pitched whine. "It kind of sounds like a dying coyote."

Mags had to smile at that. Her stomach did sound like a wild animal in pain. Because it kind of was. "I doubt you've ever seen a coyote."

"Sure I have. There were plenty running around Winnetka where I grew up."

"Winnetka! Figures." North Shore rich guy. She could've pegged it. "I knew you were the come-from-money type."

"I have three sisters. Whatever money we had, they spent. My mom was a nurse. Dad was an attorney. We were the poorest family on our block."

"But your block was rich."

He shrugged.

"You were the only boy?"

"Yep. Except for our dog, Teddy."

"Really?" Now Mags wanted to laugh. She'd been an only child, but she could only imagine how a boy sharing a house with women would feel. Outnumbered. Probably outsmarted, too.

"I'll tell you all about it over lunch."

Mags hopped on the stool behind the counter and tugged the bag closer to her, letting the steam hit her face as she rolled back the paper's edges. She could go get one of her own, but this one was *right here*. And she was starving. She grabbed a double cheeseburger and began to unwrap it. She was about to take a bite when she stopped.

"How do I know you haven't drugged this?" If a man could roofie a drink, he sure as hell could roofie a cheeseburger.

Gael scoffed. "Because all of my sisters would kill me. Skin me alive." He studied her. Then he whipped the burger out of her hands. He folded down the paper and took a big bite. She watched him sink his teeth into what she knew was a full pound of amazing, grade-A beef.

"If I did, we're both taking a nap now." He handed it back to her, and she reluctantly took it. She glanced at the half-moon of his bite on the bun and hesitated. It was almost too intimate, taking a bite of the same sandwich. It implied she didn't mind putting her mouth where his had been. Her stomach growled its protest once more, and she finally gave in. She took a bite of the burger, its juices soaking into her mouth, and moaned.

"Oh, God. That's just the best," she mumbled, mouth full. She chewed with gusto. The Romer's burger was as good as she remembered. She glanced up and realized Gael was staring at her intently. She swallowed her bite, feeling a little self-conscious all at once. "It's the best burger in town."

"This," he said, holding up his half-eaten double cheeseburger, "is a very good burger. But it's not the best."

"Name another."

"Lanier's."

"You mean La-Overpriced?" Mags took another big bite.

"Not overpriced at all," he protested. "You get what you pay for. Have you ever been there?"

Mags shook her head. She didn't eat at the expensive, Michelin-starred restaurants on Randolph.

"Well, then, how do you know?" Gael questioned, digging out a fry from the bunch and popping it into his mouth.

"I know they charge forty dollars for a burger. That's what I know." Mags believed the pricier something was, the more it wasn't worth the hype. She swallowed a bite of burger, even as the warmth of the meal began to hit her stomach, smoothing out some of her rough edges. She could feel herself becoming less hangry with every bite. She glanced at Gael. The suit was smarter than he looked. Buttering her up with food was actually a decent strategy.

"Money isn't bad, especially when it's in your own pocket." He wiggled his dark eyebrows, and Mags had to laugh. He had some charm, this suit, and she was succumbing to it, despite her best efforts. The gleam in his green eyes told her he was determined to get his way. He had the brash confidence of someone who was used to success. The burgers proved that. She finished the last of her double cheeseburger and licked a bit of cheese off one finger. Then she doubled down on the fries. He'd only gotten one large to share.

"You grew up with sisters, huh? That must've been rough." Mags lifted a fry to her mouth and chomped it whole. Then she reached for another.

"You have no idea. I think I have PTSD. Post-traumatic sister disorder."

"Couldn't be that bad." Mags picked up two more fries this time. She couldn't get enough of the salty goodness. Fries were her kryptonite.

"Kathleen—the oldest—used to punch me when my parents weren't looking. If I hit her back, I'd get double the punishment. Boys aren't supposed to hit girls. Maeve was a sweetie, unless she was hungry, and when she was hungry, she'd yell. A lot. Ava…" His eyes grew warm. "Well, Ava's twelve years younger. She's adorable and perfect, so she stole all the attention. The jerk." He laughed as he said it, though, and Mags got the impression Gael cared a lot for Ava. For all his sisters. "How about you? Any sisters?"

Mags took another fry and shook her head quickly. "Only child. Adopted. Thus the name, Margaret McHenry."

"Ah." Gael nodded slowly. "Only child? That explains so much."

"What's *that* supposed to me?"

"That you never learned to share." He nodded at the box of quickly dwindling fries. "You're hoarding all the fries."

"You should've known to get two orders. That's your fault. Not mine."

Gael pressed his hand to his chest. "You always punch a gift horse in the mouth?"

"When they deserve it." Mags wasn't going to make any apologies about the fries. Or enjoying the free burger. "Besides, *you* decided to buy lunch. If you had asked me before you did, I would've told you to buy extra fries."

"You were way too hangry for that. I think if I'd tried to ask you, you would've stabbed me in the eye."

Mags considered this, taking another fry and rolling her eyes to the ceiling. "Perhaps. But now that I know I can punch you and you're programmed not to punch me back, I might try that instead."

Gael had just taken a big bite of burger and coughed a laugh through it. He grabbed a napkin and swiped his mouth. "Hey, now. You do that, and I'll have to dredge up my old revenge tactics. Wet willies." Gael licked a finger and held it up beneath the fluorescent lights of the shop. "Mom and Dad never said *these* were off-limits."

Mags wadded up a napkin and threw it at him. "Don't even try it."

He tucked his finger away. "I'll show mercy. *This* time."

Mags felt a warmth in her belly that had nothing to do with the burger and fries. She was actually having a good time. She tried to remember the last time she'd enjoyed a man's company—with her clothes on. She couldn't, actually.

Gael considered her over the lunch wrappers as he leaned against her glass counter. He made the counter look so small beneath his elbow. The man took up a significant amount of real estate. "So, want to tell me why you hate Shaded Moon so much?"

She frowned at him. "It's personal."

He watched her intently. Interest was nothing new to Mags, who typically fought off all kinds at the seedy bars she frequented, but *his* interest was less…obvious. He wanted to know *about* her. Personal things. Not just whether or not she wore underwear, which was the question one stranger had asked her at a bar last week or the occasional racist remark about Asians that she got every now and then from people who thought they were being clever, but in the end, were just showing their ignorance.

"Why do you want Shaded Moon so badly?" she asked.

"It's Ava's favorite album of all time," he said, wadding up his burger's empty wrapper and tucking it neatly into the paper bag.

"You're doing all this…" Mags waved her hands around their lunch trash. "And bugging the hell out of me for your little sister?" She couldn't believe it. Why would a grown man even care what his sister's favorite band was? And why on earth would he want to tattoo *that* on himself?

"Well, I promised. She's seventeen. She's fighting…cancer. Again." He paused, the emotion getting to him for the briefest of seconds.

Mags felt something in her loosen, weaken, maybe. A hairline crack in that brick wall she used to dam up her emotions. She thought of her mother, how the breast cancer had been found too late. How she'd wasted away in a matter of months before her eyes. How her death had begun the downward spiral of the whole family. The medical bills that had stacked up, impossibly fast, the way it had drained their bank accounts. Then, of course, came the foreclosure. She blinked fast, shocked at how the memory hit her hard, as if it felt like it had blown its way out of the chest where she kept it locked up in her mind. Blown its way out, intent on doing damage.

So Gael had a sister with cancer. She glanced at him and could almost sense the weight of the worry on him. She remembered what that felt like all too well. He wasn't all handshakes and smiles and big banker deals, after all. Now she kind of did feel like an asshole for kicking him out of her place. And he'd come back with piping-hot cheeseburgers.

"Why didn't you say that in the first place?" she asked him.

"I was trying, but I believe you were too busy kicking me out." He patted his mouth with his napkin.

She had been a little harsh. The apology lodged itself in her throat, but she forced it out. "Sorry."

"Oh, so the tattoo queen *does* apologize." Gael grinned.

"I'm about to take it back if you keep gloating." She glared.

"Duly noted." Gale flipped through his phone's photos. "This is Ava." Gael offered up a picture of a girl who looked even younger than seventeen, hospital gown, bald. She had Gael's smile, was using it to its full advantage, grinning ear to ear, the brave one, despite the fact she looked paler than her sheets. It reminded her suddenly of her own mother's bedside. Her mother, all frail and pale, a shell of her former self. "She already went into remission once. The cancer is back. A second time."

"What kind does she have?" Mags asked, swallowing back the memory and the wave of emotion that threatened to follow it.

"Thyroid cancer," he said, voice low, as if saying it too loudly would give the cancer power, as if there was an evil wizard hiding somewhere. Mags studied the picture. She could see even more of the family resemblance—the little sister had his eyes.

"What's her prognosis?"

"The cancer spread, so not as good as I'd like." His eyes clouded. Gael tugged at his silk tie, loosening the knot as if he needed some air. Mags's attention went to his neck, to the little hollow at base of his throat. She wondered what he looked like without a shirt. Not that she should be having such thoughts about a banker. "I know you don't have to do this, but that album is Ava's favorite. She listens to it every day, and I wanted to carry a piece of that with me, to remind me of her, but also to let her know that she's not alone in this fight. I promised her I'd get the tattoo—to help her recovery."

Gael met Mags's gaze, and she could feel his determination, the importance of the promise he'd made. Now, there was no half smile on his face, no charm offensive, no salesmanship. There was just need. Pure and simple. He needed her to do this.

"What's her favorite song?" Mags still needed proof.

"What?"

"Her favorite song on the album?"

"'Blue Sky.'" He didn't miss a beat. Well, damn. That was her favorite song, too. She hesitated as she glanced down at the black paint on her nails. Was she really thinking about breaking her own rules for a suit? Just because he had a sob story? Yes, she damn well was. Her place, her rules. She could bend or break them if she wanted.

She considered Gael once more. "Okay," she said at last. "I'll do it." Hell, her heart wasn't made of stone. The girl had cancer. The suit wasn't just getting a tattoo for the fun of it.

His whole face lit up then with joy…and, she saw, relief, as his shoulders relaxed just a tad. Well, maybe he had actually been worried she'd say no.

"Can we start now?" he asked, hopeful.

"Don't push it." She glanced at the white-and-black clock on the wall. She was hoping to close up shop early today. Maybe grab a beer. But then again, Clint was working at her favorite bar, so maybe a beer wasn't a good idea.

"Please?" he asked. "My other sisters have been nagging me for the better part of the month to do this."

"And you waited until the last minute." Typical.

"You got it." He took off his jacket and folded it over one arm. She noticed how the cotton shirt accented his muscles. He wasn't a normal, flabby banker type. Not in the least.

He looked away from her. "She's in the hospital now. She's having surgery Friday. It's going to be a tough day. I want to show her something. Give her some hope before she goes under the knife. Or let her laugh her ass off at me—either one would be good for her before surgery." He took a deep breath. "She's been dealing with cancer since she was thirteen. She had four years in remission, but now she's older. She knows more about what the odds mean."

Shit. That sounded rough.

"The tattoo will be red and still healing. Ugly as hell," she warned him, but her attention was fixed on his strong fingers as they undid his shirt.

Normally she'd tell the man to piss off, but part of her—a dark part of her—wanted to see him with his shirt off.

"I don't care."

"You got cash on you?"

"I've got credit cards. And a checkbook." He reached for his coat pocket. Who the hell carried a checkbook anymore? But not that she was arguing. She far preferred checks to credit cards.

"Check. No plastic." Plastic just meant giving a larger cut to the banks who processed the payments. She didn't care to let them keep any more of her own money, thank you.

"Okay," Gael agreed. "I'll write you the check for the whole amount." He pulled out the checkbook from his coat pocket. Leather-bound, expensive, with gold foil on the checks.

He made swift work of the check, his handwriting precise as he wrote out a check to her for $10,000. He ripped it from the register and handed it to her. She took it and stared at all the zeroes, blinking fast. She'd never gotten a check that big. Ever in her life.

"How do I know it won't bounce?"

Gael laughed, big and hearty, and then handed her

a business card. "If it bounces, you can come find me here." He tapped the office address, one of the sleek high-rises downtown. She'd vaguely heard of the investment firm on it. "Or hell, go to city hall. My sister's the mayor. She'll send out the entire Chicago police force after me."

"Your sister is *Kathleen Quinn*?" The suit had political connections, too? Then again, why did that surprise her? Rich, powerful and connected. Sounded about right.

"She's the ambitious one in the family."

Judging by the Rolex on his wrist, not the only one, Mags thought. "The *mayor* of Chicago used to punch you? *That* sister."

"Still does, if she can get away with it." He let out a rueful sigh.

"Okay, we can get started today. I don't want the mayor after me," she said and nodded toward the small room with the reclining tattoo chair. The door was wide-open and the hook on the wall empty. "You can hang your coat and your shirt there."

She watched as he hung his coat on the hook and whipped off his tie. After that, his hands made quick work of the buttons on his shirt. She wondered what else they could do quickly. How else they might be nimble. She bit her lower lip as the crisp white button-down came off, and there were suddenly just miles of perfect, smooth chest. Muscular, taut, unblemished skin, ridges and valleys of muscles that invited a slow touch. Damn, what a canvas. She instantly felt her body react and had to fight the urge to whistle. The man was fine. Finer than fine. Why did he do his body such an injustice by covering it with a suit? Her eyes lingered on the V of muscle leading into his wool trousers.

Well, she thought, her mind going to all kinds of carnal places, there were worst ways to spend an afternoon other than painting a freakin' Greek god. Scratch that: Celtic god. This job might not suck after all.

He hung up his shirt over his coat and glanced back at her, arms spread in a question.

"Go on, lie down then," she told him, feeling a trickle of sweat drip down her lower back. God, it had been too long since she'd gotten laid, she thought. She was a woman who took care of her needs—who had plenty of rotating casual relationships to do just that. She'd been busy of late. Hadn't even seen Clint that much, which was probably why he'd fallen into Elena's bed. She'd have to look after herself, and soon. She was drooling after an investment banker, for God's sake. "Before I change my mind."

His eyes lit up. "Thank you so much," he said as he laid himself down on her chair, half-naked and completely and totally at her mercy: right where she wanted him.

"Don't thank me yet," she warned him. She nodded at her tattoo machine. "This is going to hurt like hell."

CHAPTER FOUR

GAEL FELT THE twitch of nerves in his stomach as he lay down on the black leather reclining chair. He watched Mags fetch a set of clean tools, eyeing the sharpness of the needle at the edge of the rotary machine in her hand, the thing that would permanently mark his skin. He'd never imagined he'd get a tattoo. But then again, he'd never imagined he'd be worried for his sister's life—a second time. She'd jokingly brought up the idea of a tattoo when the cancer hit the first time. Now that it had made a second appearance and in other places, he wasn't going to waste any more time. He'd been looking after her since she'd been born. There were twelve years and one sister between them, but he and Ava had always had a special bond. Ava had come along as a surprise to the whole family and had been the only sister to grow up idolizing him and everything he did. She tottered after him as soon as she could walk and had been his shadow almost ever since.

Mags glanced up at him, and for a second, her brown eyes held a question.

"You sure you want to do this?" Her eyes trailed down his bare chest. He noticed she wasn't looking at all at his shoulder, where she should be focusing her attention. Her eyes seemed glued to his belly button and went even lower. If he didn't know any better, he'd think she was checking him out.

"Yes," he said, even as he pressed down a small wiggle of doubt. He couldn't believe he was *actually* doing this. Couldn't believe Mags had agreed to it. *Ah, the power of cheeseburgers*, he thought. The way to a woman's tattoo machine was really through her stomach. She swiped a bit of electric-blue hair off her shoulder, and Gael suddenly had the urge to put his hands in it.

Mags sat before him now and rubbed his skin with alcohol, disinfecting the shoulder. The alcohol was cool to the touch, but her gloved fingers felt warm.

He glanced down at his bare shoulder. "Are you going to draw it first?" he asked her, uncertain.

She gave him a lopsided grin. "I do better freehand," she told him, which sent a ripple of nerves through his stomach. She was going to permanently mark him without even so much as a pencil sketch first?

"Are you sure?" He frowned.

She frowned back, a wrinkle appearing between her two perfect brows. "Are you doubting me? Because if you're doubting me, this is never going to work."

"No, I'm not..." He totally was doubting her. What kind of artist didn't do an outline first before making it permanent? "But I just thought tattoo artists drew it on, or stenciled it... That's what I saw online."

Mags let out a gruff laugh. "You looked at tattoo artists on YouTube?"

"Maybe." Yes, he most certainly did. He'd wanted to know what he was in for. Gael never did something without calculating all possible angles. He wasn't one to jump spontaneously into anything. He'd already thought about every considerable outcome before he made a move. It's what made him a famously successful investor, after all.

Plus, he'd noticed the glances she kept stealing at his bare chest...and his belt buckle, as if mentally unfastening it. He didn't need a distracted tattoo artist freehanding it while sneaking glances at his abs. Under different circumstances, he'd tell this gorgeous woman to stare away. But this one had tattoo needles in her hand.

"Hacks," she murmured to herself, adjusting the lamp above his shoulder for the best possible angle of light. She rolled her stool closer to him, and he got a whiff of something sweet. Roses? She smelled like an open field of flowers, the scent of perfume startling him. She wasn't sure what rough and gruff, blue-haired tattooed Asian biker chicks were supposed to smell like, but he wouldn't have bet on flowers. She moved the five-needled machine over his shoulder, and he found himself swallowing, hard. Gael never was one to fear pain. Hell, being the only boy meant all his sisters had never felt the need to pull their punches. And they could hit.

"Anyway, are you worried about the pain?" There was a teasing light in her eyes.

"No," he said. He'd been in enough fights growing up that he knew how to take a punch. And how to land one.

Mags laughed. "You should be," she warned, looking a little like she could be a member of some crime syndicate wielding her tattoo needles as a weapon. And then she kicked on the machine and a loud, buzzing hum like a swarm of bees filled the room. He had no more opportunity to protest the lack of an outline before she had pressed the multiple vibrating needles against his skin. He felt the tickle and then the sting of the needles piercing his flesh. He glanced over at Mags, whose face was now inches from his, and noticed her slight frown of concentration. She was completely and totally focused on the line she drew on his arm. She suddenly looked strikingly beautiful in that moment of total concentration. He admired the intensity with which she studied his arm. Suddenly, he trusted her in the zone, even as she worked permanent ink into his skin. She worked a little more and then swabbed his shoulder.

"You doing okay?" she asked him.

"Fine," he said, even as he felt his skin burn.

"Good. It only gets worse." There was laughter in her voice, as if she was enjoying this. Reminded him a smidgen of Kathleen.

He watched as a blue streak of hair fell into her face.

"You're trying to scare me on purpose," he offered, hoping that was true.

"Why? Do you scare easily?" She lifted the needle and met his gaze, her brown eyes with just a hint of a teasing light in them. Hell, she kept that up, he might get the impression she was flirting with him.

"No." He meant it. She raised a slender brown eyebrow.

"Is that a challenge?" The tattoo tool buzzed even louder in her hand.

"So, did you become a tattoo artist because you're a sadist?" He was only half joking, but she laughed out loud, a full, bright laugh. It didn't seem to match the surly expression she tried to wear most of the time. Of course, neither did that delicate chin, the sharp eyes lined with dark, dark kohl. She was a bundle of contradictions, Mags McHenry. She concentrated and the tiniest of lines appeared between her brows, but otherwise, her skin was perfectly smooth. She was gorgeous, even if she liked metal bands like the one emblazoned on her T-shirt. Maybe even because she liked metal bands.

"No, that's just a bonus." She shook her head as she focused again on his shoulder. "I've always loved to draw. But opening a tattoo shop was easier than getting a gallery show." She shrugged one shoulder. "Besides, I kind of like the idea of art that evolves. This bird that I put on you will go with you, live with you, see what you see. It's personal art, and only the people *you* want to see it, will."

"Interesting. Ava needs this, anyway. She and my sisters are all the family I've got."

"What happened to your parents?" Mags asked without looking up from his shoulder.

"Mom and Dad died in a car accident when I was twenty-one."

She hissed. "You just the king of bad luck or what?"

"You make your own luck," he said, believing it. "Everybody's got something. It's all about how you deal with it."

"Now you're making me feel sorry for you." Mags shook her head slowly.

"Good. Maybe you'll go easy on me."

Her eyes met his for a brief moment. "Maybe." A smile tugged at the corner of her lips.

She grew quiet once more. He was acutely aware of the needles poking into his skin. He glanced down at her work but could only see a few dark lines and a smear of blood as she wiped at his skin. He couldn't make out a form, if there was one to see, and looking only made him more nervous. He was at her mercy. She could write *idiot* on his arm and he'd be stuck with it.

"So, who's Clint?" he asked, unable to keep it in any longer. He'd overheard the entire exchange with the big guy. "Boyfriend?"

Mags snorted. "No."

"Somebody you dated?" Gael knew he should just let it go, but he couldn't. For some reason, he *needed* to know. He'd never been more curious about a stranger he'd just met.

"If by dated, you mean fucked, then yeah. That." Mags focused her attention again on her work.

He liked how she said that word. As if she did it all the time.

"So casual."

"Yep. That's all I do." He could feel the light tickle of her breath on his skin in between the sharp stinging sensation of the needles. She'd stopped staring at his chest and was now concentrating hard on her work. Good. When he inhaled he smelled roses again.

"Why?" Gael knew he was pushing his luck, but he couldn't help it. He wasn't opposed to commitment, but he wasn't exactly looking for it, either. He'd been taking care of his sisters—well, technically, they'd been taking care of each other—since their parents died in that car crash when Gael was a senior in college. He and Kathleen had played mom and dad to Maeve and Ava. They'd been the ones to deal with Ava's diagnosis the first time around. Needless to say, over the last ten years, he'd had enough of playing family. Wasn't looking to make another one any time soon. Eventually, sure. After Ava was well.

"Because casual is easier," Mags said. "I don't want to be tied down. Unless it's in bed."

The idea of Mags, naked, literally cuffed in his bed, made all kinds of sensations go off in Gael's brain. He felt a tightening in his groin. "Really?"

Mags laughed. "Sometimes. For fun."

So the hard-as-nails tattoo artist liked a little bondage? He wondered what it would be like, having Mags gagged and tied.

"I bet you look good in handcuffs."

Mags paused and looked at him. He wondered for a minute if he was going to get a slap in the face.

"Because you look good in anything," he amended.

She laughed.

"You trying to kiss up to me because I'm holding this?" She lifted the tattoo needle from his skin.

"That depends. Is it working?"

She looked up to meet his gaze, and for just an instant, her shoulders relaxed a tad and something moved between them. A feeling of recognition, maybe? The spark of what could be something more? For a split second, just a second, he thought he saw the flicker of attraction in her brown eyes. She looked striking then: the pucker of her full mouth, the point of her delicate chin. But it was the look in her eyes, the desire rising in her, as she gazed at him. He'd never felt *sized up* before, except right in this moment. Something animalistic buzzed between them, something primal, and he was suddenly completely aware of how close she was to him, how he could feel the warmth of her hands through the medical gloves. He itched to feel her skin against his and wondered what it would be like to taste her mouth. And then he realized she had him pinned with at least five buzzing needles against his skin. Making a move right now would be idiotic.

Or would it? Because she lifted her tattoo needles, pausing in her work. She looked at him, a flicker of want lighting her eyes. He'd seen that look from enough women to knew exactly what it meant.

But then his phone rang, the sound blaring in the soft quiet between them. He glanced at the face and saw it was Will Moriarty, one of his partners at the investment firm. The man couldn't have worse timing.

"Hello?" he answered his phone, even as the buzz continued.

"Just wanted to let you know you should crack open the champagne tonight—or the good scotch. We got the deal. It's going through."

This was the Lewis deal, the one that would bring jobs to Chicago. He ought to be celebrating. It's what he'd been working on for months. All the twisting of arms he'd done should've earned him a medal. And, yet, somehow he didn't quite feel like celebrating. He glanced down at the half tattoo on his arm and thought about his sister. In that moment, he'd trade all the Lewis deals if he could know Ava was cancer-free.

"Aren't you excited, man?"

"Yeah, I'm excited. Good for the firm."

"No, man, good for *us*. This deal is going to take us to the next level, man. You'll see."

Mags lifted her needle from Gael's arm and frowned at him. He was oblivious, blabbing into his phone about some business deal. He was congratulating one of his lackeys about something. This was what she didn't like about suits—they felt their work was more important than hers.

She rolled back her chair and put her equipment down, watching him as he sat up a little.

"You go on and open that scotch, Will." He pressed his lips into a thin line, unsatisfied with the answer. "You deserve it. And the bonus that's coming your way."

Mags stared at the outline of the bird on his shoulder. Not too bad considering he hadn't shut up the whole time and now was ruining a perfectly good session with a business call. *About money.* That was all bankers ever cared about, and why should he be any different? Just because he had a kid sister who was sick? The falcon stared back at her, beak slightly open, wings spread, missing at least a third, maybe even more like half of its body. It was a shame, too. She was in the zone.

She rolled farther away from him and snapped

off her rubber gloves. She tossed them in the trash and stood.

Now she seemed to have Gael's attention. "Hold on," he said. He looked up at her. "Just give me five minutes."

"No," Mags said, shaking her head. Gael paused, surprise flickering across his face. The man was not used to hearing the word *no*. Well, he'd better get used to it. "If you want to take calls, then do it on your own time." Mags turned, heading to the sink at the corner of the room, turning on the water and running her hands under it. She had better things to do than sit around and listen to Gael run his fiefdom. She knew she was being unreasonable. But she blamed him. He'd stirred up memories of her mother's illness, of what happened after. Some things wouldn't go back in the box once they escaped. Now she was feeling like she was just one exposed nerve.

"I'm going to have to call you back," she heard from behind her, and then Gael scrambled to his feet.

"Mags, wait." He came up behind her, stealthy, moving a little too quietly for a banker, she thought, and surprised her by laying his hand on her shoulder. "What's going on?"

"We're done here." She crossed her arms across her chest. Let Gael think she was a bitch. She was, and she didn't care.

"What do you mean, done?" He glanced at his unfinished shoulder, confused.

"I was doing you a favor by taking you in and

doing a tattoo I don't like to do." She ground her back molars together. "If you want to disrespect me and my time by being on the phone, then you can do that in another shop. Have someone else finish it for you."

Fire burned in Gael's eyes. "Are you serious?"

"Yes. I am."

"You're being unreasonable. It was one phone call." He used a fatherly tone. Condescending, too. She wondered if he used that very tone on his younger sisters. He was standing toe to toe with her now, and she was very aware how much bigger he was. But her temper didn't care.

"It's my shop. I can be unreasonable if I want."

"Over *one* phone call? A call that took less than a minute. No. I don't think so."

Mags glared at him. He glared back. Most men were scared of her. Like Clint. And Angus. Really, most men went to hide when she got mad, scurried away from her as if they worried she could cast a spell on them or rip their eyes out with her fingernails. Mags guessed she leaned on the tough-girl persona a little too hard at times. But Gael didn't even blink. He was a mountain that wasn't moving. Wasn't the least bit afraid of her.

And that was all kinds of hot.

"You can't make me finish that tattoo." She almost said it as a dare. Could he make her?

He folded his arms across his muscled chest. He chuckled, low, eyes confident. "You sure I can't?"

Looking at that taut skin across those impressive

muscles, she suddenly wasn't so sure. She craned her neck to look at his face and saw a determined gleam in his green eyes. His jaw twitched, mouth set in a line.

"I *suggest* you finish the tattoo." Mags suddenly had the image of him whipping her over his knee. Spanking her for being unruly. The thought sent an electric pulse through her.

"Why?" God, he was tall. And broad. And had such big hands. Big, strong hands.

"Because you said you'd do this. And you're not going to quit now just because I stopped paying attention to you for half a second."

"Excuse me?" Fire burned in her belly. Thoughts of him putting her over one knee vanished. "This isn't about you not paying attention to me."

"Really? Because I get one phone call and you're suddenly angry that I'm not talking to you? Seems like maybe you *do* want my attention." He flashed her that dimple again, that smug dimple, and she almost wanted to claw it out of his face. He was turning the tables on her. Not fair.

"You're ridiculous. I don't even *like* you." She balled her hands into fists.

"So why are you staring at my chest like it's a steak, then?" He grinned. "Eyes are up here, sweetheart."

Mags swallowed, hard. So he'd noticed that. Dammit. Even worse, she could feel a blush creeping up her neck. This man was making her *blush*.

"So why don't I lie back in this chair and you go back to fantasizing about what the *rest* of my body looks like naked and finish up this tattoo?"

"You're an ass." A perceptive one, but still. An ass.

"You can see that, too. If you just finish up here." He nodded at his arm.

She slapped his bare arm. He didn't flinch. She slapped it again, harder this time, and then he grabbed her wrist. Held it tight. She knew he was strong. Now he proved it. Her wrist was in a vise grip, yet it didn't hurt. He knew how to hold her just right, and that made her think about other ways he might bind her. Contain her. She sucked in a breath, eyes flicking up to meet his.

"Don't hit me," he warned her, voice low, eyes dangerous.

"Or what?"

"Or I'll hit back." His jaw twitched again. His mouth formed a straight, serious line. And it sent another shiver of anticipation that ran straight between her legs.

"I thought you don't punch girls." Her voice came out breathy. He pulled her even closer.

"I don't," he said, his voice a low growl. "But spanking…that's something else." A slow, deliberate smile curved the edges of his mouth. She almost wanted to laugh, except the serious flicker in his eyes made the laugh die in her throat. "I think I need to put you over my knee."

She swallowed, mouth suddenly dry.

"Should I bend over then?" She wanted her voice to sound strong, defiant, but it almost came out as... meek and ready. *Submissive.* Her heart pounded in her chest as her brain realized what her body already knew: part of her wanted him to tell her yes.

He stared at her for a half beat.

"No," he said. "Not yet."

Not yet. The words hung there. A threat or a promise? Now she wasn't even sure if a spanking would be a punishment...or a pleasure. Maybe it would be both.

He let her wrist go, and the fresh air hit her skin. "Get back to work."

Cool disappointment kissed the back of her neck.

"Okay," she said, giving in as she stared at the floor, struggling to contain the desire that flared in her chest.

Gael slid wordlessly back into the chair, watching her with intent, as if gauging whether or not she'd misbehave. Hell, she didn't even know herself what she'd do. Mags fetched another pair of rubber gloves and tugged them on, deliberately *not* looking at the expansive of perfect skin before her as she struggled to push down the desire that threatened to overtake her good sense. Had she wanted him to go Neanderthal on her? Drag her back to his cave and show her what a man he was? What the hell was wrong with her? Had she all of a sudden decided what she wanted wasn't a Harley-riding bad boy, but a Christian Grey type? No. She knew that was all fantasy, anyway. Suits had pure missionary sex with the lights off, didn't they? Besides, she liked tough guys, guys who were a little rough and gruff, but she'd never wanted to be spanked before.

Not until Gael Quinn had suggested it. Somehow, in his low, commanding voice, it had sounded like something she needed.

Ridiculous.

She picked up her equipment, flipping the switch, the familiar hum of the needles vibrating in tandem feeling like music to her ears. She sat down and focused on the missing edge of the bird's wing, gently following the line that would complete the final feather. She worked in silence beneath Gael's knowing stare. She'd revealed something of herself just then, and she wasn't sure it was the smartest move. What she ought to do was finish up the tattoo and get this man out of her shop before he ordered her to strip and her body did it gladly.

She worked in silence for a while, and Mags felt her brain buzzing. Normally she loved hearing the drone of the tattoo machine, but now it sounded too loud, too scratchy in her ears. Gael never stopped looking at her, studying her, and she had the feeling he knew exactly the effect he'd had on her, knew that her mind was a swirl of confusion. But she had no idea what he was thinking. Or, even worse, what he was planning to do next.

She tried to focus on his shoulder, but all she could

think about was the sexy growl of Gael's voice. The way the thrumming bass in her chest had stopped her completely. Made her lose her damn mind. No wonder he got people to invest millions in his projects. He could just *order* them to and they'd need to obey.

She tried not to focus on the way the thick muscle across her shoulder twitched a bit, a knee-jerk response to her needles. She swiped at the blood rising on the tattoo and couldn't help but sneak a glance at his broad, bare chest. She'd tattooed hundreds of men and women by now in her career, and yet she'd never been so affected by a man's body in her chair. By a man's voice. What was so special about it, anyway? The longer they sat in silence, the more she could convince herself she'd just imagined the power in it. The persuasion.

Sure, he was sexy AF. But she'd had plenty of muscled men lie there before. Fit men. Fine men. Sexy men. He wasn't any different. Except he had had a family of sisters he took care of. That made him far beyond just a body. Or a suit. Made him a brother. A provider. A father figure. Was that why she thought he could keep her in line? Was that why she wanted him to? She shook her head. Dumb. She was being dumb. She just needed one night with her vibrator to forget all about Gael and his strong hands and low rumble of a voice.

She glanced up and their eyes met, and she froze for the briefest of seconds.

Him dominating. Her submitting. The role-play

fantasy flickered through her mind before she could stop it. *I've been bad. Punish me.* The words gurgled up in her throat, but she swallowed them down. She glanced away quickly, pulling her attention away from her borderline BDSM fantasy and back to his shoulder.

Focus, Mags. You've got a damn needle in the first layer of this man's skin. One distracted move and her mistake would be imprinted on him forever. And then he'd just lord it over her head, how she couldn't stop drooling over him. How she wanted to beg him to spank her. That would be a fate worse than death.

Her real problem was that it had been too damn long since she'd been laid. And the fact that Clint was cuffed meant it might be even longer than she'd like until she could scratch the itch building inside her. Sure, she could take home her pick of men tonight, but Clint was easy. He knew what she liked. He knew she edged toward a little rough but not too rough. He didn't talk too much. He didn't pry. And, most of all, he accepted the fact without question that after he'd done what she wanted, given her the release she craved, he went home. She never wanted a man to sleep over; she preferred to sprawl out naked— and alone—beneath her own sheets. She'd have to explain all of this to a new guy. Explain why it was best to keep sex just sex. Explain that she might like to be bossed around a little in the bedroom, but she was always—and forever—the boss outside it. Mags was always amazed about how many men simply wouldn't agree to those terms.

She pushed down her desire, her want, and by sheer strength of will focused on the tattoo. It was a seemingly endless struggle, even as the sun sank below the November horizon. She barely noticed the lack of sunshine. The bright lights of her parlor illuminated every little hair on Gael's arm, her desire for him not completely gone, but she'd wrestled out of being *ever present*. She was keeping a tight rein on her stupid sex fantasies. *Just get him out. Get him on his way.*

"Okay," she murmured when the tricky part was done. She sat back and let him sit up and stretch. She glanced up at the clock and rolled her neck, feeling the stiffness there. "I think we've done enough for today. We can finish up in a day or two."

Gael glanced down at the outline of the bird in flight. "Wow. You did…" His eyes grew wide. "An amazing job. This looks just like the cover. And you just drew this from memory?"

Mags liked the way he was looking at her now, as if she was a witch who could spin spells of magic. She nodded. "It's just what I do. We'll color it in tomorrow or the next day, after you've had a chance to heal, and we can see if your body takes to it all right. But right now, you've got the bones of it on you. You can see what it'll look like." She slid off her rubber gloves with a snap and tossed them into a nearby trash can. She rolled her neck again, working out the stiffness.

Gael nodded.

"You don't even know what this will mean to Ava." There it was again, that shining look in his eye, as if she'd saved him from something. As if she'd saved *him* somehow. She felt uncomfortable, almost, with the praise. She'd been careful in her work, sure, but she was careful every time. She'd rarely seen a man so happy to have her art on him.

"You're welcome," she said, but her throat suddenly felt dry. The way he could be both commanding and grateful at the same time made her feel disoriented. *Like a true alpha*, she thought, *commanding but caring. His first obligation to protect the pack.*

She grinned, though, matching his joy, unable to help herself. His joy was contagious. She'd worked hard for him, and he appreciated it. She couldn't believe she liked his approval so much, but there it was. She couldn't believe it, but she was beginning to like this damn suit. Maybe it was because he wasn't wearing it. Not the shirt, anyway. He had on just his pants, the V of muscle near his groin disappearing beneath the expensive leather belt he wore.

"You did well. Really well." The praise. In that deep voice. She felt something in her tick on. Want, pure and hot, rushed through her veins. His approval grew like warmth in her belly.

"So I don't get a spanking then?" she managed.

She met his gaze and saw his switch had flicked on, too. She could tell, because his grin faded and his green eyes burned with his own desire.

"Do you want one?" His gaze also held a question. And she knew the answer.

"Maybe."

"Come here, then." Mags's stomach lurched. That voice. That commanding voice that she felt in her toes.

Mags moved to him. He reached out and pulled her into his lap, and she went, compliant and ready. His eyes never left hers, and his jaw twitched again, his mouth in that familiar strong line. It was the strength there, the determination that made her thighs tingle.

"Spankings are for bad girls," he told her, a glint in his eye. "You've done well. You deserve a reward."

Her mouth parted.

Yes. I'm a good girl. Reward me.

She was deep into the role play, and she couldn't get out. Didn't want to get out. She was lost in it and forgot entirely about Gael being a suit, about him being not her type, about anything but the sensual curve of his mouth. She realized she'd wanted to kiss him, taste him, since the moment he'd walked into her shop. She had done good work on his arm. And now she'd claim her reward.

She put her lips on his.

CHAPTER FIVE

GAEL COULDN'T BELIEVE it as Mags's lips parted and her soft, wet mouth opened up to him. She tasted like cherries—her lip balm, maybe—and something else, something primal, something he *needed*. His brain was still struggling with the shock of it. Because Mags—the tough, blue-haired Asian biker chick—actually responded to him. He'd been half teasing about the spankings, about playing the dominant, but damn, it had worked better than he'd ever dreamed. Here she was, firm, warm ass on his legs, her tongue exploring his mouth. The tough girl that had all but told him to go to hell now putty in his hands.

And it couldn't be hotter.

It lit up all the primal sensors in his reptile brain. They pinged like lights on a slot machine. Her blue hair fell across his cheek, surprisingly soft. Not what he'd expected from the electric-blueberry color, but that was just the first of many surprises. Besides, what did it matter? His body was in control now, and the way she tasted made every nerve ending he had stand up at attention. That wasn't the only thing at attention, either, he realized as his groin tightened uncomfortably. The need grew as he focused on her soft lips, her wet tongue and the way she kissed him, as if her sole purpose on this earth was to please him.

First she hated him. Then she couldn't get enough of him. His head spun when she moved against his groin. She seemed to know exactly what the heat and pressure would do to him. She had her hands in his hair now. Her kiss became even more frantic, more urgent, and she put both cool hands on the sides of his face. He felt the heat between her legs as she rubbed against him, the delicious feel of her weight—such that it was—on him. God, he liked it. So did his cock, which was now fully awake and ready. She tasted so damn good. He'd thought he was in control, but now, with her mouth on his, he realized he had no control. She owned him. Her tongue flicked against his own, and he had to hold back his overwhelming desire to burrow into her wet depths. That was where he wanted to be. Now.

She broke free of the kiss then and leaned back, her pupils wide in her brown eyes. Her chest heaved, as did his, and she pushed back her electric-blue hair.

He hadn't been that blindsided since he didn't know when. How the hell had she learned to kiss like that?

"I liked my reward," she murmured, a submissive twinge to her tone that made those lights in his primal brain buzz. His cock ached.

"Yes," he breathed. "Me, too."

Her dark eyes gleamed with a promise of more to come. She hopped off him and wiped a seductive finger across her bottom lip. Damn, she was pure sex.

His heart was beating so fiercely he heard it in his ears. God, she'd really rung his bell. *And made his cock stand at attention.* That usually didn't happen so damn fast. But how would he know? These days, women had been the last thing on his mind. Hell, he hadn't even kissed a woman in months. He'd been too wrapped up in the Lewis deal and in his sister's diagnosis. No time for play. Until now. And that was only because Mags demanded it. She seemed to dare him to challenge her, and challenge her he would. What the woman wanted, the woman would get.

"How about we go get a drink?" she asked him.

A drink was not what his body wanted right then. His body wanted to burrow into hers, bury himself in her and keep on going until they both had their release. But she'd turned her back and was grabbing a leather jacket from a hook on the wall.

A drink it was, then. He scrambled for his shirt.

Mags wasn't sure why she'd why she'd offered the drink. Actually, that was a lie. She knew exactly why she'd invited him out for a drink. Because if she'd stayed one more second in that tattoo parlor, she would've ripped the man's clothes off and ridden him until he was dry. He tasted like…everything she'd ever craved, everything she'd ever wanted. He was a suit. She was a rebel. She was supposed to hate bankers. Even orphaned ones with three sisters. She'd never imagined she'd love the taste of him. But she did. Too much. And who would've ever thought a banker could kiss like that?

Who would've thought she wanted to *please* a damn banker? Or, hell, that he could issue commands like that? That was the most shocking part of all. That he'd been all too happy to play alpha. And that he was damn good at it. His strong jaw, those determined eyes. He had a surprising strength in him. Maybe it was because he'd had three sisters and had ultimately determined not to let them push him around. Or maybe it was because he'd been playing the father role since a young age. Whatever it was, that quiet strength, that unmovable center, was damn hot.

He sat in the back of the rideshare with her, leg to leg, and she felt his heat through her thin leggings. She remembered the feel of the hard bulge in his lap. Remembered how the sound of his voice made her want to do exactly what he asked. A drink was the only way to put the brakes on her libido, on her wanting to serve him, except now she was stuck with the suit. Scratch that—the suit she wanted to fuck. She might as well be honest with herself on that score. Even now, she remembered the feel of his lips on hers, how they'd each fought for dominance, how he seemed to anticipate her every move…the best kind of wrestling match. Because in the end, she knew she'd give in to what he wanted. That was what scared her most.

The fact that they'd ended up going to Clint's bar, she told herself, was pure coincidence. The Bulldog was the closest bar, and it had her favorite beer. Not that any of those two things mattered. Part of her worried she was trying to flaunt Gael in Clint's face. She told herself she wasn't. That wasn't what this was about. She didn't really care if Clint wanted to cuff himself to some waitress for the winter—or for the rest of his life, for that matter. His choice. But she wasn't going to stop coming to her favorite bar because of his choices, either.

At the door of the bar, they ran into Angus, in his full bouncer glory, not bothering to even wear a jacket despite the quickly dropping November evening temperature. He was wearing a black T-shirt and a black leather vest, his impressive forearms bare, her tattoos visible, except for the fresh one she'd just finished, which was still hidden under her bandage.

"Mags," Angus said, giving her a bear hug. She hugged him back. "Didn't expect you tonight." He glanced at Gael, uncertain.

"Just craving the best IPA in town."

He glanced at Gael. "He with you?" Angus narrowed his eyes a bit.

"Yeah." She shrugged.

"ID," he commanded, and a slight frown wrinkled Gael's brow but soon disappeared. He fished his wallet out of his back pocket and showed it to Angus. Not that there'd be any chance he was anywhere near twenty-one. Still, Angus studied it. He looked at it so long, Mags wouldn't be surprised if he was memorizing his driver's license number. Angus handed the card back to him wordlessly.

"Good to see you, Mags," Angus said. "Be careful in there."

"Thanks, Angus." Mags nodded at the beefy man. It was a word of caution. Even Angus wasn't sure, she assumed, how Clint would react to her being there. Not that she cared exactly how Clint would react. It had been his choice to get cuffed.

Mags walked inside the warm, low-lit Bulldog. They settled by the beat-up old wooden horseshoe of a bar, the lights so dim you could only barely make out the tin advertisement for PBR behind the bottles of whiskey. Gael was clearly not used to run-down places. He glanced at the broken-down bar stools as if unsure they'd hold his weight. They would—probably. He'd ditched the tie and coat, thank God. Still, his freshly pressed button-down Oxford looked out of place among the ratty T-shirts and worn leather jackets sitting at the no-doubt sticky high-top tables. He looked a little like one of those congressmen who tried to look folksy by not wearing a jacket. He still had too much of an air of respectability about him for this place.

"Want to sit at the bar?" Gael asked, since the few high tops were already full. She didn't, exactly, with

Clint there, but she also wasn't going to get scared away from it, either. Besides, the only other server in the place was Elena, the blonde waitress who was serving two guys pints of beer in the corner. She was wearing black leather pants, a red crop top and too much lipstick. Mags mentally shrugged off the image. She loved this bar. It was *her* bar, and they were all adults and could act like it.

"Sure," she said, and Gael actually *pulled out a bar stool*, as if she were a lady in 1890. "You don't have to do that," she told him, but he just sent her a crooked grin.

"I know," he said, but then she sat and he slid onto the seat next to her, glancing around as if for a cocktail menu.

"They don't have a drink list," she said. "But they've got what you see there." She nodded to the bottles stacked behind the bar. "And what's on tap."

"What do you like?"

"Bone-crusher," she said nodding at the silver skull atop the tap handle. "Best double IPA in town."

Clint had seen them now. He looked surprised and, worse, worried. Fearful, even. Mags frowned. Well, she guessed when he played alpha in the bedroom, he was just faking it. He *was* scared of her. He looked like he might want to piss himself. The fear filled her with disdain. This was why she hated relationships—because everyone disappointed in the end.

He might not be sharing her bed, *pretending* to be

the tough guy he clearly wasn't, but surely her money was still good for a round. He'd cut his jet-black hair shorter than usual and was growing a goatee, a new addition since she'd seen him last. What was that? Two weeks ago? Three? She couldn't remember, exactly, but she'd known it was before the weather had turned cold. He ambled up to them, then, wearing a bar towel over one shoulder and scowl.

"Mags," he said, guarded. That fear in his eyes again. Coward. How did she ever let him into her bed to begin with? How could she not smell that fear on him?

"Clint," she replied. "This is my friend Gael."

Clint glanced at Gael as if he were a bug he wanted to crush under his boot. Gael didn't seem the least bit intimidated, either. If he were annoyed that she'd taken him to the place where her friend with benefits worked, he sure didn't show it. She would've guessed he would be the annoyingly territorial type, the kind who beat his own chest and told all the other gorillas he was the alpha, but Gael didn't seem to operate like that. Interesting.

"Nice to meet you," Gael said, holding out his hand. Clint reluctantly took it, and Gael shook it enthusiastically. Mags had to admire his confidence.

"You're not going to start anything, are you, Mags?" Clint looked worried. It almost made Mags laugh. She shook her head, slowly.

"Nah. I just want a Bone-crusher."

"Okay," he said, not seeming to believe her. He glanced at Gael. "You?"

"The same," he said. "And a shot of Jameson."

Both Mags and Clint stared at Gael a beat. "Make it two," Mags said, with a new appreciation for the suit.

Gael moved so that his knee brushed hers by the bar. She could feel an electric charge, even through her leggings, as the heat from his body touched hers. Man, she really was in trouble if some accidental footsie was getting her this wound up.

"So, that's *the* Clint, huh?" Gael raised an eyebrow, as he watched the thick-shouldered bartender grab some clean pint glasses. She glanced at him, noticed he wasn't afraid. Or the least bit intimidated. There it was: that quiet strength in him. She felt drawn to it.

"Yeah." Mags shrugged. Clint wasn't the best lay she'd ever had or the worst, but he was solidly in the satisfactory category. But he wasn't nearly as handsome as Gael, or as confident, either, as it turned out.

"So…" Gael grinned a little bit. "You treating me like arm candy? Bringing me around to make him jealous?"

"What?" Mags whirled, shocked. "You can't be serious. You're not arm candy." Though, looking at his dark, wavy, shampoo–ready hair, maybe she was wrong about that.

"Oh, sure I am." Gael flashed his dimple at her, and she wasn't sure if she wanted to kiss him or punch him. The man had no shortage of ego. It was ridiculous. "Should we fake make out? If we use tongue, that ought to make him jealous enough."

"Stop it." She gave him a sharp elbow. The idea was ridiculous. But then, wasn't part of her kind of hoping that Clint would see she didn't lose any time in moving on as well? There were other bars she could've gone to. Less convenient ones, but still. Mags watched as Clint filled their beer glasses, noting that he seemed to be trying not to listen in on their conversation, when he clearly was. Let the coward listen.

"Come on. I know when I'm being used."

"Are you always this full of yourself?"

"No. Sometimes I eat steak. Then I'm full of that," he deadpanned. God, he kept her off balance. A jokester one minute, a dom the next. But that strength was there, that immovability of his, there beneath it all. The man was made of granite. "Or you want to start a bar fight? Need some backup? Is that why I'm here? Who do I rush first?"

"God, this was a mistake." But she laughed as she said it.

"I just want to know if we're busting skulls or we're simply trying to make him jealous."

Mags threw back her head and laughed. "Don't be absurd. Jealousy is a wasted emotion. I don't believe in it."

"You don't believe in jealousy?" Gael raised his dark eyebrows in surprise, skepticism on his face.

"You'd have to be attached to something to be jealous. And I don't get attached."

"Not ever?"

"Not ever." Attachment led to pain. She'd learned that the hard way. First with her mother. Then…her father. "You the relationship type?"

Gael glanced at her. "Not if I can help it."

Now it was Mags's turn to laugh.

"Well, then, we have something in common." Clint slid two foamy IPAs in front of them, as well as two shots of Jameson. Mags took her shot glass and raised it. He met her glass in the air.

"To avoiding getting cuffed," she said.

"Amen," he answered, and the two of them took slugs of the drink, the Irish whiskey burning down her throat.

Metallica jammed out from hidden speakers in the ceiling, and Mags watched as Elena made her way past them and to the edge of the bar to pick up a round of drinks for one of her tables. She eyed Mags, a worry line appearing on her forehead. Why was everyone afraid of her? Why was everyone so worried she was going to start something? Mags might be tough, but she wasn't a hothead. She left bar fights to the amateurs who couldn't control their tempers. She was starting to think this was a mistake. She was the one being childish, after all. They should've gone to a different place. But…this was *her* bar as much as it was Clint's. Hell, it had been her bar since well before Clint showed up. Why should she be the one to run off with her tail between her legs?

She glanced at Gael. *He* was the only one who didn't seem afraid of her. Not in the least.

Gael nudged her elbow. "You okay?" he asked. Damn his sympathy. She didn't need his pity.

"Fine," she said, trying to stiffen her back a little. It was just a drink, dammit. Gael eyed Elena as she swept past them. Then he glanced at the adjacent room with the two pool tables. One of which was still empty.

"Do you play?" he asked her.

"Do you?" She couldn't help but ask, surprised.

"A little." He slid off his bar stool, and Mags followed, curious. She was suddenly glad to put some space between herself and Clint. She told herself it wasn't because she cared. She didn't. But she hated awkward. She had no time for it. Now she could focus on Gael. A suit that could play pool? This she had to see.

She took a slow sip of her beer as she watched while Gael stashed his beer on a side table and retrieved the balls from the pockets of the table. He racked them like a pro, sliding the triangle to the end of the table. The pool table had seen better days: its felt was faded in a few spots and torn at the far right edge of one hole, but it was still passable for play— or at least what passed for play at the Bulldog.

Mags watched Gael roll up his shirtsleeves and felt a little hitch in her throat. He almost looked...a little dangerous, which Mags told herself was ridiculous. Bankers weren't the dangerous type. Unless, of course, they were foreclosing on someone's family home, she reminded herself. Then they were very dangerous. But Gael looked anything but a pencil pusher or real estate thief as he chalked up the end of a cue, his forearm muscles working. He certainly seemed comfortable at the pool table. In fact, he seemed comfortable no matter where he was. That quiet confidence was sexy. More than sexy. It was... apex alpha.

She wasn't the only one who'd noticed, either. The women sitting at the end of the bar, clad in fishnets and torn denim, eyed him with interest. They'd been staring since he'd arrived at the bar but intensified their looks as he prowled around the pool table. Even Elena cast him more than a single glance. He wasn't wrong. He was eye candy. But he also was more than that.

She remembered him holding her wrist tight. The warning in his eyes. God, the memory made her want to get on her knees. Submit to him. The urge was strong. Stupidly strong. She gulped her beer to cool the fire licking at her throat.

"Would you like to break?" he asked, grabbing a pool cue from the bin against the wall and offering her the stick.

She shook her head. "You can go ahead." She wanted to see what he could do.

"You sure?" He grinned. "If I take the cue, you might not a get a shot."

Mags laughed and put down her beer. She doubted he was *that* good. How many suits ever spent time in a pool hall? Please. That wasn't where they made their money. The other women in the bar were watching him intently as he moved around the pool table.

"You can't be that good. You grew up on the North Shore."

He just shrugged one shoulder as he handed her the cue. "I was always taught...ladies first."

The way he said it made it sound like pool wasn't the thing he was talking about at all. She felt a quiver of anticipation run down her inner thigh. She put down her beer at a side table and choked up on the cue.

"Well, I'll go, then." Mags leaned over the table and shut one eye as she lined up the stick and let it rip. The balls clattered across the table, and two stripes went barreling into opposite corner pockets. Mags settled in, aiming for a blue ten. She was keenly aware of Gael's attention focused on her. She almost thought he might be checking out her ass. She hit the ball, hoping to spin it to the side pocket, but barely missed. Mags felt her cheeks burn ever so slightly. Normally she was better at this. Was she actually nervous? She didn't want to think that Gael's knowing gaze was the reason she'd missed.

"That's rough," Gael said as she handed him her pool cue. He flashed her that grin again, cocky as ever. His eyes held hers, just for the briefest of seconds. She remembered the kiss then, the sudden warmth of his tongue in her mouth, the way he'd opened a need in her to please him—a dangerous need.

"I'm out of practice," she said, wondering if she meant playing pool or flirting. Lately Mags had done very little of either. But now it was her turn to stare at *his* ass if she wanted. Which she did. She watched him walk around the table, calculating the geometry in his head. He decided on a shot, number three into the corner pocket. He leaned over and was all tight control as he easily knocked the ball into the corner. It was an easy shot, one she could've made with her eyes closed.

"Nice shot," she said.

He raised an eyebrow. "Are you patronizing me?"

She laughed. "No. Yes. Maybe."

He chuckled again, low in his throat. Then he leaned over the felt again, and she could see down the front of his shirt, the hint of the chest muscles there. She had a strong desire to run her hands across the ridge, draw her finger down the front of his belly and see if those ab ridges she'd seen in the tattoo parlor felt as hard as they looked. She suspected they would. He cracked the cue stick against the ball, and it rolled hard, smacking the side ball and the corner ball, straight into the pocket. Mags's mouth fell open.

"What the hell?" she murmured, gripping the side of the pool table. That was no lucky shot. That wasn't an amateur's play. "You're…" She struggled for the right word. "Good."

"Surprised?" Gael grabbed a chalk cube and twisted it around the end of his cue, green eyes sparkling. "Did you think I was a buttoned-up stiff who never had any fun?"

She felt a blush creep up her cheek. That was exactly what she'd thought.

He leaned back down and made quick work of the five, slapping it into the opposite side pocket, spinning the cue ball so that it didn't follow. Gael was systematically cleaning the table, setting himself up for one shot after another. The pool table fell under the power of his will. And so did she.

"You weren't kidding when you said I wouldn't have a turn if you went first." She'd thought he was all bluster. No substance. She'd been wrong. Very wrong.

"Don't say I didn't warn you," he added as he knocked the two in. Then the three. Next came the six. Now all he had left was the eight ball. It was a rough shot, a tough angle.

"Eight ball, corner pocket." He nodded toward the edge of the table.

"The side pocket would be easier," Mags pointed out. "Unless you just want to show off." She grinned, leaning up against the wall of the bar, arms crossed across her chest.

Gael looked up, raising an eyebrow. "Nah," he said. "I just like things the hard way." He hit the cue ball without even *looking* at it, sinking the eight ball in the corner as if it was meant to be there. Mags laughed, pushing herself off the wall and giving Gael a slow clap.

"I'm impressed," she said. "And it's not easy to impress me." Mags was moving closer to him, as if there was an invisible force pushing her there, a fishing line between her and Gael. Every time Gael's smile grew bigger, the line grew more taut. Reeling her in. Slowly but surely. She was no different than the balls on the pool table. Rolling to him, bending to his will.

"Where did you learn how to do that?"

"I was a broke college student," he said. "I had to earn drinking money somehow." He shrugged.

"I can believe it. Is that how you made enough money to buy custom-made suits?" She nodded at his wool pants.

"No. That came from my parents' life insurance policy. And a few lucky investments."

She stared at him a beat. "Somehow, I don't believe it was all luck." Not with him. It was will, not luck.

Gael leaned the pool cue against the rack behind Mags. He brushed her arm as he went, and she got a nose full of him: something spicy. Something sweet. Something…decidedly man. Her whole body felt on high alert. Tense, ready, waiting. She wanted to do what he wanted, wanted him to do what he pleased.

He paused, releasing the cue, his eyes meeting hers. A question was in them, a question her body had already answered. Her heart thudded in her chest, the blood rushing through her ears like a wild river. She felt her lips part and watched as he seemed to grow closer. She knew it was folly to make out with him in this bar, mere feet from Clint and with Angus at the door. If she'd been in her right mind, she would've stepped away from him. But she couldn't. Wouldn't.

Something in her blood told her this man was made for her, *meant for her*, that she couldn't turn away from this. He was too strong to resist, too solid to ignore. Gael's lips were so close now, and all she wanted was to feel them again on her own, to meet his tongue with hers, to go to a place where both their minds would think of nothing but pure need. She closed her eyes, anticipating the feel of his lips on hers, but suddenly, she felt nothing but cold air. He'd withdrawn. Her eyes fluttered open, surprised to see Clint standing there. Holding a new beer.

He thumbed back to the ladies in fishnets at the bar. "They bought you another round."

Mags frowned at them, but they weren't looking at her. "None for me?" she asked.

Clint ignored her as he slid the drink over to Gael. He took it and hesitated. "Would you like it? You can have it," he offered.

She shook her head. "No, they want to see you drink it."

Gael took it and raised the glass to the women at

the bar before he took a swig. Mags felt her throat tighten as she glared at the women. Maybe she would get into a fight, after all.

Clint, however, was still staring at Gael.

"You up for a game?" Clint asked, nostrils flaring.

"You're working," Mags said, feeling suddenly annoyed by his presence. Clint was the one who got cuffed and yet now he was being territorial? He had no right. None.

"I'm on break," Clint said, nodding toward the bar. Another bartender, a new guy that she'd only seen once before, was pouring beer. The fishnets-and-torn-jeans ladies were talking to him now. Clint's lips curved upward, but the smile didn't reach his eyes. Mags told herself that there was no way Clint would start a fight in his own bar. But, still, part of her worried. Clint had a temper sometimes.

"Sure." Gael didn't move. He was sending the signal he wouldn't be scared off. Mags almost rolled her eyes. She wasn't anybody's territory. Mags moved to the table.

"How about I beat you both?" Mags grabbed a pool cue and swung it under one arm.

"How about you let the boys play this round?" Clint said, shaking his head, never looking away from Gael. Mags nearly rolled her eyes. She hated pissing contests.

"If I can't play, then I'm getting a drink," Mags said. She glanced at both men, but they didn't seem to care about her threat to leave. It was just as she

thought: some men were more concerned about competition with one another than the woman in the
room. She hated that feeling of exclusion, that she
was little more than a trophy for one of their shelves.

Gael, seeming to sense her disapproval, glanced
quickly at Mags.

"This won't take long," he promised.

Mags didn't answer. They could take as long as
they wanted. In her mind, she'd already decided she'd
order a new beer and if she finished it and the two
men were still trying to fight for her damn attention,
she'd leave. She knew this was partly her fault. She'd
brought Gael to Clint's bar. What did she expect? For
Clint to play nice? For boys *not* to be boys?

But the fact that Gael was going to take Clint's
challenge was irksome. She felt abandoned, ignored.
She trudged to the bar, sat herself down and ordered
another Bone-crusher. It came, cold and crisp, and
she took a deep drink. She wasn't going to be here
long. She glanced over her shoulder and saw that
Gael got the first shot. That was Clint's mistake. She
smirked to herself, wondering just when Clint would
lose his temper. Mags took another swig of beer even
as she tried to put her back to the pool table. Though,
out of the corner of her eye, she watched Gael move,
smooth and unconcerned, that unshakable confidence making him steady.

Gael was taller than Clint and had a bit more muscle. That surprised her, somehow. How Clint didn't
just look smaller. He looked...weaker. On his back

heel. Maybe it was the quiet self-assurance that ran through every move Gael made. He was a man who wasn't afraid. Strangely refreshing, too. He probably wouldn't send Angus to break up with her. He wouldn't be afraid of her. That lack of fear was what made her want to submit to him, wasn't it? That was why she wanted to give him the reins—because she knew he could hold them.

She smiled at the thought and secretly rooted for Gael to clean Clint's clock. She was not surprised to see Gael wiping the table. She wondered how Clint would take it and then decided she didn't care. Gael could take care of himself.

Mags swiveled around to face the bar, still keeping an eye on the men in the mirror behind the bourbon. Not that she cared, she told herself. This was their problem. She eyed the eight ball, the only one left on the table. It was a challenging shot. Some would say even an impossible shot. The chances were slim to none he'd make it. And Clint was letting him know it.

Mags heard rather than saw Gael sink the eight ball and froze, wondering when Gael would get a pool cue across the head. She tightened her grip around her pint glass. Perhaps she ought to leave right now. Before things got ugly. Before she felt the need to try to help Gael. She braced for the fight, but instead, she heard…laughter.

She turned, puzzled, and saw Clint *clap* Gael on the back. What the hell…? She forgot her beer entirely and swiveled in her chair, watching the two men come back to the bar, laughing. Like they were best friends. She watched as Clint went behind the bar and grabbed a bottle of expensive Irish whiskey, the kind he kept for special customers, and pour out three shots. Gael slid onto the empty bar stool next to her.

"What the hell happened?" she whispered to Gael.

"Clint's buying us shots," Gael said.

"He's...what?"

But Clint appeared with those expensive shots and handed one to Gael, one to her and one to himself.

"To fucking bastards!" he said and raised his shot glass. Mags, still confused, glanced at Gael, who already had his shot glass in the air.

"Fuck 'em!" Gael cheered, and then the two men downed the whiskey. Mags, puzzled, drank hers, hoping the whiskey would help her make sense of what the hell was happening.

Clint wandered off. Mags stared at Gael. "You going to tell me why Clint's not beating you right now...and instead is *buying you drinks*, which, by the way, is something he never does?"

"Turns out, my cousin and he were in the army together," Gael said. "Same platoon. They had the same drinking salute—to fuckin' bastards!"

"You got all that in thirty seconds of kicking his ass at the pool table?"

"He has an army tattoo. He served, too, in Afghanistan."

"He did?" Mags shook his head. She'd slept with

the man countless times and hadn't even known he'd served in Afghanistan. Sure, she knew about the tattoo, but plenty of men had tattoos. She didn't ask about all of them. She realized she hadn't really cared enough about Clint to ask those questions. No wonder he'd cuffed himself to Elena. Mags saw Clint grab beer glasses and begin to fill them.

"Is he buying us beers, too?" Mags was going to lose her mind.

"Yep." Gael grinned.

Mags noticed the fishnet ladies eyeing Gael. Trying to figure out if she and he were together, and in the end, she realized, not caring if they were.

"Does *everybody* just fall at your feet? Clint and then those skanks down there?" She nodded down.

He shrugged.

"You could fuck one of them if you wanted. Maybe both of them, they way they're looking at you."

"I don't want them." He glanced at her sideways.

Mags swallowed, hard. She felt the blood rush to her inner thighs. Could the man read her damn mind? Was she such an open book? Her mouth had gone dry as she met his serious gaze. The weight of it, the power. She could feel it in her belly.

"What do you want, then?"

He leaned forward so his lips were against her ear. "You," he murmured, voice low. "I want you."

CHAPTER SIX

GAEL LEANED BACK to enjoy the look of complete shock blooming on Mags's face. He got the feeling she was a woman who wasn't surprised often, having already figured out all the angles of a situation and the people in it. She was cautious, tactical and guarded. Not an easy woman to surprise. He almost laughed but thought better of it. Laughing would probably just make her mad.

What he really wanted to do was kiss those full lips of hers, taste that hint of something sweet again, feel the power of her tongue. Make her *do* things for him. She worked so hard to be a rebel punk, a tough girl, but he got the impression what she wanted was to let all that go…for an hour or a night. Let someone else make the decisions for once. She wanted strength. She wanted someone who'd command her. She craved the discipline. That was why she lashed out so hard. She was waiting for someone to lash back.

She blinked fast, thick eyelashes framing those

brown eyes. She wasn't going to make it easy for him. His eyes traveled down to her trim waist and flared hips, clad in skintight leggings. He wanted to put his hands on her hips, show her exactly the position he wanted her in. He had a feeling she'd want that, too. Her small feet wore thick combat boots, and she'd perched one toe territorially on his stool. She could claim all the territory she wanted. He wasn't going to resist. Hell, he'd throw her a welcome party.

"You want me? You think you can have me?" she managed after a beat. He thought she meant to sound tough, except he heard her breath catch. What was meant to sound like a dare came out like a plea.

Something in him lit up then. Something primal, something predatory. He felt like a wolf watching a rabbit run away from him. There was only one thing to do: pursue.

"I know I can have you." He caught her stool beneath one foot. He dragged it closer, the legs of the stool scraping against the worn wood of the floor.

Her pink lips parted, eyes widened in surprise. She looked less like a punk chick then and more like a doll. A fragile doll. She was warring with herself—he could see it in her eyes. Trying to decide whether to give in or slap him in the face. He liked the struggle. Because he knew he'd win.

"What if I'm going home with Clint tonight?" She lifted her small chin in challenge.

He felt something dark in his belly then, dark

and nasty. He glanced at the bearded bartender, the veteran.

Elena was leaning over the bar, waiting to pick up the beer Clint was pouring for some other customers. And Mags was watching them a little too intently for Gael's tastes. For a woman who didn't believe in jealousy, she sure seemed...jealous. Gael didn't like it. Not one bit.

"You're not going anywhere with Clint."

"Who says?"

"I say." He almost thought Mags would fight him on that. But, instead, he realized, she only approved of him putting his foot down. Something shifted in her then. He could almost feel it. She reached out and grabbed his hand.

"Come on then," she murmured, voice low, as she pulled him off the stool.

"Where?"

She glanced at him, eyes full of mischief, a wicked tilt to her pink lips. "My place."

Mags hadn't been planning on inviting Gael to her bed. All she knew was that when Gael laid down the law, she wanted to lie down beneath him. That's it. As backward as that might sound, she couldn't help it. She knew it was barbaric, out-of-date thinking. But when she'd seen the flash of territorialness in his eyes, she'd felt the want, warm in her belly. She liked strong men. She'd make no apologies, either. Only a strong man could handle her. And she yearned for one who wasn't afraid. Gael might be egotistical, might even be a suit, but he wasn't afraid.

What she wanted more than anything was to lean against his strength, yield to it. Wanted a cleansing, mindless fuck, so that she could get on with her life and put this November behind her as fast as possible. Gael was the perfect option.

They were barely in the rideshare before Mags was on Gael, hands in his dark hair, mouth against his. Mags never did this, never let her feelings overwhelm her common sense, never made out with a guy in the back of a rideshare, not caring if the driver saw or cared. But she'd never felt this kind of attraction before. It was electric, addictive. It was as if all along she'd been hooked on him and didn't know it until he walked into her life.

Mags didn't believe in love at first sight, but lust—that was something she understood. Just not quite at this urgent level. She prided herself on keeping her feelings—and her desires—neatly stored away in a steel box in her brain. She let them out when *she* wanted. Except with Gael, it felt like her whole body was a Pandora's box. It wanted to open. For him.

She knew he was full of himself, knew that he was bad news, but that was what she wanted right now. Bad news. Something to help her forget Clint, help her forget it was November at all.

Gael matched her enthusiasm, his hands roaming down her back, exploring her curves, sliding territorially down her ass. Yes. *Own me*, she wanted to tell him.

His left hand slid down the back of her leggings, and she welcomed the electric contact, his heat against her lower back. She wanted his hands everywhere all at once, and the fact that they still had clothes on felt infuriating. She barely cared they were in a car, speeding to her apartment just blocks away.

When they arrived, the driver cleared his throat, uncomfortable. She didn't care. She leaped out of the car, tugging Gael out by the hand. He laughed as she keyed in her passcode at her old condo, a converted warehouse on the near west side. She and Gael tumbled into her narrow foyer lined with the eight mailboxes of the other renters.

She pulled him up the flight of carpeted stairs and at the first landing managed to get the key into the lock of her door and push inside the darkened one-bedroom. She flicked on a lamp sitting on the foyer table but wanted to keep the rest of the lights out. Her kitchen was a mess, her living room barely better. Her bedroom was the only room semiclean, and that was only because behind her closed closet door was another mess.

She hadn't been expecting company, after all. Not that she cared what Gael thought. Hell, this was going to be one night only. She wasn't going to make a habit of seeing him so he could tease her about how far behind she was on her laundry.

Laundry seemed to be the last thing on his mind

as they both kicked off their shoes in the foyer, barely stopping their frantic kiss to do so. She liked the feel of his warm hands, liked the fact that they felt like they belonged on her. He kissed her again, and she felt her spine melt into a puddle, felt her bones turn to gelatin. Eventually she had enough power to guide him into her bedroom, and he went. She flicked on a bedside lamp as she sat on her own soft bed, which took her weight with a protesting creak.

Mags tugged the buttons on his shirt, frustrated that there were so many. She just wanted the man's clothes off. She wanted to feel his skin on hers, wanted the electric current of his body against hers. Mags had never known she needed something so much, had never felt so…vulnerable…as she did right now, her hunger growing in her like a fire, the flames licking her earlobes, threatening to consume her. This would normally be the time her mind would roam—her thoughts would be half here, on the man in her bed, and half at her studio, or making up a to-do list. But Gael commanded all of her attention, every fiber of her being as she got his shirt off and saw his wide expanse of chest. Skin she knew was soft, her mark on his right shoulder, the bandage still in place. She reached up and kissed him and then broke away.

His green eyes studied her, and she felt as if he could see right through her, see to the burning flame of desire he'd lit inside her, just for him. God, she wanted him. She felt the soft bed beneath her. She just wanted him to join her there.

"Tell me what to do. Order me," she panted, her voice barely a whisper as she asked for what she needed.

He took a step back. Was he not going to play? Was he going to run for the door? She hoped not. Was the role play too much? Had she gone too far? Then came his voice.

"Get up." The command in it, the strength, made her knees shake with want. She stood, powerless to do anything else. There it was: the set line of his jaw, the determined look in his eye. God, so damn sexy. This was all she ever wanted. A man to be…in control. To not be afraid of her. And he wasn't the least bit afraid of her.

"Take off your shirt."

White-hot want moistened the thong beneath her tights. *Yes*, she thought. *I'm yours to command.* She tugged on the corner of her T-shirt and lifted it over her head, hands trembling. She tossed it to the ground.

"Take off your bra." His eyes gleamed with power. The power she was giving him. Delicious.

Her hands did as told, slipping off the straps. Unhooking the back and letting it fall to the ground. Cold air hit her nipples, making them rise. He studied them, a small smile of approval spreading across his face.

"Take off…everything else." His voice, the strength

in it, was going to make her come right there. She felt her legs quiver as she tugged off her tights and her thong. He slowly cased her full body, head to toe. She felt completely exposed. Completely at his mercy. And all she wanted to do was obey.

She loved it.

She spent her days being tough. At night she wanted to please. That was all she'd ever really wanted. Her lower back prickled with excitement. What would he tell her to do next? The endless possibilities made her tingle.

"Get on the bed." She sat down, scooting back a little. Knees together, heart pounding in her chest. What next? Her mind bounced to a dozen different possibilities.

She watched as he undid his pants, and she watched, mesmerized, as he unzipped his fly. He pulled something—a square condom package—from his back pocket before he kicked off the pants. He slid down his underwear next, and she felt shock at the size of him—bigger than she'd expected, standing at attention, ready and willing. No wonder he was so damn egotistical. And no wonder he could give orders. With a cock like that, what woman wouldn't obey?

A slow, wicked expression crept into his eyes. "Spread your legs," he told her.

She did. Slowly. Never breaking his gaze. She saw the heat in his eyes, the want. Knew that as much as he worked to keep his voice steady, he wanted her as much as she wanted him. That seeing her splayed on the bed, at his mercy, was driving him as wild as her. Her heart thumped in her chest as she lay back on her elbows, legs spread, waiting patiently for his next command. He studied her body, focused on a point between her legs.

He tossed her the condom without looking at her face. "Put it on me."

She sat up, sliding to the edge of the bed. She ripped the condom open with her teeth and put it between her lips. He hadn't said *how* she ought to put it on. But his eyebrows raised slightly in approval. She moved to the edge of the bed. She reached up and took him in her hands, gingerly at first, reverential, almost. He moaned softly at her touch, and all she wanted was to make him groan even louder. Then she put the edge of the condom on the tip and rolled it on with her mouth. He was so thick, it was hard to do, but she managed to get half of it on before her hands had to finish the job.

He grew even bigger beneath her touch, his green eyes growing sharp, needy. He tilted down and found her mouth. The commands went silent then, as his lips trailed down the side of her neck and found her left nipple, his warm tongue bringing it to an aching point. Then he worked on the other, and it was her turn to moan as her head lolled back, eyes closed, as she rode the urgent wave of need that crashed over them both. The delicate way he moved drove her nearly insane. She wanted him—all of him—now, but he was taking his sweet time, exploring her body gingerly, deliberately. He bent over her, kissing her, licking her nipples, making her whole body arch with want. She focused on his mouth on her skin, and her body felt white-hot, a single exposed nerve that he could play with as he wished.

He filled her then, spreading her open, and she wrapped herself around him, her legs clenching tightly around his waist. He moved, slowly, deliberately, and she felt like she was going to come right there, dissolve into a puddle of pure ecstasy. She felt his weight on her, his delicious weight, and welcomed it. He pulled both her arms above her head and held them tightly with one hand, wrists together. She was completely at his mercy as his mouth found her nipple again. He pushed against her, harder, deeper, and it felt like a punishment and a reward all at once.

She gave her power to him, gave her will, gave her body. She tried to move her wrists, but he held them fast. Those strong hands. That was what she wanted. She wanted those strong hands to bind her. Hold her wildness in check. Give her the boundaries she desperately needed. He pulled back and met her gaze.

"You're going to come for me," he told her.

"Yes," she breathed. Yes, she would. She couldn't help it. She was climbing a staircase, one step at a time, and he was pushing her faster. Ever faster. He claimed her, deeper and deeper with each thrust.

"Come now. Come for me." The command pushed

her to the top. She rocked her hips to meet his thrust, and then, in an instant, her whole body tensed, her toes curled, and she was coming, and she cried out, the pleasure tearing from her throat, unable to be contained. She looked down at Gael's face and saw him studying her, almost reverentially, and wondered if a man had ever looked at her like that before, like a work of art. "That's good," he told her, the praise warming her from the inside as he let her wrists go. "That's very good."

Her body shuddered with aftershocks. She'd never come that hard, that fast before. And never on command. Never, not once in her life. Mags was always coaxing climaxes from her reticent body. But not with Gael, not here in her bed. He seemed to know exactly what would drive her wild, and she wondered how he'd come about that knowledge, how many hours he'd spent worshipping other women, but then decided she didn't care.

Already she could feel she would have another one. And maybe yet another. They were queued up in her like candy bars in a vending machine. Gael put his hands on her hips, steering her to a new position. Now he moved to the edge of the bed and stood and tugged her backward so she was on her hands on knees. She was completely vulnerable now, her body was still shuddering from the aftereffects of her amazing orgasm. He swiftly took her from behind, dominating her, as he leaned down and nibbled her ear.

"Now it's my turn." His voice left no room for argument. Not that she would.

"Yes," she moaned. *Whatever you want.*

Then he took her harder, driving deeper, and she gasped with the force, the determination. The sheer will. God, he was strong. Her body molded to him, and he powered to his own end. She felt hers building once more. Was she going to come again? Her body said yes…her body might always tell him yes. She could feel him growing harder inside her, feel his want. And then, in a loud cry, he came in three deep thrusts inside her. At the same moment, she came, too, her mind blinded with pleasure. He fell on top of her, panting, his frantic heartbeat matching hers.

She had a thought then, as he lay breathing on top of her back: she might never in her life have sex this good again. She'd never given over control that completely before. Never felt so…turned on by the possibility. Sure, she like things a little rough. Liked a slap on the ass now and again, but this… This was different. This was him commanding. And her obeying.

The thought was frightening.

It's just sex, she told herself. *Nothing more. Role play. That's it.*

He rolled off her then, gently unraveling the condom from himself and disposing of it in the bagged trash near the nightstand. Then he rolled over and kissed her ever so slowly. The contact sent a quiver of want down her spine. Her body still felt spent. How could she even think about round two?

She rolled on her back, looking at the ceiling, heart still beating in her chest. He pulled her to him, noticing her secret tattoo—the one she'd done herself on her hipbone, the small, delicate zebra finch, bright orange beak open in song, his black-and-white tail feathers splayed out behind him. He trailed his fingers across it, glancing once up at her.

"This is a beautiful work of art," he told her, and she wasn't sure in that split second if he meant the tattoo or her body. The commanding voice was gone then. He was back to normal, back to friendly Gael.

"My first tattoo," she admitted. She'd worked on it for years, honing, sculpting, making it better. She still wasn't completely happy with the pattern on the bird's tail. She was still fixing it. The tattoo had evolved with her skills: beginning as a shaky outline, and then becoming the lush, colored version she now wore. Her hands slid down his bandaged arm, and she remembered that she'd marked him, too. That they both carried her art, and the knowledge was tantalizing somehow. This wasn't the first man she'd slept with that she'd tattooed. Hell, she'd tattooed most of them. But this was the first man she'd marked *for the first time* and slept with. He had miles of unmarked skin, a tattoo virgin. It made her feel almost...territorial.

He found another tattoo now, the two birds on her arm. He traced the line of her tattoo, and she felt goose bumps rising on her skin.

"What does it mean?" he asked her. "The two birds?"

She glanced down at the robins on her arm.

"The first bird, here, holding the branch in her claw, that's my adoptive mother. I did this one after she died." Mags realized at that moment that she'd never actually spoken these words out loud. Never voiced the intention behind the tattoo. That was because no one had ever asked.

"How'd she die?"

"Cancer." Mags glanced up at him. "Breast cancer. Spread to her liver."

"I'm sorry," Gael said, as if he'd had anything to do with her mother's death. Or the downward spiral of what was left of the family afterward.

"It's not your fault. It's cancer's fault. You know that."

Gael nodded. "What about the other bird?"

"The second bird is my adoptive father. He's still alive, but…" She trailed off, not sure she could trust her voice.

"Not in the picture?"

"He remarried. Moved to California. Started over again." *Forgot Mom*, she wanted to add, but didn't. *Showed me Mom was the one who wanted to adopt me. Not him.* She'd already shared too much. Hell, she was practically blabbing about her feelings. She never did that. Especially not with men she slept with. "Anyway, we don't talk much."

She thought about the number of missed calls on

her phone. Her dad had recently started calling again after a long while of nothing. Probably because the anniversary was coming up. That damn awful day in November when her mother died. That day was supposed to bring relief with it—when her mother had finally been at peace—but instead, it just brought sadness. Now, every November 20, Dad would call, and they'd struggle to fill the dead air on the phone. This year that day fell the same day as Ava's surgery.

Mags rolled away from him even as he ran his fingers through his hair. She sat up at the edge of the bed and grabbed her shirt, which she pulled over her head. Might as well set the tone, get him out of her bedroom as fast as possible. She should've gone to his place, she thought, because at least then she could leave. Now she'd have to kick the man out. And by the look of him, sprawled out and spent in her bed, she knew it wouldn't be easy. He sat up on one elbow, his muscles across his torso rippling.

"You're not going to kick me out." There was that commanding voice again. Her spine stiffened. She felt her resolve weaken. That damn voice. How could she fight it?

"I don't like sleepovers," she added tentatively. But part of her didn't want him to go. Not yet.

"Who said we were going to sleep?"

CHAPTER SEVEN

Gael woke the next morning to an empty apartment. Mags had sneaked out on him, the minx. If he hadn't been so damn tired after exploring her delicious body all night, he might've caught her. But he hadn't. He glanced around her cluttered, small apartment with the shades drawn. He pulled himself from bed and found she'd left a note on the table, beneath a dirty coffee cup.

Take care of the tattoo. Bandage should come off now.

That was it. No *thanks for rocking my world. When can we do it again?* message. Hmm.

Sure, he wasn't used to playing dominant, but he kind of liked it. Scratch that—he found it white-hot when Mags was looking at him, the light to please in her eyes. Oh yes, he liked telling her what to do very much. Like ordering her to come and then watching her body dissolve into delicious spasms. He wanted to do that again. And again.

He checked the bandage on his arm, which was

still in place, and stretched his arm, which was a tad sore from the needles. Stung a little, but manageable. He couldn't believe Mags had sneaked out on him, but then again, he could. He had a feeling if he'd been awake, he would've ordered her to stay. And she would.

What was he supposed to make of this one-line note? The complete lack of a personal touch in it was irksome. Felt like a kiss-off. *Thanks for the white-hot sex, but now I'm done. Get out.*

Damn, but he'd never met a woman so prickly, so troublesome out of bed but completely willing to please in it. The dichotomy made his head spin. Mags was a mystery. First she was tearing his clothes off, and then she was sneaking out and treating him like a one-night stand. He couldn't read her, couldn't predict her, couldn't begin to imagine what she was thinking, and that drove him crazy. He could read people, had always been able to read people, but Mags was a closed diary, under lock and key. What he did know was that he absolutely wanted to see her again. He had a flash of her, legs spread on the bed, lips parted, waiting for his next command, and his groin tightened.

Down, boy, he told it. *Not the right time.*

He gathered up his clothes from her apartment and snooped a little as he did so. Picked up a picture of her and her parents, he assumed. Her in a graduate's cap. The older white couple beaming back. Fresh-faced Asian daughter wearing her black cap and gown, straight dark hair down her shoulders, standing between them and grinning from ear to ear. Mags hadn't had blue hair then. And she barely wore makeup. No tattoos, either. Hell, she had an honor tassel on. Straight-A student, no sign of the rebel, punk girl. They looked happy, the three of them.

But then her mom had died. Gael knew how that could knock a person for a loop. A whole family, really. But she hadn't wanted to talk about it. Had shut down at the mere mention of her mom. Clearly, there was more to that story. Gael put down the photo and glanced around for a sign of any others. He found none of Mags and Clint, to his relief, or any other past boyfriends. No friends, either. Mags was a loner. He poked around her room some more but found nothing too illuminating. A pair of red patent Doc Martens. A chain belt. More clothes on the floor than hanging in her closet.

He opened the drawer at her bedside table and found a packet of condoms and a big pink vibrator. He laughed as he picked it up. Might have to use this on her next time. He flicked it on, and the batteries kicked in, humming.

He chuckled to himself. If she'd known he would be doing this much snooping, she would've never left him alone in her place. Well, served her right.

He headed to the bathroom, where the counter space was clogged with her makeup: compacts, eyeliners, tubes of mascara. Mags's tattoo shop was pristine, but her home was a mess. There was that dichotomy again. Messy and neat. Aggressive and... submissive. He shook his head. The place was a disaster area. The mess reminded him of Ava when she went through her early teen phase, leaving her stuff out on every available countertop. Mags needed someone to tell her to pick up after herself, but then again, it was probably because she wasn't used to sharing her space with anyone. No sister could get away with this kind of stuff spreading in the family's only bathroom when they were growing up. Makeup left out was stolen or thrown away. He smiled at the memory of Kathleen and Maeve arguing about a missing eyeliner, only to discover it had fallen behind the toilet. Good times.

He dug around in her bathroom cabinet until he found some mouthwash and took a swig, glancing at his tired reflection in the mirror, noticing the new stubble on his chin and the bandage still on his arm. He peeled it back, noticing the skin was still a little red and raw from the experience, but the falcon was perfect. He studied the bird of prey's eyes, which somehow seemed alive on his skin, even though he knew it was just a trick of shading she'd used, the way she'd drawn them. Thankfully, his skin seemed to be taking well to the art. No allergic reactions to the ink that he could see, no swelling.

He found himself staring at his upper shoulder in admiration. The woman had serious talent. Ava, he thought, would be pleased. Hopefully, Maeve and

Kathleen would like it, too. They'd been on board with the idea ever since Ava suggested it, but he thought that might be partly because they loved the idea of their corporate investor brother having ink. He double-checked the time on his phone. His first meeting at the office wasn't for two hours. He needed to head home to his penthouse to change, but first, he could swing by the hospital on the way to work and check up on his sister. Gael went every day if he could, even though Ava told him she was fine. That she didn't need babysitting. She'd always been tough on the outside, soft on the inside. He knew her bluster was mostly for show. But he also knew she was glad to see him. Knew that it helped, because he could see the fear in her eyes, the worry that this time the cancer would be back for good.

After getting dressed and smoothing down his errant cowlick, he headed to the hospital, a quick rideshare away. He hopped out of the car near the sliding glass doors of the hospital, walking through them and past the big fountain in the lobby. He knew the way to Ava's room through the teal and beige hallways on the third floor by heart. On his way down her hall, he nearly bumped into his sister Maeve, one of the floor nurses. She was wearing her trademark neon scrubs plastered with yellow smiley faces. Maeve always wore the brightest, most outrageous scrubs, along with her patented neon-green sneakers. You could see her coming from a mile away. If there was a power outage at the hospital, she could probably light up the whole wing with her clothes alone.

"There you are! Did you get it? I bet Kathleen twenty bucks you would, so you'd *better* have it."

"Um...hello, sis? Nice to see you, too?" He opened his arms, and Maeve gave him a quick hug. Maeve was the sister closest to his age and the one who could always be counted on to ally against Kathleen when her authoritarian tendencies got to be too much.

"Did you *get* it, though?"

"Come on. You know me." He shrugged out of his suit jacket and rolled up the sleeve of his shirt to show her an edge of the tattoo. She squealed in delight and clapped her hands together.

"Whoa! I can't believe you *actually* did it. Ava is going to love this." She threw her arms around Gael's neck again. "You're the best. *And* I'm going to rub it in Kathleen's face."

"Make sure she's not holding anything sharp when you do it," Gael quipped. He glanced down the hospital hallway. "How's Ava doing?"

"That little spitfire?" Maeve shook her head. "I almost feel sorry for the cancer. It's not going to know what hit it. Do you know I caught her playing poker with the orderlies again?"

Gael laughed a little. "Did she win?"

"She's going to clean them out if she keeps it up! I told her it wasn't fair to Dylan or Bob if she kept doing that."

"I'm the one who taught her the rules of Texas Hold'em, so I guess it's my fault."

"Sure is," Maeve said, but her voice was soft. "She's not quite feeling up to Texas Hold'em today, though." Her voice dropped. "Got some new meds and they're making her a little groggy, but she's not going to feel any pain, so that's good."

Gael nodded. The constant carousel of new meds was hard to keep track of, along with their various side effects and all the ways they might hurt her long-term. But they'd have to worry about that later. Right now, beating the cancer was everyone's focus.

"Well, go on, better go look in on the girl before she gets into more trouble. I've got to check on some other patients," Maeve said, bustling off down the hallway, her neon-green sneakers squeaking as she went.

"Will do," Gael called after her before moving toward Ava's open doorway. She had several vases of flowers in her room—some from her high school, most from him. The fact that she was spending most of her senior year here was beyond unfair. Gael hated it. Hated that she was missing out on so much. She ought to be studying for the SATs or stressing over college applications or who might take her to the homecoming dance. Not worrying about whether she'd live to graduate.

She was lying on her back, looking even paler than yesterday, her normally amber skin too ashen for his tastes. Her dark hair lay flat on her pillow, and the light in her normally bright green eyes—their father's—faded. This new round of treatment was taking its toll on her. What had started out as a sore throat that didn't go away had turned into thyroid cancer. Surgery removed the tumor, and they'd thought it was okay. Until recent tests had shown it had spread to one of her kidneys.

"Ava," he called, and the seventeen-year-old glanced up at him and grinned. "How are you?"

"Feeling like I'm about to have surgery—again." She rolled her eyes. "I'm kind of fed up with cancer."

"Me, too." He took a seat on her bed, and she leaned up to hug him. She felt frail, too. Like skin and bones. When Ava was stressed, she didn't eat. "But you beat cancer's ass once. You'll do it again."

She leaned back on her pillows and sent him a weak smile. "You think?"

"I know." He pulled a bag from his jacket pocket. "Brought you your favorite blueberry scone. Every warrior needs fuel." She tried to snatch the bag, but he held it aloft. "I'll only give it to you if you promise *not* to take the orderlies' money. No more poker."

"Did Maeve tattle on me?" Ava rolled her eyes. "Come on, I at least have to give them one more chance to make their money back."

"No more taking their money," Gael said.

"How about if we bet with chocolate? M&M's?"

Gael laughed a little. "Maybe," he said, and then he let her have the scone.

"Yum," she declared as she pulled the crumbly buttery goodness from the bag and took a big, enthusiastic bite.

"I've got another surprise for you," he said. He shrugged out of his suit jacket, and began to unbutton his shirt. He slid the collar down his shoulder, to reveal the brand-new falcon tattoo. Ava dropped the scone in her lap and squealed.

"You are kidding me!" she declared, grabbing his arm and taking a hard look at Mags's artwork. Then she glanced up at the signed CD case she kept by her bedside, a gift Gael had gotten her the first time cancer reared its ugly head and the first time she'd faced surgery.

"Not kidding. It's real."

She gently slid her finger over the line of the bird's beak. The skin was still tender, but her touch didn't hurt. "It looks *exactly* the same." She grabbed the CD and held it up to his arm.

"It should. I had Mags McHenry do it. She did the original cover art."

Ava glanced up at him, eyes wide. "Seriously?"

"She drew it from memory, too."

Ava gave a low whistle. "That's insane."

"I know. She's really talented." Gael couldn't keep the admiration from his voice. Ava didn't miss it, either.

"You like her," she said, instantly picking up on his enthusiasm.

"No," he lied.

"You do." Ava dropped his arm and clapped her hands together. "You *like* Mags McHenry."

Gael adjusted his Oxford and buttoned it up again, almost regretting ever bringing up the tattoo. A brief memory of exploring the soft skin between Mags's legs made his groin tighten. He more than liked her. That was a fact. But not one Ava needed to know. The girl was relentless when it came to matching him up. His little sister was dying to see him settled down. She kept saying it was because he needed someone else to father besides her. Someone who was *actually* a son or daughter.

"It's about time you *liked* someone. You haven't in a long time." Ava's smile faded a bit. "You need to do more than just hang out in hospitals, unless you're going to bang a hot doctor."

"Would you please stop talking about me banging anyone? You're my *little* sister."

Ava sat up straighter in bed, offended. "Who's technically six months away from being an adult. And who wants her *big* brother to have a personal life. All you do is work and fret about me. You *should* be banging some hot chick. A doctor…or a tattoo artist, or…"

Gael tried to keep his face neutral but felt his left eye twitch. Ava trailed off, studying him. "Wait a second…did you sleep with Mags McHenry already?"

"No." But Gael felt his eye twitch again. "And you

know that these are totally inappropriate questions for a seventeen-year-old to be asking."

Her mouth dropped open, and she covered it with both hands. Then she laughed and slapped at her knees. "You *did*!"

"Ava!"

"*Gael.*" She giggled some more. In that moment, she looked like a middle schooler rather than a senior in high school. "You know you cannot lie to me. I can always tell. Your left eye twitches."

He rubbed his left eye. "It doesn't."

"It *does*." She shook her head. "Anyway, I'm glad you're banging somebody."

"Who's banging someone?" Maeve poked her head into the room and then trotted in.

"Gael is banging the tattoo artist. Her name is Mags. She's Asian. And she has a blue streak in her hair. I just looked her up on Instagram." Ava held up her phone.

Maeve looked at Gael, eyebrows raised. "You're sleeping with her?"

"That's none of anybody's business."

"So, you're sleeping with her." Maeve grinned.

"See? I *told* you!" Ava cried. "Banging!"

"Would you two stop!" Gael stood and paced a bit. The idea of his sister even *knowing* about sex at all made him squirm. "And please stop staying *banging*."

"Would you rather I say boinking? Knocking boots? *Fucking?*"

"Language," Gael and Maeve both said at once.

"Whatever." Ava rolled her eyes, showing her disdain for the request. "I'm just glad you're doing something for you. Moping around the hospital all the time isn't healthy."

"You're my responsibility. I'm focused on you right now. That's all I care about." He turned and crossed his arms across his chest.

"You need to blow off steam sometimes, you know. It's okay. You should go have fun. Maeve is here, anyway, until at least midnight. What is Mags doing tonight?"

Gael raised his eyebrows. "What are you trying to do? Get me out of your hair?"

Ava pretended to be shocked. "Who? Little old me?"

"Smartass," he growled.

"Language!" she and Maeve cried, and then they both laughed. Gael couldn't help but join in. "So, when are you seeing her again?" she asked him.

Gael remembered the not-so-friendly note she'd left. And how she'd sneaked out of her own apartment.

"She's got to finish the tattoo," he said.

"That's the perfect opportunity for you to make your move!"

"What do you know about moves? And I'm focused on *you*. Your surgery is tomorrow. No distractions."

Gael felt Maeve's eyes on him. He looked up, and

they both exchanged a look of worry. Everyone was focused on Ava. For good reason.

Ava rolled her eyes in disgust. "I don't need *this* much attention. Besides, you can't multitask even a little?"

He thought about Mags's wicked mouth. Maybe he could, indeed.

a little."

CHAPTER EIGHT

M AGS SPENT THE day feeling out of sorts and not quite
herself. Even now, as she focused on a new client's
back shoulder tattoo—a crow sitting on an eight
ball—she found herself distracted, her brain im-
mersed in fog. All she could think about was Gael's
hands on her body and that damn fine man's mouth
on hers. The sound of his commanding voice. She
wanted to hear it again.

Everything reminded her of him, even this
stranger's tattoo. The eight ball. The one he'd sunk
easily at the bar when he somehow had talked Clint
into buying them all a round of drinks. The man had
a silver tongue. Hell, not just silver. Strong. Commanding. A voice she had no choice but to obey.
Plus, she'd sneaked out on him. Would he be mad?
Peeved? In the mood to punish her? And was that
what she wanted? A little punishment from his big,
strong hands?

She gave herself an inward shake. She needed
to focus. Hell, she was liable to scrawl *Gael* on this

stranger's back by accident. Mags was not the type to suffer crushes. She didn't get giggly, and she sure as hell never mooned about over a boy. Not as a kid and not as an adult, either.

It was just good sex, that's all. Nice little role play. No need to go crazy about it.

Yet the chemistry between them had been undeniable. Even she had to admit the sex had been amazing. Hell, *amazing* didn't even begin to cover it. Life altering? Her skin almost felt seared by Gael's touch, as if he'd been the one who tattooed her and not the other way around. Giving her very will over to him… was damn hot. Hotter than she could've imagined. Even now, as she worked on the crow's beak of this tattoo in front of her, she itched to call him. Wondered what he might be doing.

He'd texted her several times that morning, but she hadn't responded. She'd half hoped he'd lose interest and go away. Make the decision for her. Make it easier for her *not* to face the feelings he stirred in her, the feelings that flat out scared her. Mags wasn't used to needing anyone or anything, and she wasn't about to start now, especially with a suit. The mere idea was ludicrous. Why did he have so much power over her, anyway? She knew why. Because she gave it to him. Because she wanted him to have it. And that troubled her.

It was lust, pure and simple. Nothing more.

After a few more weeks, she'd forget all about Gael, forget about the way his body melded to hers, the way he tasted: like everything she'd ever wanted. But giving in to her cravings for the man's body would only make it harder to break from him later. She knew better than to go down that road. She much preferred friends with benefits like Clint, men who were passable, fun even, but not in control. Not dangerous. Not addictive. Gael felt like a hit of the most addictive drug she'd ever tried. She knew better than to go back for seconds.

"Ow," the man in the chair cried and shifted a little.

"Sorry," she mumbled into the man's back. Her mind had wandered and her customer had suffered. Not the best start of the day. *Focus before you really hurt somebody*, Mags told herself. She finished off the last bits of the man's tattoo and sat back, relieved she'd managed to get through it without any more snags. Gael was already disrupting her life in ways she didn't like and they'd only fucked *once*. It was one night, yet she was dreaming about him like some tween with a crush on a Korean boy band. "There you go."

The customer stood, glancing at the full-length mirror, using the smaller one in his hand to view the finished product. He nodded once, satisfied at the crow with its wings outspread on his back, and then tugged on his shirt as Mags moved to the front counter near the door. John wasn't there—again. He was more three hours late for shift today. She'd have to let the kid go. She couldn't go on like this, paying someone who didn't show up or when he did, he spent the afternoon taking smoking breaks.

The customer paid her and then left, happy with his crow tattoo, and none the wiser that Mags's heart hadn't been in the design. Mags pulled her blue hair up into a bun at the crown of her head, stabbing it securely with a pencil she found on her shop's counter. Cool air seeped in through the crack beneath the glass door, and she made a mental note once more that she needed to get to work sealing up her place. She wore just a thin T-shirt and jeans today, a poor choice for outside, which had dropped to near freezing on the edge of cold air from Canada. Winter was coming, she knew, as she watched people scurry down the sidewalk in front her shop, zipping up jackets and flipping up collars, meager protection against the cold air blowing off Lake Michigan, which lay just a few blocks to the east.

Mags's phone buzzed, and she picked it up, eyeing yet another incoming text from Gael. She didn't bother to open the notification and read it. That would just make things more complicated. And Mags didn't do complicated. She liked simple. Straightforward. Just then, the door to her shop opened, and John—her new counter guy—wandered in then, dinging the bell. She glanced at her watch.

"You're late," she said.

"Yeah." He shrugged, unconcerned. The lanky, pale kid was twenty-two. He wore a beanie snug on his head, covering his ears, and a black hoodie. His eyes were bloodshot, like he was either hungover or had been hitting a bong before he'd wandered into the store. She felt anger rising in her.

"Three hours late," she said. "And yesterday you left early. In fact, you ducked out without saying anything at all."

John glared at her, daring her to do something about it.

"You never came back after that last smoking break. Remember?" She couldn't believe she was having to spell this out. She'd almost hoped John would just never return. But she wasn't going to be so lucky. She tapped her nails on the glass. The sound felt loud.

"So?"

Mags temper flared, but she struggled to keep it under control. She needed to be the adult here.

"So, I'm sorry, John. But I need a more reliable counter guy." Or none at all. This was what she got for relying on other people, she thought to herself. People almost always disappointed. Best just to do things yourself.

John just stared at her and didn't blink.

"You're fired, John."

"What about what you owe me?" His voice was thick with menace. The kid was barely 110 pounds, so Mags thought she could take him in a fight. She'd taken a ton of self-defense classes at the Y. She knew how to flip a guy. She could flip this guy right on out of her store. But she did owe him for one day's pay—the only time he'd actually worked a full day. Mags moved to the cash register and popped it open. She counted out six twenties and gave them to him. He snatched the bills from her hand.

"Seems light to me," he said, the menace there again.

She really didn't want to pop this kid in the nose, but if he kept this up, she would. She reached out under the counter, felt the cool can of Mace there. Mags could use that if she had to.

Her door dinged again, and this time, a man wearing a suit and a khaki-colored trench coat strolled in. Gael.

For some reason, she felt relieved to see him. Relieved she wouldn't have to take this scrappy, insolent kid on herself.

Gael glanced at John, his white-knuckled fist full of twenties, and then at Mags. "Everything okay here?"

"Fine," Mags said. "John was just leaving."

John glanced at Gael, his broad shoulders and shiny shoes, and considered his options. John flipped greasy hair from his eyes. Could he feel Gael's strength? His solidness?

"You heard her. Time for you to go." There it was. The voice. The command. Mags felt the vibrations of it in the back of her knees. John felt it, too. She saw a flicker of uneasiness in his eyes. So, Mags wasn't the only one affected. Interesting.

"Whatever," John grunted, and then he stuffed

the twenties into his hoodie pocket. He grumbled something inaudible beneath his breath.

"What did you say?" Gael's eyes narrowed.

John's head whipped up. "Nothing, man," he added, and then he was already out the door and halfway across the street.

"Leave it," Mags told Gael.

Gael turned back, frowning. "What was that all about?"

"Had to fire the kid for not showing up at work. Most times John was here, he was high." Mags shrugged. "Not that I care, if you do your job. But he didn't."

Gael shook his head slowly, keeping an eye on the kid as he bounced down the street. "I still want to go talk to him." Gael's fists curled at his sides. Mags felt her stomach twitch. Maybe Gael was a damn alpha after all. Sending kids skittering off. Making her want to take off her pants.

"Leave him alone. He's just a punk kid." Mags shrugged again. "Not the first one I've fired." Now that it was just her and Gael, she realized she had no idea what she might look like. She fought the urge to smooth her blue hair and hated herself for wondering if she still had a smudge of lip tint on. Why should she care what she looked like? Whatever had happened between them wasn't going to happen again. Period. Full stop.

She'd gone too far. Now she had to rein herself back in.

"What are you doing here?" She tried to keep her voice all business. The faster she could get him out of her store, the faster she could get back to her boring old life, without him in it. That was what she wanted.

"Here to tell you I didn't appreciate waking up alone in a cold bed." He quirked an eyebrow.

"I left a note."

"Hardly good enough." Gael stuffed his big hands in the pockets of his coat, and she tried not to think about how talented they were at roving the curves of her bare body. How strongly they'd held her wrists above her head.

Damn. She wanted that feeling again. Restrained. No other choice but to enjoy it.

Why was she so attracted to the man? Was it *because* he was wearing a silk tie? She hated ties. Hated wing tips. Or did she? She glanced down at the shiny designer shoes on his feet. Mags always thought men wearing them looked…dainty. But not this one. No one would accuse him of being weak. Not with those shoulders and strong hands.

Gael moved and so did she, and they seemed to be circling her tattoo chair.

"You shouldn't have snuck out." Damn that voice of his. Now she felt like she was being scolded. Worse, she liked it. Scolding might lead to punishment. She thought of all the missed calls on her phone from her dad. Maybe she needed to be punished.

"What are you going to do about it?"

She eyed him, wary.

"I don't know. You've been a bad girl." He grinned, and there was no mistaking his meaning. Mags was already imagining herself at his mercy, his strong hands on her. Yes. This was what she wanted. She'd been fantasizing about it all morning.

"So?" She wouldn't deny it. She felt bad. She felt like…she'd gotten away with something when she'd left him snoring in her bed. She'd known he wouldn't like it. She'd hoped there'd be repercussions. She realized she'd been waiting for them, waiting for the shoe to drop, since she'd quietly shut her front door that morning. He moved closer, and she backed away, down the hall. There was the small office down there. The office with the door.

"Well, for one, you are going to finish my tattoo today."

"I'm booked." This was a lie. Her main client had canceled. She was wide-open. But if she was being bad, why not lie? Why not add another sin to the roster? She took another step back. She was baiting on him purpose. She didn't know why. Why play this game? *Because she wanted to.* She wanted to see what he'd do. See how far she could push him.

"You're going to cancel the others." That voice. Deep. Strong. Authoritarian.

"Make me."

"Don't tempt me." His jaw twitched. The line of his mouth told her he wasn't playing. Or he was. Depending on how she looked at it. She was at her office door now, the door open, the small space big enough for a desk and two chairs. She backed in and he followed, getting so close to her that her butt bumped against the edge of the desk. Now she was trapped. Her heart kicked up a notch. Blood rushed to her thighs.

She dropped her voice low, meeting his gaze, enjoying challenging him. "I said, 'Make me.'" She wanted him to. He bent down, and for a second she thought he'd kiss her, but he stopped just shy.

"Turn around," he commanded. That damn voice. How could she resist the power in it? She turned. "Put your hands on the desk."

She did, palms down against the cool wood. He cupped the curve of her butt from behind, squeezing it. A little moan escaped her.

"You've been a bad girl." His voice, like molten lava. "Say it."

"I've been a bad girl," she managed, the words scratchy in her throat.

"You need to be punished." His breath tickled her earlobe. His hot hand caressed her backside.

"Yes. Punish me." Her voice was a croak. Need throttled her.

Then he swept his hand back and made contact with the heel of his hand. The sound of the smack was loud, the hit jarring her.

"Harder," she whispered. *Yes. Punish me. I need it.*

He spanked her again, harder. And one more time.

His hand. Big and strong, pain and pleasure melded into one, so that she couldn't tell when one began and the other ended. He slapped her again, and she moaned. And then he cupped her once more, possessive. He pulled down her jeans, and she let him, along with her thong. He slapped her bare skin, and she groaned again. Yes. This was what she wanted.

Then he stopped, rubbing her hot skin, easing the contact. His hands slipped around then, to her slick center.

"God, you're so wet," he murmured, surprised. Her legs were shaking as she stared at the wall behind her desk. Yes, she was. She'd never felt so white-hot in all her life. He kicked the office door closed behind them.

"What are you going to do about it?" Her voice low, a challenge.

"I'm going to give you what you deserve," he promised.

CHAPTER NINE

GAEL SLIPPED HIS fingers inside Mags, and she gasped with want as he explored her slowly, finding her soft ridges, her G-spot, almost instantly. She groaned, her pelvis pushing against his fingers, desperate for more contact. He'd never felt a woman so wet before, never had a woman so willing. Then again, he'd never all-out spanked a woman before, either. So, firsts all around.

He still couldn't believe he'd done it. He never thought of himself as a dominant type, but something about Mags brought it out in him. Hell, she'd asked for it. She'd told him, *punish me*. Well, what the lady wanted, she'd get.

She spread her legs wider, leaning into him and his fingers, moaning.

"Yes," she whispered. "Give me what I deserve."

Her meaning was unmistakable. First, she wanted him to spank her, and now she was daring him to fuck her. Right here in her office. His cock screamed for it anyway, and he felt his groan practically vibrating with hard need. It felt like he was going to burst through his own damn fly. He unzipped his pants and freed himself, much to his relief. This was what the woman did to him. He'd noticed a small box of condoms near her desk, condoms with her business logo on them, right next to a cup of pens and a stack of business cards. He'd have to ask about the business condoms later, but in the meantime he grabbed a neon-green one from the top of the stack and ripped it open. He began rolling it down his length, and then she turned as if to help him, lifting her hands from the desk.

"Uh-uh," he said, hand on her lower back. "Keep your hands there. On the desk."

Obediently, she pressed her palms against the table and arched her back in compliance. He got harder, if possible. Damn, this woman could do things to him no other woman could. He bounced the tip of his cock against the back of her thigh.

"You want this?" Even with all the role play, he had to be certain.

"Yes," she cried, and he could hear the desire in her voice. The want drove him wild.

He entered her from behind. Pants still on, shirt lifted to his belly button. He almost came right there, right away, into her tight wetness. He felt like he'd died and gone to heaven right then. He thrust deeper, as she struggled to keep her hands on the desk. She clutched at the smooth surface, trying to maintain her balance. He grabbed her hips, possessive, keeping her steady. He thought about her sneaking out of the apartment, about the frown on her face when he'd entered her shop. He thrust again and again and again.

He reached around and found her clit with his finger, giving it a gentle flick, and felt her knees give way a little.

"This is your punishment," he told her, and she moaned. The perfect punishment. Death by pleasure.

She cried out again as he kept the gentle touch on her clit, and then she came in a pained cry of release. He came, too, the pleasure so acute it almost felt painful as the orgasm racked his body. He collapsed on her back, panting.

"*Now* you will finish my tattoo."

All she could do was nod her head once.

Fifteen minutes later, and it was as if the spanking-foreplay-hot-desk-sex had never happened. Mags was once again all business, working on coloring in his tattoo as he lay in her leather chair in the little room, the dull late-fall sunlight barely penetrating. Gael was beginning to think maybe he'd imagined the whole quickie in her office—maybe it had just been some delusion.

Above, the bright overhead light washed everything in an unforgiving light, but Mags looked even more gorgeous than he remembered. Sharp brown eyes, heart-shaped face, features a little too delicate for her tough-girl persona that she wore like a protective cloak. Her bright blue streak was pulled back up in a hasty bun that threatened to unravel, despite the yellow pencil that seemed to keep it in place. He had a sudden urge to run his finger down the delicate slope of her chin as he watched the fine bones of her hands delicately work on coloring in the falcon on his arm. The pain was worse than the last time, but maybe it was because she seemed to be focused on one spot for a long time, the shading of the falcon's upper wing.

His heart ticked up a notch, and he wondered if it was the fact that she had needles in his arm, or because she was so close to him that he could smell the faint whiff of her shampoo—something soft and sweet. Roses again. Definitely roses. He thought of the soft petals of the flower, how her skin had felt even softer beneath his hands. He wanted to inhale her, wanted to snuggle his nose into her neck and breathe in her skin. Then he shook himself. He didn't have time to think about her or anyone else. Ava had surgery tomorrow. That was where his focus ought to be. Not on this Asian rebel woman and the fullness of her lip as she bit it in concentration.

"How's it looking?" he asked, trying to peer down at his shoulder, but her head was in the way.

"Fine," she said, voice toneless.

What the hell? Did he need to spank her again? He would, if necessary. Thinking about how wet it had made her sent a buzzing through his brain.

He winced as she seemed to really focus on that

one small bit of skin, her needles merciless. But worse than that, as she bit her lower lip a little harder, he felt a twinge in his own groin. He wanted to bite that lip, too. Nibble at all her soft edges. He wasn't sure what was worse: the tattoo or lying still while she touched him. That skintight V-neck didn't help matters, either. He saw the pale slope of her breast from the corner of his eye. Remembered the softness of her body against his. How easily he'd made her groan. "How much longer?"

"Two hours. Maybe."

Two hours. That was going to be a long time to lie with a hard-on, he thought, glaring at the ceiling. He didn't know what was wrong with him. He'd had sex *just minutes ago*. Why was he all raring to go again? Normally women didn't affect him like this— making him feel like he was a fourteen-year-old boy again, with zero control over his body.

Mags kept her face a perfect mask. If she was bothered by the close proximity, she didn't let on. Hell, if she'd hated the sex in the office, she didn't let on to that, either. Except he knew she hadn't. He knew just how much her body had liked it. As he studied her face, he saw she was trying hard to appear as if she didn't care he was lying there by her. And was it just his imagination, or was she trying to answer him in the briefest replies possible?

In fact, he got the distinct impression she'd rather he be anywhere but here. She was working on him, yes, but there was an unwelcoming slant to her shoulders, to the set of her determined mouth. If he were to leave, she'd be relieved. He didn't understand it. Hadn't they shared an electric night and a white-hot quickie in her office? So why did she seem glad if she never saw him again?

He wasn't used to being ignored. Being...boxed in. He didn't like it. Plus, the fullest conversations they seemed to have were when he was ordered her around for sex. Dirty talk was great, but didn't make a relationship. Didn't help him get to know her better.

"What was it like when your mom had cancer?" he asked her.

Her head popped up, surprised and her brown eyes met his for the first time since he sat down.

"Why do you want to know?" The defensive wall went up. He could feel her shutting him out.

"Because I care." He didn't blink, didn't look away. "Because I know some of what that's like. Because most people don't. Hell, I feel like I'm on an island most of the time. My coworkers? Friends? They don't understand what it's like having a sister with cancer." For a second, he thought she'd tell him it was none of his business. But then she took a deep breath and exhaled it. She lowered the tattoo needle.

"I was just a kid—seven years old. It was hard, beyond hard, watching my mom, who was this amazing woman, slowly fade away." She glanced up and out the window. "I remember being just angry about everything. About Mom being sick. About Dad not being able to pay the bills."

"Why could he not pay the bills?"

"Our insurance only covered so much." Mags shrugged. "Dad had a decent job. A warehouse job, a decent union job with good benefits, but even that wasn't enough." Mags shook her head and bit her lip, a worry line appearing between her eyebrows. Gael felt the urge to reach out and touch her, bring her to him, but he refrained. He wanted to hear the rest of the story.

"What happened?"

"My dad took out a second mortgage on the house to pay her hospital bills. But even that didn't cover it." Mags glanced at him. "After Mom died, we lost everything else—the house, the car, everything. He eventually declared bankruptcy."

"That's why you hate suits." Gael met her eye, and the current of harsh truth passed between them. Now he finally understood why she kept him at arm's length. Hell, he wouldn't trust suits, either. Not after that.

She nodded once, swiftly. "Bank suits, hospital suits...none of them cared about my mom. They just cared about getting their money."

"I'm sorry. That's terrible."

Mags looked up at him, studying his face. She seemed surprised to find he truly cared. Made him wonder if few people bothered to ask about her life.

"It's not just the suits. Dad remarried. Moved away. He didn't want to be here anymore."

"Do you talk to him?"

"Not much." Her glance shifted sideways. He suspected that she might have a few missed voice mails on her phone she hadn't yet bothered to return. Somehow, he got the impression she was the one keeping her father at arm's length. She was the one who worked hard to keep people out. "Sometimes I don't know who bothers me more—the bank that took my house or my dad, who ran away after. But I survived. I made it on my own. People just let you down. They get sick. Or they run away."

"Not all people are like that."

"All people disappoint." There was her incisive gaze again. Sharp, defensive.

"But real connections with people, those are what make life worth living."

She fell into a grumpy silence then. A grumpy, rebellious silence. She began filling in the rest of his tattoo, the buzz of her needles loud in the silence. Gael almost thought he'd gone too far. He thought he was penetrating her hard shell, but maybe he was just pushing her farther away. He didn't know. The woman beside him with the blue hair was a complete mystery. She was so vulnerable during sex, but after…she shut down. Hid behind her emotional barricades.

Now she focused on coloring in his arm, her attention now focused on each new swipe of color. He braced himself against the pain, an annoying sting, really, and told himself this was nothing compared to what Ava would have to deal with. And there'd be the pain meds after. They were both worried about the possibility of addiction. Gael had read stories about those who'd leaned too heavily on the pain meds so many doctors seemed happy to prescribe, and what happened afterward.

It would be a long, hard road. The tattoo was such a little gesture, but one he felt he had to make. He sank into his own thoughts for the rest of the time he spent in the chair, though he was keenly aware of Mags touching him, inscribing him. He thought she should be the one to talk next. Everything he said only seemed to push her father into her shell.

"There," Mags said as she leaned back, wiping his shoulder with her clean cloth. "I think we're done."

She sat back, admiring her work, and Gael glanced down. The side of his shoulder was now fully inked, the falcon's wings across it, its talons outstretched. The damn thing looked almost three dimensional. When he flexed his arm, he almost felt like the bird might really take flight.

"Wow," he said, amazed. "I thought the outline was great, but this..." He didn't think words could do it justice. He moved his arm, and the bird moved with him. "It feels like it's alive. This...is like living art."

She cocked her head to one side. "Living art," she repeated. "I like that."

Their eyes met, and he felt locked in. Could almost see the pulse in her neck tick up a notch as she sat, frozen, next to him. Maybe they couldn't carry on a conversation about anything other than sex, but their bodies talked to one another just fine, he thought—he could feel the current of electricity running between them, buzzing and hot. He reached up and touched her face, and she didn't move, didn't speak, as he pulled her closer to him, and then her lips were against his. She hungrily deepened the kiss and he welcomed it, her tongue lashing against his. This was a language they both understood.

He broke free, though. Determined to make inroads with her on grounds other than physical. He'd crack her hard shell. One way or another.

"Want to get dinner?" he asked her as he put on his shirt.

She blinked back surprise. Dinner was not on her mind, as she glanced at his belt buckle again.

Before she could say no, he took her hand. "Come on. I know you worked up an appetite doing this. And I also know you get hangry."

She laughed a little, but he could feel her hesitate. He wondered if he ordered her to have dinner with him, if she would. But that wasn't what he wanted. He wanted her to *want* to come.

"I should probably stay at the shop. I don't have anyone to man the front." She was fine with fucking him in her office, but when it came to going out? That was another story. He wondered why.

Gael glanced at her and then his watch. "That's okay," he added. "I'll be headed to the hospital first, anyway, to check on Ava."

He saw something shift in her at the mention of his sister. "Wait," Mags called, snatching her leather jacket off the hook near the door. "I'm coming with you."

CHAPTER TEN

MAGS SQUIRMED IN the passenger seat of Gael's expensive car. She'd never ridden in anything so sleek before, and she'd only ever seen an Aston Martin on TV, usually with James Bond driving it. With Gael at the wheel of the silver sports car, she could almost imagine him fighting spies. The image of 007 in her mind reminded her that not all men who wore expensive suits were weak or cowardly.

But then, Gael wasn't weak. She'd felt his strong hands on her body, followed his direct commands with pleasure. The memory of him taking her against the desk of her own place made a white-hot flash singe the back of her neck. He was anything but weak.

Gael's hand reached out and took hers, and she let him keep it. She liked the warmth of his hand, the way he glanced at her periodically, as if checking to see if she was still there. She shifted a bit in the car, feeling underdressed, somehow, which didn't even make sense. They were in a car, not a five-star restaurant.

He pulled into the drive-in of a local hot-dog joint. "Do you mind if we pick something up for Ava?" he asked her. "It's Ava's favorite, and she hates hospital food. Her surgery is midmorning tomorrow, so she can eat and drink until 10:00 p.m. tonight."

"Sure—I love Superdawg," Mags said, feeling relieved that they were getting back to something she knew: Chicago dog with the works—pepper, pickle, onion, relish, tomato and mustard, and fries. These were things she could wrap her head around. A six-figure car was something else altogether. "But you can get food into the hospital?"

When her mom was sick, they could barely bring in cookies, much less a dinner from Superdawg. Gael glanced at her and grinned. "That's why we order extra chocolate shakes—to bribe the nurses. My sister especially."

"Your sister is a nurse?"

"Maeve is very caring and sweet. When's she's sleeping."

Mags laughed. "She's as bad as your mayor sister? Kathleen?"

"Oh, God, no. Kathleen's by far the worst." But the way he said it made her think he really did love his sisters very much, flaws and all.

"I'll just get Ava's and Maeve's now, unless you're starving," Gael said. "We can get ours later?"

"Superdawg is good for me, too," she said. "We don't have to—"

"I've got something special in mind for you."

Mags hated surprises. Usually, surprises were bad
news. "What is it?"

"You'll see. Come on. Trust me. You'll like it."
There was that commanding tone again, the one that
made the goose bumps rise up on her arms.

One bag of food and a tray of shakes later and
they were on their way to Chicago Memorial, the
smell of food making her stomach growl. Maybe she
should've insisted on a hot dog, after all. She was
beginning to regret agreeing to wait to eat.

Gael slid his expensive car into a parking spot and
then insisted on carrying Ava's dinner and the tray
of shakes for the nurses' station and managed to do
it with one beefy hand. He led her through the front
doors of the hospital. For a split second, she was hit
with memories of when her mother was sick. The
bright white fluorescent lights above, the hint of anti-
septic in the air, the squeak of nurses' and doctors'
shoes on the clean tile. She hated hospitals. Hated
their tidy efficiency, hated how people's lives hung
in the balance of all the white lab coats. Being in
one brought up all those feelings of desperation and
despair she thought she'd long buried.

"Are you okay?" Gael had paused, looking at her,
green eyes concerned. He was perceptive, she'd give
him that.

"Sorry. I don't like hospitals." Understatement
of the year.

"It's okay," he said, voice low. "Neither do I." He
reached out and grabbed her hand, and she was sud-

denly grateful for the contact. His hand felt steady, sturdy and strong. With her hand in his, she felt she could get her feet moving. She realized she'd been stopped, stock-still, near the automatic doors of the lobby. She mentally shook herself. This was for Gael's sister. She followed him to the bank of elevators and tried to ignore the annoying Muzak playing softly in the background, or the fact that the security guards near the door were eyeing her as if she planned to steal something. She got it. Her leather jacket, ample tattoos and blue hair screamed *troublemaker*. Hell, that was why she wore them. She liked putting people on notice, and she didn't usually care when people stared. But with Gael, she felt extra self-conscious.

The security guards weren't the only ones sending questioning glances their way, curious about the punk chick and the handsome man in the expensive suit. Even though he'd long since ditched the tie, there was no getting around the fact that they looked like people from two different worlds. Because they were, she reminded herself. If they ever were a couple, they'd always get strangers staring at them.

She wondered what the security guard would think if he knew she'd been splayed over a desk, bare cheeked, Gael's hand leaving a pink print on her backside just hours ago. At the memory, she felt a shiver run down the back of her leg. He'd been good at that. Too good.

"People are looking at us," she murmured, voice

low. She let her fingers go loose, and if he let go, she wouldn't blame him. They didn't look like a catalog-ready couple. Hell, they didn't even look like they belonged together. But he tightened his grip on her hand.

"Let them stare," he said, drawing her in closer. As they stood by the elevators, he drew her in for a kiss. It came quickly, but he lingered, kissing her slowly and deliberately. His message clear—that he didn't care what anyone else thought. She wasn't used to public displays, wasn't used to men wanting to own her in public. Even Clint wouldn't dare hold her hand in public. He, like many she'd slept with, felt like public displays of affection made them look weak. Normally, she didn't care. That was just one more tie she didn't need. But something about Gael claiming her mouth in the middle of a busy hospital corridor sent a little thrill through her. A little swell of pride. When he released her, a giggle popped up through her throat. An actual damn *giggle*. Was she one of those girls now?

The elevator doors slid open, and Gael led her inside. The orderly with the dinner cart eyed them with suspicion, but Gael pulled her in and put his arm around her. Mags ignored the stare and put her head in the nook of his arm, and it felt like she belonged there. She tried not to analyze the feeling beyond that. The doors opened to Ava's floor, and Gael led her to the nurses' station. A tall, dark-haired woman in bright pink flamingo scrubs lit up when she saw him.

"Gael!" she said and bustled over to give him a hug.

"Maeve! Love the flamingos. You know those are my favorite."

Gael quickly made the introductions. "Mags, this is my sister Maeve." The words came out smoothly, and Gael seemed to feel no awkwardness at all. He didn't even pause as if trying to figure out how to explain her presence. He just announced it as if she were always meant to be there. So this was one of his sisters. She lacked his green eyes, but they shared the exact same hair color and both had the dimple in their left cheek.

"Mags!" Maeve cried, instant recognition. "Ava's told me about you. You're the tattoo artist!"

"Uh, yes, that's right." Maeve's enthusiasm was almost contagious. She wasn't used to this kind of reception, especially not in a hospital.

"Oh my." Maeve stood back and studied Mags from head to toe, dark eyes shining with approval. "You're *gorgeous*, you know that? My Lord. No wonder Ava was—"

"Talking about how cool your Instagram was," Gael cut in before his sister could finish.

Mags actually felt herself blush. Normally people didn't tell her she was pretty. She hadn't even realized that was a compliment she wanted until it came out of Maeve's mouth, so authentic and real.

"No wonder Gael's got a crush on you."

Now it was Gael's turn to shift uneasily. "Where did you hear that?"

"You know Ava. She's not going to keep any secrets to herself." Maeve laughed at that, and Gael joined in.

"Well, hurry up then and take your shake before it melts," Gael prodded, offering her the tray.

She took a shake and laughed with delight. "Oh, you can bribe me any time, you know that!"

"And one of these bags of food is for the nurses' station," Gael handed her the biggest bag. "Make sure everybody gets some."

"You know I will." Maeve took the bag. "You're a gift from God. Thank *you*." She took the bag. "You've got a good one here, Mags," Maeve said before she bustled off back to the nurses' station. Gael took her hand once more and squeezed.

"So you have a crush on me?" Mags teased as Gael let out a sigh.

"Maeve and Ava will have us married off before you know it."

Normally, the very word *married* would send Mags running for the door. But instead, Mags laughed at that, and Gael joined in. "You ready to meet Ava?"

"You bet." Mags felt an unexpected jolt of nerves in her stomach—anxiety she couldn't quite explain. Why was she nervous about meeting Gael's sister? Gael seemed to sense the tension, because he gave her hand a reassuring squeeze before he pulled her to his sister's room. It was the one stuffed full of get-well balloons and flower arrangements—nearly every available surface was covered in cheer.

"Knock, knock." Gael walked in, and Ava sprang up in bed, matching his smile. Mags instantly recognized the resemblance: same dark, gorgeous hair, same stark green eyes. Her eyes lit up with such pure joy at seeing her brother that Mags felt her heart constrict. Gael was a provider, a protector. She had a sudden flash of him as a father. He'd make a good one. Then she nearly kicked herself. Why was she so quick to imagine him with a little toddler on his shoulders? Next she'd be pretending they were all going to put up a Christmas tree together. Mags's thoughts were getting entirely too domesticated.

They had fun together in the bedroom. That was it. Role play only. Not real play.

Gael hugged his sister, and she clung to his neck affectionately.

"Looks like someone got a few more balloons since the last time I was here," Gael said.

"Maeve said if I get any more, it's a fire hazard!" Ava said, and then met Mags's gaze above his shoulder. "But Kathleen told me I could have as *many as I* wanted."

"Kathleen doesn't work in the hospital," Maeve pointed out.

Ava ignored her. "You brought her!" she squealed, and Gael pulled away to reveal Ava's beaming face.

Mags wasn't sure what to do, so she held out her hand for a shake, but Ava grabbed it and pulled her in for a hug. "The Quinn family are huggers," she declared and folded Mags into a warm embrace. It felt nice, actually. Mags couldn't remember the last time she'd had a platonic hug. When Ava let her go, she declared, "So this guy has been nice to you, right? I told him to be nice!"

Mags couldn't help herself—she laughed a little. "More than nice," Mags said.

"Good." Ava studied Mags's blue hair and her stark eyeliner but then nodded in approval. "Your hair is so cool," she said. "I want to do that. Dye my hair. After the surgery, maybe!" She glanced over at Gael for approval as if out of habit. She might be an adult, but she still very much felt like the younger sister, Mags noticed.

"When you're eighteen, you can do what you want." Gael shrugged. "But you *will* have to deal with Kathleen's wrath."

"Kathleen loves me. She'd even let me get a nipple piercing, I think."

Gael frowned, looking more than a little like an authoritarian. "I'm going to pretend I didn't hear that."

Ava ignored his comment. "So? Can I see the final version of the masterpiece?" She nodded at his arm.

Gael shrugged out of his jacket and unbuttoned his sleeve and began rolling it up. The bandage that Mags had put on it was still in place. Mags felt a pang of nerves then, hoping that Ava liked it. She hardly ever doubted her work, and she knew she'd done a good job, but she wanted his sister's approval.

Mags had begun to notice that despite Ava's bright green eyes, her face was a bit pale, her eyes slightly sunken and lined with dark circles. She was putting on a brave face, but she was sick, very sick. She remembered her mother putting on the same brave face even as the cancer ate away her insides. But Ava seemed far, far too young to be dealing with any of this. Mags suddenly felt protective of the young woman.

As Gael gently pulled off the bandage, Ava's eyes grew wide.

"Whoa! That's amazing," she said reverently as she studied Mags's work. Gael's skin was still a little red and raw, but in a few days, she was confident that it would seem that the tattoo was meant to be there. She felt a warm swell of pride in her work. She never thought she'd feel that way looking at this particular drawing again. Not after what the band did with it. All those damn hats and shirts and posters. But despite all that, it was still *her* work. Her design. And the joy that it brought Ava made her feel good.

Mags was so used to taking care of herself—only herself—that she'd forgotten what it was like to have family depending upon her. She'd always thought of family bonds as things that were difficult. Her father, when he was around, before he'd gotten remarried, had always been difficult. But she was starting to understand that bonds could also be sweet.

Gael sat on her bed and shared a packet of fries with Ava. He nodded for Mags to take a seat at the bedside, and the three of them had a little hospital picnic. Mags was amazed about how calm Ava was, how poised, despite the fact she was facing serious surgery in the morning. She dug into the hot dog like a starving college student.

"So good," she murmured between bites. "This is *so* good." She closed her eyes, savoring the Chicago dog. "I'm tired of bland chicken and soggy broccoli." She rolled her eyes. "How is a girl supposed to get well eating that?"

"Cheese fries will cure what ails you," Mags said and offered up some melted cheese dipping sauce. Ava enthusiastically dunked a crinkle fry into it and then popped the fry into her mouth.

"I'm cured!" she exclaimed and giggled. It was hard not to be affected by Ava's bubbly, warm personality, her zest for life. Someone like her shouldn't be sick, Mags thought. She ought to be out with her friends, having the time of her life.

Ava glanced at Mags. "So, how did you end up doing the Shaded Moon cover? Did Gael tell you that's, like, my favorite album of all time? Of course, it's their only album so far, but still."

Mags took a deep breath. She thought about the band, about how they'd promised to promote her work and about how they ended up replicating it instead, pocketing all the cash. There'd been those excuses about how song downloads wouldn't begin to pay for studio time, how merch was the only way to make a living in the music business anymore. If they'd just told her ahead of time, discussed it with her before they'd printed all those shirts and hats, she might've been on board. But they hadn't. The betrayal still stung.

"I knew people who knew them," she said. "They used to hang out at the same bar I went to. The Bulldog."

Gael raised an eyebrow. "Does everyone go there?" he teased.

Mags shrugged. "Just the important people." She glanced at Ava. "Anyway, they asked if I would design the cover, so I did."

"That's so cool. *You're* so cool." The unabashed admiration in the girl's eyes made Mags a little uncomfortable.

"No, *you're* the cool one. Look at all these flowers!" Mags nodded around the room, which was stuffed full of balloons and several layers of plants and some wilting flowers. "You've got a lot of friends."

"*He* sends me most of them." She pointed to Gael.

Mags glanced at Gael with surprise. It was a thoughtful gesture, keeping her room full of cheer.

"Not just me. Her whole class signed that giant card." He nodded to the poster board–size get-well card propped up in the corner.

"That's because *you* made them sign it," Ava said. "He pestered the school until they did it."

"They were happy to do it. They miss you."

Ava rolled her eyes to the ceiling, unconcerned. That made Mags somehow like her even more. "You all are making too big a deal out of this. I'm going to be fine."

Mags caught the worry line that appeared in Gael's forehead, the way he stiffened ever so slightly, as if hoping he could protect his little sister from all the medical bad news in the world with sheer force of will.

"Yes, you are," Mags agreed. "You're tough. And I know tough." Both Gael and Ava laughed a little. Gael flashed her a look of gratitude. "Maybe when you've kicked cancer's butt, your brother might be okay with letting you get a tattoo, too. On the house."

Ava's face instantly lit up. "Really? You'd do that? For me?" Ava's whole face radiated joy. Gael's, however, darkened with disapproval. She'd overstepped.

"Maybe," Gael said. "A small one. *Maybe.*"

"Sorry—" Mags backtracked. "I should've asked your brother first. It's his call." Mags wasn't used to asking permission. She suddenly felt like she'd mucked things up without meaning to. This was why she didn't belong in sweet families. She didn't fit. Her mom had been the sweet one of the family. And cancer had taken her before she'd been able to teach Mags how to be sweet.

"It's okay." Gael shrugged one shoulder. "Just so long as she knows it's a *maybe*."

"Please? Pretty, pretty please?" Ava begged, like a toddler in the toy aisle at Target.

"You have to be eighteen first," Gael said.

"My birthday is in mere months. So then can I?"

Gael frowned. Clearly, he'd been hoping to stall longer than a few months. That much was clear on his face. "Maybe," he said.

Ava deflated like a punctured balloon. "Maybe always means no." She glanced at Mags.

"It doesn't," Gael protested, sounding very much like a dad. She liked it. It was a shade warmer than The Tone he used in the bedroom. Warmer, but still with an underlying steel to it. "It means *maybe*."

"Fine." Ava stuck out her tongue, and at that moment she looked very much the teenager. Not a sick teenager, just a teenager, chafing against authority, determined to get her own way somehow. Mags remembered that feeling. It wasn't so long ago she was a teenager herself. A teen who'd had to take care of her father for the most part. He'd been in rough shape after her mother died. It had just been her and him then. At least, before he remarried and moved halfway across the country. She pushed those thoughts away. No use dwelling on them now.

"We getting some sass in here?" This was from Maeve, who'd poked her head in and overheard the last bit. "If you want my opinion, no tattoos until you're twenty-one."

"Not you, too." Ava crossed her arms across her chest in protest.

"Look, I'm just trying to save you from this." Maeve pulled up her left scrub pant and showed Ava a small tattoo just above her left ankle. It was of Scooby-Doo.

Gael let out a frustrated breath and squeezed the bridge of his nose between two fingers. "Not the Doo."

"I was a little bit of a jerk after our parents died," Maeve explained. "Might have gone through a rebel phase."

Mags understood that. She was still in one.

"I was seventeen and wanted to shock this guy."

"Oh, you shocked me all right." Gael shook his head.

"He lost it. Grounded me for a month."

Ava giggled a little. "But I'm not getting Scooby-Doo."

"I think she means that whatever you get you might outgrow," Gael added, giving Maeve a little nod of thanks. Maeve let her pant leg fall down, covering the tattoo once more.

"I can't even wear shorts without people commenting on it." Maeve shook her head. "So best not to get a tattoo until you really know what you want."

"She's right," Mags added. "I get plenty of people who ask me to alter old tattoos. And then there are the people who need to get their exes marked out. That happens a lot."

"Think you could do anything about the Doo down there?" Maeve asked her, pulling up her pant leg once more. Mags gave it a quick look.

"Maybe," she said, studying the lines of the tattoo. "I might be able to turn it into something, but it would have to be much bigger than what you have there. Come on by the shop sometime, though, and I could sketch something on you. Give you an idea of what it might be."

"I knew I liked you," Maeve said, beaming. Then she cut a look to Gael. "You better be nice to this one."

"*That's* what I said!" Ava cried.

"Do your sisters always boss you around so much?" Mags asked.

"Yes!" Ava and Maeve both replied.

"And we're not even as bad as Kathleen," Maeve added.

Mags had to laugh. It was all so…adorable. Sweet, even. These women cared about Gael. Wanted to see him happy. Made her feel like she wanted to be one of them. Sign her up for Team Gael.

"Well, hate to break up the party…" Maeve trailed off, glancing at the white clock hanging on the wall above the TV. "But it's that time. Miss Ava needs her sleep. She's got a big day tomorrow."

"I can stay," Gael said quickly, reaching for Ava's hand. Protectively. "I can wheel in one of those reclining chairs. Sleep here with you."

Mags got the idea it wouldn't be the first time.

"No!" Ava insisted, voice loud. "You need to take Mags home. Maybe stop and get a drink on the way there. One of us needs to have a little fun."

"Ava. I don't have to—"

"No buts!" Ava held up one finger, green eyes blazing.

"Oh, you're getting the finger wag now," Maeve teased. "You know that nobody wins against the finger wag."

Gael hesitated. "You sure?"

"Positive! I will be furious if you spend the night here. And you know I should be calm before the big event. Now get out!" Ava pointed to the door. Still, a huge grin lit her face. "I'll see you tomorrow, big brother."

Gael leaned in to give her a hug. "I'll be here bright and early."

CHAPTER ELEVEN

MAGS SAT IN the passenger seat of Gael's expensive car as he drove through the darkened streets of Chicago. She felt strangely comfortable when he reached out and took her hand. He brought her wrist to his lips and kissed the inside of it. A little jolt of sensation went up the length of her arm. She wondered how his lips had that kind of power over her and then remembered how they'd felt all over her body. A shiver ran through her.

"Thank you for coming to the hospital. I think it meant a lot to Ava."

"I don't know about that. I think I might have gotten her hopes up for a tattoo."

Gael chuckled, meeting her stare across the gearshift. "Don't worry. She's always wanted one, anyway. And it's not that much longer until she's eighteen."

"I don't meant to stir up trouble."

"You didn't," Gael said quickly. Mags's stomach let out an unruly growl then, loud enough to be heard clearly in the small expanse of the car. Gael raised his eyebrows in alarm.

"We need to get you fed before you get hangry," he said. "Otherwise, you might kick me out of my own car."

"I might," Mags teased. The grumble of her stomach sounded almost embarrassingly loud now. "Where are we going?"

"You'll see."

A few moments later, they pulled up in front of the valet stand at Lanier's, an überfancy burger and steak restaurant known for their forty-dollar burger.

"I can't go here," Mags exclaimed, feeling panic well up in her throat.

"Why not?"

"I'm not dressed for it." She glanced down at her shredded jeans and her combat boots. This was a four-dollar-sign restaurant. Sure, they served burgers, but they did it on the fine china. She doubted there'd be any blue-haired, tattoo-laden punk girls inside. "Besides, how can a forty-dollar burger *possibly* be worth it? I just don't believe it."

"It's worth it," Gael said. "Besides, I'm paying."

Mags rebelled. She couldn't let him buy something so outlandish. "No way. This is too much."

"You didn't have to go with me to see Ava. It's my way of saying thanks. So you're going to let me do this."

There. That tone. She felt it in her belly. God, the man's mere voice turned her on.

"Okay," she relented.

Gael put the car in Park. "Valet's already coming over. We'll need to go. And you look great. It's not a formal place."

She didn't understand how it couldn't be. A forty-dollar burger? She imagined waitstaff dressed in tuxedos carrying some stuffed burger on a silver tray. Stuck-up and ridiculous. But the valet was already opening Gael's door, and he was sliding out. A second valet had opened her door, and now cold air was blowing in against her thin leather jacket. She couldn't just very well sit there. So she swung her legs out and reluctantly followed Gael. He'd be sorry once they got in and the maître d' gave her one of those you-don't-belong-here looks and told them both to leave.

The opaque glass outside the modern-looking restaurant gave nothing away. They slid through the revolving doors, and instantly, Mags was hit with the sound of AC/DC playing over the restaurant speakers. What the...? It wasn't the white-tablecloth, fancy restaurant she'd imagined at all. It looked mostly like...a normal bar. A little too modern for her tastes—the restaurant had a sleek glass bar and a line of expensive liquors behind it—but still. The old, worn oak tables with modern lines weren't that pretentious after all. And Gael had been right about her outfit. Near the hostess stand stood a crowd of people from all walks of life—business casual, business formal, completely casual and even punk, she noted as she caught the eye of a woman with purple hair—waiting in the small lobby. The place wasn't big—including the glass bar and the tables around it, she'd guessed it might seat sixty people, tops.

"The wait will be too long," she protested. Her stomach growled again, registering its official complaint.

"No, it won't." Gael made his way through the crowd and caught the hostess's eye.

"Gael!" she cried and gave him a big hug. A ripple of unease passed across the back of Mags's neck. The woman was gorgeous: a dark brunette with curves that wouldn't quit. She wore a very low-cut V-neck minidress that held up her breasts as if on a tray, and she was hanging on to Gael for a beat too long. Not that Mags should care, she reminded herself.

"Mags, this is Felicity," he said, making introductions. "She's the owner of Lanier's."

"Nice to meet you," Felicity said, enthusiastically shaking Mags's hand. She thought the woman might shake it right off.

"I know you don't take reservations, but—"

"For you, there's always an exception to be made," Felicity gushed. "Come in—we've got a table there near the kitchen."

Mags raised an eyebrow, realizing they'd just leaped to the front of the line ahead of what looked to be a more-than-an-hour wait. As they followed the svelte hostess through the crowded, small restaurant, Mags squeezed his arm.

"We're getting the royal treatment," she said, wondering if Gael had a relationship with Felicity. She wondered if it was just sex or something more. Had he made her laugh? Had he bent her over a desk and spanked her, too? She wouldn't like that if he had. Not one bit.

"How did you two meet?" Mags asked Gael, knowing she was fishing for information she shouldn't dig for.

"I did her a favor a little while back," Gael said.

"Favor?"

"More than a favor," Felicity cut in, eyes shining with gratitude. "He saved us. Remember that beef recall last year?"

Mags did, vaguely. The entire country pretty much went without beef for a month.

"We serve burgers, and pretty much only burgers, and we'd have gone under, if it hadn't been for an emergency loan from this guy." Felicity stood before an empty table at the end of the bar, and Mags slid into one of the seats as the hostess placed a menu in front of her, ugly thoughts popping into her head. How did Felicity repay that kindness? She didn't want to know. Then she reminded herself she didn't believe in jealousy. Jealousy was a wasted emotion. Except it didn't feel like a waste. Not right now. Not looking at Felicity grinning at Gael.

"I wasn't going to let the best burger restaurant in town go under," Gael said.

"Plenty of banks would've—that's what Simone always says," Felicity said. She met Mags's gaze. "Simone's my wife."

"Oh," Mags said, taken off guard, her face coloring. Okay, so now Mags felt like an idiot.

"He's one of the good guys," Felicity told her, sincere. "I'll send a server right over."

Mags glanced at the menu in front of her and wanted to hide behind it. Good, yes. Good at ordering her around her bedroom and making her like it. He was damn good at that. But did she really want to let in the fact he was more than that? More than strong hands and a domineering voice? She distracted herself by looking at the menu, but then she saw the prices marked there and nearly choked. Forty dollars for a burger wasn't even the start. Fifteen dollars for a beer? Twenty dollars for a cocktail? If she offered to pay even half her share, it would be her eat-out budget for the week, most likely.

"This is a bit…pricey."

"I'm paying," Gael said quickly.

"You don't have to," Mags said. After all, she could order water and a side of fries. Just that would likely be twenty dollars.

"No arguments." That voice again. There was no fighting with it. No matter how much she wanted to. It just hit some spot in her brain, made her numb, unable to resist.

"Why are the fries so expensive?" she murmured, almost to herself.

"They're truffle fries."

"What are those?" Mags hadn't heard of them before. But then, she didn't do fine dining all that much.

"Truffles are a rare mushroom. They're hard to grow and hard to find, but delicious."

"Twenty-dollars-per-side-of-fries delicious?" Mags didn't believe it.

"Mags. Trust me." Gael grabbed her hand across the table and squeezed. The warmth and strength in his palm calmed her. It reminded her that she'd trusted him in bed, and that had worked out just fine. Better than fine.

That made her feel slightly better. "Okay," she said, reluctantly. "But I don't need a whole burger. We could split one?" Then, it would be just be forty dollars and not eighty.

"Nope." Gael shook his head. "And we're getting garlic and regular truffle fries. You'll thank me."

Mags wasn't so sure. She wasn't used to spending so much, so freely. But she also knew that changing Gael's mind would be like moving a mountain. And she knew he'd spank her if she resisted too much. But she might like that. A lot.

Gael watched Mags devour the last of her burger hungrily and felt...good. Whole. He liked taking care of this fiercely independent woman who seemed so determined to let him know she *didn't* need taking care of. Even though everybody needed a little TLC now and again, and Mags most of all. Beneath that rough exterior, he knew, was a sensitive soul. He'd seen the way she'd looked at Ava, seen the way she'd tried to cheer the teen. She cared, even if she wasn't letting on that she did.

Plus, the way she'd been so vulnerable in bed showed him that there was a completely different side to Mags. One he wanted to get to know better. Even if he had to punish her with lashes across her backside to do it.

"So, this *is* the best burger. Am I right?" He'd waited until she'd nearly cleaned her plate. But he had to gloat. Just a little. She'd been so determined to hate Lanier's based on the cost alone. But there was a reason it was named the best burger in town.

"Okay, okay." Mags held up her hands in defeat. "You're right. This was a damn amazing burger." She swiped at her mouth with the linen napkin and sighed. "I still don't know if it's worth forty-two dollars, but it was like nothing I've ever had before. And these fries? It's not truffle oil—it's crack. Has to be, because I can't stop eating them!" As if to prove her point, she reached to the plate in front of her and grabbed a short fry and popped it into her mouth.

"I told you they're addictive." Gael grinned. He liked watching Mags enjoy herself, fill her belly, have a good time. A light shone in her brown eyes, and for a second, she forgot to put on the hard shell she wore 24-7. Gael got it. Growing up poor without a mom did things to a person, but that didn't mean she had to stay that way forever. Gael had seen her at her most vulnerable, naked in his bed, and she didn't wear a hard shell then. She didn't wear any protective layer at all. It was when she was most herself. Then and now, when she forgot, just for a second, that she was supposed to keep him at a distance.

The bill came, and Gael paid it with ease, careful not to let her see the total. With the cocktails they'd added to the tab, the bill was much larger than the one at Superdawg. Gael glanced at his watch. It was getting late, too. He had to think about getting up early for his sister's surgery. At the very thought of that, his stomach tightened. He was worried about so many things—worried about the recovery time. Worried if Ava's one kidney could do the job of two. Worried most of all that the surgery wouldn't take out all the cancer, that another tumor was hiding somewhere, unseen.

"We'd better get going," Gael said, even as Mags finished off the last fry on the table. "I'll have an early morning."

Mags studied Gael. "Right. Ava's surgery." She paused a beat. "Do you need company tonight? Or would you rather be alone?"

The way she said it was so matter-of-fact, as if she didn't have a preference herself. There was that wall again. That shield. He should tell her he was fine—

after all, he'd need to be up early in the morning to get there well before the surgery. But he wanted a respite. Actually, he needed one. A distraction from the real worries weighing him down.

"I'd like company," he admitted. She reached across the table and held his hand.

"Okay," she said.

Mags couldn't believe her eyes as she walked into Gael's enormous penthouse condo. It was bigger than the entire floor of her apartment building, which held four units. The sleek new floors and shining kitchen made her feel practically underdressed.

"Curtains," he called to his smart device, and the sleek drapes automatically opened, revealing his million-dollar view. Miles of Lake Michigan stretched out before them, the dark water glistening underneath the full moon. She gaped at the view, but he barely seemed to notice.

"You live here?" It felt almost like a museum, some kind of display about how rich people lived.

"I do." He tossed his jacket onto the large leather sofa in the glassed-in living room that looked directly out to Lake Michigan. The view alone was worth millions. She wasn't sure if she ought to touch anything. It felt like everything ought to be cordoned off behind red velvet rope. Mags walked to the window, amazed at how high up they were. The traffic below looked like it was made of Matchbox cars, toys moving back and forth down the street. She stared at the small cars below, the people so tiny she could only see them as dots walking on the sidewalks far below. She wondered what it was like to live up here, like a king looking out over a fiefdom.

Most women would be swayed by this kind of view, by this expensive place. Most women would find it attractive, but Mags was not most women. The penthouse and its spectacular view just made her nervous. She remembered the Waterford crystal paperweight on the banker's desk at the bank that had foreclosed on her dad. That and the sterling-silver Tiffany letter opener made her wonder how many houses he'd foreclosed on to afford the extra-nice desk accessories and the diamond pinkie ring he wore.

Gael came up behind her, wrapping his arms around her waist. She leaned back into him, glad for the contact, because she suddenly felt unsteady on her feet. She wanted to feel his body against hers, forget about the differences between them. Because standing in his expensive penthouse, she was more aware than ever that they came from different worlds. She twisted in his arms and found his mouth, kissing him fiercely, trying to say all the things she wanted to say with a kiss.

Mags didn't want to look at the view anymore. She didn't want to think about how much his furniture cost. She only wanted the feel of his hands on her skin, to connect with him in the only way that mattered. After all, this wasn't about moving into his penthouse. It wasn't about trying to make their lives fit together. This was about sex. It would be good of her to remember that. She was making it all more complicated than it needed to be. Why did she even care if she felt out of place in his home? She wasn't planning on living there.

She just wanted him to order her around. Dominate her for an hour or so, and then she could go back to her own life, her own tattoo shop, where she belonged.

Mags devoured Gael, her need suddenly urgent, and her brain shut off, which was bliss. Because no matter how different they might be, their bodies spoke the same language. Their bodies knew exactly how to communicate, how to cut through their economic brackets.

Gael lifted Mags into his arms as if she weighed nothing, and her breath almost caught in her throat. She wrapped her legs around him reflexively, and he tightened his grip, his strong arms beneath her butt. The man was literally sweeping her off her feet, carrying her near blind to his bedroom, and she couldn't be more delighted, couldn't be more ready to give him control. She didn't want to think anymore. Didn't want to worry. Didn't want to spin the thoughts in her mind about what might or might not happen. She just wanted to be in this moment.

Gael carried her to his bed, laying her gently down on his plush, king-size platform with the expensive goose-down cover. She didn't want to think about the thread count of the man's sheets, but lying on his bed felt like reclining in a puddle of soft, rich goodness. Gael freed her mouth and gently undid the button of her jeans, sliding them down her legs slowly, his green eyes never leaving hers. She saw want there, hot and sharp, but he was moving carefully, deliberately. With her jeans on the floor, he tugged down her thong, careful to run a finger over the tattoo on her hip bone, kissing it delicately.

"Lie back," he commanded. Desire bubbled in her, threatened to run over. That damn voice. God, she loved that voice. She lay there, naked, vulnerable and waiting for her next command. He soaked in her body, admiring her curves. "Touch yourself."

He spread her knees with his hands, and then she reached down, tentatively at first, and laid the first stroke there. He watched, and the more he watched, the hotter she got. She'd never done this before, never been *ordered* to do this before. This was something she saved for herself, alone. But him watching made it better somehow. Made it hotter. And here, on his massive bed in his beyond-expensive penthouse... she wanted to do this. And more. She didn't want to admit that the money and the view of Lake Michigan meant a thing to her, but they did. They affected her. Here on his expensive sheets, as she met his gaze and touched herself, her clit swelling with need beneath her finger.

He unzipped his pants and dropped them to the floor, his muscled legs moving out of them. She paused in her movements, eyeing the growing bulge in his boxer briefs.

"Keep going," he demanded, green gaze finding hers. "Don't stop."

She started stroking again, shivering as she did what she was told. God, she liked it. Liked being told what to do. But only by him, she realized. No one else.

He unbuttoned his shirt and dropped it to the floor. She sucked in a breath. God, his chest. So perfect. The ridges of muscles she'd felt beneath her hands. Perfection. He moved closer.

"Stop," he commanded, and she did, she released herself, even as she felt the burning want. Her body cried out for her to continue, demanded the sensation, protested the abrupt end. But obey him she would.

He let her suffer there, for just a moment.

"What now?" she asked him, tentative, a bit of a plea in her voice. Her whole body vibrated with the anticipation of what he'd do next, of what he'd ask her to do.

He settled down between her legs, taking his time, a wicked look crossing his face. "Now," he commanded. "Now you're going to come for me. Harder than you've ever come for anyone."

Then he was between her legs. His tongue caressed her as if she were a delicacy, and a thousand different sensations skipped up her spine. Her finger was no match for his tongue, and every nerve ending came alive beneath his gentle touch. She almost thought he intended to prove that to her with this little exercise.

She was a slave to him, completely and totally. Her body would do anything he asked at this point. All it wanted was that warm, wet tongue. Every thought in her brain vanished, and her body was one throbbing nerve, pulsating, exposed. She tangled her hands in his thick, dark hair. She'd never in her life had a man so giving…so completely into her, so willing to put aside his own climax for hers. She'd never imagined a suit could be this selfless, or, hell…this damn talented. He took his time with her, savoring her, bringing her to the very brink. Her back arched, pressing her pelvis to his eager mouth. She couldn't think, could barely breathe, the desire taking hold of her, smothering all other need. Then his tongue demanded her climax, and she gave it to him, fully, completely. She was blinded with pure pleasure, so complete, so full that she almost thought the very climax might break her in half. A shout escaped her throat, a shout that almost felt like a prayer. Or a cry for mercy.

She wasn't sure which.

Because she'd done what she was told. She'd come hard. Harder than she'd ever come in her damn life.

Mags sucked in a breath, her heart pounding in her chest like a loosened shutter in a hurricane.

"That's my good girl," he growled. And then, as she lay before him, spent, unable to move, he tugged off his boxer briefs. She was wet spaghetti in his bed, but he was rock hard and ready. She felt swollen all over. How could she take him now? He'd shattered her body, blown it apart with his tongue.

"I'm…" She was going to say *exhausted*. Spent. Done for. But he had the condom in his hand and was rolling it down the length of him.

"Oh, you're not done yet."

"But… I came so hard." Her voice was almost a whine. A protest.

"You'll come again." It was a command and a prophecy. Then he pulled her to the edge of the bed on her side. She went, without protest, sliding on her back. He stood at the edge of the bed and entered her slowly, inch by inch, her body that she thought couldn't do this accepting him. Welcoming him. She moaned again, unable to help herself. In that moment she was his, completely, totally, as her eyes flicked open and she met his gaze. He held her legs, clutching her in his big, strong hands, a vise grip. He wasn't letting go, and she didn't want him to. She wasn't sure how much of this she could take. She felt her body might tear apart from the force of another climax. And, yet, she also felt it building in her. Felt it with every thrust he made, felt it in the very core of her.

She wanted this. Wanted him. Wanted this man more than she'd ever wanted another man in her life. She'd never felt like this before, never felt such a searing need. Something in her chest shifted then, something moved. A brick of her wall coming loose? She didn't know. But she was opening more than her body to him in that moment, and she couldn't stop herself. She held Gael's gaze and felt like she might fall into it. His eyes projected an unspoken promise. He'd catch her if she fell. He'd be the steady hand she'd never had in her life. And for the briefest of seconds, she realized she could be his, too. She could steady him. If she'd just allow herself the possibility.

Then she let herself go and fell tumbling over the edge into a sweet oblivion, her whole body seized with her climax, a shout escaping from her lips. Gael matched her, thrust for thrust, before he, too, came. Gael collapsed on top of Mags's chest, spent and winded, and she could feel his heartbeat, as wild as hers, against her chest.

Mags lay there for she didn't know how long, feeling drained and boneless, happy to be in a bubble with her eyes closed and nothing but his comforting warmth against her, the steady swell of his chest with breath. She wanted to stay there forever, cocooned in the safety of him, but she knew eventually she'd need to pull herself away before she got too comfortable.

This was role play, wasn't it? Just sweet release. Nothing more.

She opened her eyes and saw the sleek bedroom, the glassed walls beyond which lay the dark void of Lake Michigan, lit only by the smallest bit of moonlight. This wasn't where she belonged, she realized. She needed to get back home, to her tiny apartment, her scrubby rental, away from the expensive chrome of Gael's penthouse.

She sat up.

"I need to go," she told him.

"Wait," Gael said, clutching her softly by the wrist. "Please stay."

"I…" Mags was about to say *can't*. Though she knew what she meant was *won't*. It was all about self-preservation. She'd let herself be too vulnerable just then. She needed to find the brick that had come loose in her wall. She needed to cement it back in place. Mags felt unsteady—wobbly, even. Because this wasn't just role play. It was becoming real. Too damn real.

Gael's need shone clearly on his face, and Mags knew he wasn't a man used to needing things. She hesitated—a beat too long, it turned out.

"Come here." That voice. That damn voice. He pulled her closer to him, and she went, her heart aching a little. If she stayed, she knew she'd get too attached. Because she wanted to—it was that simple. It wasn't just the penthouse making her uncomfortable. It was him: his very presence, the way he looked at her now, offering her something different, something…complicated. But something amazing at the same time.

"I—I shouldn't stay. I don't…spend the night. Those are my rules." Rules that suddenly seemed ridiculous right now, sitting in Gael's bed, nose to nose. She could smell him, the hint of his spicy cologne and the smell of his skin beneath. She wanted to lose herself in that scent, tuck herself into his arms beneath his comforter and let his scent blanket her all night long. And that was why she ought to go, because those thoughts were insane. She couldn't *be* with Gael. A suit would never marry a tattooed punk girl, or vice versa.

Plus, she'd promised herself she'd never get married. She knew that love didn't last. It was foolish to think you could promise to love another person forever when you didn't know when cancer or, hell, any other tragedy might strike.

"There's that wall again," Gael murmured, focusing on her face.

"What wall?" Mags felt exposed. How did *he* know about her wall? Did he also know about the loose brick?

"The one you put up between us when I get too close."

Mags shifted, uncomfortable. "What do you mean?" Why did she even care what he meant? She ought to go. Now. Before she got too entangled in the man's brain. In his sheets. In his whole life.

Gael sat up on his elbows. "All your defenses come down when we're in here." He patted the bed. "Did you know that? You're completely *you*, completely open when your body is against mine." Gael stared off out the big plate-glass window toward the lake. "But most other times, you hide behind your wall. Trying to keep everybody else out."

Mags toyed with the edge of Gael's sheet, suddenly feeling guilty and then wondering why. Why did she feel bad? It wasn't like she'd promised Gael she'd be emotionally available. In fact, she thought she pretty much warned him the opposite would be true.

"I have my reasons for keeping people out."

"Because everyone you've ever really loved disappointed you. I get it." Gael sat up in bed, the sheet falling away and revealing the expanse of his bare chest and the dark ink of his new tattoo.

"Not everyone," she protested, but then she realized Gael was right. Pretty much everyone. "My mother couldn't help that she got sick."

"No, but she left you all the same. Even though it wasn't your fault. And your dad, you said he got remarried? Moved across the country?"

Mags nodded. She thought about how he used to call every month, but when she stopped calling him back so soon, eventually, he'd stopped calling regularly. Now she could pretty much only count on hearing from him on the anniversary of her mother's death. That would be tomorrow. But for Mags, remembering her mother only one day a year just didn't seem fair. It wasn't enough. And she resented her father for it.

Gael stared at Mags a beat. "I'm not wrong, am I?"

She slowly shook her head.

"Look, I think… I think we could *be* something." Gael ran his hands through his thick, dark hair. "I've never met anyone like you before. I feel like I've known you forever, even though we just met. Didn't you feel that? When we first kissed? Like we were somehow made for each other?"

"You're a pretty damn good kisser," Mags admitted.

"But it's more than that. I think it's more. Or could be. If you let it be."

Mags felt her chest tighten. She wanted it to be more, that was the problem. Unlike all her other friends with benefits, Gael seemed so steady. So real. So made for her. She couldn't deny the truth in his words. The first time they'd kissed, she'd known he was different from the others. Hell, the first time he'd ordered her around, she'd known he was different. Known he wasn't afraid of her.

But she didn't want something different. She wanted simple. Uncomplicated. She didn't want to be cuffed.

"I just don't think I want that," Mags said. "It's easier if things aren't complicated."

"Simple things are nice," Gael said. "But they're also simple. There's no real satisfaction in simple."

Mags glanced at Gael's face, at his sincere green eyes, and wondered if what he said was true.

"Now isn't a great time for me, either," Gael admitted. "I need to be focused on my sister, on her getting well. I shouldn't even be thinking about a relationship."

"Then why are you?" Mags almost feared the answer.

"I didn't plan this. I didn't plan any of it." Gael shook his head as he reached out and caressed Mags's forearm. "But I can't stop how I feel. I'm falling in love with you."

CHAPTER TWELVE

HE WAS CRAZY. He couldn't be falling in love with her. They'd only just met, dammit. Mags stared at Gael, feeling like someone had punched her in the stomach and all the air had been pushed out of her lungs.

"You can't be in love with me." She felt that wobble again, the missing brick in her wall. It felt like one more word from him and the whole damn thing would topple.

"Why not?"

"We just met." It was insane. Beyond crazy. They'd known each other a matter of days. He barely knew her.

"People fall in love at first sight all the time. I waited a couple of days." Gael flashed her a grin, but she felt dizzy. Disoriented. Normally, when men began to profess their feelings, she only felt annoyed. But Gael was different. And that scared the hell out of her. She didn't feel annoyed at all. She felt…warm inside. Bubbly, even. And wobbly.

Definitely wobbly. He was *falling in love with her*? The suit? She couldn't believe it.

"But we're so different." That was the understatement of the year. Just glancing around his penthouse suite, Mags couldn't even begin to imagine living his lifestyle, much less being a real couple.

"So? I'm pretty sure they call that something." Gael snapped his fingers. "Right—opposites attract?"

"Of course they attract. They don't *fall in love*." Mags crossed her arms across her chest. She wore her shirt, but her jeans were still somewhere on Gael's floor. She'd need to get them if she was leaving.

"Sure they do," he said. "We are." The way he said it, so confident, so sure, nearly made Mags's head spin. Was she falling in love with him? She almost laughed aloud at the idea, but then something deep inside made her pause.

"You think I'm falling in love with you."

"You haven't stormed out yet, so I think my odds are good." Gael cocked his head to one side, his dark hair a riot on his head. There it was again in his eyes, that confidence and solidness. A man who wasn't scared. Maybe that was it, she thought. He knew what he wanted. Wasn't afraid to ask for it. And he wanted *her*. And she wanted to put her hands on him again, feel his silky hair in her hands. She felt the urge to crawl into his arms and stay there. Was that love? Or was it just loneliness? She realized she didn't know. She'd spent her entire adult life avoiding love, avoiding anything approaching love. She wasn't even sure she'd recognize love if it knocked on her front door.

Gael pulled her close and kissed her. She wanted to resist him, to resist everything he'd just said, but her body responded to him as if she had no control. She kissed him back, her mind a whirl of contradictions: *I need to go home. I want to stay. I should leave. I don't want to.* Then Mags thought of her mother. Of how she'd tried so hard to make them a family, but how after her death, the family fell apart. What good was wanting to connect with people if they would just leave you?

Mags pulled away. She was about to tell Gael this, about the futility of love, of it all, when her phone rang. She glanced at the face of her phone. "Chicago police?" Why were the police calling?

"Hello?" she answered.

"Margaret McHenry?" a stern-sounding woman said.

"Yes."

"This is Officer Lopez. There's been a break-in at your tattoo shop. A smash and grab. The convenience store owner next door called us. He also gave us your number. Can you come down to the store now to help us identify what might be missing?"

Mags's heart lodged in her throat. Why would someone want to rob her place? She didn't even keep much cash in the drawer. "I'll be right there." Mags hung up, hands shaking.

"Everything okay?" Gael asked, concern in his green eyes.

"I don't think so," Mags said. "Someone broke into my shop. I've got to go." She sprang up, hunting for her jeans. She needed to go, needed to see what damage had been done to her store. She found her jeans on the ground and snatched them up.

"I'm going with you," Gael said.

"That's not necessary," Mags protested as she wiggled into her pants.

"It is necessary," Gael said, and he was already on his feet, pulling on his shirt.

As he pulled up in front of Mags's tattoo parlor, Gael felt his stomach tighten. It was worse than he'd thought. The entire front glass window of the shop had been smashed in. It seemed angry, unnecessary. Someone could've simply broken the glass door and turned the bolt from the inside to go in. There wasn't a need to break the entire front window. Unless whoever did it was sending some kind of message. Gael frowned at that thought.

Gael parked his car behind the flashing lights of the police SUV near the front of the store. Mags sat in his passenger seat, nearly frozen to the spot, her mouth agape as she stared at her store. Gael grabbed her hand and squeezed it, but she was already fumbling with the door handle and leaping out onto the curb almost before the car had stopped moving. Gael threw the car into Park and turned off the ignition, following her to the police officers, who were taking photographs of the storefront. Mags herself stood near the broken glass, hands on her head in shock.

"I can't believe this," she murmured, shaking her head. "Who would do this?"

"That's what we were hoping you could tell us," said a tall, thin woman wearing a Chicago police officer's uniform. Her nearly black hair was pulled back into a tight bun at the nape of her neck. "I'm Officer Lopez."

"I'm Mags—er, Margaret McHenry."

The two women hastily shook hands. "This is… uh…" Mags stumbled as she looked at Gael. Then she opted not to give him a title. "Gael."

"Gael Quinn." He took the officer's proffered hand and shook it.

"Wait—as in brother of the mayor?" Officer Lopez said.

"That's the one."

"I heard you're bringing some big deal to the city. Lots of jobs coming." Officer Lopez sized him up with a single downward gaze.

"That's the idea." His partner, no doubt, had already had a few celebratory glasses of champagne, or even fancy dinners around town to celebrate. Gael preferred to see how the deal unfolded, how it all went. He knew even the most promising deals could go sideways. He studied Mags, saw how she worked hard to keep her composure. Seeing her beloved shop in pieces struck her deeply.

"Can I go in?" Mags didn't seem to care about deals, not that Gael blamed her. Her store hadn't just been robbed. It had been vandalized. The tattoo chair had been thrown on its side, the mirror near the front lobby broken. The glass countertop had been cracked in several places. Whoever had done this had been angry. Very angry.

"Yes, actually. We were hoping you could tell us what might have been stolen."

The front door to her place was propped open. Mags went right on through, past the register, which had been dumped on the ground, the cash drawer out and empty. Gael felt his stomach seize. He didn't like her jumping into the vandalized store alone, even if there were police around. He was fairly sure no burglar was lurking in the back hallways, but he still wanted to go with her.

Gael was fast on her heels as she ran to the back office, a tiny room barely big enough for a desk. She dropped to her knees by the desk and opened the cabinet door near the base. It swung open to reveal an empty shelf. Then she let out a cry that almost sounded like a wounded animal's.

"My safe!" she cried, pointing to the open drawer under the desk. "It's gone!"

"You had a safe?" Gael asked, and suddenly the pieces fell into place. Mags hated banks and suits. Gael had only ever seen her take cash from clients. She'd asked him for cash or a check. And he'd never seen a Visa or MasterCard sign. Hers was a cash-only business.

"The safe was heavy, but two guys still could've carried it." She shook her head as if she ought to have seen this coming. "I hid it in the cabinet, careful not to let anybody know where it was." She stuck her fingers deep into her blue hair. "I thought I was being careful, anyway."

Gael didn't know about the safe, and he'd been to her shop twice.

"How much was in it?" Gael asked, dread knotting his stomach.

"All of my month's earnings so far. At least eight thousand, plus your check." Mags glanced up at Gael, eyes flashing fury. "It's all gone now."

"Do you have insurance?" Officer Lopez asked gently. She'd been standing behind the two, notepad in her hand.

Mags shook her head. "For fire and damage to the shop, but not for the cash." Mags buried her face in her hands. Gael reached down and cupped his hand on her shoulder. She felt so tiny then, so small. Her bones were so delicate. Her skin so soft. He wanted to comfort her, tell her it would all be okay, but the words would sound weak in that moment. How could he say for sure everything would work out? Someone had trashed her shop. She'd be closed down at least a month while she made repairs, and maybe longer. And then there was the problem of the missing cash. He wanted to ask her if she had a safety reserve tucked away somewhere—hopefully in one of those banks she hated so much. But now wasn't the time for that.

"I'm sorry, Margaret—er, Mags, but can I ask you a few more questions?" Officer Lopez tapped her notepad with the tip of her ballpoint pen. "Just want to see if you have any surveillance, anything we could use?"

Mags shook her head. "The other two stores on the block have cameras," she said. "I know Mr. Ling's next door covers most of my shop. I think he's the one who called you guys."

"Yes, we'll be looking at the footage." Officer Lopez flipped her notepad. "But I have to ask, do you know of anyone who might have a vendetta against you? Ex-boyfriend? Someone who'd want to do this?"

Mags looked taken aback. "I don't think so. My ex, Clint—I mean, he broke up with me. He didn't hold any grudge." She shook her head and bit her lip. "I can't imagine who would do this."

Gael was struck with a memory.

"What about that kid who worked for you? What was his name? John?" Gael remembered the scowl on the kid's face when he'd seen him in Mags's parlor the day she'd fired him. Then there'd been that parting shot, the insult mumbled beneath this breath. This looked like something he'd do.

Mags folded her arms across her chest. "I never thought he'd do something like this." She shook her head, looking at the empty cabinet near her desk. She glanced toward the front of the store, where big shards of broken glass lay gleaming on the tile. "But maybe I was wrong."

Mags felt numb. She stood with her arms crossed, staring at the broken glass on her floor, the knocked-over tattoo chair, and still not quite believing this had happened, not quite believing that John—or whoever had done this—had such hate for her place that he'd want to do her so much damage. She couldn't even begin to wrap her mind around it. She'd been at this location for years, had always been a good neighbor, had friends all over town, but right now she felt very, very alone.

In fact, she'd never felt so alone, so vulnerable before in her life. Except the day her mother died. She glanced at her watch and realized it was just past midnight. *Well, this is just great*, she thought. Another shitty thing to remember that happened on this day. She was really, really beginning to hate November. The flashing blue lights of the police SUV outside still bathed her floor. The officers had gone next door to get the surveillance tape, promising to return with a few more questions.

But now she surveyed the damage to the shop, wondering when she could get started cleaning up the mess.

"How can I help?" Gael stood behind her, phone in his hands, as if ready to call for backup if needed.

"I don't know," she admitted. The problem seemed too big for him. Too big for her. How was she even going to start with this mess? "I don't even know what to do first. Clean? Call the insurance company? And then there's the problem of this." She spread out her arms across the big, broken window. "It's like a big welcome sign to looters. And there's probably still a few things here worth stealing."

Like her tattoo needles. The ink. Even the cash register, which had been battered but not entirely broken.

"I know guys," Gael said. "They can get over here and board this up. They can get the glass out."

"I can do that myself." Mags never asked for help. She wasn't used to needing it. And part of her didn't want it. When the world smacked her down, she was the one who got up herself. She never asked for a hand up.

"I know you can. But why? Let me help you."

But that would mean letting him in, wouldn't it? That would mean letting him have a piece of her. That would mean admitting to him and to herself that this wasn't the casual take-it-or-leave-it relationship she'd planned. But then, she already knew that. Already knew what they had went far deeper. She already knew she needed him. And that scared the hell out of her.

"No. I can do it myself." She was being stubborn. Stupid, even. She should just ask for the man's help.

Yet, on the anniversary of her mother's death…it just felt like a betrayal. Of her mom. Of herself.

"You can't do this yourself. You need help, and I want to give it to you." Gael sounded frustrated, and why wouldn't he be? He was just trying to do her a favor. And she wasn't letting him. She knew he didn't deserve this from her. He was just trying to help. She was the one with the problem. She was the one who wasn't accepting the help. And that said more about her than it did about him. "Don't be so damn proud. I can help. I want to help. All you have to do is let me."

"No." She sniffed, hard, hoping the growing anger in her stomach would burn out the tears threatening to spill. The tears just enraged her more. She wasn't going to cry. She wasn't going to let herself cry.

"What about the bills at the end of the month, or beginning of next? If your cash is gone, then you'll need a bridge loan. You've got utilities, a lease, I assume, to pay?"

She knew this already, but hearing it out loud felt like a blow. She had no idea how she was going to do any of that. There were the utilities to pay, and then the rent would be due, and there was no insurance to take care that because she'd opted out of that kind of coverage. And she'd been the one not to trust banks, to have kept a stupid amount of money on hand. She'd thought she'd been clever, keeping it hidden, but the ease with which two guys had executed a quick smash and grab might easily put her

out of business. But she didn't want to face all that
right now, and she sure as hell didn't want to think
that Gael was her only way out. She'd never been
so vulnerable, so in need before, and she hated the
feeling. She also hated that his money could be the
answer she needed. The money she'd so despised the
moment he walked in her door.

"I'll figure something out." She'd have to hit up
friends for loans, maybe. Or, God forbid, go to an
actual bank. She had no idea if they'd even lend her
money at all.

"Just let me help."

"If you help, then I owe you." Mags felt tears sting
the backs of her eyes. Stupid tears! Since when was
she so weak? It was because she felt helpless. It was
because she was letting Gael in. Leaning on people
made her weak. She'd not felt so hopeless since the
day her mother died. She couldn't do anything about
that then, but she'd sworn she'd never let herself be
so vulnerable again. She'd have control over her life.
But right now, nothing seemed in her control. "And
I don't owe anybody."

"I'm not just anybody."

"Yes, you are. You're just another guy I happened
to sleep with, okay? I told you not to make a big deal
out of it, but you are. We had some nice little role
play, but that's all it was, okay? Just a game." The
words slipped out of her mouth before she could stop
them. They were a lie. He wasn't just another guy

she'd slept with. She knew that. It wasn't just role play, either. It wasn't a game.

"Just a game," Gael repeated. She'd hurt him. Really hurt him.

She wanted to tell him she didn't mean any of it. That maybe he ought to punish her. Spank her. Whatever he wanted to do to make this right. Because he wasn't just another guy. He wasn't just a notch in her bedpost. Why was she lying to his face? Because she felt cornered. Because lashing out was her only way to feel like she was in control again. Even if that meant pushing Gael away. But now, as she saw the real pain in his face, she realized this wasn't role play. This was real.

"I get it." A volume of disappointment lay in those three words. She hated it. Hated disappointing him most of all. All she wanted to do was please him. All she wanted to do was kiss him and make it all better.

"No. Gael. It's not like that."

"No. Look. I get it. I'm going to go." The way Gael said it sounded like he wasn't just giving up on trying to help her now. He was giving up on her.

What the hell was wrong with her? Why couldn't she just say what she meant? Why couldn't she let her guard down even a little bit? Maybe Gael was right. She only let down her guard in bed. Nowhere else.

"Gael, please..."

But he was already heading out the door. "It's late," he managed. "I have to be at the hospital early anyway. For Ava."

Ava. Fuck. With the insanity of the last hour, she'd forgotten that she wasn't the only one having the worst day of her life.

"I... I'm sorry, Gael," she managed. It sounded weak, even to her own ears.

"Not your worry."

The words hit harder than they should. Not her worry. None of her business. Yet... she wanted it to be.

Gael glanced out the window where the officers were headed back to her shop. To ask the final questions, she assumed, or tell her what they'd found on the surveillance video next door.

Mags badly wanted to tell him that she wanted him to stay. That everything she'd said had been wrong. That she wanted to make it right. But none of the words came. They all lodged in her throat, a tangled mess.

Gael reached out and grabbed Mags's hand. He brought it to his mouth for a kiss. "Goodbye, Mags." There was that voice again. The strong one. The commanding one. He was telling her goodbye, and he meant it. She watched, legs useless and frozen, as he walked out of her shop. She wanted to call out to him, but the jumble of all her unsaid thoughts choked her. She felt like crying. She willed those damn tears back down where they came from. But this time, they didn't listen.

CHAPTER THIRTEEN

MAGS SPENT THE night cleaning, trying to keep her hands and her mind busy, as she swept up broken glass and picked up the cash register, closing the open drawer. She righted her toppled tattoo chair, only to discover that one arm of the chair was now broken. The thieves had to have stomped it on purpose to cause that kind of damage.

She thought about the security footage from Mr. Ling's store. The police had let her watch it, but the cameras hadn't caught much: two guys in black hoodies. One definitely tall, skinny and white, which might have been John, or it might have been someone else. The officers were going to try to see if they could enhance the video, and they had plans to interrogate John as well. They'd told her before they left around one in the morning that they'd be in touch.

Officer Lopez had clapped a hand on her elbow. "We've got a lot of evidence and good leads, like a partial tattoo on one of the perps. Better than most smash and grabs. We'll do our best to find who did this."

The kindness from the officer made Mags even more emotional, and she felt like she didn't deserve that kindness. She'd lashed out so much at Gael, which he hadn't deserved. It wasn't the first time, either, that she'd pushed away someone trying to get close to her. She pushed people away and then mourned their loss. Hell, if she were honest with herself, she spent her time assuming people would abandon her, and she'd push them hard enough until they did, proving her right. She realized she'd relished that feeling, of feeling superior, of being right, except that in the end, what satisfaction did it really give her? She was alone.

And now she was standing by herself in her shop, the weak sunlight of the morning beginning to stream in. She felt hollow. She felt exhausted, too. Her muscles burned with the hours of cleanup. Her back ached. This would've been easier if she'd let Gael help. But that felt like defeat. It was stupid, defied reason, but she'd learned a long time ago that leaning on people just led to disappointment.

She glanced at the gaping hole where her window used to be, the cold November morning air whisking in, chilling her, despite the fact she had on her leather jacket, gloves, hat and a chunky scarf she'd found tucked in her desk drawer in the back. The thieves hadn't bothered to take the knitted wool, and she'd put it to use. A few brown leaves were already swirling into her shop. She almost wanted to cry. Why did picking up all the glass matter? Mags's place was wide-open, a sitting duck for anybody else who wanted to come by and help themselves to her things.

The unfairness of it all struck her then. Her mother's death, her father's abandonment, the universe helping itself to her feelings, taking what it wanted. She'd spent her life fighting against anyone who'd take anything from her again, and in one night, two men had changed that. Bashing through the glass, taking her cash, her dignity. Maybe walls and barriers were just illusions, after all. Maybe walling herself off didn't actually protect her from anything. Maybe she should just sit on the floor, lie down and give up. She felt tempted. Everything felt so futile. She'd pushed away the only man who had ever really seemed to care for her, and why? To keep the illusion of her walls intact? To pretend she didn't need anyone, when she damn well knew she did.

She'd needed her mother. She'd needed her mother, and her mother had died. She'd needed her father, but he'd left her. She needed Gael. But she'd pushed him away. That was on her.

Then she saw a white, unmarked delivery truck pull up out front of her shop. Curious, she watched a man bundled in a jumper, wool beanie and work gloves jump out, clipboard in hand. Delivery for Mr. Ling, she wondered? But then she saw two other men get out of the truck, roll up the back and begin lugging out large pieces of plywood. The man in the beanie came to her door and waved to her. She opened it, curious.

"You Ms. McHenry?" one of them asked.

Mags nodded. "Who's asking?"

"Gael Quinn sent us. Said we should board up the window?"

Mags felt her chest swell with all kinds of emotion: gratitude, shock, relief. She was so tired, so damn bone tired, and the help had come at just the right time. Even after she had pushed him away, he was still taking care of her. Still looking after her.

Right then, she didn't care if she'd be in Gael's debt. Didn't care what it might cost her. She was just glad to see the men here to board up the broken window. In minutes, they had the first board up and were working on the second.

Her phone rang then, and she brightened, whipping it out of her back pocket and hoping to see Gael's number scroll across her screen. She'd apologize to him; she'd tell him she'd been an idiot; she'd tell him how very, very glad she was to see his guys pull up in front of her shop.

Instead, she saw her father's number. Today was the day, after all. The anniversary of the day her mother died. She instinctively wanted to send him to voice mail. But something made her hesitate. She was feeling so alone. So…abandoned.

"Hello?"

"Hello?" her father breathed, sounding surprised she'd answered. Part of her was surprised, too. It had been so long since she'd heard his voice, except in the occasional voice mail. But she recognized it. "Maggie? Is that you?"

She cringed at the nickname only her father and her grade school friends called her. She'd been Mags since high school. Not that her father would know that. He'd long since checked out of her life by the time she shortened her name.

"Yes, Dad. It's me." Mags felt emotion welling up in her, breaking free of the airtight container she normally stored it in, a potent cocktail of resentment, sadness, anger and...guilt.

"Honey, I'm so glad you answered. I've called so much."

"I know. But... I've been mad at you."

"For moving. I know."

"For forgetting Mom. For making me feel like *she* was the one who wanted to adopt me."

"Why on earth would you think that?"

Mags clutched the phone hard against her ear. "Because after she died, you moved away. Because you got remarried and wanted to get as far away from me as possible."

There, the truth finally.

"No. Oh no." She could hear the emotion in his voice. "No, I wasn't getting away from you, sweetheart. I love you. It's just...everything reminded me of your mom. After I met Amy, well, it just made sense to follow her out to California. Make a new start. I wasn't running away from you."

Something loosened in her chest then. Another brick in her wall crumbling? Possibly.

"I wanted you as much as your mother did. I've always been so proud of you. Of all the things you've accomplished. I've missed you so much."

"Yeah," she said, glancing around her empty store. "I've missed you, too."

"This is a hard day for you and for me, but Mom would've wanted us to go through it together. Mom would be so proud of you. All that you've accomplished! All that you've done. You still doing tattoos?"

"Oh, Dad." Mags felt the tears burn her eyes. She thought of how awful she'd been to Gael. How needlessly cruel. And the worst part was that she was just hurting herself in the process. "I think Mom wouldn't be proud of me at all." Then she told him about Gael, about Ava's surgery, about the break-in. About how he'd offered to help and she'd rebuffed him.

"Sounds like you like him."

"I do," Mags admitted. "More than like him. Maybe even…love him." There, she'd finally said the truth out loud. The truth she'd been trying to ignore ever since the man had walked into her damn store. Maybe she hadn't fallen into hate at first sight after all. She'd fallen in love that first day and had been fighting her feelings ever since.

"Then you should go to him. You know how hard surgery days are. You know the risks. Just being there will help him."

"But I think I messed it all up. I don't know if he'll forgive me." But she thought of the men he'd sent. She suspected he would forgive her. That was the scary part.

"He will," her dad said, sounding much more confident than Mags felt.

Gael sipped his coffee as he sat by his sister's bedside, both of them quiet as they waited for the staff to come in and wheel her to the surgical floor. Yet Gael's mind was a million miles away. Actually, not a million—just fifteen or so, at Mags's tattoo parlor. She'd told him she didn't care about him, not in the way he cared about her, and he'd just have to live with it. Gael didn't understand how she could deny what was between them. It was like claiming the sky was purple. Yet she'd made her feelings clear, and he'd respect them.

That didn't, of course, prevent him from calling in a favor to one of the many construction crews he knew around town. It wouldn't cost them much to hang up the plywood, secure her place from looters. She needed the help even if she was stubbornly refusing it. He wasn't going to let her spite herself out of pride. The fact that she'd made it clear to him that he wasn't someone she cared about stung, but he still wasn't going to let her twist in the wind. Wasn't going to abandon her when she needed help. That wasn't the kind of man he was.

"Hello? Gael?" Ava said, waving her hands in

front of him. He blinked fast, rousing himself from
those frustrating thoughts.

"Sorry."

"Thinking about her, aren't you?"

Gael shrugged. "That obvious?"

"I can read you like a book." Ava grinned. "Hey,
on the bright side, Mags gives you something else
to think about besides my dumb old tumor." Ava
laughed a little. She always joked around when she
was nervous about something. It was her way of hiding her fear, Gael knew.

"True. Who wants to think about that old thing
anyway?"

Ava grinned.

A soft knock game at the hospital room door, and
Gael turned, expecting to see the hospital staff ready
to wheel Ava to the operating floor. Instead, he saw
Mags standing there, blue hair hidden under a knit
cap, gray wool scarf wrapped around her neck.

"Mags!" Ava beamed. She threw her arms wide,
and Mags came over and gave her a hug. "We were
just talking about you."

"No, we weren't," Gael said, giving his sister a
look that he hoped would convince her not to cause
trouble.

Mags produced a small notebook from behind her
back. "Just a few tattoo sketches," Mags said. "Not
for now, of course." She glanced uneasily at Gael.
"But something you can think about as you heal."

"This is so cool!" Ava flipped through Mags's art

book, the colored drawings leaping off the page. Gael might not approve of a tattoo just yet, but he sure did like the look of joy on his sister's face. Attitude was so important going into surgery. All the doctors had told him that. And giving her something to look forward to on the other end of it was just smart.

Gael met Mags's gaze and tried to communicate his gratitude, but one look at her big, light brown eyes, framed by those thick dark lashes, and his breath caught, just for a second.

Two hospital orderlies came to the door then. "Ava? It's time," one said, coming into the room.

"This is it," Gael said and gave Ava a big hug. It was difficult with the IV in her arm and her heart monitor, but he managed. "You're going to do great."

She handed him Mags's tattoo book. "I'll see you on the other side," she said and lay back down as the orderlies wheeled her out and away. Gael turned to Mags then, giving her his full attention.

"I'm surprised you came." Gael couldn't help but feel a sprig of hope bloom in his chest. Had she come for him? Or did she just feel sorry for Ava?

"I wanted to…" Mags swallowed. Talking about her feelings was really like pulling teeth. She bit her full lip, hesitating. "Thank you for sending those guys. They boarded up my shop, and it helped. A lot."

"Good." Gael wasn't going to make this easy for her. She was the one who'd told him he was just one more notch in her bedpost.

"I… I'm sorry," Mags blurted before Gael could say another word. "I really messed up. I…was such an ass."

Gael laughed a little. "You kind of were."

"Hey! I'm trying to apologize here." Mags moved closer to Gael so they were both standing in the middle of Ava's empty room. Gael was close enough now to smell Mags's signature scent. Roses. The flower as delicate as her lips. Which he wanted to taste right now.

"I'm listening." If she asked him to spank her, he just might. She kind of deserved it.

Mags took a deep breath. Gael noticed her hands were shaking. His own heart ticked up a notch.

"I lied to you. You're not just another guy." Mags swallowed, hard. "I don't know why I lied. I was scared. I gave up so much to you… I lost control… with the role play."

"No, you didn't." He shook his head slowly. "You *gave* me control. You never lost it. It was always your choice to make. I never ordered you to do anything you didn't want to do."

She seemed to realize the stark truth of this. "You're right."

"I know I am."

She put a hand on her forehead. "This is just a really rough time of year for me. It's not an excuse, it's just an explanation." Mags took a deep breath, and Gael waited for her to exhale. "My mother died on this day."

"Today is the anniversary of your mother's death? Why didn't you tell me?" Gael was stunned. It was the kind of information she should have shared. What else was she keeping to herself? Maybe she did need a good spanking. A long one.

"Sure, I'll just mention that my mom died of cancer on the very day your sister is having *surgery* for cancer. That's a great thing to bring up." Mags curled her hands into fists at her sides.

"Okay, fair enough. I get why you might not want to mention it. But, still, you should have."

"I'm telling you now. Look... I... I don't let people in."

"I know." Gael studied her. "You don't trust outsiders. You barely trust insiders. I know. I get it. Your mom died when you were young, and when you leaned on your dad, he let you down, too."

Mags suddenly looked like she might cry.

"But it doesn't have to be that way. You don't have to live your whole damn life as a tribe of one," Gael said. "Technically, it's not even a tribe."

"I know." Mags took in a deep breath. "I never wanted to be with anyone, you know. I always told myself I'd never get married, never settle down, but you changed all that." She blinked fast. "You and your damn fine self waltz into my tattoo shop, into my life, talking about my walls. Ordering me around and me liking it. About how I'm keeping people out, and you're right. I have been. I didn't want to let you in, but now I realize that there's no way I'll ever truly keep you out."

Gael felt his ears buzzing.

"I'm falling in love with you, too, Gael," Mags said. She blinked fast, tears glassy in her eyes. He'd never been more moved by a woman before this moment. He couldn't help himself any longer. He reached out for her, and she came to him.

"It's about time," Gael murmured, and then he pulled her into his arms and kissed the life out of her.

CHAPTER FOURTEEN

MAGS SAT WITH her head against Gael's beefy shoulder in the waiting room of the hospital. It had been several hours since Ava's surgery had begun, and they'd gotten a couple of updates from Maeve. Gael had entwined his fingers in hers and squeezed her hand every now and again, a gentle gesture of gratitude. Mags had thought she'd feel caged, confined, after admitting she was in love with a man, but she found that being cuffed wasn't as awful as she thought. It kind of felt...nice.

She felt foolish, really, for fighting commitment for so long. But then, she told herself, she'd never really considered settling down until she'd met Gael. He was different. He was strong, steady, and he wasn't afraid of anything life had to throw at them. Cancer, burglaries—he was a calm port in the storm. One that she hadn't realized she'd needed until then. Plus, he damn well didn't let her get away with anything. And she needed that.

Mags cradled Gael's hand in both of hers, and

in that moment she realized he wasn't just her port, but she was his as well, a place for safety, a place for support. She liked being with him now, helping him wait through the anxious minutes and then hours as they waited to hear about Ava. She liked taking care of him. That was what had been missing her life. Someone she could care for and who could care for her back. Love wasn't just a one-way street like she'd thought.

She'd spent all those years worried about keeping people out, but Gael had been right. She'd only succeeded in making herself an island, lonely and alone.

"Are you okay?" Mags asked Gael.

"I just wish the damn doctor would come out already. The surgery is taking too long." He glanced anxiously at the clock.

"It's not too bad. They said it could be up to four hours. We're just over three."

Gael frowned. "Yeah, but a simple, quick surgery should've been two hours. Or less. Kathleen has already called five times." He raised his phone to show her. "She has a police press conference this morning. She'll come here after, but that doesn't stop her from pestering me."

Mags could feel the anxiety growing in Gael. Could almost feel the fear. She knew that feeling. Knew exactly how bad it could get when someone you loved was in danger.

"You don't know anything yet," Mags said. "The worst thing you can do is get ahead of yourself."

Gael grew silent a moment and then glanced up at the big clock in the waiting room. He frowned again. Every second that ticked by was another reason to worry, Mags knew. How often had she waited for her own mother to come out of surgery? She knew the feeling all too well. She also knew what happened when surgeries failed to stop the cancer.

"Do you need to go see about your store?" Gael offered. "You can, you know. If you need to go. You don't have to stay."

"Are you out of your damn mind?" Mags squeezed Gael's hand. "I'm not going anywhere."

Gael laughed and squeezed her hand back. "Thanks," he said, his voice a low murmur. "I guess I'm in the tribe of one now?"

"Damn well better believe it. Everybody else is the outsiders now. Once you're in my tribe, you're *in*. I'm not going anywhere."

"Good."

Mags tilted her head up to kiss him, and he kissed her back. The flame between them ignited instantly, like a gas burner coming to life. It took all Mags's force of will not to jump into his lap right here in this waiting room. They broke the kiss, eventually. She wasn't going to have sex here in the hospital, no matter how much she wanted to tear this man's clothes off.

"When this is all over," Gael said. "Let's just you and me go find the nearest bedroom and…"

"I was thinking the same thing. Maybe we could

find one on a beach. Maybe one of the bungalows on the sea? I saw a picture of those once."

"No interruptions," Gael said. "And all the room service we want. I like that idea." He wrapped an arm around her shoulders. "I also like the idea of you in a bikini."

"You might like me out of one even better."

Mags liked this, liked flirting, liked distracting Gael from the fact that his sister was fighting for her life in an operating room not far from here. Because what was the point of dwelling on the worst-case scenario? Worst case always knocked you on your butt whether you planned for it or not. She'd had months to get ready for her mother's death, and it had still knocked the wind out of her.

"So where would we go? Hawaii?" Mags asked.

"Fiji," Gael said with some certainty. "They have the best beach bungalows."

"You've been, then? With some gorgeous woman already?" Mags felt her blood pressure tick up a notch.

"Is that *jealousy* in your voice?" Gael had the gall to actually look amused. She'd wipe that look right off his face.

"No. I don't get jealous." Mags lifted her chin in defiance.

"*Sounds* like you're jealous, though."

"No. It sounds like I just want to get away from the impending Chicago winter and go somewhere warm."

"So this is just a matter of convenience for you, then?" A grin tugged at the corners of his mouth.

"Yes."

"Liar." Gael tucked his fingers beneath her ribs, and she couldn't help but giggle. Other worried faces in the waiting room turned to them, and she suddenly felt foolish. Her laughter died, and she settled back into her seat. This wasn't the place for laughter. Gael took Mags's hand again and squeezed it.

The automatic doors near them opened, and Ava's doctor came out. Mags felt her own stomach tighten as she tried to read the woman's blank expression.

"Dr. Carter?" Gael was already on his feet, ready for the news.

The auburn-haired doctor smiled, and Mags felt the tension in her shoulders relax for the first time since they'd sat down in the waiting room. She knew that doctors delivering bad news never smiled.

"I talked to Maeve but wanted to let you know Ava did great. We took out the kidney, the one that had been overtaken by the tumor. She's in recovery." Dr. Carter's smile faded a bit. "The reason it took a little longer than we expected is that we found another tumor. On her other kidney."

Gael squeezed Mags's hand, hard. Mags felt her own heart leap to her throat.

"But—" Dr. Carter lifted a hand "—we're pretty sure we got it, too. And saved the kidney. We're not 100 percent certain, but there's a very good chance she'll have a full recovery."

"No more cancer?" Gael asked.

"We're hoping we got it all," Dr. Carter said.

Mags felt like a weight had been lifted, and as she watched the joy come into Gael's face, she knew he felt the same. Gael gave the doctor a hug. "Thank you, thank you so very much."

The doctor left, and Gael pulled Mags into his arms, lifted her up and spun her around.

"She's going to be okay," Gael said into Mags's neck. He put her down on her feet and beamed. "You're my good-luck charm."

Mags almost laughed out loud. "I'm not anybody's good-luck charm."

"You're mine." His eyes shone with love, with joy. She laughed a little. Then he dipped his head down and kissed her so deeply, she felt it in her toes. He pulled away, and Mags didn't even care about the people staring. Let them stare.

CHAPTER FIFTEEN

One year later

IT MIGHT BE NOVEMBER, but the weather wasn't anything like fall, Mags thought as she glanced up briefly at the bright sun hanging over the Pacific. She shaded her eyes and leaned back on the wooden dock of the little bungalow in Fiji, feeling the warm sun tanning her skin. She wore a white string bikini, and most of her hip tattoo was visible, as were the others on her arms. But she'd reverted back to her natural hair color. No more blue streaks. No more excessive eyeliner or super-punk-chick vibe. She was just...her again.

She'd realized she'd been rebelling for the better part of her life, and now that she had Gael, she didn't need to work so hard at going against the grain. Now, here she was in the middle of paradise. Their bungalow was at the end of a long dock, and privacy was theirs. They could sunbathe in the nude if they wanted. Sometimes they'd go most of the day without even getting dressed.

Gael popped his head up out of the crystal-blue water, droplets flying every which way.

"I saw an octopus down there! A real octopus. He was only about six inches long, but still…" He pushed the goggles to the back of his head and grinned, his bright white teeth even whiter against his amber skin. He held on to the edge, smiling like a little kid.

"Ava is going to freak when I send her the picture I took." He dropped the waterproof camera on the deck. "Seriously, she's all into them now. Since they're on Shaded Moon's new album."

Mags just laughed and shook her head. "How did they go from falcons to an octopus? I'll never understand those guys."

"I'll never understand why they didn't ask you to do the second cover."

Mags snorted. "Because they knew I'd tell them to go to hell."

Gael wagged his finger, droplets flying. "No. You'd tell them you want an ironclad royalty contract."

Mags cocked her head to one side. "True. But it's better this way. I don't want to draw an octopus."

He dropped his snorkel on the dock and climbed up next to her, chiseled muscles in his chest and arms working as he pulled himself up. He lay down on the dock next to her, breathing hard, water glistening on his chest. The sight of him never failed to stir want in her, and as he lay back, she eyed his broad chest, her eyes lingering on her tattoo on his arm. She rolled over on him, wet body against dry.

"You can't just lie there half-naked and expect me not to do something about it," she teased him.

"I was hoping you'd notice," he growled. He covered her mouth with his, and instantly her body lit up, the switch thrown. They'd had sex more times than she could count since they'd arrived on the island a few days ago, but her body was never satisfied. She always wanted more. More of him. More of his hands. More of his cock. More of his chocolate voice, ordering her around. Asking her to do things she'd never dreamed of doing. Hot, wet, crazy things.

Of course, the craziest thing was that she'd had him all year long. She'd cuffed herself to this man and hadn't grown tired of him as she feared. He'd also not abandoned her, either. He'd been there through the year's ups and downs, including the arrest of John, her ex-employee, and his brother for vandalizing her shop. Gael had insisted on helping her rebuild her shop. Now, the shop was better than ever, and armed with surveillance cameras and the best security system money could buy.

She broke free from the kiss, and he grinned, his green eyes an even lighter shade beneath the Pacific sun. She'd never get tired of those eyes. She knew it now, that somehow, they'd always make her shiver. She'd never imagined a relationship could be so fulfilling…that the love and affection would just grow and deepen. She'd spent a lifetime feeling like her dad had forgotten her mom, abandoned her for a new relationship, but now Mags realized that he had only been trying to heal the best way he knew how. She'd kept everyone out, and he'd let someone in. Now that she'd finally taken out enough bricks in her own wall, now that she'd finally let Gael in, she'd grown to understand that in a new way.

She now knew that being bound to someone wasn't about being a prisoner against one's will, about feeling trapped—it was about feeling safe. Feeling at home. Never in a million years would she ever have imagined being in a relationship with a suit, but, frankly, they just fit together. They belonged together.

"I need to call Ava," Gael said. "I promised her I'd check in."

Mags laid a trail of kisses down his neck. She tasted the salt water of the sea and his skin. God, she loved the taste of him. She thought she always would.

"Mmm-hmm," she said as Gael set up his phone for a video call. Ava answered on the second ring. She looked healthy and beaming, a gorgeous eighteen-year-old who had been cancer-free for a year.

"You checking up on me, big brother?" she teased, grinning from ear to ear. She was in her college dorm, and a bevy of Shaded Moon posters could be seen behind her. She still loved that band.

"He completely is," Mags said, tipping her face to the screen. "Don't let him get away with it."

"Hi, Mags! You look so tan already!" Ava gushed.

"More like burned, but thanks." Mags grinned.

"Anyway." Gael cleared his throat. "I saw an octopus, just wanted to tell you."

"Oooh! An octopus!" Ava squealed. She was a freshman at Eckerd College in Florida, studying marine biology. Everything marine was fascinating to her, and Gael, Mags knew, couldn't be prouder of his sister. She'd made up all her lost school time well before graduation and managed to get into the first college of her choice. The girl was on fire.

"I'll send you the picture."

"Do. Also. Look, Mags! The tattoo looks great!" Ava pulled up her T-shirt sleeve and showed Mags an identical tattoo of the falcon she'd done on her brother's arm. "Thank you for doing it. It's healed up nicely."

"My pleasure." Mags beamed with pride. She'd been glad to do it. She'd given Ava the tattoo on the anniversary of being cancer-free, after a minor fight with Gael about how big it ought to be.

"It looks good," Gael admitted.

"Oh, I know it does." Ava snapped her fingers at the camera. "You don't have to tell me that!" She paused a second. "Aren't you forgetting something, Gael?"

"Oh. Right. I promised I'd ask Mags."

"Ask me what?" Mags glanced at Gael and then Ava. What were these two Quinn siblings cooking up behind her back?

"So…winter is coming up," Gael began, a teasing smile on his lips.

"Yes?"

"And… I mean, this might seem sudden."

Mags frowned. What the hell was he going to ask her? As it was, they practically lived together, hardly spending a single night of the week apart. She'd even started delivering packages to his condo, since he had a doorman that could keep them safe. He'd given her a key to his place many months ago. So now what?

"Spit it out, Quinn."

"Well… I mean…" He looked at the sky. "Maybe we should date. Or something."

"Gael!" Ava cried through the phone. "Be serious!"

Gael put the phone on the dock, using his snorkel as a stand.

"I think we're beyond that now," Mags said. If he kept this up, tonight it would be *his* turn to get lashes across his butt.

"Are we?" Gael blinked fast, trying to look innocent but only really succeeding at pushing her buttons. "Well, then, maybe…*just* maybe, we should think about…"

From behind his back, Gael produced a black velvet box. Mags's heart completely stopped. What the hell was this? She felt the hammer thumping in her chest.

"Maybe we should think about getting cuffed,"

Gael finished, and he opened the box. Inside was the biggest freakin' diamond Mags had ever seen, a square princess cut, completely surrounded by smaller diamonds. It was the most beautiful thing she'd ever seen in her life.

She was absolutely speechless. Marriage? She hadn't even really considered it. No, that was a lie. She had thought about it. Thought about it on any number of loud Saturday nights at the bar or lazy Sunday mornings in Gael's bed. She'd thought about it more than she'd like.

"You're proposing?"

"The ultimate cuff," he said. "It's three carats." He nodded at the ring. "But, Mags McHenry, my life hasn't been the same since I've met you. You're the most caring, most loving, most giving woman I've ever met. You took a chance on me, and for that, I'll forever be grateful. There's no one else I'd rather spend the rest of my life with than you. You're everything I could ever ask for in a partner. You were with me through the bad times with Ava and the good. You are the most loyal—and the most stubborn—woman I know. I want to spend this life and the next life with you. Please. Do me the honor of being my wife."

"I... I don't know what to say." She was still stunned. Still not believing it.

"Say yes!" Ava cried, clapping her hands together.

"Yes. Say yes." That voice. His voice. The one that never failed to flick a switch in her.

"Yes," she said, blinking back tears. "Yes, yes, yes!"

Tears stung her eyes. Mags wanted nothing more than to be a part of the family Gael, Kathleen, Maeve and Ava had created. Hell, to one day even add to it with children of their own. She saw a future that she couldn't wait to meet for the first time in her life. Being cuffed didn't seem like a prison sentence at all. It seemed like something beautiful, something filled with hope and love.

"Put the ring on her finger already!" Ava cried from the phone.

Gael slid the ring on even as Ava cheered. "I helped pick out that ring, just so you know."

Mags watched it as it sparkled brightly under the bright sun. It caught the light and threw it back out, sparkling as if it were on fire, as if it knew the passion burning in Mags's heart.

"You did a great job," Mags told Ava.

"Yes, you did, now scram," Gael told his sister.

"Fine, fine. I'll go. I know you want to make kissy faces." Ava stuck out her tongue. "Congrats, you two crazy lovebirds."

Then she ended the call, and the phone went dark.

"I hope you plan to do more than just a kissy face," Mags said.

"Oh, I do. Damn well I do." Then Gael pounced, rolling her down on the dock, his lips meeting hers, hungry but gentle, and the kiss held a promise of many, many more to come. Mags felt the very last brick of her wall crumble then, crumble to dust, as Gael deepened the kiss, as his hands roved her back and found the string of her bikini. She'd never felt freer than right then, with Gael's mouth on hers and his hands on her body. She couldn't wait to spend the rest of her life with him. She couldn't wait to start.

Gael broke free of the kiss for a second, his eyes meeting hers. "Thank you for making me the luckiest man alive."

"No, silly," she said and shook her head as she traced his cheek with her finger. "You're the one who's made me the lucky one. You knocked down my damn wall."

"You better believe I did. Now, what should I do next?"

"Tell me what you want." She quirked her eyebrow in challenge.

"I want you to kiss me," he said in that voice. That commanding, no-nonsense voice. God, she loved that voice. All she wanted to do was obey.

And kiss him, she did.

* * * * *

HOLIDAY HOOKUP

JAMIE K. SCHMIDT

MILLS & BOON

For my husband, Tom, who tries new and engaging
ways to help me finish the book.

CHAPTER ONE

SELENA THOMPSON EYED the clock while she put her vegetarian lasagna into the oven. It would be ready to eat when her client Blaine Stephens arrived in his penthouse suite at the Maui Wellness Center. He'd be tired from the long flight, so he might not want the heavy meal, but she hoped the comforting aroma of the garlic and sauce made him feel at home.

It was still a few weeks before Christmas, but she wanted to get him into the holiday spirit early. His dossier said he needed it. And she knew from experience that healthy and delicious food was a great mood enhancer.

Checking her notes, she reviewed that Blaine was here for two weeks of relaxation, meditation, and to rewire his diet of fast food to more healthy options. That left her favorite Christmas fudge out, but maybe she'd make him a small batch of sugar cookies. "Everything in Moderation" was her motto. There was also an asterisk at the end of the report that he was pretty much forced to come to the Maui Wellness

Center by his business partners because of a stress-related incident at work.

Selena liked a challenge. After a quick Google search, she found out that Blaine was a software engineer who was working on a self-driving car, and that the latest tests were disastrous. He was gorgeous, with ice-blue eyes and short dark brown hair, but he was a hothead. Quick to shout and get physical, with coworkers and reporters, it was no wonder he had been exiled here.

But she had also found out that he loved Italian food, hence the lasagna in the oven. She hoped he would still eat it when he found out it was made with tofu instead of sausage. The Maui Wellness Center pushed a vegetarian menu and a strict no-junk-food policy. They promoted clean eating and living, even during the holiday season. Fortunately, she wasn't an employee. She was a contractor and her boss didn't care what she cooked as long as the client was happy. In this case, Selena wanted to walk the fine line of keeping Titus a.k.a. "Tight Ass" Dukes, the general manager of the Maui Wellness Center, and Blaine Stephens happy. Titus was a strict vegan and an even stricter CrossFit devotee. If she hadn't worked under a chef from hell during her early years, Titus would have caused her to have a nervous breakdown.

Selena already felt bad about Blaine having to deal with him. As a self-proclaimed workaholic, he would be in for the hardest two weeks of his life without internet and Titus wouldn't budge a bit on that. Selena figured Blaine would last three days before checking out and heading to the nearest luxury chain hotel. She had been hired by his business partners to be his personal chef for the two weeks he was here, so he had better choose a property that wasn't part of the destination vacation club that held her contract. Otherwise, she'd be following him like a veggie-pushing stalker.

Wiping her hands on a dish towel, Selena walked out on Blaine's private balcony. The cost of this penthouse suite for two weeks was more than she made in a year. It had a beautiful view of the ocean, and at sunset it would be a wonderful place to decompress. Since she had some time until the lasagna came out of the oven, she poured herself a glass of pog—pineapple, orange and guava juice—and sat out on the balcony with her Bullet Journal.

She crossed off today in her countdown to Paris with a mental *fuck you* to Anton Koslov. Her former mentor was the voice she heard in her head every time she made a mistake in the kitchen. Anton made Gordon Ramsay look like Fred Rogers. If Blaine thought she was going to quail when he threw a temper tantrum, he would be greatly surprised. Selena had been forged in the fire of Anton's kitchen. She had eaten abuse with a pleasant, *Yes, Chef!* It had been five years since she was his sous chef in San Francisco, but there were days when she was under pressure in the kitchen that she could still feel him over her shoulder. He had run his Michelin-starred restaurant Bolete like his own personal fiefdom and had treated her like the lowest serf. Nowadays, he traveled the country with his Food Network show and promoted his merchandise like a late-night infomercial hawker.

Back then, Anton had hated that she had good ideas and that she had gotten most of her education at Miami-Dade's culinary school and by working in corporate cafeterias.

"You would never make it at Le Cordon Bleu," was one of his favorite sneers.

When Selena quit Bolete out of self-preservation, she wanted nothing to do with a commercial kitchen for a long time. But she had a burning desire to go to Paris and enroll in Cordon Bleu just to prove the son-of-a-bitch wrong. She was planning on taking additional courses while getting her MBA in international hospitality and culinary leadership. Unfortunately, she needed more money for a move to France. Luckily, her Miami-Dade contacts came in handy and told her that real estate mogul Kirk Diamonte had an opening for a personal chef for his destination vacation properties. Selena liked the idea of moving from place to place every few weeks, and after whipping up a coq au vin for Kirk, she had the job.

Maui was her favorite island. Kirk managed a bunch of properties on Maui that he rented out to the rich and famous, but he also contracted chefs, concierges and other service personnel to local resorts when needed. The Maui Wellness Center was set on a semiprivate beach, and when she wasn't in the kitchen cooking, she could do whatever she wanted. It made dealing with crazy clients and general managers like "Tight Ass" Dukes bearable. That and no matter what happened, she'd be gone in two weeks for another exotic location. For the moment, that suited her. But it wasn't what she wanted long term.

Turning to her dreams-and-goals page in her Bullet Journal, Selena added to the brainstorming list of names she was compiling for the restaurant she wanted to open after she graduated from Cordon Bleu.

"Chanterelle—just to piss off Anton." Bolete was a Russian mushroom. "The V Spot." Selena chuckled. *V* for vegetarian, but her dirty mind took it to G-spot or virgin spot. Tossing her pen on the table. She needed to get laid. Moving from one gorgeous vacation property to another every couple of weeks didn't make it easy to make a meaningful connection, but she had excellent luck with one-night stands. Lately, though, that had seemed rather empty and she chose abstinence, which sounded nobler than it actually was. And, of course, this time of year there was mistletoe everywhere and no one to smooch.

The door to the condo opened and Selena shot to her feet. "Can I help you?" she called out, feeling a little guilty about lounging around the gorgeous suite.

Her friend Mikelina Presley shouldered her way in, carrying two large shopping bags. Mikelina was assigned to be Blaine's concierge for his stay. Like Selena, she moved around to whatever property Kirk needed her at. They had gone to high school and college together and had remained close.

"Yeah, take these." Mikelina handed her the bags. "I've got to make a few other trips. Be right back."

Selena put the groceries away while Mikelina brought in box after box of stuff. She glanced at the labels for the pantry items, and while they weren't the ones she would've chosen, Mikelina did a good job of balancing what Blaine wanted versus what the Maui Wellness Center allowed.

Mikelina's job was to prepare the condo for the client, making them feel at home and providing them with just about anything they asked for. Some of the requests were as mundane as snorkels and bathing suits, or a candy dish of green—and only green—M&M's. And then there were the unique requests. Selena's favorite was a client who had requested that all the lightbulbs be changed to ones that gave off red light.

Mikelina came back in, carrying large tote bags. "It smells wonderful in here," she said.

"Thanks. What on earth are you doing? He's only going to be here for two weeks."

"Titus wants everyone who celebrates Christmas to have decorations up. I drew the line at a tree, though."

Luckily Titus and Kirk hashed out all the details of Blaine Stephens's stay, leaving Mikelina and

Selena to do their jobs without any micromanaging. Still, Titus made it a point to stick his nose into everything.

"Do you need a hand?" Selena asked.

"Always. Can you swap out the towels for these higher thread counts. Just store the others in the laundry room."

"Not a problem," Selena grabbed a stack of towels. "Were there any weird requests?"

"Aside from the wireless password?"

Selena snorted. Good luck with that. The Maui Wellness Center rooms didn't have a television, computer hookups or internet access. The only thing the condos had was a killer sound system that relied on CDs.

"He likes junk food," Mikelina said, as she artfully spaced beach-themed snow globes and Santas in Hawaiian shirts around the rooms.

"I saw the blue corn chips and salsa. Nice compromise," Selena said. "I'll probably make him some of my pineapple salsa and serve it over some mahi-mahi tomorrow for him."

"Stop," Mikelina said, holding a hand to her stomach. "You're making me hungry."

"Is Bastien starving you?" she asked. Bastien was Mikelina's fiancé and they probably spent all their spare time in bed rather than doing something as mundane as eating.

Mikelina twisted the honker of an engagement

ring on her finger. "He's been so busy lately, I barely see him. Help me with these lights, would you?"

As they strung up delicate white lights over the sliding glass door, Selena said, "If you want to give me the keys, I can show the client around. I've got to stay here until the lasagna's done anyway."

Biting her lip, Mikelina said, "I really shouldn't, but it's all very straightforward. Same old, same old. Are you sure you don't mind?"

"No, not at all."

"I'd really appreciate it. It would give Bastien and me a few extra hours for dinner together."

"Go." Selena waved her hands. Someone should have a little romance in their life. If it couldn't be Selena, she wanted it to be her best friend.

"Okay, here are his keys. Show him how to use all the appliances and the stereo. Go over the emergency procedure with him."

"I got it. Don't worry about me. I've done this before." Having no cell phone access, it was imperative that the guests were assured that help was only a button away. There was an operator standing by twenty-four/seven to assist the guests.

Handing her a list, Mikelina said, "Here is the itinerary that the client's business partners suggested for him. He's under no obligation to do them, of course, but I've reserved a spot for him just in case."

"Sunrise yoga, surfing lessons, beach massage, bedtime meditation," Selena read. "Hell, if he doesn't want to go, I will."

Mikelina shifted from one foot to the other. "I have a bad feeling about this guy."

"Like danger bad or disaster bad?"

"Both."

"Why?" Selena set the list on the counter.

"Blaine Stephens punched out his partner because the car they'd been working on didn't do what it was supposed to do."

"He's lucky he's not in jail."

"Yeah, well rich men with connections don't go to jail, they go to places like this." Mikelina finished wrapping a tasteful garland down the staircase railing.

"Must be nice," Selena said. "I don't think he's going to punch me. My cooking can soothe the savage beast."

"I believe it, but he's going to be difficult. Especially since his partners wanted him to detox while he was here."

"Is he having problems with drugs or alcohol?"

Mikelina shook her head. "Not that I could find out in my research. His drugs of choice are work and the internet. He has anger-management issues and I'm afraid he will get verbally abusive."

Selena shrugged. "He's got nothing on Anton Koslov."

"You shouldn't have to deal with that. Not anymore." Mikelina had been really supportive during her Bolete days, even when they had been on opposite sides of the country.

"As long as you don't think it's going to get physical…"

"It won't," Mikelina said.

"Then don't worry about me. If I can handle myself on a busy line, creating several complicated dishes while a wannabe Vladimir Putin insults everything from my cooking to my legitimacy both in and out of the kitchen, I can take care of a high-strung corporate shill."

"Well, just call me if you need me. Or if he's looking for more activities to do. The only thing we can't provide him is a computer and internet access, but I'm sure he can find a way around that." Mikelina sighed. "I hope he doesn't go that route. His partners sent him here for a reason."

"I'm his chef, not his jailer. But I'll push the excursions and see if I can get him to concentrate on rest and relaxation."

"Thanks, so much." Mikelina handed her more Christmas knickknacks and hurried out the door.

While Selena went upstairs to place the decorations, she wondered what it would be like to be sent to a place like this, all expenses paid for two whole weeks, just for having a bad attitude. She resisted the urge to flop on the big king-size bed and take a nap.

It would be paradise, she decided.

But for now, she had to work for a living, always stuck in various paradises on the outside looking in. Blaine Stephens would be a challenge. By the end of these two weeks not only would he enjoy her meals, but also takeout and delivery wouldn't taste as good. Selena could forever change his outlook on healthy eating. If she had to work for her dream one unbeliever at a time, she would. After all, if she could convince her father to eat Brussels sprouts, Blaine shouldn't be a problem.

CHAPTER TWO

BLAINE STEPHENS KNEW he needed a vacation. And he had planned to take one after the holidays and as soon as the Pilot Project was completed to his satisfaction. But with the French Expo coming up in a few months, he didn't have time to screw around Maui, breathing out of his eyelids and eating tofu. Especially since in their latest test, their state-of-the-art, future-is-now, driverless car had run over a dog, an old lady in a crosswalk, and had run a red light in simulation. It was a disaster, even if the casualties were all virtual. Someone had leaked the footage to the media, complete with him losing his ever-loving shit on his business partner Paul Miller.

To be fair, Paul threw the first punch. Blaine had made sure Paul wouldn't do that again, although if he had known someone had their camera filming them, he might have acted differently.

Blaine flexed his hand. His knuckles still hurt from punching the lazy prick in the face. It had been worth it to wipe that defensive pout off his face, even though he probably should have taken the high road and shrugged it off.

Paul had been in the wrong so many other ways. He should have run more tests. He should have documented the errors. He should have kept his hands to himself. Just because Paul was the Miller in the Stephens-Miller Corporation, that didn't give him the right to solve their differences playground style.

Mitchell had been caught in the middle. Paul was his best friend and Blaine was his brother. They had built their company together ever since they graduated from college. Mitchell was also the boss and had reprimanded both of them.

Although sending Blaine to a new age wellness center might seem like a reward, it was in fact a brilliant revenge, even if it was on a private beach in Maui in the middle of December.

I'm going to give it to you straight, his brother Mitchell had said. *You're a frickin' time bomb. You need to go far, far away until you get your head on straight.*

I'm fine, Blaine had said.

You're an important part of this launch, but your job is done.

Obviously not, Blaine had replied, gesturing to Paul who glared at him from across the room. It wasn't as if he was going continue to fight with him, but Paul acted like it, giving him a wide berth.

You need to take a step back—a few steps back and let us do our jobs.

I can help, he had said.

You're making it worse, Mitchell said, not pulling any punches. *You haven't slept. I don't even think you've been home in the past two weeks.*

That was the problem of starting a business with family, they brought up personal stuff. Where he slept and when had nothing to do with the problems the new car was having. *This launch is very important.*

I'm not disputing that. I don't want it at the cost of your life or sanity.

That's a little dramatic, Mitch.

Is it?

Blaine hadn't had a cute comeback for that. The heart-attack scare had been hard on their family. Their parents were very upset. Blaine had collapsed in front of them. He couldn't remember feeling so much pain. It had all been in his chest and Blaine had a hard time breathing.

It turned out to be nothing, Blaine said, feeling the need to defend the momentary weakness. His body had betrayed him, and Blaine wasn't sure how to stop it from happening it again.

It turned out to be stress related, his brother pointed out. *Look, I'm not pulling you off the project.*

I'd like to see you try, Blaine had said, standing up so fast his chair had toppled over. Paul had jumped back like a scared cat.

Are you going to hit me too? A muscle worked in Mitchell's jaw.

He hadn't brawled with his brother since they were kids, but Blaine had been tempted.

Mom, Dad and I have booked you on an all-expense-paid trip to Maui as a Christmas present. Two weeks of sun, sand and relaxation. Mitchell had handed him the brochure to Maui. *You go there. Be a good boy, and then come back here refreshed for a nice family Christmas and then you'll be back on track.*

I'm on track now, Blaine had complained.

Our parents are very worried about you. Stop being such a selfish ass and accept this gift, that I would take from you in a heartbeat.

You can have it, he said.

Sure. Rub it in. Spend two weeks eating like an adult and working on your health. If you don't want to do it for yourself, do it for your dear old mother. She hasn't stopped crying about how it would kill her to bury her youngest son.

Now that's hitting below the belt, Blaine had protested. *I admit I overreacted and maybe I haven't been as diligent about sleep and eating, but I need to be here.*

It's two weeks, not two years.

Blaine had argued up until the day of departure, but it got him nowhere. His family guilted him into getting into the limo and being driven to the airport. He took vicious pleasure that as soon as he was in the air, it had started to snow heavily. Serves them right.

On the plane ride, Blaine slept the full ten hours

to Maui. It was the longest he had slept in…years. He even dozed in the car from the Maui airport to the resort, waking up when the driver opened the trunk to get his bags. Blaine felt worse after all that sleep, but he was starving. The first thing he'd do once he got settled was call for delivery.

"I got this," Blaine said, peeling off a hundred-dollar bill for the driver. He wasn't even sure what was in the two big wheeled bags. Mitchell had some-one pack for him, not giving him an inch of leeway to wiggle out of this trip. He had said the concierge will get him anything that they missed. How about a cell phone that worked? Blaine scowled at his phone. No internet connection available. He knew he was on an island in the middle of the Pacific, but he had seen signs of civilization. They passed a Walmart just after leaving the airport.

Grumbling, Blaine picked up a bag in each hand and carried them up the stairs until he got on flat ground and then he rolled them into the lobby. Not that he needed one, but he didn't see any porters who would normally be all over him for a chance to carry his bags for a tip. The lobby was open-air and he wondered what happened when it rained. He didn't see any computers or electronics. Just benches and clusters of vibrantly colored flowers everywhere. Squinting around, he looked to where he could check in. A security guard approached him.

"Aloha."

"A-aloha," Blaine responded, wondering if he was

going to get another lei put around his neck. They did that at the airport, and he had waited until he was in the car before taking the flowers off his neck because he didn't want to offend anyone.

"Can I help you, sir?"

"Yeah, I'm checking in."

"Name?"

"Blaine Stephens."

The guard checked his iPad and scrolled. "Penthouse suite. Follow me, sir."

Blaine rolled the luggage to a cluster of elevators, wondering if the iPad was magically connected to the internet.

The security guard slid a key card and a set of elevator doors opened. When it opened, the guard waved him in. "Your concierge is waiting in your suite to get you acquainted with the wellness center."

"Great," Blaine said.

The doors closed and the elevator shot up fast and efficiently. He stared at his reflection in the polished chrome doors. Man, he looked like he'd been rode hard and put away wet. He rubbed his hand over the stubble of his chin. Maybe a few days in the sun wouldn't hurt. With a mellow bing, the elevator doors opened up into a luxurious suite. Standing in the hallway was a gorgeous brunette. Now that's what he called service. He only wished he didn't look like such a bum.

She had long black hair that was tied back in a

braid. Gray-blue eyes smiled at him, and she extended her hand.

"I'm Selena Thompson. I'll be your personal chef for these two weeks." The chef's jacket hugged her curves and he knew that he would eat anything she gave him as long as he could watch her move around the kitchen.

"Blaine Stephens." He shook her hand, admiring her firm grip. Letting go before it was obvious that he liked holding her hand, Blaine became aware of a tantalizing aroma. His stomach growled in protest that it wasn't indulging in whatever that was. "Is that lasagna?" Blaine asked with an appreciative sniff.

"Hot out of the oven. Why don't you drop your luggage off in the bedroom and come and sit at the table?" She pointed up. "Top of the stairs. Do you need a hand with your bags?"

"No, I got this." He gave her a grin and hoisted the bags up. It didn't matter how heavy they were, he didn't want her to think he was a wimp. He jogged up the stairs and made it through the bedroom door before staggering under their weight.

Shit, he was winded. Blaine rubbed the center of his chest and made a face.

He took a few minutes to freshen up. While he didn't break out his electric razor, he finger combed his hair and straightened out his clothes. When he came out, he was disappointed that she had set out only one plate. After sitting down, he placed the cloth napkin on his lap.

"Would you like to join me?" he asked.

"I'll sit with you for a bit, but I'm not allowed to eat with the guests."

"Sounds like a silly rule." Blaine was too hungry not to dig in.

"Can I get you some wine? I've got a nice spicy red that will complement that dish."

He nodded, trying not to drool cheese out of his mouth. Selena went into the kitchen and he heard the pop of a cork and the long glug of wine being poured. Was she pouring him the whole bottle? This place rocked! He was going to make it a habit of punching Paul out, if the punishment was being sent here.

Selena came back with a decanter and two glasses. "The wine has to breathe for a few minutes to fully enjoy it." She poured sparkling water into one of the glasses from a bottle that was lodged in an iced bucket on the table.

Sitting down across from him, she pulled out a journal. "Would you like another piece of lasagna before we begin the orientation?"

He looked down and realized he had gobbled it down. "I should give it a minute. That was the best lasagna I've ever tasted."

"It was vegetarian. That sausage was actually tofu."

Blaine stared at her in confusion. "Wow, I never would have known."

"I'm sorry I didn't tell you sooner. I was supposed to, but..." She smiled shyly. "I was distracted."

He was distracted too, by the laugh lines around her eyes and her plump, kissable lips. "Are you my concierge too?"

"Actually, that's Mikelina. She was called away tonight. I told her that I would give you the rundown of the place since I was going to be here to serve dinner anyway."

"Thank you," he said.

She slid the key card over to him and told him that would be how he accessed his room and the elevators. "I also have the key to your room. I will come in three times a day to make you breakfast, lunch and dinner. However, you can go into privacy mode, which will stop me from entering."

"I doubt that will be necessary." He followed her over to the door.

Selena showed him how to set it to private. It looked like all she did was wave the key in front of it a few times. Part of him wanted to take it apart and see how it worked.

"So my own private chef, huh? I can have whatever I want to eat?"

"As long as we can find the ingredients. Being on an island makes it a little more difficult to get some of the more obscure delicacies."

"Like what?"

Selena gestured and they sat back down at the table. "We've got plenty of sushi and fresh fruit. Lobster and Wagyu beef, on the other hand, will take a few days."

"Put me down for that."

She jotted in her notebook. "Although keep in mind, as a wellness retreat, the emphasis will be on whole foods, with a trace of decadence."

"I like decadence," he said. "What I don't like is boredom."

"Have you been to a wellness resort before?" she asked, pouring him a glass of wine.

"No, and to be honest, I thought I was in for a week of drinking coconut water, eating bamboo shoots and navel-gazing meditating with an aging hippie." Blaine was enchanted by her small laugh.

"We can make that happen, if that's what you'd like."

"I'll stick with wine."

"Red wine has many health benefits. It's all about moderation."

"I'm not good at moderation." He twirled his fork. "Could I get another piece of that lasagna?"

"Absolutely, even though I know you're going to go out of your way to pick out the tofu."

He chuckled. "I'm going to suspend my disbelief and pretend it's sausage."

"Whatever gets you through."

Blaine liked her smart mouth, and he liked her cooking. She slid another serving on his plate. "There's another two pieces in case you would like some for dinner tonight. But most clients sleep right on through until the morning."

"I won't be able to sleep," he said. Sleep had never

been a priority for him and now that he was here, his fingers itched to be on the keyboard or on his pretty chef. "And while the lasagna is good, I'm eager to try something else for dinner."

"Like I said, I have a key and if you're asleep, I'll just come back in the morning."

"I'll be awake." He'd make sure of it. Checking his phone, it was three in the afternoon local time, which was nine at night his time. "Come by around seven." It would be like a midnight snack for him. He was used to eating late. He'd often be running code and testing. Something Paul should have also been doing. Pushing aside his aggravation, he concentrated on Selena's pretty face. He was here to relax and have a good time, damn it. Still, his finger tapped on his email and he was rewarded with a spinning disk. No signal. Fuck.

"What would you like for dinner?"

You. "Cheeseburger and fries."

"All right," she drawled. "What time would you like me to serve breakfast tomorrow?"

He'd rather that she didn't leave, but he didn't think a personal chef actually slept in the suite. Usually, he skipped breakfast or made do with a coffee and a stale doughnut from the breakroom, but he didn't want to miss another chance to talk with her or to have a gourmet meal prepared for him. He hadn't realized how lonely he had been until it was just him and Selena alone in the room together.

"How about eight?"

Selena nodded. "Your benefactors gave me a list of meals to prepare for you, but I wanted to get your opinion. How does eggs Benedict over taro-root muffins with asparagus on the side sound?"

"Hold the asparagus and sub in bacon and we're all good."

"No," she said with a sweet smile.

"You wanted my opinion," he said. "I'm not a vegetable-for-breakfast type of guy."

"You've never had my asparagus."

"Does it taste like coffee and a Boston cream doughnut?"

"It tastes like asparagus. Nutty and buttery and you'll want to dip the spears into the egg yolk."

Blaine wasn't sure he would want to do that at all, and forced his dirty mind not to translate that into a sexual innuendo. "What's taro root?"

"It's a local vegetable."

"What does it taste like?"

Selena blinked. "Like taro root."

At least she didn't say it tasted like chicken. "What's it similar to?"

"It's a root vegetable, like a potato."

"Can I just have a potato?"

Rolling her eyes, Selena said, "Yes, but part of your journey these two weeks is to expand your culinary horizons. If you hate something, I'm not going to force you to eat it. But won't you at least try it?"

"You're making me feel like a kid who doesn't want to eat his vegetables."

Selena raised an eyebrow. "No, if I was doing that, I'd tell you I was giving you a 'no thank you' helping."

Blaine finished the lasagna. This time around he could tell by the texture that it hadn't been sausage, but the flavor had still been there. Maybe tofu wasn't so bad. But the longer he kept her talking, the later she stayed. It was nice to have a glass of wine and dinner with someone, even if she wasn't eating and was technically being paid to be there.

"I'll eat just about everything, but I'm a meat-and-potatoes guy. I'll forgive you the tofu once, but I don't think I'd like it again."

"Why?"

"Why?" Blaine repeated while he thought about it. He sipped his wine. "Stubbornness?"

She laughed again. "At least you admit it. I've stocked the fridge with healthy snacks just in case you get hungry in between meals. Mikelina filled the pantry with most of the items you requested."

"Most?"

"Make me a list of anything that's missing or anything on the menu that displeases you. I'll use the default menu unless you say otherwise."

"Were the chips and beer out of the question?"

"I could make potato chips for you. And there is a selection of beer that the Wellness Center has permitted." She handed him a folder. "Everything you need to know is in here. Cleaning service will come in at two p.m. every day and I will be here for about an hour for each meal to prepare and serve it. If you're not out and about, I suggest taking a swim at that time or hanging out in the hot tub, so we're not in your way." Selena gestured to the patio.

"Any chance we can take the wine over there and you'd join me in the hot tub?"

Selena blushed. "I'm flattered. And tempted, but it's probably for the best if we keep things professional."

He liked the tempted part. It made him feel less like a lecher. He supposed she got hit on a lot. "If you insist," he said. "I'm going to get changed and go in."

She stood up. "I should be going anyway. You have a vacation to start."

Disappointment flashed through him. In desperation, he racked his brains for a way to make her stay for just a few more minutes.

She hesitated, as if she was thinking the same thing. Or maybe that was wishful thinking on his part. "I'll just put the food away then," she said. "Don't worry about the dishes, the housekeepers will take care of them tomorrow."

"I have a few more questions. I won't keep you long. I'm not sure about this whole food nonsense." That was a good stall tactic. He could see that she was passionate about cooking in the way her spine straightened, and her gaze sharpened.

"Okay," Selena said. "I've got to warn you. I'm going to cook you good food and you're going to enjoy it."

"I'm looking forward to it." He went to the bedroom and shucked off all his clothes. After grabbing the Turkish robe off the hook in the bathroom. He wrapped it around himself.

When he came back out, she had soft jazz playing on the stereo. He couldn't help himself. He got hard. All he could think about was pulling off that chef's jacket and dancing around the living room with her in his arms. His toes curled into the soft rug. It had been a long time since he'd been with a woman. For the past year, it had been all business, day and night.

"We're going old school with technology." She showed him how to use the stereo, but he wasn't paying attention. He was more interested in the curve of her cheek and the soft scent of her perfume. She smelled like the sweet plumeria flowers from the lobby.

"I can't believe I can't get Wi-Fi or a cell signal," he said, moving away from her before he made her uncomfortable. He poured himself another glass of wine and went out to the hot tub.

"Let me show you how to adjust the settings." Selena showed him how to control the heat and the jets. He had her set them on high, so the bubbles obscured what was under the surface.

"What else did my benefactors have in store for me?" he asked, before taking a sip of wine. If Mitchell and Paul could see him now, they would be green with envy. Thinking about them made him wish for his phone to check his emails. But his phone was as good as a brick right about now. His laptop still had code and blueprints on it, but without being able to dial into the company's VPN he was limited on what he could work on.

Selena stared into his eyes for a little longer than necessary and he wondered if he should try for a kiss. "Let me get my notebook."

When she hurried back inside, Blaine dropped the robe over a chair and stepped down into the deep hot tub. Sitting on the built-in bench, he sank up to his ears. The wine and the heat of the water filled in all the ragged places inside him and he was shocked at the lethargic feeling that came over him. He had slept for twelve hours; how could he still be tired? It was still daylight. He wondered what sexy Selena had in store for the rest of the day.

What was he going to do for the rest of the day?

She pulled up a chair to the hot tub, her notebook in hand.

"Why don't you sit on the edge and dangle your feet in?"

"That's not very professional," she said, but she looked at the water longingly.

"Fuck professional," he said. "It's just you and me. And I won't tell."

A slight shiver passed through her, and he wondered if she was feeling the same attraction he was.

She smirked and he caught a little bit of the wild child she was hiding. "I suppose it wouldn't hurt." After kicking off her shoes, she rolled up her pants and sat opposite him. Dangling her feet in the water, she reached up for her notebook.

"I'm going to be bored out of my mind, aren't I?"

"Your family gave Mikelina a suggested list of activities that you might like. She's gone ahead and signed you up for these events, but you don't have to do them if you don't want to." She passed him the notebook and he read through them.

"Yeah," he snorted. "Not my style."

"Like the asparagus, you should at least try it."

"I'd like to go on a helicopter ride over the volcanos, take surfing lessons, maybe parasailing. I need something to spike my adrenaline or I'm going to go insane. Are there any challenging hikes?"

"Sure. Pe'ahi on the North Shore is a good place for that, plus waves are insane. Just for watching, though, unless you're a professional surfer." She reached for her notebook and jotted his requests down. "I can pass your suggestions along to Mikelina, and she'll make the arrangements. I'll tell her you want to keep busy, but in a relaxing way."

"That sounds like an oxymoron."

"Not really. You're on Hawaii time now, bruddah." She flashed him the shaka, the thumb-and-finger sign that all islanders did.

He gave it back to her. "I think I'm going to need a shark-tooth necklace."

"We can get that for you." Selena scribbled it down.

"I'm not keeping you from another client, am I?"

"Nope," Selena said. "I'm all yours for two weeks."

"Outstanding," he drawled, loving the way her face flushed when she realized what she'd said.

CHAPTER THREE

SELENA COULDN'T BELIEVE she had said that. She wrapped up the rest of the orientation and hurried out of there with her shoes in her hand. Smooth, she berated herself once she reached the lobby. She hadn't expected Mr. High-Strung Corporate Shill to look like a pirate in person, with the body of a Viking, and ice-blue eyes she shivered with cold just looking in them.

It was going to be a long two weeks. She had been *this close* to joining him in the hot tub. As it was, the vision of his chiseled ass as he dropped the robe to get into the tub was going to be featured in her late-night fantasies. She had been peeking from the kitchen. Selena could only hope that jet lag caught up to him by the time dinner arrived. He made her feel reckless and like breaking all the rules. Starting with eating with a client and ending with fraternizing with him all night long.

Selena went to the local market to get the ingredients for the cheeseburger and fries he ordered. Of course, she was going to make them her way. The Lahaina market was walking distance from the wellness center. There were lights on the palm trees, but that was as holiday as it got here. This was a local place, hidden from the tourists. Sitting on the bench, she watched the surfers and tried to dredge up a smidgen of the attraction she felt with Blaine Stephens. No luck. She kept seeing his intense eyes and gorgeous smile. She should have gotten in the hot tub with him. Well, he was going to be there for two weeks. Maybe there would be another opportunity. It would be her Christmas present to herself.

She treated herself to a root beer shaved ice with a splash of sweet condensed milk topping it to cool off. But she took too long savoring it while people-watching. It melted all over her hands. When she was done with her sticky treat, she went into the public bathroom to clean up.

Kelli Ann, one of their snorkeling instructors, was in there and it looked like she was trying her hardest to stop crying.

"Kelli, what's wrong?" she said.

"Titus just fired me," she sobbed.

That jerk! "Why?"

Kelli shook her head. "It was innocent. I was just taking the client out by Molokini Crater. We had a good day of snorkeling and then he wanted to do some sunbathing on the boat."

"What's wrong with that?" Selena said, washing

her hands and drying them on raspy brown paper that was in the dispenser.

"He wanted to do it in the nude."

"Okay," Kelli said. "Clients are weird. They have weird requests. Did you feel safe?"

"More than safe."

Uh-oh.

"I joined him, and we wound up having sex."

Selena hid a wince. "Well, you're two consenting adults. I don't see the problem." Although fraternizing with the clients was against the rules, she didn't think it was a fireable offense, especially if no money exchanged hands. It wasn't professional and usually added more problems than it was worth, which was why she wasn't bouncing on Blaine in the hot tub right now.

"It was with Tyger Li, the front man for the Volcano Bois."

"Nice," Selena said, not knowing what else to say.

"Very nice. Except, he's got a big mouth and Titus overheard him telling his band members how awesome it was. Next thing I know, Titus fired me without references because he's not, quote—running a brothel—unquote."

Leave it to Titus to overreact and then fire someone a few weeks before Christmas. "That sucks. Is there anything I can do? I can give you a reference, if you need it. You're a kick-ass snorkeling guide."

"Thanks," she sniffed. "I hope the rumor of why I got fired doesn't get around."

"I won't say a word." Selena crossed her fingers over her heart.

"I slept with him because I wanted to. He didn't expect it. I wasn't paid for it. In fact, we're going out to dinner tonight."

"Good for you." Selena hugged her. "Then don't worry about a thing. Hold your head up high and enjoy your romance while you can."

They exchanged numbers and Selena went to the vegetarian market to pick up the ingredients she would need. Kelli Ann's story should have been a warning to her. She couldn't afford to get fired for eight more months. But instead, Selena was picturing making love to Blaine under the warm Maui sun. Although, if she got fired—and that was a big if since she technically worked for Kirk and not Titus—she could start her life in Paris sooner. Of course, enrolling in culinary school would have to wait until she secured a job and housing. She had been hoping to be sent to Paris before her contract was up so she could do some scouting around.

But what if the sex wasn't good? It would be awkward cooking for him for another two weeks. What if it was just all right? Then he'd be wanting to play grab ass while she was cooking in the kitchen. Nah, it was easier to find a lover that she could walk away from if it got too difficult. She had a feeling Blaine's middle name was *difficult*.

After making her purchases, Selena strolled back to the wellness center. Unlike other properties, the staff had their own studio apartments on site. She put the groceries in her fridge and went to find her Bullet Journal, but it wasn't in her purse.

She must have left it in Blaine's suite. Selena didn't want to call and bother him. He had to have some down time to decompress from the long plane ride and get settled. But her fingers itched for her journal. It had all her plans for her restaurant and Cordon Bleu in it. Looking at her phone for the time, she had to be back over there in two hours anyway. She could wait the two hours. But she wasn't sure what she was going to do if the journal wasn't there. Staring at her phone, she wished that she could text him. While she had the password for the Wi-Fi and her phone could be a personal hotspot in an emergency, that wasn't common knowledge.

If the clients knew all the staff had the internet, they'd be mobbed.

Maybe Blaine would be asleep, and she could sneak in and out and he wouldn't even notice.

Selena flipped through a magazine and tried to relax, but she couldn't. She wound up taking a long shower, making sure to shave and then cover herself with soft lotion. She wanted to be prepared in case things between her and Blaine did escalate. Grabbing a new chef's coat, she took the groceries and headed over to the penthouse. So what if she was over an hour early? She could tell Blaine that she needed the extra time to prepare. She'd be in the kitchen, completely out of his way—once she got her journal back.

"Selena!"

Oh no. Not him. She plastered a fake smile on her face and willed the elevator to come down fast. "Hello, Titus."

"What are you doing?"

"My job," she said between her teeth, still smiling.

He peeked into the bag and beamed. "What are you making?"

"The client had a special request for dinner."

Titus consulted his tablet. "Mr. Stephens requested a vegan meal?"

"He requested a bacon cheeseburger and fries."

"Good girl," he said, and patted her shoulder.

She managed not to flinch. The elevator finally came, and she stepped back into it.

"We'll talk more tomorrow," he said, with a wave.

The elevator doors closed.

"Not if I see you first."

All she needed was that asshole on her case. The elevator doors opened, and she stormed into the penthouse, still fuming about Titus's hand on her shoulder. She was in the kitchen before she realized that she hadn't even seen Blaine. Before she got started, she looked around the first floor for him. He had gotten out of the hot tub and was sitting under the wide umbrella in a sling-back chair. At least, he had put on a bathing suit. It looked like something Mikelina would have picked out for a client who requested the swimming package added on to the room. She glanced around and sure enough there was a towel, and snorkeling gear. She wondered if Blaine would have suggested naked sunbathing to Kelli Ann.

Probably.

Selena cut a look at him and saw he was reading her journal.

"Hey," she said, using the anger that was still simmering over Titus. "That's mine. You have no right to read that."

"You handed it to me. I thought it had all of my itinerary and menus in it."

It did. And he had her there. "Once you realized there was more, you should have put it down and stopped reading it."

"I would have, but I'm fascinated. Your idea for a restaurant seems solid. I couldn't do any forecasting or checking because—" He picked up his phone and dropped it on the table. "I can't access the internet."

She held out her hand and he gave her back the journal. He pretended to dangle it as bait for her to come closer, but let her have it without a fight when she snatched it out of his hands.

"Is it seven o'clock yet?" he asked, stretching.

"Not quite. I have some prep work to do in the kitchen for your dinner."

"I'm bored. Do you mind if I watch?"

"Yes," she said. "My kitchen. My rules."

"Fine," he said. "Can we still talk if I sit out in the dining room? Or will I be bothering you?"

She could play the hard-ass, but she had no busi-ness even being right here. "Yeah, sure." She slipped the journal back into to her purse, wondering if she had anything embarrassing in there.

"Who's Anton? He sounds like a dick."

"He is," she said, leaving him sitting at the dining room table as she went into the kitchen.

"Boyfriend?"

"Barf. He was my boss."

"I want to Google him, but I can't. I want to do some work, but I can't."

She poked her head out of the kitchen. "You're here to relax, not work."

"I relaxed. I soaked in the hot tub. I lay out in the sun. I read a book."

Selena glared at him and went back into the kitchen to mix up the beans with the other ingre-dients.

"I was thinking of hitting the bars tonight."

Ignoring the little stab of jealousy that she had no right to feel, she said, "That's nice."

"But I don't have the internet to look up clubs and none of these brochures advertise anything like that."

Continuing to work, she made a sympathetic noise that she didn't really mean.

"I don't suppose you could show me around town."

She thought back on Titus. "Not tonight."

"That's not no," he pointed out.

"Yeah, it's just the general manager fired our

snorkel instructor today for screwing a guest and I bet he's on high alert for other indiscretions."

"This wouldn't be screwing, though. Would it?" He appeared in the doorway.

"Out." She pointed with the spatula.

"What's that contraption?" he asked, pointing to the steel cutting machine she had set up on the counter.

"It's a mandoline. It's going to make your fries have the ridges in them." She looked up. "Are you interested in cooking?"

He gave a half shrug. "I don't have time for it. Do you want to come back to Michigan and be my personal chef?"

She smirked. "You couldn't afford me."

"I bet I could."

When she frowned at him, he gestured to her purse. "Looking at those numbers, I could buy you out of your contract and pay you what Five Diamonds is paying you."

"No offense, but if it's between exotic properties all over the world and… Detroit? I think Cabo San Lucas and its ilk win out," she said, peeling the vegetables.

"Detroit's not so bad."

"How much snow did you guys get last winter?" she asked.

"Only ten inches," he said.

"Yeah, it went down to ten degrees in Maui."

"Fahrenheit or Celsius?"

"Celsius."

Blaine looked at the ceiling and his mouth moved as he calculated. "That's fifty degrees Fahrenheit."

"Brrr," she said and fake shivered.

"The kitchen would be nice and warm," he said.

"Ha ha," she said. "Seriously, you saw the book. After my contract is up here, I'm Paris bound."

"Why?"

"I thought you read the journal." She chopped the onions into a fine dice and then switched to the herbs.

"Damn, you're fast with that knife. Remind me not to piss you off."

"I'd never stab you with this knife."

"That's good," he said.

"I'd use one of those ginzo ones." She pointed to the stocked knife block.

"Great," he said. "So why Cordon Bleu?"

"So I can learn to cook." She sprinkled the herbs and spices into the bean mixture and let that sit while she rubbed the vegetable over the mandoline's edge, making a pile of ridged, frenched fries.

"What are you doing now?" he asked. "Because that sure looks like cooking to me."

"It's different when you're a professional chef. I need to work on my glazes and my sauces are for shit." Great, now she was parroting Anton.

"I'd like to be the judge of that."

She smiled up at him. "I'll take you up on that.

Now go sit down so I can concentrate on getting your meal together."

Miracle of miracles, he left her alone and she was able to time it, so everything was finished and hot at the same time. When she walked out into the dining room, he was scowling over his computer.

"Hit Save, because I'm going to close the top of that and if you don't move fast enough, I'm going to get your fingers," she said.

He slammed the lid down himself. "It's not like I can do anything." He pushed it away from him across the table.

"That's the point." Selena placed the plate in front of him. On the surface it looked like a cheeseburger with fries. She smiled sweetly at him. Blaine regarded her with suspicion.

"This isn't beef, is it?" he said.

"Just try it."

"Please tell me these are at least French fries."

"As you can see from the ripples in them, they're crinkled cut."

Blaine took one and chewed it thoughtfully. "This is not a potato."

"It's a turnip."

"What do you have against potatoes? It's a vegetable."

"You can have a potato tomorrow. I just thought you should expand your horizons. I'm a very good cook. I've worked at Michelin-starred restaurants."

He took another fry. "What's the burger? Tofu?"

"Black bean."

Blaine opened the sandwich and peered inside. "This looks like bacon and cheese. I'm going to go out on a limb and say it's not."

"The bacon is seasoned seitan, a wheat gluten, and the cheese is made from cashews."

His lip curled up in a sneer.

Selena heard Anton's voice in her head. *Stupid, woman. Can't even make a simple meal. You're pathetic.*

"Take a bite, wimp," Selena snapped.

Blaine raised an eyebrow. "The turnips are good. I still prefer potatoes."

She couldn't help but feel her old mentor over her shoulder, judging her and finding her meal lacking in presentation and taste. "Noted," she bit out. Why did she suddenly feel like crying?

With a fatalistic sigh, he took a bite of the burger. She watched him as he chewed thoughtfully. He took another bite. "It's all right," he said, grudgingly.

"Outstanding," she said to him. *All right, my ass. It was masterpiece.* Selena grabbed her purse and left, leaving the mess for the morning. Wishing she could slam the door, she had to settle for stomping into the elevator. She hoped he choked on that delicious burger and that Anton would stay the hell out of her head.

CHAPTER FOUR

NORMALLY, BLAINE WOULDN'T be caught dead doing a sunrise yoga class on the beach. But he was up, his body still trying to adjust to the time change and he was jonesing to check his email. Of course, there wasn't an internet to connect to, and the wellness center had a block on cell phone signals unless you had the password. He strolled down to the where his paper map—how quaint—showed where the class was taking place.

Things were looking up. He was the only man there. Straightening his shoulders, he sucked in his stomach. He might not be thrilled about being benched for two weeks, but there was a lot to be said for getting laid on the beach. His eyes were immediately drawn to a curvy brunette, who had her long hair up in a high ponytail. Her spandex shorts clung to her ass and Blaine rushed over to take the spot next to her.

"Hey," he said, and then froze when he saw it was his prickly chef. She was wearing a sports bra and he fought to keep his eyes from dropping to her cleavage. So that was what was under that chef's jacket. Yowza.

"I'm surprised to see you here." She continued with her stretching after a brief sneer in his direction.

"Told you. I don't sleep." He caught his ankle in a runner's stretch and was surprised he didn't pitch face-first in the sand. When was the last time he went running? Probably before the Pilot Project. "Look, I didn't mean to be a dick last night. Your food is fantastic. I just like to break balls. I could see it was a sore spot with you and I figured I'd yank your chain a bit."

She regarded him for a minute. He gave her his best self-deprecating grin.

"It's okay," she said finally, giving him a small smile. "I guess I don't have much of a sense of humor about my cooking. I get a lot of pushback from guests who want fried, fatty and heavy food for every meal. And let's not forget the ones who hate vegetables because the only way they've had them was boiled to death."

"I can't lie. I'd rather be at work, but if I had to be trapped at a resort in paradise, there's no one I'd rather have cook for me."

"You figured that out after two meals?"

"You had me at tofu lasagna." He put a hand over his heart and gave her what he hoped was a sincere look. Blaine was laying it on thick because he didn't want her to be mad at him.

She smiled widely at him. "I'm so glad you decided to try yoga."

"Me too," he said. He hoped he had been forgiven about teasing her about the cheeseburger. It hadn't been Wagyu-beef good, but it had been tasty.

"What do you want for breakfast?" She raised her arms over her head and stretched to one side and then the other. "You didn't seem too thrilled about my eggs Benedict."

"Pancakes, bacon and sausage," he said, just to be a buster.

"How about orange crepes with bacon?" she countered.

"Real bacon?" He squinted.

"Nitrate free."

"Deal."

"But you've got to work for it." She gestured to the yoga class. "I want to see you sweat."

"You do, huh?" he grinned at her sudden blush.

"Okay, people. Aloha," the perky instructor said, clapping her hands to get their attention. She stood in front of a festive display of a Hawaiian Santa on a surfboard with a flock of light-up flamingos in front of him.

"Aloha," the class responded back.

This was going to be the easiest bacon he'd ever earned. He might even squeeze in a nap while they did asanas to the sun and sand. Or maybe he'd admire Selena's sleek poses as discretely as he could.

Instead, for the next hour he twisted and bent,

holding poses until his muscles were shaking. Yoga was not for the weak. Next time he had the bright idea to exercise, he was just going to jog along the surf line. He'd at least have a chance of looking like a stud and not a loser. By the time they got to the last pose, he just remained on his knees with his chest in the sand and his face on the ground. He managed not to whimper like a downward dog.

"You okay?" Selena said in his ear.

"I'm just going to stay here until lunch."

"You don't want to do that. You'll miss my crepes. Come on, I'll help you up and treat you to a power smoothie."

He turned his head—even that hurt. He pried one eye open. "Will that make all the pain go away?"

"No, but the hot tub should do the trick."

"Oh yeah," he said. Groaning, he pushed himself up to his feet.

She grabbed his arm to steady him.

"I got this."

"Just checking, tough guy."

They walked slowly back to the elevators. He hoped she didn't think he was a weakling just because the yoga class rang his bell. Blaine might not have kept up with his jogging, but he used the company's weight room every day. He'd flex for her, but it hurt too much.

"Here you go," she said when they got to the elevator.

"Where are you going?" He cupped her elbow.

"I was promised a power smoothie, whatever the hell that is."

"I need a shower first."

"Shower at my place. I'm just going to hop into the hot tub."

She looked down at herself. "I need to be in uniform if I'm in your suite."

"Who's going to know? It's just after the ass crack of dawn."

"It won't be when I leave."

"Okay," he said. "But if you want to keep a spare set of clothes in the suite, I'm okay with that."

"Why would I do that?" Selena crossed her arms.

Blaine shrugged. "Wishful thinking."

"Keep wishing. I'll be up soon."

He watched her walk away before calling the elevator down. Damn, she had an ass that wouldn't quit. He got into the elevator and his legs decided standing was overrated and he slumped against the walls. Staggering out into his suite, he chucked off clothes until he got to the balcony. Easing himself into the hot tub, he jammed it on full force and submerged. When he ran out of breath, he gradually floated to the top. Staring at the sky, he wondered if it was as blue in Michigan under all the smog and pollution. He wouldn't want to trade a place like this for Detroit either.

It was almost lunchtime there. He would have grabbed something from the food trucks outside his building or maybe a sandwich from the cafeteria before eating at his desk. He wondered if Paul was redoing the trials again and this time documenting what was wrong with the code.

This was stupid. He could fix it in a few hours if he had that information. As he was stewing in the hot tub, he was also getting angrier. He was an adult. If he wanted to spend a few hours of his vacation making sure that he wouldn't be under an avalanche of shit when he got back, that was his prerogative. He had to get out of the resort today. There had to be an internet café around here somewhere. If he only could search and see where the closest one was. Maybe he could have his concierge Micky-something look that up for him?

"Careful," Selena said, coming out onto the balcony with what looked like a piña colada in her hand. "Your face is going to freeze that way."

She was dressed in crisp linen slacks and a denim chef's jacket. Strands of black hair curled around her face, escaping that braid of hers.

"How many of those things do you have?" he asked, gesturing to her jacket and taking the glass from her.

"Tons," she said.

"I liked you in your yoga outfit."

"I'd wear that all day if I could."

"I'd let you, if you come work for me. Of course, you might be a little cold." He took a sip. It was a virgin piña colada with something creamy and vanilla tasting in it. "Why is the rum all gone?" he said in his best Captain Jack Sparrow impression and waggled the glass at her.

His smile froze on his face at the flash of raw lust that crossed her face.

"Come here," he said, every aching muscle in his body forgotten as the blood rushed to his cock.

"I've got to get breakfast started," she said breathlessly, and rushed back into the kitchen.

Blaine let out a slow breath. There was no way he imagined that. Unless all the vegetables and exercises were making him hallucinate. He wasn't ruling anything out. But because he was too sore to go chasing after her, he sipped his pitiful piña colada. It was pretty good even though it didn't have any rum in it.

Leaning his head back, he tried for a Zen moment of relaxation, but his cock was throbbing too hard as he played back that sizzle in her gray-blue eyes. He wanted to wrap her long braid around his fist and pull her in for a kiss or hold her steady while she slid those sweet red lips up and down him.

"Blaine?" Selena cleared her throat.

He put everything he was feeling in his gaze and she swallowed hard. "Breakfast is served."

Without breaking eye contact, he lifted himself out of the hot tub and stood there dripping wet and naked in front of her. Her eyes fluttered closed, but her breathing was shallow. He leaned in close and whispered in her ear.

"Thanks."

Grabbing a towel, he then wrapped it around his

waist. The crepes and bacon smelled like heaven and he was tearing into them before he consciously realized what he was doing. Just feeding one hunger instead of another.

Selena poured him a cup of coffee. She was steadier than he felt right now. "Did you give a thought about lunch or does the chicken stir fry sound good?"

She sounded good. He stared up at her. "Are you going to make me eat that brown rice shit?"

Her lips twitched, and the tension popped. "I could be persuaded to serve it over jasmine rice."

"I'm good at persuasion." Blaine stood up and his entire body felt a thrill when she didn't move back. "What do you want?"

"The list is long." She giggled nervously and took a step back.

He let her go, even though it went against all of his instincts. Blaine wanted her, but he was very aware that she was technically employed by his business partners and in essence, him. She would have to make the first move, even though it would kill him.

"Let me think about it," she said.

"Take all the time you need." Blaine watched her leave, trying to erase visions of him making love to her over every surface of the penthouse suite.

It took him a few moments after she left to remember he still had bacon to finish. Returning to the dining room table, he poured himself a refresher on his coffee and sank into the chair. His phone was useless, so he flipped through the paperwork Selena left him last night.

He confirmed that there weren't any computers, internet access, or televisions on the property. He did have an in-room phone, though, in case of emergencies or questions. Taking his coffee over to the phone—a handset with a rotary dial, how quaint—he picked up the receiver and dialed zero for the lobby.

"Yes, Mr. Stephens," a soft male voice said.

"Yeah, I need a car brought around."

"Would you like to book a tour of the island?"

"Not today. I need to get out for a few hours."

"What would you like to do?"

Blaine stared at the phone. He wasn't used to twenty questions. "I'm looking for an internet café."

"I'm sorry, sir. We don't have a shuttle or a service for that."

Holding on to his temper with an iron grip, Blaine said, "I don't care. Just get me a car. I'll find one myself."

"If there's something you need, we can arrange it to be delivered to your suite."

"Deliver the car to the lobby and that will be fine," he said in measured tones.

"I'm sorry, sir. I can't do that."

"Sure you can. I've got a credit-card number. Hell, give me an outside line and I'll get one myself."

"That's against the rules, sir."

"Let me speak to your manager." Blaine was about to go "all Karen" on this guy.

"Of course, sir. One moment."

Seething, Blaine slammed his coffee cup down on the table. A muscle throbbed in his eye and pain lanced through his chest. He tried to calm down. He was overreacting again. This was all just a misunderstanding. He wasn't a prisoner here. He could come and go as he pleased. He didn't care what his brother and Paul cooked up for him as a punishment. He was a damned adult and if he wanted to have a plate of nachos and a beer while surfing the internet, he was going to do it.

"Mr. Stephens, this is Titus Dukes. I'm the general manager here."

"Look, I don't want to be a jerk. I need a cab, or a car—I don't mind renting one. I just need to go for a drive."

"That can certainly be arranged."

Blaine's locked muscles relaxed. See? Maybe his brother was right. He had sun, sand and surf. If he could finagle some hot sex, he'd come back to Detroit a new man.

"Where would you like to go? You have a surfing lesson at eleven."

"I do?" He went to go back to the table to see his itinerary, but the short cord on the phone stopped him. Damn thing.

"Shall I reschedule?" Titus asked.

"Yeah, that would be great. Tomorrow would be good." Today, he just needed to see what was going on with his company.

"Are you looking to do some shopping?"

"Yeah," Blaine said. He wasn't going to get trapped into admitting he wanted an internet café. That way led nowhere.

"Very good, sir. Your car will be ready in the lobby in fifteen minutes."

"Thank you," he said. But Blaine had a feeling he had been outmaneuvered.

CHAPTER FIVE

THE LAST PERSON Selena expected to see wandering
around downtown Lahaina was Blaine Stephens.
Even if he hadn't had a surfing lesson, touristy shopping areas didn't seem like his style. She, at least,
had an excuse. Mikelina and she were shopping for
stuff to put in welcome baskets that one of Mikelina's clients had requested. It wasn't Selena's job, but
it gave her an excuse to talk to her about the crazy
attraction she had to Blaine and just what the heck
she was going to do about it.

"Can you believe this?" Mikelina said, holding
up a pair of kitchen mitts covered in mushrooms
and Anton Koslov's Bolete logo. "He's everywhere."

"He's always been a whore," Selena said, shaking her head. "If they paid him enough, he'd put his
logo on dog food."

Mikelina wordlessly showed her a bag of Bolete
gourmet dog food.

"I can't." Selena threw her hands in the air. Realizing too late, that she was attracting attention, she

looked up and caught Blaine's eyes. She couldn't comprehend the flush of excitement that washed over her as he determinedly made his way over to them.

"Hello, hottie alert coming in fast," Mikelina said.

"That's Blaine."

"The pirate Viking?" Mikelina squinted to get a better look. "What the hell are you waiting for?"

"Professionalism?"

"Overrated. Besides, he's as hot for you as you are for him."

"How on earth can you tell?"

"Honey, he's plowing through the crowd like a drowning man and you're a life preserver." Mikelina put a pair of pineapple oven mitts in her basket. "I've got this. You're going to have your hands full in a minute."

"You think?"

"I'll be disappointed in you, if you don't."

Selena and Mikelina exchanged grins.

"Hi," Blaine said, slightly out of breath. He looked a little manic.

"Are you all right?" Selena asked.

"Mr. Stephens, I'm glad to meet you. I'm Mikelina Presley, your concierge." She held out her hand and Blaine shook it. "Was there something wrong with your surfing lessons?"

"Yeah, no Wi-Fi. I don't suppose you can get me something or somewhere, where I can connect to the internet?"

Mikelina shot her a look. "I'm sorry, sir."

He held up his hand. "I get it. It's against the rules." Blaine turned those ice-blue eyes on Selena and she caught her breath. "Can we talk?"

"Sure," she said.

"See you later," Mikelina said, and then behind Blaine's back gave her two thumbs up.

Blaine's fingers were warm on her upper arm and Selena resisted the urge to move closer hoping he would accidentally brush the side of her breast. God, she was pathetic. "What are you doing here?" Had he followed her to convince her to spend the day with him doing more interesting things than cooking and yoga?

"There's got to be an internet café around here somewhere."

Selena deflated. Of course. "Not around here. They want you shopping, not taking up space for a paying customer."

"I'm a paying customer. Please, you've got to point me in the right direction. I still don't have cell service. I just want to check my email and see how work is coming along."

"It's been what? Forty-eight hours? I think they're good."

"Are you going to help me or not?" Blaine said.

She sighed. "Fine. I think I'm enabling your workaholic tendencies, but I'm also not a fan of the cold-turkey method of dealing with addiction."

"I'm not an addict."

Selena looked at him up and down. "You're one shake away from coming apart."

Blaine straightened. "I am not."

"Come on." She started walking back to her scooter. "I know an internet café a few blocks away."

"Thanks," he said, following her. "I owe you."

"I have to ask, did you even notice the banyan tree?" She gestured to the large tree above them. It was covered in white lights for the holiday. At night it was magical.

"It's hard to miss. It takes up the whole block."

"Don't you want to know more about it? Can't you appreciate the beauty?"

"I read the brochure in the car."

She shook her head. "Did you even take the time to admire the beautiful view of the ocean? You know if you go out past that channel, you might see humpback whales?"

"Yeah, it's nice."

"I can't believe you. Most people would kill to be here in Maui away from work and all their responsibilities for two weeks."

"Most people don't have a make-or-break product launch in February. Most people's projects haven't gone viral in the world's most embarrassing video."

"It wouldn't have gotten so popular if you hadn't decked your head engineer."

He stopped in his tracks. "You saw the video?"

"It has like five million views. Everyone saw the video."

"Would you buy the car?" he said.

The thread of dejection in his voice got through to her. "What car?"

"What do you mean, what car? The one that hit all the obstacles."

Selena shrugged. "It was a video of a car. We didn't see the prototype. If the prototype did that, I'd say you've got something to worry about. That was just good publicity."

"You have a funny idea about good PR," he said, but he resumed walking and he didn't look as desperate anymore.

"Get on," she said, throwing her leg over her Vespa.

"You want me to ride bitch on a scooter?" he said.

"I'm going to forgive you for that sexist remark because you're obviously starting with the DT's." She gave him a challenging stare.

After looking around, he must have realized he didn't have much of a choice. He got on the back and wrapped his arms around her.

Oh my.

"Go fast," he said in her ear. "Speed turns me on."

She choked on her laugh and carefully and slowly pulled out into the street. His arms made her think of more private things they could be doing, but the feel of his solid body against her felt right. Selena wanted him to turn her on and had a sinking suspicion that it wouldn't take much.

"How did you get here?" she asked.

"I took a three-hour tour of downtown Lahaina

and tipped the driver a hundred dollars to go away until it was time to pick me up."

"You're incredible."

"Incredible is that general manager of your resort. He's got a hard-on something fierce for rules and regulations."

"Yeah, Titus is a special type of control freak. He runs the wellness center with an iron fist. Fortunately, I'm a contractor, so while he's technically my supervisor, I only have to deal with him in small doses. I just have to put up with him for the next two weeks and then I don't have to see him again until I'm assigned back here for the next rich internet junkie who needs a personal chef."

She wondered if he was even interested in her or if he was just looking for a hookup and he'd be putting the moves on anyone, Mikelina, Kelli Ann. Was she just convenient?

He squeezed her tight. "You're going to be the best thing about these two weeks."

"You're just saying that because I'm giving you internet." She parked in front of the café. "You owe me a bubble tea."

"Anything you want, it's yours," he said, helping her off the scooter.

She decided to take him up on that and ordered a macadamia-nut brownie with her bubble tea. Blaine just got a black coffee. As she waited for her tea, she watched him walk to the bank of computers and pick one out. He wore his T-shirt tight and fitted. Selena could admire the strong muscles of his back and shoulders. Damn, but she wanted him. To hell with the rules. She was already breaking one by bringing him here. What were a few more? She wanted to eat dinner with him and join him in the hot tub. She hadn't felt this way about a guy in a long time. She wanted some fun. Blaine wasn't the only workaholic here. How many times had she come here and worked in her journal daydreaming about her restaurant? She was sick and tired of waiting for her life to start. She wanted an adventure and Blaine seemed more than willing to indulge her.

"What would Titus think of that?" he said, pointing to the brownie when she sat next to him.

"He'd hate it. But not as much as he'd hate this."

Taking a deep breath for courage, she leaned forward and planted a kiss on Blaine's mouth. Shock held him still for a moment. Then his arm went around her, and he deepened the kiss. Her body thrummed in pleasure. She wanted to feel his body slide against hers. Yeah, she didn't care if Titus found out about this. The worst he could do was remove her from the property and complain to Kirk Diamonte. It wouldn't be a great thing to happen, but she was willing to take the risk.

She was melting from the sweet feel of his mouth when he broke it off.

"Want to surf the internet that badly?" she asked, disappointed. Her lips felt puffy and the rest of her was restless.

"No. I just don't like the audience."

Blushing, she looked around to see that everyone in the café was staring at them. Clearing her throat, she shifted away from him. "All right then."

"But this is to be continued. You can bet your very sweet ass on that."

She leaned in and whispered in his ear. "I told Mikelina to put condoms and lube in your room."

Blaine choked on his coffee. He reached down and grabbed her hand. "Let's go."

Tugging free, Selena went back to her brownie. "You still have an hour or so until your babysitter comes back for you. Get it out of your system."

"I'm having a hard time concentrating."

She put her hand on his leg and squeezed. "Good."

Blaine kissed her again, sending shivers through her body. Yeah, this was one of her better decisions. When he reluctantly turned to the computer, she bit into her brownie with relish. She even shared a bit with him while he took turns muttering and scowling into the screen. After pulling out her own notebook, she jotted down menu items for her restaurant. She was so engrossed she didn't know that Blaine was watching her, until he pushed a strand of hair over her ear.

"I was able to access my email, but I can't log on to Stephens-Miller from anywhere but my laptop."

"Oh well, I guess you'll have to go surfing and snorkeling for two weeks." Selena patted his cheek. "You poor thing."

"I had a few extra minutes, so I looked up Anton Koslov."

She made a face. "You should have surfed porn instead. It would have been more pleasant."

"You worked with him?"

"Unfortunately."

"He never went to Cordon Bleu."

Selena drank from her bubble tea, then chewed on the tapioca pearls. "Your point?"

"My point is, you don't work for him anymore. You've got a dream job. You're an excellent chef. Why are you letting this dickhead still get to you?"

Straightening her shoulders, she said, "I prefer to think of it as motivation."

"So you want to graduate from Cordon Bleu to spite him? Honey, I got news for you. He wouldn't care less. In fact, I'm betting he doesn't even remember you."

Selena hated talking about Anton. It made her feel inadequate.

"What you should be doing is saving up for that restaurant of yours."

"Thanks for mansplaining my life to me." Rolling her eyes, she stood up and put her trash in the garbage and walked out. Blaine must have had to rush to close out of what he was doing in order to catch her just as she started up the scooter.

"I didn't mean to make you upset. I'm trying to help."

"Help?" she scoffed. "Blaine, we met yesterday.

Just because you read my journal doesn't mean you know me."

"I'd like to know you," he said.

"Then, let's just take this day by day."

"And night by night?" he asked.

Selena hesitated. Did she really want to do this? Jump into a two-week stand? Looking him up and down, she knew that she did by the way her heart pounded and the way her nipples tightened when he looked at her.

"I'll see you back in the penthouse for lunch," she said.

"Just tell me one thing." He jammed his hands into the pockets of his shorts. "Did I blow it big time?"

"You almost did, but not quite."

The smile he gave her sent her hormones into overdrive.

Yeah, totally worth risking getting busted by Titus.

CHAPTER SIX

BLAINE STILL COULDN'T get a freakin' cell signal. It was like the universe was conspiring against him. And yet, he had a date with his personal chef that was making him want to run back to the wellness center instead of waiting for his driver to pick him up. He should have brought his laptop with him. Although, the corporate firewall would have probably freaked out on him and denied him access when they saw the ISP address of the café.

He had to admit, the weather was perfect. Detroit had over a foot of snow and here he was sitting on a stone wall, looking at green-blue waves crashing into a frothy white surf. It was mesmerizing. Being forced to do nothing didn't suck as much as he thought it would, especially when he had Selena to look forward to.

It had been fun to read her journal, even though the decent part of him knew it was an invasion of privacy. It had given him an intimate look at her hopes and dreams and he really should return the favor to even the score between them. But he was an open book. Hell, she saw what he was all about on You-Tube. It bothered him that she couldn't see that going to Cordon Bleu was a waste of time and money. She could get her MBA much cheaper stateside. Or to hell with the MBA, get real-life experience in running her own business.

Her restaurant idea had franchise possibility written all over it. After going into one of the shops, he bought a leather journal with a tortoise on the cover and a trashy pen that had a picture of a lady in a bikini, whose bikini faded away when you tipped the pen. While he waited for his ride, he did some calculations for a first-year budget for Selena's restaurant. He was so engrossed with what he was doing, when his driver came up to him, Blaine was startled to realize it was lunchtime.

"Ready to go, Mr. Stephens?" the driver said.

"Yeah." Blaine stretched and walked back to the car. It had felt nice to have the sun on his back and to hear the crash of the waves. And while he still wasn't satisfied with the lack of information in his inbox about the Pilot Project, he wasn't about to give up on finding out what was happening with his company. But for now, he was content to wait out the two weeks.

When they got back to the wellness center, a man was waiting to greet him. He seemed as tightly wound as his muscles, which were displayed with a rash guard and matching shorts. Blaine really hoped

Mikelina hadn't set him up with an exercise program with this douchebag.

"Mr. Stephens? I'm Titus Dukes." He held out his hand.

Blaine tried not to smirk that he pronounced his first name like *tight ass*.

"How was your shopping experience?"

"Life changing," Blaine drawled and pushed past him.

"You have a phone message."

Blaine frowned.

"It came through an hour ago. It wasn't urgent, but your mother wanted to speak to you once you were back from your excursion."

"Why didn't she call my cell?" he asked.

"Guests of the Maui Wellness Center are unable to make calls in or out on their personal units."

"You've got a cell blocker on my phone?" Blaine took a threatening step forward, but then the cell phone beeped.

"As you agreed when you signed our liability paperwork."

That served Blaine right for not reading it. He should have realized his brother Mitchell was up to something by the way he had smirked.

Titus handed him a cell phone. "If you press five, you'll be able to hear the message. I can allow you a ten-minute call."

"That's generous of you." Blaine pressed five and his mother's voice came on asking him to call her.

He looked at the phone. It appeared to be Tight Ass's personal cell. "If you'll excuse me?" Blaine said.

"Of course." Titus went behind a desk and shuffled some papers, but he didn't go away too far.

Blaine walked through the lobby and took a seat on a bench facing the beach. Titus followed at a discreet distance, like he had expected Blaine to take off running with the phone. Calling his mother's number, Blaine stared off into the waves. Maybe he should have gone surfing after all.

"Hello?" his mother picked up.

"Hello from Maui," Blaine said, forcing a cheerful tone into his voice.

"Blaine! I'm so glad to hear from you. How do you like the resort?"

"It's all right," he said.

"Just all right?" her voice fell.

Blaine cursed himself. She paid a lot of money for this. He didn't have to be such a bastard about it. "I'm still shaking off the jet lag. I took a tour of Lahaina today and did yoga."

"Yoga?" she said. "You did yoga?"

"Yeah, and I've got a personal chef who's making all my meals. So they're taking good care of me, Mom."

"I'm so happy. I just want you to relax a little. All that stress you're under is no good for you."

"Well, I sat out in the sun by the water today and I'm heading back to my room for a good meal and a nap." After what he hoped was earthshaking sex.

"I wish I was there."

Blaine winced, glad she wasn't privy to his thoughts. "I think you and Dad would like it here. You should book a trip. Is it snowing?"

"Ugh," she groaned. "Worse. It's icy sleet and absolutely frigid."

"It's about eighty-five, but there is a strong breeze coming in from the west."

"Rub it in," she said. "You better enjoy it while you can. It's going to be a quick two weeks."

"Yeah, it'll be over before I know it." Strangely, that didn't fill him with the relief that he thought it would.

"And don't worry about the Pilot Project. Mitchell and Paul have completely scrapped the camera-sensor programming and are starting fresh."

"They what?" he said, jerking to his feet.

"Alice!" Blaine heard his father yell in the background. "You're not supposed to talk with him about work."

"What do you mean, they're starting fresh? There's nothing wrong with my code."

She gave a nervous giggle. "Oh, I must have heard it wrong then. Don't mind me. You go out there and do something fun and enjoy that beautiful weather. I've got to go."

"Mom." Blaine saw Titus coming over to him.

"Love you!" She hung up.

"Love you too," he muttered, and handed the phone to Titus before he could ask for it back.

"Is there anything else we can do for you today?" Titus said.

All of a sudden, he wanted to punch the smirk off of Titus's face. "No." He headed for the elevators, his mother's words still clanging around in his brain. He forced his fists to unclench.

"Mikelina has scheduled you for a luau tonight."

Blaine stopped dead in his tracks. "I thought Selena is cooking dinner for me tonight?" That definitely put a dent in his earthshaking sex plans. He wanted a marathon session, all night long. Stopping to go to a luau, solo, didn't appeal to him at all.

Titus scrolled through his phone. "No, but if you would like, I can schedule her to make a dessert. Perhaps a late-night tea and digestive."

Blaine was going to cancel the luau, but Titus frowned at him and Blaine remembered that Selena said one of her coworkers got fired for sleeping with a client. He didn't want to make Titus suspicious of what he had planned for Selena. "Sure," Blaine said, forcing a smile.

"Have a nice afternoon," Titus said.

Blaine waited until the elevator doors closed before giving him the finger. The knot between his shoulders eased when the doors opened up to his penthouse. That hot tub was calling his name, but then he caught a scent of sesame oil and he gravitated to the kitchen.

Selena had her back to him, but her fist was

jammed in her back. The other hand was stirring in the wok.

"You all right?" he asked, the pulsing rage he had been feeling turning into a simmering blaze of lust. He wanted to lean her over the counter and take her deep and slow.

She jumped. "I didn't hear you over the sizzle."

"I get that a lot," he said, winking and smoothing a hand over his hair.

"I was talking about the onions, but you do you." She rolled her shoulders. "I'm just a little stiff."

So am I. Blaine tried to discreetly adjust himself.

"This Italian marble floor is gorgeous, but killer on my back."

"Maybe I can treat you to a little massage." He wiggled his fingers.

"Speaking of massages, you're booked for one tomorrow afternoon at three. It's on the beach not far from where the yoga was this morning."

"What part of *I need a little excitement* was Mikelina missing?"

"She also has rebooked your surfing lessons to tomorrow morning, followed by cliff diving off Black Rock, and weather permitting you'll be hiking at Pe'ahi, taking a helicopter ride around the island and—" Selena walked over to her journal and flipped a few pages. "—zip-lining through Makawao."

"That's more like it," he said.

"I'm glad to see you embracing your vacation."

"I'd rather be embracing you."

"We'll get to that," she said with a sexy smile that he felt right down to his cock. "Why don't you relax for a bit and I'll call you when lunch is ready?"

"I'll be in the hot tub."

He didn't even bother with the robe this time. Stripping off everything, he settled into the hot tub. Blaine sank down into the water and leaned his head back. This would have been perfect if he didn't keep hearing his mother tell him that his brother and Paul had trashed his work and were rebuilding the camera sensor on their own.

He'd be the first to admit there was a problem. After all, a camera sensor would have picked up the dog and the little old lady. There wasn't time to start over from scratch. As he stewed about the problem, he knew he could at least put them on the right track if he had access to his computer.

"Lunch," Selena said, tossing a robe over the chair.

She watched him as he got out of the tub with a greedy look in her eyes. "You sure lunch can't wait?"

"Are you hungry?" she asked.

"Not for food." He ignored the robe and stalked toward her.

"It can wait." She stepped back into the room. "I hope you don't mind that I activated the privacy locks."

"I don't mind at all."

He grabbed her and was surprised by a sharp buzz.

Selena rolled her eyes. She pulled her phone out of her pocket and looked at the number. "That's Titus. He probably wants to make sure I'm not up here with you."

The rage came back. "Why is that any of his business?" He really didn't like that guy.

"He's uptight. I told you he fired a friend of mine for sleeping with one of the guests."

"That's a little harsh." It was as expected. Titus was checking up on her.

"That's Titus for you."

"More like Tight Ass."

"Let me just shut this off." She put it on the table and then shrugged out of her chef's coat. "Now, where were we?"

"Wait, you have cell signal?" He had assumed Tight Ass had blocked everyone's cell phone.

"Here we go." She rolled her eyes. "Yes. All staff do."

"I need you to make your cell a hot spot so I can log my laptop onto the internet." It would just take him an hour to straighten this mess out.

"No." She crossed her arms over her chest, and he noticed that she was wearing a very thin T-shirt over a bikini top.

"No?" he said. "Why not?"

"Because, you came here for a relaxing vacation. You're not going to manage your stress if you're working full-time."

"I promise it won't be full-time."

"Blaine, I wasn't born yesterday. I have nephews. I've seen them play video games for eighteen hours straight, go to sleep, wake up and do it all over again. That's you, only it's work, not play."

"How about we make a deal?" he said.

"This ought to be good." She went into the kitchen and started plating up lunch.

Well, he was hungry now that he thought of it. And he'd be able to concentrate on having a good time once he could straighten this camera-sensor problem.

"I could go to a cybercafe and do the same thing, but that's not very relaxing."

"Uh-huh." Selena narrowed her eyes at him.

"What if I pay you what I would pay them, and I work a few hours after every meal? In the meantime, I'll do all the rest-and-relaxation stuff that you want."

"This could cost me my job." She nudged him back to the table and set a brightly colored chicken stir fry in front of him. It smelled amazing.

"If it does, I'll pay you what you would have made if you hadn't been fired. Actually, I'll do that anyway." He speared a chunk of chicken and a pepper on his fork and popped it in his mouth. "Damn, this is good."

"I'm glad you like it," she said dryly. "So let me get this straight. You're going to pay me six months' salary, for the use of my cell phone as a hot spot so you can connect to the internet for the two weeks that you're here? Are you nuts?"

"Desperate. This place would be a perfect vacation, but I can't be disconnected for two weeks."

Selena nibbled on her lip. "I thought the most rule breaking I'd be doing was having sex with a client. Providing you with internet would be like me ordering fried chicken for you."

"In for a penny," he said, shrugging. "In for a pound. I'm okay with take-out chicken."

"I will wash your mouth out with soap," she snapped.

"Look, the bottom line is I'm not going to be able to relax unless I can see what's going on at my company."

"The moment you do, your business partners will be calling up the resort and we'll both be busted. Only designated phones have cell service at the center. Titus will revoke my privilege in a heartbeat."

"I can be discreet."

"Can you?" Selena glared at him. "Can you really?" She gestured, and he realized he was sitting there buck naked.

Blaine decided to brazen it out. They just had to agree to this one thing, and then the fun and romance could get back on schedule. "You've got nothing to lose. Set me up on the internet and I'll wire the six months into your account. If my brother decides to be a punk and your cell phone gets blocked, the money is all yours."

Selena walked away from him, and he realized the afternoon's activities had suddenly shifted.

"I don't want to jeopardize your job, though," he said, trying to regain the mood. "We can talk about this later. Why don't you grab a plate and join me for lunch?"

"It was a hard enough decision for me to decide to sleep with you," she said. "I hadn't planned on going rogue."

"I don't want to put any pressure on you," Blaine said. "Why don't we talk about this later? Much, much later."

Selena sighed and put her chef's jacket back on.

Blaine closed his eyes. He was an idiot.

"I need to think about this," she said, giving him a sad smile as she slipped her phone back into her pocket. "Enjoy your lunch."

CHAPTER SEVEN

SELENA WAS SO FRUSTRATED, she wanted to take Blaine's laptop and toss it in the ocean. She wished he didn't look like a cross between Johnny Depp's Captain Jack Sparrow and a Viking. She wished he wasn't obsessed with his job. Heck, while she was wishing, she should have wished that vegan cheese tasted like real cheese.

This whole thing was a bad idea. Tomorrow at breakfast, she'd tell him that over the eggs Benedict and asparagus. He'd need the protein for the surfing and cliff diving anyway. Selena would keep him at arm's length for the rest of his vacation. There would be no more ogling over his dripping-wet body coming out of the hot tub or about running her hands all over his tight ass. Trying not to be dejected over Blaine's rejection, Selena didn't realize Titus was coming the other way until it was too late.

"I've been trying to reach you," he said, smiling widely.

"I had my phone off," she said tiredly. "What do you need?" Aside from a shave-iced enema.

"Mr. Stephens would like a digestive and some tea after the luau. I was thinking maybe a fruit custard."

Untightening her jaw, Selena said curtly, "Sure. I'll get right on that."

Titus reached out for her, but she sidestepped him. "Selena, I was speaking with Kirk this morning."

"How is he?" she said, politely.

"He's having a good time with his new bride."

This time, Selena's smile was real. Kirk had married Mikelina's mother.

"Anyway, I told him that I would love to have you here under me at the wellness center."

"What?" Selena wasn't sure she heard him correctly.

"When your contract is up, I'd like to hire you to work for me full-time, on a permanent basis."

Oh hell no.

"Or if you'd like to make that happen sooner, I could buy out your contract."

"No thanks," she said. "I don't like staying in one place for a long time. I get bored easily." There, that should be a good enough excuse.

"Think about it." Titus raised his hand to touch her shoulder and she scurried back away from him. This was not happening. She couldn't get the one guy she wanted into bed, but the one guy she wouldn't sleep with if he was the last man on earth was hitting on her.

* * *

Selena was hoping to finish up the fruit custard and be the hell out of there before Blaine came back, but she heard the elevator just as she was pulling the dessert out of the oven.

"Shit," she muttered.

"Aloha," Blaine said, coming into the kitchen with something rolled up under his arm. He was wearing a screaming red Hawaiian shirt with Santa Clauses all over it.

Her lips twitched. "You look festive."

"Getting into the holiday spirit," Blaine said. "This is for you."

He handed her what he had under his arm. It was a thick kitchen mat. "Why?"

"Put it by the stove, so you can stand on it instead of the hard floor. It rolls up like a yoga mat so you can take it with you from job to job."

"That's really sweet," Selena said. "Thanks." Now she felt bad about the fantasies of stomping on his phone and laptop that she had been amusing herself with while she had been cooking.

"I'm sorry for this afternoon."

"It's fine," she said, taking a deep breath to tell him that she changed her mind about having sex with him. Selena wished he wasn't so damned good looking.

"I also scheduled you for a massage tomorrow. The same time as mine."

"What?" She blinked at him.

"I figure you've been working so hard, you deserve a little pampering."

"I'm not supposed to…" she trailed off.

"You went to the yoga class. I figured it would be all right to have a massage."

Selena thought about it. She really could use one. And he was right. Titus didn't have a problem with them using the amenities on the resort as long as it didn't interfere with their jobs.

"That was really thoughtful of you. Thank you."

He held out his hand. "Come on—I've got one more surprise for you."

Intrigued, Selena took his hand. It was strong and warm, and she still wanted to feel him touch her all over, damn it. This was a bad idea, but she followed him out to the living room where he turned on the stereo. The soft strains of Christian Dibiasi's guitar filled the room.

"I love this album," she said as Blaine took her in his arms.

"I know," he said in her ear, his lips tickling her earlobe. "Mikelina told me."

"Traitor." She laughed huskily. She hadn't told Mikelina that Blaine had blown it by being internet crazy, so maybe that was a little unfair to call her a traitor.

Blaine rested his cheek against her forehead as they swayed to the music. Selena pressed in close to him, enjoying the hard planes of his body. If he didn't mention the internet or work, she would stay for a bit. There was no harm in that. The moment he started up again about it, she would leave. That was a good compromise.

"Take this off," he muttered, unbuttoning her chef's jacket.

She let him slide it off her shoulders. Her T-shirt was thin, and she still had on her bikini top from this afternoon.

"You won't need this either." Blaine pulled the hem of her shirt up. She lifted her arms to make it easy for him.

"This has to go," she said, unbuttoning the obnoxious shirt.

Her bikini top was next.

She groaned at the feel of her hard nipples against his chest. Blaine kissed her and she forgot all the promises she made to herself and how much this was a bad idea, because she could kiss him forever and not get tired. Breathing was overrated anyway. While his mouth plundered hers, she stroked the hard muscles of his back. They danced slow, rubbing against each other. Her slacks collapsed to the floor joined shortly with his pants. Reaching down, Selena slid her hands under his boxers and grabbed a handful of his chiseled ass.

Blaine retaliated by dragging his nails over her silky panties.

"Off," she muttered against his mouth and soon they were dancing naked in the living room.

"Upstairs," he said, unwilling to stop kissing her

as they made their way up the stairs. Almost at the top, he stopped and cupped her breasts in his hands. She held his head as sucked on her nipples. Entwining her leg around his, Selena ground herself against his thigh.

"I could come like this," she gasped as he held her tighter, still ravaging her breasts with his tongue and teeth.

"Okay," he panted, going back to her mouth. Tugging on her tight nipples, Blaine inched up the stairs. His cock was hot and hard against her stomach.

"Want you," Selena muttered, writhing on him.

"Let me," he said when they reached the landing. He pressed her against the wall and pushed his hand between their bodies.

At the first touch between her thighs, Selena gasped. When his fingers rubbed her clit, she clung to his shoulders. "Yes," she said, scraping her sensitive nipples up his chest.

"Come," he said, covering his mouth with hers.

He played with her slow until she was nearly screaming. Clamping her thighs together, she rode his fingers to a body-shaking orgasm that left half moons in his shoulders from her fingernails.

"That's it," he said.

She reached down for his cock and stroked it fast.

"I will come all over your hand," he warned.

"Do it," she dared, wanting to make him come as hard as she did.

They made it to the doorway of his bedroom. Him

playing with her breasts and her rubbing him into a frenzy. He came, hot, sticky and shaking.

"Fuck, yeah," Blaine said and pushed her down on the bed.

Spreading her legs wide, he looked as she squirmed from the heat in his gaze.

"You're driving me crazy. You're so damned beautiful." Leaning down, he licked her up and down. "You taste so sweet."

"Blaine," she moaned.

He tongued her pussy, each stroke making her shiver. He sucked on her folds and then went for her clit. Selena shrieked and held his head between her thighs as they quivered against his cheeks. She bucked and ground herself into his mouth.

"So good. So damned good."

This was worth every bit of trouble she could get into.

"Don't stop," she begged. His tongue driving her closer and closer to the edge.

He moaned deep into her and her fingers left his hair to clutch at the bedspread.

"More, more." Selena turned her head. She could see the moon over the waves crashing in the distance. Blaine's tongue was flicking at her clit and she could barely form words. She came and he groaned, not stopping licking and sucking until she twitched and her breath hitched with each sensitive stroke.

"You said Mikelina got condoms." Blaine's voice was ragged.

"Here," Selena sobbed out, stretching to the bed-side table. Two boxes. Bless her. She tore one open and with shaking fingers took one out.

Blaine unwrapped it and slid it on his cock.

Eager for him, she wrapped her legs around his waist.

He drove into her, his hard length filling her. She clutched his shoulders as he thrust deep. Rocking her into the bed, Blaine kissed her again. The headboard knocked into the wall and the bedsprings creaked. Her hips rose to meet each thrust.

"Faster," her swollen lips murmured against his.

Blaine picked up the pace and for a moment, she thought they'd break the bed when the end of the bed lifted up and slammed down.

Blaine's harsh grunts drove her to a place where all she needed was this driving pleasure. Gripping his ass, she encouraged him deeper, harder, faster. She came for the third time, clamping around him. Slowly coming back to earth, Selena reveled in his body as it clenched and jerked as he came inside her.

After collapsing next to her, he tied off the con-dom and lay on his back. Selena threw her leg over his and cuddled in close as their harsh breaths came back to normal. Okay, so all the rules just went out the window. There was no way she was going to stop having sex with Blaine. She wanted every minute of the next two weeks with him to be spent in this de-licious haze. But she wanted all of his attention and that would mean she'd have to give him some internet time or he'd obsess about his company. This was a no-strings thing and she definitely didn't want to like him too much However, she had some standards. He needed to relax more than he needed to work. Fortunately, sex was very relaxing.

"I'll let you use my cell phone as a hot spot as long as you agree to do all the relaxation activities that Mikelina has scheduled for you."

"What?" Blaine panted out, still sounding dazed.

She reached up and tilted his chin toward her. "Between that and me, you'll be too busy to be a workaholic these two weeks."

CHAPTER EIGHT

BLAINE WAS SURE when Mitchell and Paul told him to go jump off a cliff, this wasn't what they had in mind. Nevertheless, he was here standing in line with about twenty other crazy people on top of a huge volcanic rock, aptly named Black Rock.

He was wearing board shorts that he would usually never be caught dead in. Thanks, Mikelina. And his muscles were sorer than he'd like to admit. A marathon night of sex and then trying to stand on a surfboard this morning made his knees weak. In a good way. Feeling the hot Maui sun on his shoulders, he rolled his neck around to get out the kinks. Thanks, Selena for rubbing suntan lotion all over his body before they left so he didn't have to worry about getting sunburned.

Against his nature, Blaine found himself relaxed and happy. He had to keep reminding himself not to get too involved. He had no time for a relationship right now. Although, his face hurt from grinning so much when he thought of her. And from squinting into the sun. He'd have to ask Mikelina to get him a pair of sunglasses. He could see his gear on the beach below and wasn't even remotely concerned. There was nothing to steal. His cell phone was useless, so it was locked up in the penthouse with his laptop. Blaine had been too busy enjoying breakfast with Selena to even think about work. He'd get to it later. Much later. If he could keep his eyes open.

From up here he could see the entire stretch of the Kaanapali strip. The beach was littered with tourists with their brightly colored blankets and beach umbrellas. Out in the water, powerboats zipped up and down carrying colorful parasails. The water was so blue and endless, it seemed to go on forever until it hit the sky. He couldn't get enough of the view. It was nothing like Detroit, Michigan, which was probably the whole point.

As the line to jump off Black Rock shuffled closer to the edge, Blaine wondered what the guys in the office were doing right now. It would be about closing time for normal people, although Blaine would just be grabbing a quick bite to eat and then working for at least five more hours. The time change still took some getting used to.

He was looking forward to heading back to the penthouse for lunch after doing a couple of cliff jumps. He couldn't wait to see Selena again. Even if they didn't have sex, and he was really hoping they would, he enjoyed talking with her. He wanted to help her with her restaurant ideas. And he was determined to break whatever hold that Anton Koslov chef had on her.

And then it occurred to him that he would also be able to log into work today. At least for a few moments before his afternoon massage. Blaine smirked. The thought of him taking a massage during the workday was ridiculous, but if it was as awesome as he thought it was going to be, maybe he'd consider taking daily massages at the office.

It wouldn't be the same as being on the beach in Maui, but it could be a way to get the people off his back who were trying to get him to relieve his stress. Now that he thought about it, Mitchell and Paul could probably use a midday massage, as well. Once he had his computer access back, he might just send a masseuse for them to the office, with his regards.

When it was his turn to jump, Blaine decided that he wanted to be all in for the moment. He pushed aside work and the memory of Selena's sweet kisses, concentrating instead on the feel of the rock beneath his toes. He took in a deep breath. That cliff wall was unforgiving. He hesitated, doubts creeping up on him.

The smell of his coconut suntan lotion hit his senses as the sun reddened his shoulders anyway. Looking down into the water, he knew it was deep enough. He saw the other men and women come to this edge and jump. Still, there was an irrational part of him that thought he wouldn't jump far enough, and he would tumble off the cliff, hitting every exposed piece of skin on the hard lava rock on the way down.

The fear exhilarated him, challenged him, but it would not win. He bent his knees and pushed his arms back preparing to launch himself far out. What if he belly flopped? That would really hurt. Maybe he should just jump straight and land feet first. What if he dove too deep and he scraped the bottom? What if he got caught the riptide?

Oh, just shut up.

Blaine pushed off, and for a moment he was flying. Then he realized, he better get into form. Otherwise, he was going to crack his neck or hurt his back. He sliced through the water as perfectly as jumping off his high school's diving board. He took a moment underwater to enjoy the warmth instead of the frigid cold of a chlorine pool. As he floated beneath the surface, colorful fish flew in every direction away from him. When he broke the surface with a victory fist in the air, people cheered. He didn't even care if it was for him or not.

Swimming farther away so the other jumpers wouldn't land on him, Blaine headed for the beach. He wanted to towel off and then climb up the rock and do it again. Blaine was delightfully surprised to see Selena in a pink bikini standing by his gear. She was clapping furiously for him.

"You did great," she said.

"It was awesome." He scooped her in for a kiss, loving the way her hands tugged his hair. Selena held him close for a hungry kiss that was all heat and passion. His body stirred, and he figured he didn't really need to jump off the cliff a couple more times. He felt the same excitement holding her in his arms. But as his fingers tickled up her spine toward her bikini tie, she pushed him away.

"Do it again."

"I plan to." He brushed another kiss over her lips.

"I mean jump."

"I'd rather jump you."

"Later," she said. "Let's see you cannonball off the rock this time."

"If I do, will you go out to lunch with me?" he said. "I know you're supposed to be the one doing all the cooking this week, and I wouldn't pass up one of your lunches for the world, but I have a powerful need to drink mai tais and snack on ceviche with you."

Selena pressed her body against his.

"Or we could go back to the penthouse. I have another powerful need I want to explore with you."

She slapped his ass. "You had me at mai tais and ceviche," she said. "Let's see what you got on the rock." She pointed.

"Why don't you come with me?" he said, pulling on her hand.

"Nope. No way. No, no." Selena dug in her heels. "I'm not jumping off that cliff. It's a long way down."

"Yeah, but it goes real fast. Come on," he said. "You'll love it."

"Blaine," she protested. "I'm afraid."

"I got you." He tugged again and she went with him reluctantly. "We'll jump together, holding hands. We'll hit feetfirst, and it'll be just like diving into a pool."

"Pools aren't usually a good ten feet over my head with a killer rip current."

"That's what makes it so much fun."

They climbed up the rock path together and got in the back of the line. Blaine slung an arm around her waist. "I'm glad you're here."

"I wanted to be with you," she said. "I'm glad you don't mind. I couldn't stop thinking about you. I figured I could spend time all by myself until you got back for lunch, or I could stalk you."

"Stalk me anytime. Besides, this is better than work."

Selena hugged him. "I'm glad to hear you say that."

"I'm a workaholic, not an idiot. Work will be there later tonight. The sun is only up for a few more hours."

"That's almost poetic."

"I'm working on embracing the island life."

"Good." She rested her head on his shoulder, but shivered as the wind blew hard. It was a warm wind, but he still wished he had a towel to wrap around her.

"I hope I didn't upset your menu by postponing lunch."

"Nah, we'll just have the mahi mahi for dinner."

She tensed. "That is, if you want me to stay for dinner."

"If you could get away with moving in for the next two weeks, I'd be all for that."

"I don't think I can keep that from Titus, but—" she looked at him through lowered eyelashes "—I could keep a few chef jackets there handy. Just in case."

"Just in case." He nodded and squeezed her tight.

"I'm a little nervous," she said as they crept closer to the edge.

"That's part of the fun. The way your heart is beating now, and all your senses are heightened, that's what being an adrenaline junkie is all about."

"Do you get the same kind of rush working overtime in Detroit?" she asked.

"It's similar," he said. "When I solve a problem that no one else can or when I create something new that no one else has ever seen before, it feels a little like this."

"I never really thought of it that way. I guess I feel the same way when I nail a dish perfectly. When there's just the perfect amount of spices and seasoning it feels like I could fly."

"And you know that no one on this earth could have done it better or the same way that you just did."

"Exactly," she said, gripping his hand.

"You don't have to do this, if you really don't want to," he said.

"I want to." She still looked nervous, but the look she gave him was full of trust.

He swallowed hard. When was the last time anyone looked at him like that? If he didn't watch out, he would fall over head-over-heels in love with Selena.

"Nothing's going to happen to you. Not while you're with me. Not while I'm here to protect you. On the count of three." Blaine squeezed her hand. "One, two…"

"Three." They said together, and then they were airborne. The flying sensation was intensified by her scream-laugh and the way her hand tightened on him.

"Don't let go," she said.

And then they were in the water. The force of hitting the surf should have jolted their hands apart, but there was no way Blaine was going to let go of her. They kicked to the surface and there were more cheers. Blaine was enamored by her laugh and the way her eyes shone with happiness. They swam away from the dive site and played in the water splashing and swimming.

"Did you bring your snorkel equipment?" Selena asked him, trying unsuccessfully to dunk him.

"No, but I wish I did. Would you like to go snorkeling with me?" He grabbed her and she wrapped her arms and legs around him.

"Sure, if you don't mind me encroaching on your vacation. I'd love to spend some more time with you."

They floated parallel to the beach, away from the snorkelers and the other swimmers.

"You're not encroaching. I enjoy your company. I'm glad you're here. I had just been thinking it would've been awfully lonely to experience all of this by myself."

"There was nobody you could've taken with you back home?"

"Not really. I'm sure there would be plenty of volunteers."

"Modest." Selena snorted.

"I don't mean because of me. Who wouldn't want to go on an all-expenses-paid trip to Maui?"

"You," she said as the waves pushed them along.

She fit in his arms like she belonged there. "I'm getting used to the idea," he said.

"You didn't have an old girlfriend or friend with benefits you could have called up?"

Blaine shook his head. "There hasn't been a lot of time for girlfriends. I haven't been in a relationship in a good year or so. Too much work. My old girlfriend would rather my plane crashed than go anywhere with me."

"What happened there?" she asked.

"The usual. I worked too hard. Too long. Didn't take time to spend with her. It was totally my fault. My only excuse was we had to get the Pilot Project started and underway. It had always been our goal to show it at the French Expo next year. It's not a good excuse. And I guess she thought that it would always be one more project and that my work was more important than her."

"Was it?"

"Yeah. I know that sounds really shitty, but at the time I didn't want a relationship. I told her that, but I think she thought I would change my mind or that she could wait me out."

"How about now?" Selena said.

"Now I'm seeing the benefits of not working so hard."

"That's progress." She slid her bare foot up his calf. Her hand slipped into his bathing suit. His cock immediately sprang to attention. "Do you think you can tread water while I get you off?"

"I'm willing to try it." Blaine was cheating. He could touch on his toes. He held her close and looked into her eyes while she grabbed him.

"I like how you feel in my hand." Selena stroked him slowly.

He kissed her salty lips. "I wish I could touch you, but I'm not that coordinated." Blaine groaned. "I'd probably drown us both." He slipped his suit lower. She cupped his balls in one hand, while tugging on him. "That's amazing."

Her breathing picked up. He could see she was enjoying herself and it shot pure pleasure straight through him. "I don't want you to make me come."

"Why not?" she pouted.

"Because I want to come fucking you so hard, I

won't be able to hear you scream over the bed frame knocking the walls."

"Let's go." She let go of him and tugged his suit up.

"Not so fast." He turned them so his back was to the beach, sheltering her from sight. "Put your legs back around me." Blaine shifted until his cock was pressing between her legs.

"Yeah," she said, grinding against him.

He floated backward until he could touch ground. No one else was around. Pushing up her bikini top, he pulled her in close and sucked hard on her nipple.

"Oh," she moaned gripping his shoulders.

He rubbed his cock against her bathing suit. Her little cries egged him on. Letting a sweet nipple out of his mouth with a loud pop, he thrust against her. Her eyes were unfocused as she writhed against him.

"God, you're beautiful," he said. "I want you to come just like this." He went back to her breasts, sucking and licking them. His body moved as if there weren't two layers of suits between them.

"Blaine," she whispered, her grinding motions going frenzied. Gripping the back of his head, she moaned in his ear. "I'm coming."

"Good." Satisfaction rolled through her.

Her entire body shook and then went limp.

"Fuck," she said, shuddering. "That was amazing."

"You're amazing." He cupped her breasts, thumbing her nipples. "I'm going to keep you up all night again tonight. Can't help myself."

She wrapped her arms around his neck and kissed him as he settled her bikini back in place. He couldn't get enough of her. But rather than rushing her back to the penthouse, he wanted to know more about her. All the details of her life that her journal hadn't told him. He wanted to know more about this restaurant she had planned and why she was still letting her old boss drive her actions.

He wanted everything. And she was going to give it to him.

CHAPTER NINE

Sitting in a lounge chair at a low-slung table filled with tropical fruits, sushi, and of course, ceviche, Selena leaned back and let the sand trickle in and out of her toes while she stared at Blaine. He was so damned handsome, he made her stupid. She felt like a giggly teenager. She knew he was still hard from their shenanigans in the water. And all she wanted to do was go back to the penthouse and make love to him all night long—after she finished her mai tai.

He had insisted on taking her to the beachside restaurant where they could watch the ocean and dig their toes in the sand. It was nice. She wasn't used to going out on an actual date anymore. One-night stands were for sex, not for casually sipping drinks and talking. Selena hadn't expected him to still take her out for lunch after she had jumped him in the water.

"What are your plans for Christmas?" Blaine asked. He trailed his fingers up her arm and her nipples tightened in reaction. "Or do you have to work?"

"No, I'm heading home to Florida for Christmas, after this assignment. I'm flying out to Ocala and spending it with my sister's family. She's got two boys—my parents should be there too." Selena smiled fondly. She couldn't wait to see all of them.

"Christmas in Florida? Is it even Christmas if it doesn't snow?"

"Yes, we take turns shaking detergent flakes out the window, so it looks like winter." Selena clinked glasses with him. "We can't all have massive drifts of snow to go sledding on."

"Or ice to slide all over the roads." Blaine popped some ceviche in his mouth. "I've always wondered, how does Santa get in, if he can't come down the chimney?"

"We have a special gold glitter key that allows him to come through the front door. And instead of the cookies and milk, Santa gets a margarita with some oranges."

"No cookies? That doesn't seem fair."

"My brother-in-law's diabetic. It would have been nice to spend Christmas with my family here, though." She looked around. Florida was nice, but it wasn't Maui.

"Would you rent them rooms at the wellness center?"

The thought was laughable. "They wouldn't be caught dead in a place like that." Or even eating at a restaurant like the one she planned to open. "Too many vegetables. My father, especially, would piss and moan at the menu."

"I don't feel so bad for giving you such a hard time about the veggie burger." Blaine grinned.

"It's not that my father doesn't like to eat vegetables—he just never gives them a thought. His mother had boiled the heck out of them, until they were mushy and tasteless. By the time I introduced him to roasted carrots and cauliflower and stuff like that, my parents no longer wanted to be bothered spending time in the kitchen. So the only time that they eat healthy is when I make them dinner."

"And with you cooking for rich people all over the world, I bet you don't get to do that as often as you like."

Selena nodded and took a sip of her drink. "It's true. My dad has medical issues and Mom's not in the greatest health either. I worry about them because they rely on take-out food too often. Like someone else I know." She fed him a bit of mango to take the sting out of her words.

"The food is not this good in Detroit. Maybe you should open up your restaurant there."

"I could open it up anywhere. My restaurant is going to take the fast-food world by storm. I'm going to offer inexpensive and healthy to-go foods. But more important, they're going to be so delicious, you're not going to even want any other fast-food brands."

"That's a tall order, but if anyone can do it, you can." He clinked glasses with her.

"Yeah, all I have to do is finish up my contract, empty my bank account and graduate from the Cordon Bleu. Then my life can start." Selena heard how bitter that sounded and shook her head.

"What happens then?" he asked.

"I'll settle down, get a real boyfriend and do what I love."

"What's that?" he asked, sipping his drink.

"Making people happy and healthy with my food—without having to pick up and start over every week or so."

"I still don't think you need to get an MBA from Cordon Bleu, Paris to do that."

"Maybe not," she said, pondering the possibility. "It seems like a long time until my life can start otherwise."

"No time like the present to work long hard hours for your company," Blaine said. "Ask me how I know."

"I can't believe you're all chill just sitting here, knowing that you have access to the internet back in the penthouse suite," she teased.

"Well, part of our deal was that I would take advantage of the rest, relaxation, and try all the new things and activities that you and Mikelina worked so hard to provide for me. So, here I am."

"I'm glad to see that you're being so reasonable."

Selena narrowed her eyes at him. "Why do I think this is not going to last?"

Blaine shrugged. "I guess you'll just have to enjoy it while it lasts."

"I intend to."

"Do you have your notebook on you?" he asked.

"Never go anywhere without it." She patted her purse. "Unless, I forget it in my handsome lover's room." She leaned forward for a boozy kiss. It was great.

"And they call me a workaholic. At least I didn't take my laptop to the beach." He ran his thumb over her lips before returning the kiss with a much more lingering one.

She broke away first this time. She didn't trust herself not to engage in major public displays of affection if she didn't. Clearing her throat, she asked, "What about my journal?"

"Well, since I haven't had a chance to do my own work, yet. I was thinking about this restaurant idea of yours."

"You were thinking about my restaurant?" she said, confused.

"I really like the idea that you had sketched out. I think you have the good chance for a franchise opportunity. Tell me a little bit more about it."

"What you read and what I just told you are really all I have. It's a fast-food restaurant selling vegetarian options made in a healthy manner with ethically sourced produce."

"That's a buzzwords dream," he said. "But doesn't really tell me what type of food you'd be making and how."

"Well, you're familiar with fast food."

"Yes, one of the four food groups, right? Quick, cheap, tasty and bad for you?"

"Exactly. So, let's say you're on a road trip and you're hungry, but you don't have time to stop for a full meal. Normally, you'd look for the quickest place that you can get in and out and then get back on the road. That means you're eating in the car on the go and usually it's a burger, fries and shake. With my restaurant you'd get carrot sticks, a veggie burger and a fruit smoothie."

"It sounds simple, but is it going to be cost prohibitive?"

"Oh, he's throwing out the financial words. It's getting serious in here. Wouldn't you rather talk about the ukulele lessons Mikelina has planned for you later this week?"

"Ukulele lessons? Are you freaking serious?"

"You promised." Selena wagged her finger at him.

"You did that just to distract me. Let's talk financials."

"Why? Are you thinking of investing?" She cocked her head at him.

"I might. Talk to me like I was."

"Blaine, I don't want your money. It's bad enough I'm accepting a bribe to use the internet. I'm only doing that because it's getting me closer to my goals to go to Cordon Bleu, which now I'm wondering if I need. I suppose the money also provides me a buffer in case Titus happens to stroll by and sees you and me necking on the beach."

"Necking on the beach sounds fun. And you're distracting me again."

Selena drank more. "I haven't figured out the financials yet," she admitted. "I haven't gotten that far because it's still about four years away. And by that time, who knows what will be going on with the organic farms."

"And what has Cordon Bleu got that you can't get in the States."

"Prestige. I'll be taking classes with world-renowned chefs."

"Won't those be in French? Do you even speak French?"

"*Un peu*, a bit."

Blaine grabbed her arm and started kissing up her wrist to her shoulder. "Tish, you spoke French."

Selena laughed and gently shoved him away. "I loved watching *The Addams Family* when I was growing up. Morticia and Gomez are relationship goals."

"Sometimes I feel like Wednesday and Pugsley are my sibling goals." Blaine said.

"Yeah, because sending someone to Maui for two weeks is equal to your sibling attempting to guillotine your head off," Selena said.

"Do you have any brothers and sisters?" he asked.

"Yes, I've got a perfect older sister. She lives in Ocala with her husband and two boys. I'm the cool aunt who comes over and makes homemade pasta."

"Lucky kids," he said. "I always wanted to be an only child, but I've got my older brother, Mitchell."

"Why did you want to be an only child?"

"Because you can keep all the French fries that fall out of the container into the bottom of the bag."

"What?"

"Didn't you and your sister fight over rogue fries?"

"What French fries? My parents would never take us to a fast-food joint."

"Where did you go when you got all A's on your report card?" he asked.

"I never got all A's. But if I got a good report card, I didn't get punished."

"Oh, your parents were one of those."

"What do you mean?" Selena finished her drink and was feeling buzzingly happy.

"I bet, if you got a 98 on your test, they asked what happened to the other two points?"

"It's like you were there during my childhood."

"My parents were never like that, but somehow I grew up to be that," he said, with a small chagrined look. "I don't take other people's failures well."

"I saw that, along with five million other people."

Blaine groaned. "Do you think that will ever be swept under the rug and forgotten?"

"No. The internet and YouTube are forever. But

the good news is something more interesting will come along soon, and then you'll be off the hook. At least until your car gets on the market."

"It'll get there," he said, tapping his fingers on the table.

"Finish up your mai tai. You're beginning to lose your vacation vibe, Mr. Serious."

"You're right." He guzzled it and then reached down to hold her hand. "So we established that I don't have a girlfriend because I'm a workaholic. Why don't you have a boyfriend?"

"I'm never in one place for more than two weeks," she said.

"But you come back to some of these places throughout the year, right?"

"Yes, but I never know where I'm going until the week before. And trying to keep a long-distance relationship going is tough under normal situations. It's just easier to keep things casual. And lately casual hasn't been doing it for me. Not that I'm expecting this to be more than casual," she said quickly. "I don't want to scare you away." That was the last thing she wanted. The mai tai was making her blab more than usual.

"I'm not scared," he said. "Casual is good, but the not so casual, long-distance relationships could work, if both parties were invested and there was the payoff at the end."

"What you mean payoff?"

"If there was an end in sight. Like if we both

knew that in two years we'd be permanently in the same place at the same time. Then a two-year long-distance relationship is doable, knowing that after two years, we'd be together full-time."

"Unfortunately, I don't know where I'm going to be after Cordon Bleu."

"But while you're at Cordon Bleu, you'll be in Paris. Isn't that in the city of love and romance?"

"I suppose it is. Maybe you can punch your brother in the face next time, and get sent to Paris while I'm there."

"It's a date. As long as you don't have a boy-friend."

"And as long as you don't have a girlfriend."

Selena switched to water as she ate her ceviche, content to sit there and have her shoulder touching his as they faced the ocean. Looking out at the waves crashing in, she was getting sleepy.

"Do you want to go on the helicopter ride with me?" Blaine said.

That woke her up. "I've never been."

"What do you mean you've never been? How many times have you been to Maui?"

"A bunch over the past five years. But it never really seemed something I wanted to spend all that money on."

"What do you do between jobs when you're not cooking dinners?"

"I do food shopping, meal planning. I practice

my cooking. I read a little bit. You know, the usual things. What do you do when you're not working?"

"I don't remember."

"Well, we're going to find that out again the next two weeks." She squeezed his hand.

CHAPTER TEN

THEY BARELY MADE IT back to the Maui Wellness Center in time for the massages. Blaine held on to her arm when they got to the beach area where the large pavilion tents were set up, the linen panels closed and tied down on all four sides to give guests privacy during the massages.

"Where do you think you're going?" he asked.

"You have your massage. I have mine." Selena gestured to two different tents.

"On the contrary, or should I say *au contraire, my chérie?*"

"Gomez, you spoke French." She pulled his hand up to her lips and did five quick kisses on his wrist. Then she looked around. "We have to stop being so obvious. Otherwise I'm going to get caught and Titus will yell at me."

"Leave Tight Ass to me. In the meantime, I changed our individual massages to one couple's massage by the beach."

"You're kidding?" She smiled.

"Nope, come with me." Blaine knew from the confirmation message that was slipped under his door this morning that they were in pavilion five. He untied the rope securing the tent door closed and walked in.

Two massage practitioners dressed in white Maui Wellness Center uniform were just finishing setting up their tables. Their name tags said Keoni and Malia and they each looked like they could tear a phone book in two with their bare hands. A diffuser was puffing out a mild tropical scent and inside the pavilion tent looked like a magazine photo shoot of a cozy high-end spa.

"Do you prefer a man or a woman massage therapist?" Blaine asked. He didn't care, so he asked for both and figured he'd take whomever Selena didn't choose.

"Woman please," she said. Malia smiled and walked over to her. That worked for him. Blaine was relieved. He knew it was strictly professional, but he didn't want another man's hands on Selena.

The massage practitioners pulled a curtain to give them privacy to get undressed and get on the tables. Blaine shucked off his bathing suit and shirt and lay face down, naked under the thick, sun-warmed sheet. He imagined that Selena was doing the same. It was soft and peaceful just lying here. His eyes immediately drooped. He hoped he wouldn't start snoring. When the curtain opened, he turned his head and saw that Selena was smiling at him.

"Are you ready to begin?" Keoni asked.

"You bet."

"I'm ready too," Selena said.

For the next hour, Blaine was rubbed down, with deep-tissue stimulation. It was pain and then relief as his coiled-up muscles released. Then when he was a puddle of goo on the table, Keoni put hot rocks up and down his spine, stimulating the chakra centers, whatever the hell they were.

Blaine had to admit when it was all over, he felt as loose as jelly and horny as hell. But not for Keoni. It was from the little sounds of pleasure Selena made during her massage. It made him more than ready to continue a different type of massage with her.

Wrapped in a plush cotton robe, Blaine tipped Keoni and Malia each a hundred-dollar bill and waited until they left the cabana. The waves were loud, even over the wind that flapped the linen walls of the structure. The heat of the sand was soothing to his bare feet.

"How was that?" he asked, placing a hand on Selena's oil-slicked back.

She shivered. "Blaine?" she said groggily.

"Just relax," he said, pouring warmed oil in his cupped hand. He let it drizzle down her spine, smiling as she quivered.

Stroking down her back, Blaine rubbed her in slow rough circles. He loved how she felt under his hands. "Do you like this?"

"Mmm-hmm," she said.

He eased the sheet down her curves until she was completely naked. Pouring more oil on the base of her spine, he smoothed it over the soft mounds of her ass. He spread her thighs, his thumbs pressing hard circles over them. Blaine's breath caught as she trembled. He could hear her breath coming in short gasps.

"You feel amazing," he said, trailing his fingertips up and down her slippery inner thighs.

"Blaine," she moaned.

"We're all alone," he said. "And you're all mine." He rubbed his hands all over her body, gliding and lingering. He would travel all the way up her inner thighs and then slide away. When he couldn't stand her little whimpers any longer, Blaine decided to put both of them out of their misery and rub the thick wetness between her legs.

Selena cried out and instantly tried to muffle it. She was slick and ready to be loved, but he fingered her slowly and tenderly, sliding in between her slick folds and teasing her clit.

"I've been wanting to do this all day."

The sound of her wetness made him long to sink himself inside her. The only reason why he hadn't made love in the water was he didn't think it would be comfortable for her. Blaine wanted her to feel nothing but mind-blowing pleasure. With one hand stroking up and down her back, he tickled her clit until she was writhing underneath him. She screamed into her arm when she came and he easily slipped two fingers inside her, pumping them gently.

"Turn over," he said, his fingers still inside her as he helped her lie on her back.

With his fingers penetrating her lovingly, he drizzled oil over her stomach and rubbed circles over her chest and belly. Blaine was so intent on the feel of her beneath his palm, he didn't realize Selena had worked his robe open until she took him into her mouth.

"Yes," he hissed out, freezing with one hand around her breast and his fingers knuckle deep inside her.

"Mmm," she moaned, pulling him deeper inside her mouth.

He pushed forward, his hips jerking in need.

Selena sucked him as he slowly worked her with his fingers. Her wet, hot mouth was driving him crazy. He went back to her clit to make her just as frenzied as he was. Her sounds of pleasure were muffled, but when she came, her thighs pressed his hand, trapping it as she rode out her orgasm that had her swallowing reflexively.

"Coming," he gasped, trying to pull away.

But she grabbed his ass and kept him there.

Blaine's entire body shook as she let him come. He was still moaning softly when her thighs released his arm and he slid out of her mouth.

"I don't have any condoms," he growled.

"In my purse," she said, pointing.

I love you.

He almost said it. It would have been a reverent

prayer, but not a joke. But it was too soon. He was too sexed up to be taken seriously. And yet, there was something about her that shook him. After putting on a condom, he walked to the foot of the massage table and yanked her to the edge.

Selena gave a giggle that was cut off when he put her thighs against his chest and held them there while he thrust inside her. Tight heat engulfed his cock, and he lost himself in slow lovemaking. This was exactly what he needed.

"Blaine," she groaned his name, arching into each deep stroke.

"Selena," he groaned back. "You feel so damned good."

The sweet friction built up until he was impossibly hard. He rocked into her faster, making her breasts bounce in a rhythm that was driving him toward an explosive release. He could hear voices on the beach. The pavilions weren't as private as being indoors, but Blaine was confident they wouldn't be interrupted. Still, the slight possibility made the already exquisite feelings have a touch of danger to them.

Selena's hands clawed at the sheet underneath her. Her mouth opened wide in a silent scream and he watched the orgasm shake through her as he pounded into her with fast strokes. The sounds of her arousal and how she tightened around his cock eroded his control. Blaine took her harder and she arched her hips, the rest of her limp and shivering. Selena offered herself to him and he accepted the sweet surrender. He came growling like a beast, hoping no one would come investigate. Lights flashed under his eyelids and he forgot how to breathe as he came deep inside her. He could barely remain standing. Yet, he couldn't leave her side.

"That was incredible," she sighed.

He wasn't sure he'd be able to form words. There wasn't room for both of them on the table, so he picked her up in his shaking arms and lay down with her on the soft blanket covering the sand floor.

They lay entwined in each other's arms until Keoni said from outside the pavilion, "Uh, guys, if you're still in there. I've got another appointment in five minutes."

CHAPTER ELEVEN

SELENA WAS FEELING so relaxed, she thought she would fall into a boneless heap. If Titus saw her right now, he would knew know that something was up. But Selena didn't have it in her to care. She went upstairs with Blaine, holding his hand. She was looking forward to hanging out a little bit more with him.

But as soon as they got up to the penthouse suite, he dragged out his laptop and looked up at her with puppy-dog eyes. Sighing, she plugged in her phone and turned it on so that it was a hot spot. She gave him the password. She didn't know where Blaine got his energy, but the last thing she wanted to do was stare at a computer screen.

She looked around the penthouse and noted that the cleaners had done a spectacular job as usual. She made a note to tell Titus what a good job they were doing. Titus tended to only care about the complaints, and not enough about when people were actually excelling at their jobs. That was another reason why she didn't want to work here permanently. Seeing Titus on a day-in-day-out basis would have been terrible enough, but to always have to be worried that she wasn't good enough or that she had to strive to do better and better each day? That was a pressure that she left behind her when she quit Bolete.

"Can I get you something to drink?" she asked.

"If you can put on a pot of coffee that would be great." Blaine looked up briefly to smile at her before immediately going back to his computer.

Selena wondered if she had made a terrible mistake. After making the coffee, she poured it into a carafe and brought it out to him. She handed him a large mug and then went out by the hot tub area. She would give him until dinner was ready. That would be a solid three hours. And then he was cut off for the rest of the day whether he liked it or not. Taking out her notebook, she started thinking about what Blaine had said about concentrating on her restaurant first and building it up, so that it could be franchised. It was so against what her life plan was, though. She had a hard time accepting that it would be a good thing to do. For the longest time, her plan was work hard, save money, go to Paris, graduate from Cordon Bleu and then the restaurant.

It was a refreshing idea that her life could start any time or that it had already started, and she wasn't aware of it.

Dinner tonight was going to be the mahi mahi and pineapple salsa that she had originally planned for lunch, but she was stumped for a side dish. A salad was the obvious choice, but it didn't spark within her. Dessert was going to be the leftover tart that they didn't demolish last night after spending an enthusiastic time in bed. Flipping to Blaine's lists, she saw he requested potato chips. And while the blue corn chips that Mikelina got him were tasty, they weren't the same. She decided that she had slacked off enough today and Blaine deserved a treat. She would make fried potato chips to go with the fish.

But first, she needed a nap. Jumping off cliffs and being made love to were hard work. Putting on a layer of sunscreen, she looked back and saw that Blaine was still hard at work. Feeling relaxed and hopeful about a possible new relationship with her life goals, Selena eased the lounge chair back and let the lingering afternoon sun bake into her.

The sunset and the slight chill in the air woke her. She had slept much longer than she had wanted to, and she hurried into action. Luckily, the mahi would only take a few minutes to cook.

"Hey," she said as she passed by Blaine to get to the kitchen.

When he looked up, his eyes were tired. He had been frowning hard at the screen.

"Is it time already?"

"Almost," she said. "I overslept. Are you hungry? If you don't mind waiting, I can make potato chips to go with the fish. Or we can have a salad."

"Chips?" he said. "You had to ask?"

"That's what I thought. You've got an hour. So finish up what you're doing because the internet is going down once dinner is down."

Blaine grunted. "Titus called a few times, but I let it go to voice mail."

"Good," she said. "There's nothing he needs to talk to me about. If it had been an emergency, he would've kept calling. How are things at the office?"

"Not as bad as I thought they'd be," he admitted. "But I'm glad I was able to take a look at the some of the code with fresh eyes."

"Sixty minutes and counting," she said. "And then you're cut off for the rest of the evening."

"Cut off?" He smirked. "As long as it's just from the internet, that's fine with me."

She felt herself blush at the hot look he gave her. "Yeah, just from the computer."

Retreating into the kitchen, she washed the potatoes and then cut them thin on the mandoline. She poured peanut oil into a deep-dish frying pan and waited for it to heat up. Once it did, she put a layer of the potato slices in until they browned and crisped. After placing them on a paper towel to drain off some of the oil, she repeated until she had a large bowl full. Satisfied, she dusted them with Himalayan salt and set them aside.

After taking the mahi mahi filets out of the fridge, she dipped them in a bowl of whisked eggs and then into a plate with panko crumbs until they were evenly coated. She lightly coated the grill pan with olive oil and added the flaky fish.

"Smells good," Blaine said from the doorway. He looked rumpled and tired. She worried that all the fun from the day had been leached out by the few hours on the computer.

"How are you doing?"

He stretched. "I'm good. Hungry."

"Excellent." She started chopping vegetables up for a salad. It wouldn't kill him to have both the salad and the potato chips. "Would you like white wine for dinner?"

"That depends. You are joining me for dinner, right?"

"As long as you still want me."

"Always," he said huskily and came up close to her to drop a kiss on her lips. "I'll open the wine." He took the wine out of the fridge and poured them each a glass.

"To us," he said, clinking glasses with her.

She allowed herself a small sip. It was crisp and tasted like peaches. It would accompany the dinner perfectly. "Thanks. Now, let me put on the finishing touches."

Blaine brought the wine and glasses to the table and then set it.

"You don't have to do that," she said. "That's my job."

"I'm greedy for your time. The sooner this is done, the sooner I can have dinner with my gorgeous chef."

She mixed up a citrus-vinaigrette dressing and allowed herself to pretend that this was her home, with her man. That this could be her life. It was a heady experience. She plated up fish and salad and brought that out first. Then came back with the bowl of potato chips and serving tongs.

"These are fantastic," Blaine said, stuffing his face with the potato chips.

"I figured you deserved a treat."

They ate in companionable silence, holding hands across the table like they had been lovers for more than just a few days.

"I'm glad I met you," he said, finishing up his fish. "I never thought I'd want to be with someone as much as I want to be with you."

Selena nodded. "I feel the same way. I'm used to being alone. I like it that way. But I'd rather be with you." Even though she knew this was temporary, had known it from the beginning, a part of her wished that they had more time to be together.

"I know what you mean. It's weird. If I was back in Detroit, I would eat while working and not think anything of it. I can't remember the last time I'd even tasted my food."

"That's a horrible way to live."

"It definitely was beginning to take its toll on me."

"It could have been worse," Selena said, rubbing her thumb over his hand.

"It was worse." He rubbed his hand over his face. "I should have never hit Paul. It felt good though.

Too good. Like I could get used to using my fists to solve all my problems. I don't want to be like that."

"That's why you're here. To learn how to deal with things a little more productively. I'm glad I didn't have to pry the internet out of your cold, dead hands." She nodded to where her phone sat on top of his closed laptop.

"I was looking forward to dinner with you. Plus," he admitted, "I was getting aggravated because the interns and some of the junior engineers where doing their work in a different way than I could have done it."

"Acknowledging that you're a control freak is the first step," she said. "Ask me how I know."

He sighed. "I guess I have to do the navel gazing."

"Beyond that, when you get back to Detroit, you might want to talk to a therapist too."

Making a face, Blaine put another dollop of chips on his plate. Selena resisted the urge to tell him to eat his salad first. She wasn't his mother. All she could do was give him the best choices and let him pick. She ate her salad as an example.

"I don't have time to talk to a shrink."

"You need to make time for yourself. Two weeks in Maui isn't going to cure you of your anger issues or vanish the stress from your life. It's a good start and you can discover new coping tools, but in the end, it's going to be up to you to continue things once your vacation is over."

"I don't want to talk about it being over," he said.

"There are still several days that I'm going to have you all to myself and I don't want to waste a moment."

"Talking about your health isn't wasting moments."

"Being here with the sand and the surf and the less frenzied lifestyle, I'm reflecting more that maybe I missed out on a whole bunch of life while I was busy working."

"It must be a day for revelations like that," Selena said. "Before I nodded off on the balcony, I was taking in what you said about working on the franchise instead of going to Cordon Bleu. Maybe I should rethink my plans."

Blaine leaned forward. "I know that you want to show Anton Koslov that you're better than he is." He held up a hand. "I know that's a sore subject for you. I'm sure he's a real jerk who deserves to get his nose rubbed into it. But you can rub his nose into it by being successful and not caring what he thinks."

"I'm not sure why he bothers me so much. Even after all these years, I have nightmares about being back in his kitchen. I guess it's because Anton's that little voice inside me that criticizes me and tells me that I can't do things."

"Why do you listen to him? Why is that voice so important?"

She toyed with a romaine leaf on her plate. "I don't know. Maybe because I secretly think he's right?"

"He's not," Blaine said.

"The rational part of me knows that," she said. "But the irrational part of me is still coming to grips with it."

"Then I'll have to convince the irrational part that Anton Koslov is full of shit."

She smiled at that. "And was your company saved by you spending valuable nap time checking your email?"

"I checked my email in the cybercafe. Today, I actually got through the firewall and was able to access my files from the cloud." He shook his hands over his head. "Hallelujah!"

"That better not mean that you downloaded them to your hard drive so you can work on them offline when you should be enjoying that sun, sand and surf you were just mentioning."

"It's like sleeping with a teddy bear," he said.

"Would that have made more sense if we were drinking mai tais and not wine?"

"You sleep with a teddy bear for comfort, right?"

"Not for a long time, but yeah." She cocked her head at him.

"It lets me sleep at night, knowing that if I get one of my brilliant ideas, I can open up my laptop and get it out of my head, so I don't forget it. Besides," he said with a slow grin. "I like checking up on my brother and Paul when they think I'm not looking."

"Do you think they're having fun without you?"

"I think they're running my company into the ground without me," he said.

"Sounds like you've got an angry voice in your head talking shit too."

"I guess I do."

He reached across the table, so now he was holding both of her hands. "You're staying over tonight, aren't you?"

"I didn't bring my toothbrush," Selena said shyly.

"I had Mikelina bring over a few overnight essentials," he said. "I could get used to this concierge thing. She's like a fairy godmother."

She owed Mikelina big.

"I'd love to stay."

"Good. Because you're going on the hike at Pe'ahi with me tomorrow morning after breakfast."

She gaped at him. "It's not fair to let your company pay my way on these trips. And I got news for you, your fairy godmother is charging your account for all the little items you're having her deliver. I don't want you to get sticker shock when you get the bill."

He scoffed. "I'm not worried. I've worked countless hours of overtime for them—unpaid. It was their idea to send me here. If they're regretting the bill, they've only themselves to blame."

"Are you sure no one is going to get mad?"

"It's my company too. If anyone has a problem with it, they can take it up with me."

"As long as it doesn't require punching anyone out."

He let go of her hands to hold one hand up in the air and other one over his heart. "I promise."

"Then I'm all yours."

"I like the way you think." Blaine put on some more jazz and sat back down across the table from her.

After they finished the wine and their plates were empty, Selena gathered them up and set them in the sink.

"I'll put on the coffee." Blaine followed her into the kitchen with the glasses and the empty chip bowl.

"None for me, thanks. I'll be up all night."

Blaine put what he had in his hands in the sink, as well. After lifting her up on the counter, he brought her in for a deep kiss.

"You're going to be up all night anyway," he said against her mouth.

Hot damn.

"Well, then bring on the coffee."

CHAPTER TWELVE

THE NEXT MORNING, Selena made oatmeal and Blaine didn't even bitch about it being healthy for him. She served it with macadamia nuts and fresh pineapple spears. They had spent the night making love and cuddling. Selena's cheeks hurt from grinning so much.

He didn't have time to log into the computer after breakfast, which played along perfectly with her plans. She was feeling very satisfied with herself, and she should have been paying attention to her surroundings after they left the elevator. She missed Titus bearing down on them. The only thing that saved her was that she had thrown on her chef's jacket before she left. That and she and Blaine were not holding hands.

"Selena," Titus barked. "May I speak to you for a moment?"

"Sure." Selena gave Blaine an apologetic look and slung her bag over her shoulder.

"Is something the matter?" Blaine asked, stepping into Titus's personal space.

"I need a word with Selena. This doesn't concern you, Mr. Stephens. She'll still be able to fix dinner for you tonight. What was on the menu again?" Titus looked at her expectantly.

"I'm going to do a tomato-eggplant bruschetta topped with mozzarella and a basil-macadamia-nut pesto."

"Is that going to be filling enough?" Blaine wrinkled his nose at her.

"It's basically a pizza," she said, exasperated. She didn't need his help. She needed him to get to the car that was taking them to Pe'ahi before it left them stuck at the wellness center all day. And with Titus on high alert, she wouldn't get a chance to sneak back upstairs until she was supposed to be there.

"Throw in a couple of beers and you got a deal."

"There's a six pack of Coconut Hiwa Porter in the fridge."

"I'd want a lighter beer for the pizza."

Holding in a sigh, she reached into her bag for her notebook. "How does Bikini Blonde Lager sound from the Maui Brewing Company?"

Blaine gave her the shaka and then finally got the hint and left them alone.

She wasn't worried that Titus was going to lay on her about fraternizing with the customers, because he would've have opened up with that. He got off on slut-shaming his employees. Just another reason she'd rather go back to the Miami Diner where she started her career than work at the Maui Wellness Center on a full-time permanent basis.

"I heard a rumor that you used to work for Anton Koslov, the famous chef."

Selena managed not to roll her eyes. "That was a long time ago."

"He's coming to visit this weekend. And I want you to cook for him."

"No." Selena hated the fact that the thought filled her with a cold fear, and she had to physically lock down her knees from shaking. "I'm not interested."

Titus frowned. "I thought you'd like to reconnect with your old mentor."

She'd rather stick a fork in her eye.

"Why don't you see if Leif is free? He's got some good skills in the kitchen and I'm sure the chef would appreciate his island delicacies. Leif's *malasadas* would sweeten even the most twisted and evil heart."

"Those are awfully fattening."

"Yeah." Selena sighed. She wondered if they could convince the driver to stop for the doughy sacks of sugar that exploded with flavor and melted in your mouth.

"Just one dish?" Titus asked. "You always get rave reviews on your ahi poke bowl. It's a simple and easy dish and I want it to be part of the chef's experiences in the wellness center. I cleared it with Kirk Diamonte, and I'm prepared to offer you a five-hundred-dollar bonus."

"Five hundred for one meal?" That would buy

a textbook at the Cordon Bleu or some really nice wine. Selena liked the irony that it would be going toward her Paris fund. And the little voice in the back of her head said, *Your ahi poke is your signature dish. Wouldn't it be nice to get a compliment from the old bastard?* And it was so damned easy. It was practically foolproof to make.

"Now that I think about it, maybe it would be a good idea to connect with Chef Koslov," Selena said. "Text me the details. And I'll make sure I've got enough for servings for whoever else is going to be there."

"Where are you going now?" Titus said. "We could discuss the menu."

"I got a few errands to run before I have to come back and make dinner for Mr. Stephens."

"You two seem to be having a good time together."

"Yeah, he's great." *Great in bed.* "He has a nice sense of humor, and it's a pleasant to cook for someone who appreciates what you're doing."

"So he's enjoying the healthier choices that you're making for him."

Selena shifted from one foot to the other. She really wanted to get going to Pe'ahi and watch the waves with Blaine, but she didn't want to be too obvious that she was blowing Titus off. Otherwise he might follow her to the car and then they'd be busted.

She gave what she hoped sounded like a carefree laugh. "I can't say that I've totally transformed the junk-food junkie, but at least he doesn't put his nose up at any of the vegetarian dishes that I serve him."

"His family was very concerned about his stress levels and eating habits. Would you say that in the past few days, you've seen a difference in his attitude?" Titus opened up his iPad and looked poised to take notes.

"I can't really say because I haven't known him previously, but he does seem to have embraced the island's lifestyle."

"That is a good sign, because his family was worried that he was working himself into a heart attack."

"Heart attack?" Selena nibbled on her lip, suddenly feeling guilty about letting him have the laptop to work. He should be resting.

"You did see the YouTube video, didn't you?"

"It was one of the first things I did when I realized that I had been assigned to him."

"Has he shown any loss of control or anger-management issues?"

She thought about the YouTube incident, but wasn't going to narc on Blaine. She would just have to keep an eye on him and make sure that he went to the meditation sessions and the ukulele lessons. Like she had told him, it wouldn't be a magic pill to fix everything in his life, but it would help. Shaking her head, she said, "I just cook his meals. It's hard to be mad at somebody feeding you."

Titus leaned in and muttered under his breath.

"He did get a little snippy with the staff when they wouldn't give him a car or access to the internet."

"Well, he is tech geek with a lot of money. He's not used to hearing the word no or being offline. So I can imagine that he was irritated, especially if it wasn't his choice to come here."

"He didn't have to agree to our terms."

"From what I understand, his family coerced him into coming here." Selena didn't want to sound like she was defending him, but it was the truth.

"His mother is driving me crazy," Titus admitted. "She calls me on a daily basis wanting an update even though I've given her a copy of his itinerary. I've told her that he's not allowed to use the phone because it will interfere with his de-stressing."

"What's she so worried about?" Selena wondered.

"From what she told me, Mr. Stephens collapsed shortly after the punching incident."

"I'm sorry to hear that," she said. She made it a point to ask him what the heck was up with that. He was too young for a heart attack, or at least, he should have been too young for a heart attack. Sometimes it didn't matter how old you were if you had been abusing your body for years.

"I know he was under a lot of stress at work," she said.

"And that's why we have to be diligent that he concentrates on relaxation. I told Mikelina to sign him up for some deep meditation classes in our serenity studio."

"He should like that," Selena said, hiding her smirk. She could hear him complaining about it now.

"Well," Titus said reluctantly. "I won't keep you. I'll text you the information about Chef Koslov's dinner party. Have a nice day." Titus paused for a moment, and she got the impression that if she had wanted to extend the conversation, Titus would be more than willing to stick around. Instead, she waved and hurried off to the parking lot, hoping he wouldn't follow her.

Blaine better not have left without her. She wasn't going to go all the way up to the North Shore without some company. At first, she didn't see the car outside the lobby and her heart sank. But a whistle caught her attention. Blaine stepped out of a car and waved at her before ducking back inside.

"Sorry! I feel like mission impossible over here trying not to get caught," she said as she got in the backseat with him.

"It's all part of the exciting adventure. Uncle Rollo over here—" Blaine gestured to the driver. "—he says he can only take us so far to Pe'ahi, but he's got a cousin that could rent us some mopeds to take us down the dirt road leading to the beach area."

"More like the rock area," she said. "And we're still going to have to park the bikes at the top of the hill and climb down." Selena had only been there once, and she almost twisted her ankle. But the sight of the roaring waves was worth it, especially during December when the swells got up to sixty feet you could watch a crazy surfer drop fifteen feet straight down and still catch the wave.

"It's all good," Uncle Rollo said. "Me and my cousins will take care of you guys." He shot them a shaka and then they were off, cruising down the road to the north coast of the island.

"What did Tight Ass want?" Blaine asked.

"He was worried about your health."

"I'm touched," Blaine said, putting a hand over his heart.

"Your mother's worried about you. She's been calling him every day for updates."

"My mom has him spying on me?"

"He's not doing a good job, otherwise she'd be getting a much different report than you've been eating all your vegetables."

"She's been a little overprotective lately."

"Can you blame her?"

Blaine narrowed his eyes at her. "What do you mean?"

"What happened when you collapsed? Was it a heart attack or stroke?"

"Hell no." He shifted uncomfortably in his seat. "I ignored some warning signs. I had been dizzy. I hadn't eaten much that day. I think my blood sugar tanked. The next thing I knew, I was on the floor. How I didn't manage to crack my head open is a mystery." Blaine rubbed her shoulder. "But I'm fine. I got checked out at the hospital and there's nothing to worry about. I told that to my mother, but she didn't believe me."

"That was serious."

"I know."

"You need to make your health a priority, not work."

"That's what I'm doing," he said. "And I'm glad you're here to keep me on the straight and narrow."

"Is that what I'm doing?" she said tartly.

"Among other things." Blaine gave her a wicked smile. "Any chance that we can hop in the water once we're there? I didn't bring a swimsuit. Maybe we could go skinny dipping?"

Selena snorted. "No. That water is for watching not for swimming, unless you're crazy."

"I'm a little crazy."

"And it's not private at all. There will be a ton of people there."

"I'm not shy either."

"I noticed," she drawled. "If you want to go swimming there are a lot better beaches that will have lifeguards, along with some surf breaks. We'll go there instead. Pe'ahi is nicknamed Jaws because the rocks are like teeth that will chew you up."

"Eh, not really, but close enough," Uncle Rollo said. "If you want to swim, I'll take you to D.T. Fleming. You might even see a sea turtle."

That sounded nice to Selena.

"No," Blaine said. "I need a little excitement. Pe'ahi sounds perfect."

Selena rolled her eyes.

"Then I guess surfing is out," Blaine said.

Now it was Uncle Rollo's turn to snort.

"Considering your first lesson was yesterday, yes. Even if you were an experienced surfer, only professional surfers should be out there. It's dangerous, even when the waves aren't fifty feet high.

"Besides," Uncle Rollo said. "The way to do it is to be towed out, by a Jet Ski if you really want to get to catch a wave."

"Don't encourage him," Selena groaned.

"If the riptides don't kill you, the waves will slam you into the rocks and drown you."

"Okay, then." Blaine said. "Believe it or not, I don't have a death wish."

"I know, but you're still looking for some excitement, right?"

"It's been an exciting week. I suppose I could just sit and enjoy the waves."

"Don't worry, by the time we get to the waves you're going to be begging to sit down and relax for a bit. It's a strenuous hike. But if you're still not filled with adrenaline by then, maybe we could do some rock climbing and get a nicer view."

Blaine intertwined his fingers with hers. "As long as you're with me, I know I'll have a good time."

Uncle Rollo let them off just as the road started getting narrower and muddier, but his two cousins were waiting for them. They paid to rent the motor bikes to go the rest of the way. There was no way she was going to ride tandem on the back of Blaine's bike. She liked to be in control of her own moped, especially when the roads were slick and treacherous.

"It's about a two-mile drive," Uncle Rollo said. "Just leave the bikes at the top when you get there and hike down to the beach area. And when you're ready to come back, give us a call." Uncle Rollo held out his phone.

"No can do," Blaine said. "I've got a cell blocker on my phone."

"I got the number," Selena said. "Thanks, Uncle Rollo."

"Have a good time." He waved and sat down to talk to his cousins as they got on the bikes.

As they zipped along the trail, the hot sun beat down on her head and neck. She was glad they weren't walking the two miles because there wasn't any shade anywhere. The heat would've made walking this almost impossible. Puttering along as fast as she dared on the muddy track was fun. She and Blaine playfully raced each other until they had to back off because of a rut or a slippery patch in the road. She almost dumped the bike a couple of times.

Blaine, even though he was a city boy, was doing all right on the motorbike. As they went farther down the trail, they passed a few people who were crazy enough to be walking. Others were on motorbikes or ATVs. Selena was glad that Blaine was enjoying himself, throwing out a shaka and then looking back to grin at her, when she was still maneuvering around, trying not to fall off her bike or hit someone.

"Careful," she said. "People might think that you're a native and start asking for directions."

"I'll just tell them to follow me. Because that's where the party is."

Selena had to laugh. It sure was.

They parked the motorbikes on the top of the hill. Ahead of them was a huge field of sugarcane and there was barely a path. "I feel like I'm in a horror movie," Blaine said.

"It does have a bit of a *Children of the Corn* vibe to it," Selena said, pushing aside stiff branches of the sugarcane.

Eventually they came to the end of the field. Straight down was a steep winding path that led to the rocky beach area. They passed several couples who had stopped to regret the fact that they were only wearing flip-flops on their feet. The leaves on the trail were wet and made the trek very treacherous.

"I should've brought my ice skates," Blaine said.

"Just watch your footing," Selena said. "The last thing we want to do is haul you back up that hill and across that long road on a stretcher."

"That's what I appreciate about you," he said. "Always looking on the bright side of life. I told you that I'm fine."

They eventually got down to the rocky beach area. There were a few people sitting on the black rocks looking out at the waves. Some had picnic blankets. Others were drinking beers.

"That's one hell of a view," Blaine said.

"Are you hungry? I packed some sandwiches and snacks in my backpack."

"Why didn't you tell me? I would've carried that for you."

"It wasn't heavy. You're the one carrying the water. If we had been walking, though, I certainly would have made you carry it."

"Give it to me now, because I want to climb up those rocks."

Gladly," she said. Looking up, and up, and up. "Do we have to?"

"Can you see up there?"

"No."

"Then neither can anyone else. I like the idea of being out here, and having you all to myself, with just the wind and the crashing of the waves."

"I'm game if you are." She handed him the backpack. "Make sure you use the rope that they've got tied up down here. Just in case the rocks are slippery."

Selena wasn't much of a rock climber, and she wasn't much of a thrill seeker either. Unless you counted the thrills coming from sleeping with a man she'd only known a couple days. She felt the flutter of giddiness in her stomach. She wasn't like this. Normally when she did go on nature hikes, it wasn't to make love in the open air. But she had to admit that the idea appealed to her. Blaine appealed to her. She knew she was falling for him hard, and even though it had been a crazy few days so far, she liked everything that he suggested doing.

The climb was hard enough that her heart was thumping, but it was worth it. They climbed up to a flat rock ledge. There were more footholds to climb above them, but she wasn't brave enough to attempt that. Below them were jagged rocks and the crashing surf. Selena couldn't see the beach below until she lay flat on her stomach and peeked over the edge.

Sitting up, she could see the surfers in the distance being towed out by the Jet Skis in order to catch some of the bigger waves. But they looked like small figures in the distance. She couldn't make out any discerning features, so the only thing they had to worry about was somebody on a Jet Ski with binoculars. And they were more interested in saving the surfers from drowning to death than they were looking around trying to spy on couples planning on having sex on a rock.

CHAPTER THIRTEEN

BLAINE WOLFED DOWN the sandwich she made for him. Selena had used crushed chickpeas and watercress as a filling. It was tasty. He didn't even miss his meatball sub with extra cheese. Well, maybe he did a little. But he'd never tell her that. Or that he was jonesing hard for a Philly Cheese Steak. She'd probably make him one with textured vegetable protein, whatever the hell that was. And even worse, he'd probably like it.

"I call that my chickpea of the sea mix."

He groaned.

She nibbled on her southwestern-flavored tofu salad. He drew the line at that.

"What's wrong with egg salad?"

"Nothing. Eggs are very nutritious. This is just a different sandwich filling. It doesn't always have to be the same three things."

"What three things?" Blaine was missing her homemade potato chips. But he settled for a granola bar instead.

"Deli meat," Selena ticked off the list on her fingers. "Egg salad, chicken salad."

She had a point.

He stared out into the rolling blue waves, impressed by the huge crash of white foam that the waves made up on the beach—not that you could really call it a beach. There was some black sand, but mostly it was made up of rocks.

"Mother Nature is a scary bitch, isn't she?" he said.

"I wouldn't want to piss her off." She folded the cloth sacks that she had stuck the sandwiches in to avoid using plastic baggies. Even their water bottles were the refillable kind.

It was a different mindset over here. He'd have thought nothing of getting his to-go lunch wrapped in foil or in a foam container. Blaine would have finished his lunch and tossed it in the garbage without a second thought. Except there weren't any trash cans around here and he was glad for that.

Leaning back against the cliff wall, he closed his eyes briefly. He hadn't wanted to admit it, but the climb had taken a lot out of him. He wasn't as in shape as he thought he was, company gym membership aside. He rubbed at an aching pain in his calf.

"Come here," he said once they were done with lunch. Selena scooted over and sat between his legs, leaning her back against his chest. He wrapped his arms around her and breathed in the sweet scent of her hair. It smelled like the spearmint-and-eucalyptus shampoo that Mikelina bought for him. Selena smelled like him and he liked that on a primitive level. These past few days had passed so quickly, it felt like an erotic dream. He didn't want it to end and as much as he wanted to get back to the Pilot Project and that damned stupid camera sensor, Blaine needed to cram as much fun into the next week and a half before he'd have to give her up forever.

That caused another pang. This time in his chest. Even the lure of Christmas didn't soothe the unease he felt about leaving her and Maui. He wondered if a long-distance relationship would work. Would it bother him that she was cooking for billionaires in Tahiti, Milan or anywhere that didn't have a foot of snow? Would she even be interested in trying to continue whatever this was? Or did this even exist because they were on vacation time instead of reality time? He'd like to find out.

Maybe the past few days were catching up to him, but he felt like he could drift off to sleep right here. As it was, he didn't think he was up to climbing down the rock anytime soon. But the good news was he didn't have anywhere else to be. Except that didn't feel like good news. He had to stop from berating himself for not checking in to work for a few minutes before they left. He wondered if they figured out the blind spots in the cameras yet.

"You're quiet," he said, when he realized he was brooding for a while.

"Just thinking about something else Titus said."

"Ugh, don't let that asshole take up any more of your time."

Giving a half laugh, she said, "Yeah, well speaking of assholes, guess who's coming to the wellness center this weekend?"

"My brother?"

She turned her head back to look at him. "You're expecting your brother to visit?"

"No, but you said asshole and my mind immediately went to him."

"Your brother is an amateur compared to Anton Koslov."

"He's coming here?" Blaine said. "Want me to punch him for you?"

"Yes. No. I thought you were working on that?"

Shrugging, Blaine said, "Some people deserve it."

"I'm not arguing that. I'm arguing that you think you're the designated hitter."

"The offer is out there. That's all I'm saying. I know a great way of avoiding him. You can hang out in my room. Naked."

"That's altruistic of you," Selena said. "But Titus wants me to cook him dinner."

"I think I have a recipe that involves chocolate Ex-lax."

"Don't even joke about that."

"So are you going to do it?"

"It's five hundred bucks."

"I'll give you five hundred bucks not to," he countered. And he would too. There was no reason she had to risk her old boss ripping into her. She didn't work for him or for Titus.

"That's very generous, but I said I'd do it."

"Why?"

"I thought the money was the deciding factor, and the irony of using it for Cordon Bleu. But now that I'm thinking about it, I want to do this for me. If I'm ever going to stop letting him rent space in my head, I've got to face him down with my best dish—something I know has thrilled and delighted countless clients."

"Have you made it for me?"

"Guess what you're having for dinner tonight? You're going to be my guinea pig."

"What is it?"

"It's a surprise."

"Normally when people say that, I know I'm not going to like it. But you haven't made me a bad meal yet, so I'll let you get away with the secrecy." He hugged her in close and kissed her cheek, which was the only part of her face he could reach at this angle. "I'm sure I'm going to love it."

"Just a little hint, is there any fish you don't like?" she asked. She knew Anton was deathly allergic to shellfish, but luckily, she knew from experience that he didn't have a problem with tuna. It was hard not to tweak the recipe in her head. She didn't want to mess with a well-tested recipe, but on the other hand, could she make it better?

"I'm not a fan of tuna fish."

Selena winced. "What about ahi?" She held out her hands about a two feet part. "The big tunas."

"I don't think I've ever had it. Is it like salmon?"

"Salmon has a stronger flavor and a different texture and mouthfeel. How about sushi?"

"I try to avoid gas-station sushi, but when it's catered, I like it."

"Gas. Station. Sushi? It's like you're speaking English, but I don't understand. Why would you purchase sushi from a gas station in Detroit?" Selena heard the shrill note in her voice and tried to dial it down a notch.

"Exactly."

"The sushi you're going to get from me, or pretty much anywhere else on this island, was happily swimming a few hours ago."

Blaine shrugged. "I'll try it. What does Chef Dickhead like?"

"He's picky about his fish, but I know a place that has the freshest around. Plus my homemade *furikake* seasoning will blow his mind."

"Did you just say you have furry khaki seasoning?" He snort-laughed.

"Yes," she sighed. "It tastes like chipmunks in resort wear."

"Now I can't wait to try it."

Banging her head against his chest, she said, "That's all you're going to remember about this dish, isn't it?"

"Maybe," he said, tucking her hair over her shoulder so he could put nibbling kisses on her neck. The quick intake of her breath made him slide his hand up her shirt. Holding her breasts in his hands, he flipped up her bra and rubbed his palms over her nipples. Selena arched into him, giving him better access. "Do you like that?"

"Yes," she said shakily, her hands on his knees. "Let me touch you."

He lifted his mouth from that sweet spot on her neck. "Not just yet. Unbutton your shorts."

She did and shimmied her shorts down a bit. Pulling her up his body a bit, he stroked his hand down into her panties.

"Blaine," she said.

"No one can see up here." He kissed up to her ear. "I can't keep my hands off you. I want you to come while we watch the waves."

She was hot and wet when his fingers reached between her legs. He tickled them through her folds before circling on her tight bud. Jerking against him, she tilted her head so he could plunder the other side of her neck.

Reaching back, Selena tugged on his hair and squirmed against him. He moaned and rolled her nipple between his thumb and forefinger, while his other hand stroked her into coming. Her hips raised and twitched and she moaned filthy words under her breath. Painfully hard, Blaine kissed up to her ear again.

"I dare you," he said, and she drenched his hand as her orgasm shook through her.

He released her and eased his shorts down. Selena turned over and bent her head over his cock. She took him in her mouth, licking around him. Now it was his turn to grip her hair and gasp out at the ocean. As she bobbed her head up and down his shaft, he fought not to come instantly. He wanted to enjoy her sweet attention and the way she sucked on him hard and slow.

"Fuck," he groaned out. The rhythm of her mouth on him made it impossible for him to keep it together. It felt too good. Too exciting. Too much. He bit his lip from roaring out his pleasure. "Oh, sweetheart. Oh, baby. You're incredible."

She chuckled and his eyes slammed shut. He licked his fingers, tasting her and that was it. He came in great shudders. Selena took all of it and kissed the tip of his cock when she was done. Handing him his water bottle, she smiled at him. "You all right?"

"Huh?" he said dazedly and let her button him back up.

After fixing her clothes, she took a long drink from her water bottle and cuddled up next to him. "I like the view, but I've got to say your bed's a lot more comfortable."

"You're the one who wanted to get me out of my comfort zone," he said, stroking her hair.

"I didn't think I'd wind up with road rash from it." She showed him a scrape on her hand.

Blaine kissed it. "I'm sorry."

"Don't be. Are you ready to head back? My back will be sore if we sit up here any longer."

"Sure," he said. "Let me go down first?"

"Why? So you can catch me when I fall?"

"No, so I don't land on you when I do." He was only half joking. Standing up, he made a show of bending to pick up the backpack, but he was really testing his knees. So far, so good. Down had to be easier than up, right? Keeping the rope that some kind soul had tied off to one of the rocks in ready reach, Blaine began the careful trek down.

Up had been easier because he could see where he was going. But through hugging the wall and ignoring the shooting pain in his leg, he managed to get his feet back on the ground. He stood close to help Selena, but wound up being distracted by her ass as she came down. She had no problem. They held hands and took it slow back up the path to the motorbikes, but by the time they reached the top, Blaine felt dizzy. He sat on his bike and finished the water bottle while Selena called for Uncle Rollo so he'd be waiting for them.

The feeling hadn't quite passed when they started up, but he kept it slow and steady. By the time they got to Uncle Rollo, he had a blinding headache. He had never been so happy to slide into the backseat of an air-conditioned car.

"You don't happen to have any ibuprofen in that magic backpack do you?"

"Never leave home without it," she said, digging into it. She handed him two tablets and the rest of his water. "You okay?"

"Headache," he said, closing his eyes. Leg ache. His back wasn't too happy with him and all of a sudden, he was exhausted. The next thing he knew they were back at the Maui Wellness Resort and Selena was shaking him awake.

He blinked and sat up. "That was quick." After reaching into his pocket, he tipped Uncle Rollo a hundred. "I appreciated the motorbikes. They were a lifesaver."

"No problem, *brah*. If you need me, just call." He handed both of them his business cards.

Selena was out of the car before Blaine could get out and open her door. He was moving slowly, but his aches and pains had eased slightly.

"You need some help?" she asked him.

"I think I need a day off. I'm going to have Mikelina cancel my activities tomorrow and just spend the day relaxing in bed. I might go in the hot tub if I'm feeling adventurous."

"I'll let her know, Mr. Stephens," she said with a fake bright smile. Then she nodded to him and walked away.

What the hell? Why so formal?

"Did you enjoy Pe'ahi, Mr. Stephens?" Titus Dukes said from his left.

Shit. He hadn't seen him standing there. How

much had he seen? Blaine was pretty sure he hadn't had his arm around Selena.

"Good. Tiring. I might have pushed myself a bit."

"We can move your sunrise meditation to a sunset one tomorrow?"

"Sure," Blaine said moving toward the elevators. He couldn't care less about his schedule tomorrow. He was having a hard time keeping his eyes open. Stifling a yawn, he was glad to see that Titus had faded back under whatever rock he crawled out from under. All he wanted to do was face-plant on his bed for a quick nap and then take a nice long shower to get all the kinks out of his muscles.

Maybe he should see if Keoni and Malia did house calls.

CHAPTER FOURTEEN

SELENA WALKED UP to the bedroom when Blaine didn't answer her when she came in. He was sleeping deeply and peacefully. She covered him up with a light quilt and let him sleep. Since she had already bought all the ingredients, she made her *furikake* seasoning and set it aside. Then she prepared the ahi tuna in bite-size chunks and made the rice. By the time everything was done, Blaine was still out cold.

He needed his sleep, so she put plastic wrap over the poke bowls and set them in the fridge. They'd make a nice light lunch. After shutting off all the lights, she smiled wistfully up the stairs and let herself out. She knew Blaine wouldn't mind if she crawled into bed next to him, but she didn't want to disturb his rest. His body had finally forced him into taking what it needed. Selena guessed it started with the good food and exercise and now sleep was the next thing Blaine required.

Titus was waiting by the elevator and looked at his phone when she came out. Had he been waiting for her? Maybe it was a good thing Blaine was tuckered out.

"Did Mr. Stephens like his Wagyu beef?" Titus made a face and shuddered.

"Yes." Selena figured the best lies were the shortest ones. And it wasn't really a lie. He was going to enjoy it for tomorrow night's dinner instead.

"Did he seem sick to you?"

She shook her head. "Tired, maybe."

"I hope that's all it is. I wish he hadn't ordered the steak tonight."

"I'm going to give him my ahi poke tomorrow for lunch."

Titus brightened. "That's a good idea. A test drive for Friday night."

"When is Chef Koslov arriving?" So she could avoid him like the plague.

"He's arriving that morning and leaving Sunday. We're hoping to hire him to do cooking classes for our guests who are interested in learning how to eat healthy."

Reason number one thousand and one that she would never work here.

"Where were you today?"

"Why?" she asked. It was none of his business. He saw her leave Blaine's penthouse after breakfast. Blaine wasn't on property for lunch, so she didn't have any duties as far as Titus was concerned.

"I was looking for you. I thought we could go paddleboarding."

Eek! "I went to see some friends Upcountry." Another lie—sort of. Blaine was a friend. And they had been Upcountry.

"Some other time," he said.

She should really shoot him down and tell him that there wasn't a chance in hell of that happening, but she didn't want him to get offended. And no matter how nicely she said it, she knew Titus didn't take rejection well. Maybe she could drag Mikelina with her. "Sure," she said and pretended to yawn. "I should get to bed early. Have a good night."

Her skin crawled as she felt his gaze on her as she walked away.

The next morning, she let herself in to make Blaine his breakfast. This time, she could hear him snoring from all the way downstairs. After heading right to the kitchen, she started the coffee. She was cubing pineapple and mangos when he stumbled in fresh out of the shower, wearing nothing but a towel.

"I overslept," he said groggily.

"You needed it."

"What day is it?" Blaine stretched.

She admired the view. He had a great body. "Thursday morning. You had a decent night's sleep."

"No wonder I feel like Rip Van Winkle. Can you hook me up?" He tapped his vein.

"Coffee or the internet?"

"Both, but I can get my own coffee."

She let him pour his own cup while she set up her phone for a hot spot. "One hour."

"Yes, ma'am," he said sitting at the table.

She placed a bowl of yogurt topped with fruit and nuts in front of him.

He eyed it. "That's it?"

"Well, you did miss dinner last night. What would you like?"

"An omelet?" Blaine asked hopefully.

"Just cheese?"

"Can I have Spam in it?"

"No." Selena resisted the urge to hit him with the spatula.

"It's the national meat."

"Calling it meat is a stretch."

"It's canned ham. What's wrong with that?"

"So many, many, things."

"Fine," Blaine groaned. "How about toast and bacon?"

"That I can do. Do you want a glass of juice?"

"I can do that." He went to get up, but she waved him down.

"Sit. This is part of my job."

She brought him a glass of pog, but he didn't even look up from the screen. As she prepared his breakfast, she could hear him tapping on the keys and muttering under his breath.

"How are things in Detroit?" she asked, placing the food he requested in front of him.

"Shitty."

"Aren't you glad you're all the way over here?" She took his empty yogurt bowl and refilled his coffee.

"Thanks," he said absently.

She brought her own yogurt bowl and sat at the table with him. "Mikelina left your helicopter ride on the schedule for today. Since you requested the open-door ride, they book up fast and she wasn't sure she could rebook you."

"What time is the flight?" Blaine asked, digging into the omelet without looking up from his screen.

"Three-thirty. It's ninety minutes."

"Are you going with me?"

"You're solo on this one, sorry." She smiled and drank her coffee.

"Are you afraid of heights?"

"I like my helicopters with doors on them."

"We could switch it," he said.

She wondered if he was even tasting the omelet. He ate it fast, glaring at the computer screen.

"No, this is your vacation. It's going to be amazing. Make sure you take your phone. You'll be able to get some great pictures. Just don't drop it." She shuddered.

"I always wanted to fly a helicopter. Do you think they'll let me take the stick?"

"Absolutely not."

"Shucks," he said, winking at her.

"I'm really proud of you for agreeing to switch

the sunrise meditation for the sunset. It's gorgeous on the beach and very peaceful."

"Are you at least going with me to that?"

"I'll fall asleep." She laughed. "I was with Mikelina the last time I went, and she had to elbow me because I started snoring."

"Dinner then?"

"Absolutely. How does steak *frites* sound?"

"Perfect as long as *frites* is a fancy way to say potato."

"It is. And for lunch, you get the poke I made us for dinner last night."

"I bet your poke is okay," he said rhyming the words.

When she just rolled her eyes at him, he poked her. "You could have pokayed me last night."

"I don't think you would have felt it if I had."

"Can I poke you now?" He closed the laptop and held out his hand.

"You don't have anything scheduled to this afternoon." Selena stood up and took his hand.

"That's what you think. I've got plenty of plans and they all revolve around you naked."

"What a coincidence," she said, draping her chef's jacket over her chair. "My plans for this morning have you naked, as well."

"Outstanding." He dropped the towel. But instead of pulling her upstairs, he brought her out on the large balcony.

"I thought you'd have had enough of the great outdoors from yesterday."

He dragged a large air mattress out from the side of the balcony and flopped it down by the hot tub.

"Mikelina is keeping secrets from me," Selena said.

Blaine took a folded cotton bedspread from one of the lounge chairs and spread it on the mattress. "Still got those condoms in your purse?" He lay down on the air mattress and started to stroke himself.

Selena couldn't look away. His eyes were staring at her with such lust while he rubbed his cock, it was clear that he was thinking of her.

"Like what you see?"

She couldn't speak, so she just nodded.

"Take off your clothes and come join me." He patted the spot next to him.

"I'll just go get the condoms." She backed up and stumbled into the door.

"Careful."

After pressing her hands to her hot cheeks, Selena grabbed a condom from her backpack and hurried back. Blaine was still lazily stroking himself. "I want to see those gorgeous tits of yours."

She pulled off her shirt and unhooked her bikini top. Tossing it on the chair, she walked slowly to him peeling off her shorts and panties. Kicking them clear, she went to lie next to him.

"Not yet," he said. "Come here. I want to taste you." He moved so she was straddling his face.

"Oh," she said, lolling her head back as he fitted his mouth between her thighs. She couldn't help rocking on him as his tongue penetrated her. Blaine gripped her hips and encouraged her to move as he licked her fast. She felt wicked and decadent, so she reached around and took his cock in her hand. It was clumsy, but she was too busy gasping and sighing as his talented mouth brought her to the edge.

Blaine lifted her off him. "Get the condom."

She scrambled for it, desperate to have him continue licking her to orgasm. As soon as her fingers grabbed it, he pulled her back. "Put it on me."

And then he went back to tonguing her. She managed to slip it all the way on him on the third try. The scrape of his beard against her sensitive parts was her undoing and she shook as she came. Before she could take a breath, he had moved her down and encouraged her to sit on his cock instead of his face.

Selena took all of him in, greedily.

Blaine groaned and she savored the sound as she bounced on him. His hands were all over her body, pinching her nipples, gripping her ass, massaging her breasts. Selena loved the thickness of him as the friction built another wave of pleasure that threatened to crash over her as if they were in the middle of Pe'ahi instead of down country.

"Selena," he cried out, fingers digging into her hips as he thrust up into her.

Steadying herself on his chest, she dangled her breasts in his face until he sucked on her nipples. She leaned over so far, he almost slipped out. But then he surged up and she was flat on her back. Wrapping her arms around his head, she reached up to kiss him. He made love to her fast and hard. She could barely tell when one orgasm started and the other finished. All she knew was she could kiss him forever. Breathing was overrated. Boneless, she sighed and hooked her legs around his waist. Each thrust of his powerful body sent her into overdrive, quivering and crying out his name.

When his entire body stiffened, she held him tight as the last strokes of his orgasm shook through them both. They lay there panting and kissing, not ready to let go of each other just yet.

After their breathing came back to normal, Blaine said, "Let's take this upstairs until lunch. Otherwise I'm going to have to meditate through an uncomfortable sunburn."

Selena reluctantly rolled out of bed when both their stomachs grumbled.

"I guess that's my cue."

"Stay," he said, with a sleepy half smile.

She hopped into the shower and then padded naked downstairs while Blaine lay on the rumpled bed with his arm over his eyes. She retrieved her change of clothes from her backpack and after wiggling back into her tennis shoes, she went into the kitchen to see how her ahi poke survived the night.

It looked good and she set it on the counter to

take the chill of the refrigerator off. She dumped the old coffee and made a fresh pot. After bringing the plates to the table, she smiled as she saw Blaine coming down the stairs, again freshly showered and wearing a towel around his waist.

"Déjà vu," she said.

"This is the best *Groundhog Day* ever," he said, sweeping her in his arms for a kiss.

"What do you think?" Selena gestured to the pretty plated ahi and vegetable dish.

"Looks great. Is this the dish you're going to serve to Chef Dickhead?"

Selena didn't know why she was nervous about having him try it. He sat down on the chair and smiled up at her. "Can you turn on the hot spot?"

Really? That was his first thought? She sighed. Of course it was. Grabbing her phone, she turned it on as he was reaching for his laptop. It really was rude to be on the computer or a phone while they were eating, but she had already set the precedent and it didn't seem like an argument she was going to win anyway.

"I made you a light lunch because you're going to have a heavy dinner."

"Can't wait for the steak *frites*." He rubbed his hands together and accepted the cup of coffee she offered him.

She also set a pitcher of iced tea on the table and poured them each a glass while he booted up his computer.

"So what's in this anyway?" Blaine said, poking around with his fork. "Or do I really not want to know?"

Forcing down a thread of annoyance, Selena pointed with her fork at each of the ingredients. "Ahi tuna, edamame, onion, seaweed—"

"Wait, what? Like that stuff that floats around out there." He pointed toward the window.

"Yes and no. I tossed it with sesame seeds, lemon juice and rice vinegar."

He poked at it suspiciously.

"Avocado," she continued on.

"That's a lot of green."

She frowned at the bowl. "Do you think?" Presentation was everything. She bit her lip. The edamame, seaweed, and avocado did tend to overshadow the red tuna.

"I'm sure it's good." He speared a piece of tuna and chewed.

"Well?"

"Hands above the gas station."

Selena touched the twitching muscle under her eye.

"I'm kidding. Relax. It's fresh and tasty. I'm not a regular eater of this stuff, but it's a nice simple dish."

Simple. She leaned back in her chair. He was right. There wasn't any skill in this dish, just the blend of flavors that any chef familiar with the cuisine could do. She held a hand to her throat. She needed to make this better.

Blaine didn't seem to notice as he ate it with one hand and scanned his laptop with another. If she couldn't distract him with her dish, she didn't have a chance in hell of impressing Anton.

She tasted her food. Blaine had hit it on the head. Too much green to be visibly appealing, but still fresh and simple.

She wanted to bang her head against the table. It was a good thing she had tried this out on him first. After taking out her journal, she skimmed some of the new menu item ideas she had jotted down for her restaurant. Were they too simplistic too?

You have little talent for originality.

Flinching as if she had felt the snap of the dish towel that had accompanied that zinger, Selena's fingers gripped her pencil so hard she almost snapped it.

"How was the helicopter ride?" Selena asked him. She had stayed in the penthouse because she could pace and think better up here. Not to mention his kitchen made a better test kitchen, especially after she and Mikelina had a glass of iced tea on the balcony and planned a few menus to wow Anton with tomorrow.

"Radical," he said, giving her the shaka. The wraparound mirrored sunglasses and shark necklace that Mikelina had gotten for him made him look like a surfer dude.

"How does dinner at seven sound?"

"Awesome!" He said in a cosmic breathy voice as he shot her double shakas.

"I will bop you on the head with a wooden spoon if you don't knock that crap out."

"Kinky," he said in his normal voice and tossed the sunglasses on the table. "Can you set me up on the internet?"

That was their deal. Selena thought that by giving Blaine access to the internet, it would be like it was in the cybercafe—they'd sit down next to each other, flirt a little bit, he'd play around for a little while and then he'd go back to rest and relaxation. But it was entirely different. It was like he became a different person when he plugged in. She turned on the hot spot while she went to cook, like she usually did.

"My day was productive." *Not that you asked*, she added silently.

"Oh yeah?" he said, as he fired up his computer.

"I spent the day figuring out what I was going to make for Anton."

"I thought you were going with the poke?"

"No, you're right. It's too green and simple."

That got his attention. "I didn't say that." He stared at her, concerned. "I'm not a sushi guy, but it tasted great to me. What does Titus say?"

"He's vegan. No fish, no dairy, no cheese."

"That's nuts."

"He can eat those, but he won't eat honey."

Blaine shook his head. "To each, their own, I guess. What did you decide to make?"

"I'm going back and forth on whether just to doctor up the ahi bowls or try something new."

"I'm sure whatever you make will be delicious and he'll be lucky to have it."

"I was going to do an octopus poke."

"I'm not eating that." Blaine said.

She looked at him smugly. "Your palate isn't ready for that yet."

He muttered something that sounded strangely like a prayer. She left him to the computer and went to make him his steak-and-potatoes dish that he'd been craving all week. A good meal didn't have to be fancy, she thought as she seasoned the steak and set it on the grill. It was the little touches that elevated it. Like the fresh chives she snipped into the sour cream or the light rub she put on the steak. Or in the case of her poke, the soy sauce, sesame oil and onion. Anton always did hate her sauces. Maybe she would fiddle with that and add some heat. A spicy Japanese *toban-djan* sauce might do the trick.

That didn't solve her too-green problem, though. She liked the edamame for the crunch and the avocado for the creaminess. Although, the red and green could be plated like a wreath. She could keep all her ingredients, just make it more Christmas-like. That would completely work. She went out to tell Blaine, but he was muttering into his computer again.

An hour later when she came out with the steak and oven-baked potato fries, he didn't even look up.

He just grabbed his fork and knife and started shoveling food in.

"Blaine?"

"Yeah," he said, not looking up from his computer.

"Do you want to have dinner together?"

"Yeah."

But he didn't look up from the computer and his plate was in his lap.

Selena got a glimpse of the man he was at home, and it wasn't the exciting vacationing Blaine that she had been attracted to. This was what Detroit Blaine looked like. She preferred Maui Blaine, even with the dumb sunglasses and shark necklace. This was definitely not healthy.

"I'm going to shut down the hot spot."

His head went up. "No. Not yet."

"Blaine, the goal of this was not for you to cram eight hours of work into the one hour that you got the internet."

"They're changing my camera program around, and they're getting it all wrong."

"And what do you think they're going to do when they find out that you're reviewing their code instead of decompressing?"

"See, that's the brilliance of my plan," he said. "I'm directing one of the interns to pass along all my comments as if they come from him."

"Is that even ethical?" she asked.

"Probably not. He's a smart kid. Ethics Schmethics. The way I figure it is I'm showing him what the errors are, and he's just passing along information. He gets to take the credit and get extra training in how to spot errors."

"That's between you and human resources. Time's up." She reached for her phone.

"Five more minutes?"

She sighed. "It's like I'm babysitting my nephews."

He grinned up at her. "Touché. But I really do need five minutes just to send this one email."

Giving up, she waved her hand but went into the kitchen to start the timer. She debated eating standing up in the kitchen, but decided that was passive-aggressive. This was partly her fault anyway.

CHAPTER FIFTEEN

BLAINE THOUGHT THAT ukulele lessons were probably the lamest thing he's ever heard of, and this was after he almost broke his nose falling face-first into the sand after meditation last night. He wasn't looking forward to two hours of playing a miniature guitar, but a deal was a deal. Selena gave him the internet time. He'd give her the relaxation time. He wouldn't have minded making a fool of himself if she was sitting next to him. He'd gladly strum her a corny love song.

Selena wasn't going to be around much today because she wanted everything to be perfect for that jackass she used to work for. She had set him up with breakfast and lunch and said that she'd see him for dinner. Then with a quick kiss goodbye, she was out the door. He knew the resentment he was feeling was ridiculous. If they were going to try a long-distance relationship, he'd have to get used to the idea of never seeing her.

Of course, if he hadn't spent so much time working out the coding errors in the new camera program, they could have enjoyed some more time together. He did feel guilty about that. But they needed that camera to be perfect for the expo in France in February. His company was counting on the preorders from that show to stay in business. Blaine really thought that they had nailed it this time. Merry Christmas to Stephens-Miller!

So he sat down on a beach blanket cross-legged with a bunch of the other guests. Their ages ran from eight to eighty. Although there were a couple of cute women in bikinis, the only woman he was interested in was Selena. She looked sexier in her chef's jacket than these girls did in their colorful flowered bikinis. The group was under a shaded pavilion. This one, however, was open on all four sides. Blaine could hear the ocean and smell the coconut suntan lotion that reminded him of Selena. He considered flagging down a waiter for a piña colada, but it just wasn't the same without the rum.

"Aloha!" a petite Hawaiian woman said.

"Aloha," they parroted back.

"I'm Auntie Freda. And I'm going to teach you how to play the ukulele." She and a helper who could have been her grandson passed out the instrument to everyone. "I bet you don't know that all of you already know how to play the ukulele. Go on," she encouraged. "Give it a try. Those are your instruments. You get to keep these."

For the next couple of minutes, the class plucked

and strummed at the strings. His family must've paid a fortune for this trip. Well, if that was the case, he was going to learn how to play a happy Hawaiian Christmas song. And when he got home, he would treat all of them to a solo concert with his positive attitude and new energy.

Sure enough Auntie Freda said, "Today, we're going to learn '*Mele Kalikimaka*,' the Hawaiian Christmas song made famous by my boyfriend Bing Crosby."

Blaine dug into learning the chords, and a strange thing happened. As he concentrated on getting the notes right, strumming the ukulele felt relaxing. He had a moment to grin at a picture of himself sitting at his desk in Detroit with his feet up on the desk playing the ukulele. As far as stress-relieving exercises go, this beat the hell out of yoga.

It wasn't as exciting as jumping off Black Rock or having dynamite sex on a rock while the ocean raged around you. But it was nice, and he had to remember to thank Selena, Mikelina and his family for the opportunity to broaden his horizons. After his first lesson, Blaine was feeling pretty good about himself. He stood up and stretched, and the thought about going for a quick dip in the ocean sounded like a good idea. He'd have to bring the ukulele back to his room and get changed into his bathing suit, but it wasn't a far walk. Still strumming the ukulele, he headed back in that direction when one of the older gentlemen in the class stopped him.

"Excuse me. You're Blaine Stephens, aren't you?"

Blaine stopped playing. "Yeah? Do I know you?"

"No, but I'm a reporter."

"No comment." Blaine grimaced.

The reporter chuckled. "Yeah, I get that a lot."

"I suppose you saw me on that disastrous YouTube video." Blaine took a deep breath to issue the apology that their public relations firm made him memorize.

"How could I?" the reporter said. "You've been here all morning." The man pulled his phone out of his pocket and tapped. He showed him a video starting up.

"How do you get cell service?" Blaine asked.

"I'm staying at the Hyatt." He pointed. "High speed is thirty bucks a day. Can you believe that shit?"

"Totally worth it. I'm staying at the Maui Wellness Center. They put a cell blocker on my phone. I can't get any service."

"So you don't know," the reporter said.

"Know what?" Blaine asked, frowning as the video came up and he recognized his brother and Paul standing next to their prototype on the track they built in back of the factory. The actual fucking car. This was not a computer simulation and from what he could tell, this was the car they were bringing to Paris.

Paul smiled for the camera and held up the controls.

"No. You idiot. No."

In the video, Paul activated the drive command and the car took off around the track. It took the first turn well. Blaine felt a cold sweat form in the base of his back.

"Slow the thing down," Blaine bit out.

It whipped around the second turn, fishtailing a bit.

"What the hell is he doing?"

The third turn was the car's undoing. It had not backed off on the acceleration. It spun out of control and flipped over a half a dozen times while technicians ran for cover.

"I'm going to kill him," Blaine muttered.

"Can I quote you on that?"

Blaine gripped the neck of the ukulele in his hand and turned menacingly to the man when he got tackled to the ground from something behind him. He tried to wrestle up, but the goon who held him was hella strong and outweighed him by a good hundred pounds.

"What the hell? Get off me," Blaine said, struggling.

"All right, that's enough," Titus said to the reporter, who was fumbling with his phone to take a picture. "Unless you'd like to surrender your phone, I suggest you leave now without any pictures."

"You can't stop me. I can take as many pictures as I want."

"Let me up," Blaine gritted and he was hauled to his feet, but he was still in some kind of martial arts hold that didn't allow him to wiggle or power his way out.

"You are now on private property and I have my guest's privacy to consider."

"Fine." The reporter stormed away.

"Let's get him under cover of the trees and bushes so they can't get him with a zoom lens," Titus said. "Right this way, Mr. Stephens."

"Let me go," he gritted out.

"As soon as you're back safe and sound in the center."

Blaine wasn't sure how safe or sound any of them was going to be when the big guy holding him let go. The three of them squeezed into the elevator and then Titus keyed it so it whisked up to the penthouse. He suddenly stopped struggling. What if Selena was still there? What if she had left her things in plain sight? He forced himself to calm down.

"I'm all right now," he said, as the elevator doors opened.

The security guard let him go. "No hard feelings, *brah*," he said.

"None taken." The guy was a good head and shoulders taller than he was and almost twice as wide. No wonder they barely fit into the elevator.

"I think I'm going to take a nap and…meditate," Blaine said, blocking Titus from coming in any farther.

"That seems like a good idea, Mr. Stephens."

Titus handed him back his ukulele and then he and the security guard were gone.

Whirling around the room, Blaine grabbed his laptop. He was going to find Uncle Rollo and they were going to drive to a cell phone store, and he was going to buy a new one with a long-minute plan so he could scream at his brother. Then he was going to go to the Hyatt and book a room where he'd gladly pay a million dollars a day for internet so he could straighten this mess out. He should have done that at the beginning of the week. Instead, he let himself get bogged down with bullshit. He was so angry he could scream. Paul was lucky he was over four thousand miles away.

As he was searching for his power cord, he noticed that Selena left her purse here. Her notebook and her phone were next to it. She must have been distracted about her meeting with Chef Dickhead.

He grabbed her phone and swiped it open, mimicking the pattern he'd seen her use to unlock it. Jackpot! He dialed his brother's phone and got his secretary. "Get my brother on the phone, please."

CHAPTER SIXTEEN

MIKELINA WALKED WITH Selena up to the suite where Anton was staying for moral support. "Are you sure you're ready for this?"

"Of course," Selena scoffed. *Of course not.* She was braced to experience a torrent of abuse. She wished she didn't feel so sick to her stomach about it.

"You want me to stick around?" Mikelina asked.

"No, that's all right. I'll call you when it's all over."

"No matter what happens, Selena, you are an amazing chef. You've cooked for princes, movie stars, musicians, politicians and everyone in between. No one—*no one*—has ever complained about what you've served them."

"I know that, and you know that, but Anton Koslov doesn't know that."

"He doesn't matter." Mikelina hugged her. "You are enough."

"I got this." Speak it until you believe it.

Mikelina nodded and stepped back.

Selena straightened her shoulders and after a slight knock, walked in. Anton and a woman half his age looked up as she entered the dining area.

"Good evening, my name is Selena and I'll be your chef for tonight."

There was a hint of recognition in Anton's eyes, but then he dismissed her. Anton and his guest sat at what the wellness center called a community table. They were on one side and she, the chef, was on the other. They would watch her prepare their meal in front of them.

Because that wasn't gut-clenching terrifying.

"I'll be back momentarily to prepare the Maui Wellness Center's Christmas Poke."

"Very well. You don't need to speak with us to do that, do you?"

"No, chef," she said, with forced serenity.

His eyes narrowed on her again, but he didn't say anything.

She went into the refrigerator and pulled out the sushi-grade ahi and the rest of her ingredients. Before she got started Selena wanted to talk to Blaine, just to hear his voice. But she realized in her haste to get all the ingredients here, she didn't have her purse on her. She must have left it in his penthouse.

Get in. Make the Meal. Serve. Get out.

Blaine had spoiled her by breaking up her routine and allowing her to eat with him and then hang out and having fun afterward. This wasn't fun. This was a job. She was going to prove to Anton once and for all that she wasn't the hot mess in the kitchen that he thought she was.

She'd taken care to buy only the freshest ingredients of the highest quality. Her knives were sharpened. She was ready to face the dragon.

It took her two trips from the kitchen back to the table because she didn't want to risk juggling things and having them fall to the floor. One last trip to wash her hands and grab her knives and she entered the dining room like she was on one of the television food cook-offs.

Mikelina had already asked the housekeepers to set their plates out so all Selena had to do was serve Anton and his guest from the table. She turned on the mini burner so she could warm up their sake and also the rice. No one wanted to sit through rice being boiled, so Selena had made it this afternoon and seasoned it with her *furikake* flakes.

Earlier, she had also set up the cushioned mat that Blaine had given her in front of the table. It was a comfort to not have to worry about her back complaining while she expertly crosscut the tuna. After making quick work of the fish that was caught this morning, she put the ahi in a large serving bowl with her spicy Japanese sauce to marinate while she worked on the rest of the meal. She had soaked her Maui onion in water and rice wine vinegar so the coarse chop didn't make anyone cry and it would sweeten the taste of it. She added the onion to the fish and gave the mixture a quick stir.

When the sake was ready, she poured them each a small cupful and left the decanter out so they could help themselves to more. Risking a glance at Anton, she saw he was more interested in his phone than in what she was doing. His friend, however, watched her avidly. Selena gave her a small smile. She couldn't imagine what it would be like to date him and the woman had her deepest sympathies.

In another bowl, Selena dressed the seaweed with her oils and seasonings, then added a handful of scallions that she quick chopped. With a toss, she used her tongs to form wreaths on their plates. The avocados were next. Selena expertly pitted them and then used a special cutter to scoop each side into equal pieces, which she fanned out like the wreath's bow. Turning the ahi and onion mixture over until it was coated completely in the *toban djan,* she scooped it on the plates in the center of the seaweed wreath. She lightly salted the edamame and then added that to the dish, as well. She topped it with crushed macadamia nuts and then pushed the plates toward Anton and his guest.

"Bon appétit," she said.

"That will be all." Anton dismissed her with a wave.

She gathered up her cooking supplies and returned to the kitchen. Poking her head out, she watched their reaction to her meal. The woman dug in with gusto and made happy noises. Anton poked one ahi cube into his mouth and chewed slowly and contemplatively.

Packing her bag, she wondered what he thought. As she was leaving, she stopped briefly at the table. "Chef Leif Tanaka will be here momentarily to make you his island-famous malasadas." She looked at the young woman. "You're in for a treat."

"Thank you," she said.

"Please leave us," Anton said.

Out of habit, she headed toward the door at the command in his voice. But then she remembered he wasn't her boss, and this wasn't his kitchen. After opening the door, she turned back one last time.

"Is everything to your liking?" she asked.

"It's delicious," his companion said.

"Yes, yes. It's fine. Now please go away."

Selena wasn't sure how to take that, but in the past, he had thrown the food at her and then smashed the dish on the floor to express his displeasure at one of her meals. So she guessed he liked the poke.

With one final glance as the door was closing behind her, Selena saw that Anton had cleared his plate and was sipping on his sake while listening avidly to his companion. Selena left in a hurry wondering if love had mellowed Anton out or if he was only that much of a bastard in his own kitchen.

She did a little dance and a fist pump. She gave Leif a shaka as she passed him and immediately headed up to the penthouse to see Blaine. Except the privacy lock was activated. She couldn't get up.

What the heck?

She couldn't even call Mikelina and give her a

heads-up because her phone was up in the penthouse. And she didn't want to risk Titus finding out she didn't have her phone by using the lobby phone. And without her purse, she couldn't go back to her apartment and put her things away. Annoyed, she walked around the compound to see if she could find a friendly face who would let her use their phone.

And of course, she ran straight into Titus.

"How did everything go?"

"Great," she said. "Leif is in there now."

"I'm glad I ran into you." He sighed and looked around. "I don't like doing this. Do you want to go somewhere more private?"

"No," she said. She definitely did not.

"I realize you were nervous about cooking for Chef Koslov, but your phone has been draining our resources all day with all the phone calls and internet."

"Is that right," she said between her teeth. "I had no idea. I'm so sorry. It won't happen again."

"I know it won't. It's never happened before. I just wanted to make you aware of it so that it doesn't happen again."

"Thank you for telling me." She forced a smile.

"But if it makes you feel better, if we can land Chef Koslov it will all have been worth it."

"Definitely," she said.

"Where are you heading off to now?"

"Well, I was going to go cook for Mr. Stephens,

but he has his privacy lock on and I'm not sure if I want to disturb him."

"That's a good idea. Let me do it. He's already mad at me."

Intrigued, Selena followed him over to the front desk. "Why is he angry at you?"

"Long story. But if I don't like his attitude, you're not going up there alone."

"What? Why?"

Titus held up a finger. "Mr. Stephens, I'm so sorry to bother you, but Selena is here with me. Do you require her to cook for you tonight?... Are you sure you're up for the intrusion?... Very well." Titus hung up. "He seems better. But if he even raises his voice to you, I want you to come right down."

"What happened?" Selena said.

"Mr. Stephens had an altercation on the beach today. I can't say more as it would be a breach of confidentiality. Please don't mention it to him. And whatever you do, please don't rile up his temper."

"Okay," she said slowly.

"Call me when you're done," Titus said.

None of this made sense. But this time when she went to call the elevator it came right down for her and shot her up to the penthouse.

It shouldn't surprise her that he was on the computer and that her phone was sitting in the center of the table, plugged in. To his credit, he looked up when she walked in. "Sorry about the privacy lock."

"You need to get the hell off my phone and the

internet. I just caught hell from Titus for being on it all day."

"Sorry," he said, reaching for the phone.

She got to it before he did and shut down the hot spot. Scrolling through her outgoing calls, she saw they were all Detroit numbers. "What the hell happened today?"

He rubbed his hand over his face. "Later. How did everything go with Chef Dickhead?"

"It was strangely anticlimactic," she said.

"Is that good?" He stood up and came over to her. Blaine gave her a big hug. She hadn't realized how much she needed that hug.

"It is now." Selena buried her face in his neck, breathing in the scent of him.

"Have you eaten anything since breakfast?" he asked.

"No, I was too nervous to eat. Now, I'm like, what was I even worried about. I'm not even sure he remembered me. He didn't mention anything. You were right. He's just a jerk from my past. I'm light-years beyond him and his snide remarks."

"Good," he said. "We're going out to celebrate."

"Celebrate?"

"You faced off against your personal demon and came out victorious. I say that deserves a fancy dinner."

"There's only one problem with that," she said, reluctantly coming out of his embrace.

"What's that?" He kissed her sweetly and she swayed against him.

He really knew how to scramble her brains, but she liked it. Rubbing his shoulders, she broke off the kiss. "Titus is pacing the lobby waiting for me to come down because he's expecting you to explode like a grenade for some reason."

"Oh, that," he said, resting his forehead against hers.

"Come on," she said, leading him into the kitchen. "You can tell me about it while I make dinner."

"Can I at least help with dinner?"

"I'm not letting you anywhere near my knives until I know what's going on."

She wound up making a spaghetti dish with a light oil sauce and vegetarian meatballs. Blaine didn't dare make a comment. As they prepared dinner together, he told her everything that happened after his ukulele lesson.

"Is the car totaled?" she asked.

"It's spare parts at this point. Production is going to have to work overtime for us to still show it in February." He gave a shaky sigh. "It doesn't look good. Our competition is going to beat us to market if we don't have it at the expo. We're going to lose a lot of money."

"I'm so sorry," she said.

"That's why I was on your phone and the internet all day. I'm sorry. If I had known it was going to blow back on you, I would have gone to the Hyatt like I had planned. But I didn't want to waste the time."

"Were you able to accomplish anything?"

"Not as much as if I had been there in person."

"You deserve this vacation. You need to take care of you. It's just as important as the February expo."

"I can wait until after February. The car can't."

"Can you?" Selena handed him his bowl of pasta. "Maybe. Should you? No."

"I know you think I'm backsliding, but I'm not. You and I have a date to go zip-lining through the jungle tomorrow."

"I don't see how me screaming over a one-hundred-dred-and-fifty-foot drop is going to relax you."

"What can I say? I like to hear you scream." He took a deep breath. "Besides, depending on what I hear in the morning, I might be cutting my stay short."

"You can't," she said, clasping his hand.

"Offer still stands to come back to Detroit with me."

She laughed, but realized he was serious. Whoa. Selena didn't dare hope he meant that he wanted her as anything other than a chef with benefits.

"You were hired to be my chef, right? I'll fly you down."

Figures. "My contract says Maui," she said quietly.

"I'd like to continue to still see you," Blaine said. "Even if you're not my personal chef."

Wow.

"That's one heck of a long-distance relationship. Especially when I don't know where I'm going to be from week to week." She was stalling and she knew it. She wanted this. She didn't want whatever this was to end, but she wasn't sure they had enough to last being apart.

"Are you willing to try?" They held hands across the table as he looked deep in her eyes. She could see the affection and sincerity in them.

"Yes," she said simply. Of course, she had doubts but she wasn't going to jinx this.

CHAPTER SEVENTEEN

WHILE DRINKING HIS morning coffee with Selena, all Blaine wanted was to call his brother or get on the internet and check out what progress had been made in the past twelve hours. It didn't matter that it was a Saturday. It didn't matter about the time difference. It certainly didn't matter that they couldn't fix a car in less than twenty-four hours. He felt powerless, useless and it made him angry. But he recognized that being four thousand miles away in Maui with a beautiful woman by his side and an adventure of a lifetime ahead of him, that he just needed to let go.

"I figured we take a breakfast to go," Selena said. "I made spam, eggs and cheese on a toasted English muffin."

"You put spam in my eggs." He kissed her hard on the mouth. "You must love me."

The fiery blush in her cheeks, and the fact that she didn't correct him, warmed his heart. Maybe they didn't need to go zip-lining to have a fantastic adventure. He was about to suggest staying in bed all day when her phone rang.

Rolling her eyes, Selena picked up the phone. "Yes, Titus. I finished with Mr. Stephens's breakfast. Right now I'm at Whalers Village doing some shopping. I'm sorry, I've got plans for today. Maybe next time."

"That's sexual harassment," Blaine said. "You should tell your boss what's going on."

"It's nothing I can't handle. He doesn't ever cross the line. And I should be more firm with him and reject him. But he doesn't take rejection well. And I really don't want to deal with the little ways he could make my life a living hell. At least if he thinks he still has a chance, he won't pull the dick moves I've seen him pull on other people."

"That is illegal," Blaine said. "What the hell is your boss' name? I'll tell him."

"Just mind your business. Be thankful that he accepted that you calmed down and are no longer a rage machine, so he feels he has to linger downstairs to make sure that you don't Hulk Smash everyone you come in contact with."

"Blaine Smash." He slammed his fists on the table, making the coffee cups jump.

"The zip-line company provides us lunch. So, I'll just pack snacks and our water bottles."

"Okay, let me carry the backpack this time."

"Sure," she said.

She left the penthouse first, dressed in her chef

jacket. He hated that they had to hide their relationship from Titus. But he understood that when he went back to Detroit, she still had to deal with him. But hopefully not for a while. He didn't know where she'd be sent to next.

He didn't want to ruin their day, telling her that he had decided no matter what news he got he was going to go back home. He was going to miss her.

If she didn't want to stay the extra week in Maui, he'd make sure that she got home to Florida all right. Part of him wished that she could go home and spend Christmas with him. But after knowing each other only a week, it seemed a little premature to ask. Still, he knew he'd be thinking about her all during Christmas dinner, and probably would spend most of Christmas Eve night FaceTiming her, if she allowed it.

Selena wasn't waiting for him in the lobby, but he wasn't expecting her to, just in case Titus didn't buy the fact that she was in Whalers Village. Blaine headed down the strip where the van was picking them up to take them to the zip-lining tour in Makawao. Climbing into the air-conditioned van, he was happy to see that she was already there. He dropped down into the seat next to her and took out the brochure to look at the farm where they would be doing several zip lines.

He wished his phone wasn't blocked. He was determined not to ask Selena if he could use her phone to call his brother, but he was thinking about it. The only things that stopped him were that her hand felt good inside his, and that he didn't want to subject the other passengers in the van to the loud argument he was going to have with his brother if he hadn't done the things Blaine told him to do.

After forcing himself to put the sight of the spinning and demolished car out of his mind, he could still see it when he closed his eyes. It replayed in his mind over and over again. They had been able to salvage the engine. Most of the electronics had been smashed to smithereens and Paul Miller was given strict orders to remain out of Blaine's sight for the time being.

"Stop thinking about it," Selena said.

"What gave me away?" He smiled ruefully at her.

"All your muscles are locked. Your jaw is tense. And I swear you're grinding your teeth."

"I should've brought my ukulele."

"We can try meditating," she said.

"I'll just fall asleep."

"That might help out too. After all," she leaned in and gave him a lingering kiss. "We didn't get much sleep last night."

"You'll never hear me complain about that." Especially since after he left Maui, the sex would be few and far between.

He forced himself to admire the view outside the windows. Everything was green and blue. When he went back to Michigan, he was going to miss that almost as much as he missed Selena. Right now, everything there was gray, white and frigid. And indoors. Blaine's whole life was going to be indoors until February. That was why it was so important to him to enjoy this last weekend together. Even though he had another week before he had to get back, there was no way that he could survive without the internet and checking in on his company. He wouldn't put Selena through that. He didn't want to get her in trouble, but more important, she didn't deserve to have all of her good cooking and companionship go to waste by a surly bastard whose life couldn't begin with her until this car was either pronounced dead or they showed it at the February expo. In a lot of ways, it felt how she was with her Cordon Bleu dream.

"Now that you don't have Anton Koslov as a monkey on your back anymore, are you still going to Cordon Bleu?"

"It is a lot of money," she said. "I'm still thinking about it. It's been my plan for so long, doing anything else right now would feel rushed. I still have my contract for the next six months and that will give me some more time to think about it. Maybe I'll re-up my contract with Diamonte."

Blaine's hand clenched hers a little too hard.

"Ow, what was that for?"

"Sorry. I was hoping that after your contract, if you weren't going to Cordon Bleu, you might want to come to Detroit."

"Yeah, it's possible. But that's also six months away. I'm willing to try, and I want this to work. But

I don't want to move my whole life from Florida to Michigan if it's not long term."

"I get it. I don't like it, but I understand."

"This week has been easy."

"Easy? You've got a weird idea of easy."

"I mean to fall in love."

He brought her fingers up to his lips and kissed them. "Is that what this is?"

"It feels like it. But it's also hard to have a fight or a major disagreement or see the ugly side of things, when you're in paradise." She gestured with her hand at the pristine foliage outside the window.

"We have fun together," Blaine said. "We could have fun anywhere. It just happens to be prettier here than Detroit right now."

"I don't have anything against Detroit. I've never been there. I actually like snow. One of my favorite times as the chef was at a ski resort in Vail."

"Michigan isn't Vail," Blaine said. "There are a lot of things I think you'd like there. Museums, the Lions and the Tigers."

"No bears?"

"That's Chicago." He bumped her shoulder with his and stole another kiss.

"You forgot the most important thing that would be there. You."

He smiled. "Good answer."

When they got to the zip-lining company, the guides spent about an hour going through the safety regulations and explaining the course and what was expected of them. Blaine felt a little dorky in his helmet and harness, but he would never go without the safety equipment. The first zip line they went on was one of the shorter ones. They would get increasingly longer and faster, as they followed the trails. He loved the feeling of flying through the jungle. It was another thrill ride for his adrenaline-junkie personality. It was quick and fun, and he was hooting with laughter. Selena was screaming and laughing, as well. When they got off the line, they hugged and kissed.

"I love to see honeymooners," one of the guides said.

Blaine didn't bother to correct her, and it warmed his heart that neither did Selena. They walked to the next zip-line site. Blaine felt that twinge in his leg again and his chest felt tight, but he took a few deep breaths and he didn't think much of it. The next zip line had them careening over a large canyon and for a moment he did have one of those thoughts of what would happen if the rope broke.

It was a long way down. The thought made him think of the crash again. He could see his car hitting the third turn too fast and going airborne, rolling over, and over, and over again. He worked two long years on the car. He was there when they built it with sleek fenders. He designed the chassis, and had watched them paint it.

When they spray painted the logo on the hood, Blaine finally thought all his hard work was going to pay off. He had thought it was embarrassing when the video of the car had run over all the obstacles. It was beyond mortifying when the actual car failed in its first test run around the track. It should have never gotten up to the speeds that Paul had pushed it to.

Paul liked to show off. Paul didn't want to take things slow. Blaine was an impatient man. Paul made him look like the tortoise to his hare. Paul wanted to do everything in one test. Any scientist could tell you that couldn't be done. Any engineer would've known that can't be done. Paul should've known better. Again, his company, his car and his life's work were being jeopardized by Paul Miller's stupidity.

"Blaine, are you all right?" Selena said, holding on to his arm.

"Yeah, I'm fine." He realized he was still dangling from his harness on the zip line.

She helped him to unhook and they walked down the path to where the four-wheeler was waiting to take them to the next zip line.

"Sorry, I must've been daydreaming." His head was pounding. He slung his backpack and dug around for his water bottle. He took a long drink.

"Here, wipe your brow. You're sweating," Selena said, handing him a bandanna.

"Thanks. It's hot out here." He took a step forward and stumbled. "I'm all right," he said. "I'm just a little unsteady on my feet."

"Let's sit down for minute," Selena said.

"I'll sit on the four-wheeler," Blaine said and then

gave her a wink and reached out to hold her hand. He barely made it to the four-wheeler. His breath was coming in short pants. He felt just like when he was about to pass out in Detroit. It wasn't a heart attack, then. It wasn't one now. He repeated it, trying to stop himself from panicking.

"Selena," he started to say, and then as he stood up from the four-wheeler, his knees gave out under him and everything went black.

When Blaine came to, it hurt to open his eyes. He was lying on a cot in an air-conditioned room. He felt a pinch in his arm and saw he was hooked up to an IV. He must be at some type of infirmary. He hoped he hadn't banged his head. It didn't hurt anymore, but he was really tired. Selena was sitting in the chair and after a few minutes of listening, he realized with horror she was talking to his mother.

"He was doing really well, but then some idiot showed him the video of the car and it really set him back." Selena looked up and caught his eye.

He shook his head and put a finger to his lips.

"Blaine just woke up. I'll let you speak with him while I get the nurse." She handed him her phone and left the room.

Making a face at Selena, Blaine said with forced cheerfulness, "Hi, Mom, how did Selena get your number?"

"You used her phone to call your brother and she

tracked him down and your brother gave me her number."

"I'm fine."

"I know exactly how you are. Selena and I had a nice chat with your doctor. You're having stress related attacks. The whole reason we sent you to Maui was so you wouldn't have another incident."

"I didn't punch anyone," he said weakly.

"Not funny, Blaine."

"I'm working on it. Did Selena tell you I did yoga and too ukulele lessons? I'm trying." Blaine leaned his head back into the pillow.

His mother made a hmph sound. "I like her. You work fast."

"Mom." Blaine closed his eyes.

"She sent me some pictures of you. You look like you're having fun. She also showed me some pictures of the two of you. She's very pretty."

"Mom. I'm literally lying in a hospital bed."

"No, you're in the ranch's clinic in Makawao. You've got a saline drip in your arm, but they'll probably be in there shortly to take it out. Once you sign some papers promising you won't sue the pants off them, they'll probably let you go."

"I'm coming home Monday."

"That's a stupid idea."

"I can't stay here while Paul and Mitchell destroy everything I've worked for."

"It's a setback. Don't be a drama queen."

"Mom." Blaine just couldn't deal with her right now.

"You have another week in paradise before coming back to the mess. Enjoy it. Get to know your girlfriend better. Enjoy that she's cooking you three meals a day because once you're married that's going to stop."

"Mom." He sounded like a record skipping a beat.

"She's treating you right and there are people who care about your health. Please stay there another week. If not for you, do it to spend some more time with Selena."

Selena walked in with the doctor. "I've got to go, Mom. I'll see you soon."

They were out of there in a half hour. The ziplining company had an employee drive them back in their car so Blaine could recline the seat back.

"I'm sorry I screwed up our day," he said.

"You scared me."

"I'm sorry," he said.

Running her fingers through his hair, she leaned forward and kissed his forehead. "Promise me that you'll take it easy. Nothing but meditation and hot tubs for the next few days."

"You got it." He was feeling sleepy, so he drifted off feeling her soft touch on his head.

When they got to the wellness center, she put her arm around him and helped him to the elevator.

"What if Titus sees?" he asked.

"I don't care," she said.

He did, but the damage was done. They were in the elevator. He let her lead him up to bed, but she resisted when he tried to pull her down with him. "You need to rest. I'll be back tonight to make you dinner. How does eggplant parmesan sound?"

"It sounds perfect."

She brushed a kiss over his lips that left him wanting more. "Rest and we can revisit that kiss if you're feeling up to it later."

"Count on it," he said.

He was dimly aware of her leaving. He must have slept because a buzzing in his pants jolted him up in surprise. Reaching his hand in his pocket, he pulled out Selena's phone and saw it was his brother.

"What?" he snapped.

"Are you near your computer?"

He groaned. "No, what did you do now?"

"I think we figured it out. We figured it all out."

Blaine jumped to his feet and pounded down the stairs.

CHAPTER EIGHTEEN

WHEN SELENA COULDN'T find her cell phone, she didn't immediately panic. She must've left it upstairs in the backpack or maybe in the pocket of her chef jacket, which was currently stuffed in the bottom of her laundry duffel bag. She had been spending so much time at the penthouse, she was behind on her chores. While Blaine was resting from the zip line, she needed to do some laundry.

There was a knock on her door.

"Come in," she said, thinking it was Mikelina. She regretted her decision when Titus walked in.

"I've been calling you and you haven't been answering."

"I've been busy. What do you want?" Selena was getting tired of his keeping-tabs-on-her bullshit and she didn't care if she snapped at him. She had a hellish day worrying about Blaine.

"Yes, I've noticed how busy you've been with Mr. Stephens." He frowned and crossed his arms. "I shouldn't have to remind you that the Maui Wellness Center forbids fraternization with clients."

That was it. She didn't care how much of an ass he was going to be to her, she had been dying to set him straight for a long time. "I shouldn't have to remind you, that I'm a contractor and I do not work for you. I work for Kirk Diamonte. My job is to cook three meals a day for Mr. Stephens. And I've done that when the schedule required it. You have no reason to fault my work or ask me questions about my personal life. But now that you're here, what are you going on about?"

"You were in Makawao today with Mr. Stephens."

"So?" She pushed past him carrying her large duffel bag full of laundry and her detergent. "Out," she said with a jerk of her head.

Titus backed up, but she saw that he had two security guards with him. "What's going on?"

"When I was told that one of our guests was hurt off-site, I called to inform his emergency contact. Imagine my surprise when she said that his girlfriend—you—had already told her, and that she had spoken to her son already. That was your first mistake."

"It wasn't a mistake."

"But you couldn't stop breaking the rules, could you. I warned you about using the internet. But it's not you, is it?" Titus looked down at his iPad. "It says you're online right now." He picked up his phone and dialed. "Your phone is ringing, but I don't hear it."

"I must've misplaced it. It's probably back inside."

Selena didn't know why she was lying. They both knew exactly where her phone was.

"Your phone is being used as a hot spot."

That asshole. After promising her that he would rest and stay off the computer for the rest of the day, as soon as her back was turned, he used her distraction with the day's events to do what he wanted anyway.

"I can't have a contractor breaking the rules of the Maui Wellness Center and putting our guests at risk. Kirk agrees with me. He's waiting to have a similar discussion with you. Please pack your things and go. I'm shutting off all access now, so Mr. Stephens is out of luck. Both for overnight activities and for internet use. If you're not off the property in one hour, I'll call the police."

"I was hired by Mr. Stephens's—Blaine's family to be his personal chef," she said.

"You will be replaced."

She couldn't even call Kirk to tell her side of the story because Blaine had her phone. Maybe Mikelina could give her his number.

Titus stood outside her door while she packed and escorted her off the property flanked by the two security guards. It didn't take her long to pack up her things. She had two suitcases; her knives and her phone were upstairs with Blaine.

"I need to retrieve a few things from the penthouse."

"I'm sorry. You are no longer allowed in the guest rooms anymore."

"I have important things that I need for my job up there."

"Leave us a forwarding address and we'll make sure they get packed up and sent to you."

"No," she said and went toward the elevator.

Titus snapped his fingers and the two security guards blocked her.

They smiled at her apologetically. "Sorry. You have to do what he says."

"Fine." Her hands were shaking, and she was on the verge of tears.

In addition to wanting to chew out Blaine, she was terrified that she was going to lose her important knives, and that her bakeware would be damaged in the mail. She didn't want them shipped haphazardly. She wanted to take them with her, but there was nothing she could do with the two large guards flanking her as she dragged her suitcases through the lobby. She couldn't even call Blaine, because the wellness center wouldn't put her through.

She had to wait until she flagged down a taxi. "This is a crazy request," she said, "But can I borrow your phone to make a call? They kicked me out. They wouldn't even let me get my phone. They fired me."

"Don't cry, sister," the driver said and disconnected his phone from the charger.

First, she tried her phone, but it rang and rang and went to voice mail. It figured. He'd never answer her phone. But once he figured out he was cut off from

Wi-Fi, he might get curious enough to answer an unknown number.

She racked her brains for a few seconds trying to remember Mikelina's number. Selena was so used to just tapping on her name and having it automatically dial her number. But Mikelina had the same number ever since they went to school together, and Selena managed punch in the numbers.

"Please answer. Please answer. Please answer," she said.

"Who's this?"

Selena was relieved, even though it wasn't Mikelina. "Bastien, it's Selena. I got fired. I don't have my phone. I need help."

"Fired? Where are you?" he asked.

"I'm down the road from the center. Can I speak to Mikelina?"

"She's in the shower now, but let me tell her that you're holding and what happened."

"Where do you want to go?" the driver said.

"Bastien," she called. "Are you guys staying at the wellness center?"

"Shit no." Bastien barked out a laugh. "I need internet access, and I like to watch TV."

"I've got nowhere to go tonight. Can I stay with you guys until I make other arrangements? It won't be long."

"Not a problem—come to the Wailea Beach Hotel. Penthouse."

Penthouse. Of course. "Okay," she said. "Thanks.

I'll explain everything once I get there." Selena handed the phone back to the driver. "Thank you."

"Your boss seems like a real asshole."

"I seem to attract them."

Blaine looked up with a grin when the elevator doors opened. But then the smile slid off his face as he recognized Titus and a male chef standing in the hallway.

"Where's Selena?" he asked.

"Selena's contract has been terminated."

"By whom?" Blaine said. "My brother hired her, not you."

"She violated the terms of her contract and has been escorted off property. I'm here to collect her things and mail them to her."

Titus looked at the phone on the table and snatched it up. "What else?"

"Go to hell. I'll bring her things to her. Give that back."

"It's not your responsibility."

"Put it back on the table." Blaine shot to his feet.

"If you put your hands on me, I'll have you arrested."

Blaine pointed to the table and Titus tossed the phone back on it. He straightened his polo shirt and said, "Leif will be your chef for the rest of your stay. He'll follow the menu that Selena had submitted."

"This is bullshit. Where is she?" Blaine asked, clenching his fists.

"She left in a taxi. Too bad you can't call her. I hope it was worth it," Titus said and made the mistake of turning his back on him to leave.

The old Blaine would've tackled him. The old Blaine would have liked nothing better than to wipe that smug smile off his face. Blaine even went as far as to shift his weight and clenched his fist. He was drawing back his hand when he realized that this time, he could get into some serious trouble. Titus would call the cops.

Selena had tried to stop him from resorting back to bad behavior, and even though he failed her terribly, he wouldn't give Titus the satisfaction of having him arrested. He forced his fingers to relax and Titus left with all his teeth. This time.

"How does eggplant parmesan sound tonight, Mr. Stephens?"

"No," Blaine said. "Just go."

"Is there anything I can get for you before I go?"

"Can I use your phone?"

"I'm sorry, sir…"

"It's against the rules," Blaine said, at the same time Leif did. "Yeah, thanks. I know."

Once Leif left, Blaine packed his bags. He wasn't going to stay another minute in this shit show of a wellness center. He made sure he had everything Selena left in the suite. Her knives, her phone, her bakeware and her clothes.

He had been such an idiot. He never should have gone online again. He didn't think that Titus would notice. He got her fired and now she was out there somewhere with no phone. She'd call her phone eventually. And when she did. He would be ready. But first, he had to get out of here, get the block taken off his phone or buy a new one.

He heard the elevator opening and he cracked his knuckles. This time Titus wasn't going to get a second chance if he failed to give him what he wanted. But when he got there, he saw it was Mikelina.

"How is she?" Blaine asked.

"She's upset. She needs her phone, but she's more worried about her knives."

"I have them here. Everything that she kept here is in this bag. I was going to bring them to her. I wouldn't let Titus have them."

"Thank you," Mikelina said. "That will mean a lot to her."

Mikelina had brought bags and packed Selena's things in them, carefully.

"Did she get fired from Five Diamonds?"

Mikelina nodded.

"Damn it. I've got to talk to her. Where is she?"

"She's staying with me and my fiancé for tonight."

"Does she need money? I can help. Please let me help. I'm checking out of here tonight. I can get us a room. Two rooms. She must be so pissed off at me. I'm so damned sorry this happened."

"Selena knew the risks and the consequences of her actions. But thank you again for not letting Titus take them. He's a vindictive prick."

"I'll call her as soon as I get cell service back." He had made a point of putting her number in his phone.

Mikelina bit her lip. "She's really mad at you right now."

"I deserve it, but I can explain."

"I don't need to know." She held up her palm. "I can't stay long, otherwise Titus will be on my case too. Give her a few days to calm down."

"I'm leaving tonight." There was no way that he could stay here for even a few more days knowing that Selena was in trouble. "I should've flown back sooner." He shook his head. "I don't want to leave it like this. I have to see her."

"Fine. I'll tell you what. Go to the lobby at the Wailea Beach Hotel at nine p.m. tonight. If she wants to see you, she'll be there. But if she doesn't, you'll have to accept that."

"Thank you." He sagged in relief. "I'll be there."

"She might not be."

That's what he was afraid of.

CHAPTER NINETEEN

"YOU DON'T HAVE to see him if you don't want to," Mikelina said.

"Yes, I do," she said. "You know I do."

"I have no problem with sending him on his way," Bastien said.

"Thanks." She gave them both a hug. "For everything. But I need to at least say goodbye to him."

"Is it the big goodbye or is it see you later?" Mikelina asked. "Because I think you should at least hear him out."

"I will." Selena had spent the last few hours getting her life back on track. She did laundry, borrowed Bastien's laptop and looked for apartments in Paris that she could afford. She had a few that she was going to visit in a few days, but she probably would have to get a roommate. She was still working out the details.

Her conversation with Kirk Diamonte hadn't been what she expected, though.

"Did you break the rules?" he had asked.

"Yes, but…" was as far as she got.

"Did you provide your client with internet access?"

"I did."

"My hands are tied, then. I can't demand that you finish out your contract there. If you want to cook for him at another of my properties, I can make the arrangements."

She had blinked in surprise. "You're not mad at me?"

"Selena, you've been with me for several years. We're lucky to have you. If you broke the rules, I trust that you had good reasons."

"I'm not fired?"

Kirk had scoffed. "No. I've been hearing rumors that Titus takes advantage of his position in several alarming ways. I'm removing the Maui Wellness Center from our property catalog."

"If it's all the same to you," Selena had said. "I'd like to end the assignment. Do you have anything in the Paris area? I'm headed that way."

"I'll see what I can do," Kirk said. "No matter what happens though, I'll give you a good reference."

At least, she was technically still employed and she had a tentative line at a new gig. It was more than she had expected. She had let Titus get to her and that pissed her off. Nobody got to rent space in her head anymore. Not Anton, not Titus, not Blaine.

At nine that evening she went down to the lobby and almost went right back up when she saw Blaine on his laptop.

"Seriously?" she asked.

He jumped up. "I have a room here. I couldn't stay at the wellness center a moment longer."

"Congratulations on getting the block off your phone," she said dryly.

After closing his laptop, he put it in his bag. "Do you want to go up to my room for some privacy or do you want to get a drink at the bar?"

"Let's start in the bar," she said, not trusting herself to keep from jumping on him as soon as they were alone. She was mad, but they were about to be apart for a long time. Possibly forever, depending on how this conversation was going to go.

They took a table with the ocean view. Tiki torches lined a walkway down to the beach. Blaine ordered a beer and she chose a glass of wine.

"I'm so damn sorry," he said.

"For what?" Selena was curious what he thought his biggest mistake had been.

"For getting you fired."

"I'm not fired."

"But Titus…"

"He can kick me off the property, but my boss is Kirk Diamonte, who your family paid to hire me."

"So technically, you're still my chef?" Blaine got a thoughtful look in his eyes.

She smacked his arm lightly. "You should be sorry for lying to me."

"I didn't lie." He looked affronted.

"You were on the computer as soon as my back was turned."

"My brother called."

"So?"

"He said he found the solution to the car's problem. I wouldn't have been able to sleep until I saw if he was telling the truth or not."

"Was he?"

"So far so good."

"Congratulations," she said.

"I'm worried about you," he said, reaching across the table for her.

She let him hold her hand. "Don't be. I'm going to be fine."

"Come back to Detroit with me for the week."

"And do what? Watch you work? Cook your meals in the company's cafeteria?"

"If you want. Or you can hang out in my apartment. I'm not ready to say goodbye to you."

Selena felt the ice around her heart melting. "Technically, I am still on the job."

"Don't do it for the job. Do it for me."

She sighed. "I'm an idiot, but I guess I'm not ready to say goodbye to you either."

"Titus is such an asshole."

"No arguments from me."

"Are you angry at me?"

"It's a real mess. I was angry at you. But mostly I'm angry at myself. I broke the rules and I didn't want to face the consequences."

"Yeah, but I forced you to break the rules."

"You didn't force me to do anything. It was a trade. I wanted to help you relax, eat healthier and realize that you have a lot more to offer than just being a corporate drone—even if you do own the corporation. And I wanted the money that you were offering for the internet service."

"The moment I saw you, I thought you were smart, gorgeous and someone I wanted to spend a lot more time with."

She shivered when he stroked his fingers over her arm. "I still want to spend time with you."

He closed his eyes in relief. "I thought I blew it."

"You almost did," she said, but she was smiling to take the sting out of her words.

"Will you come to Detroit?"

Selena looked across the bar, not really seeing it. "I was planning on booking a flight to Paris," she hedged.

"What?" Blaine leaned back in his chair. "Why?"

"I decided to start the MBA course. It'll take five months of classes and five months of practical experience. And many more years to pay it off, but that's beside the point."

"I know Chef Dickhead tried to destroy your career and you feel Cordon Bleu is a way to stick it up his ass..." he began, but she interrupted him.

"It's not about Anton anymore, not since I made him dinner. I really want to graduate there and get my MBA in international hospitality and culinary leadership. It's ten months and then I'll start my restaurant. That's my decision. I'm sorry if you don't like it."

"I think that's a waste of time and money."

She leaned forward. "It's not your time or money being wasted."

Rubbing his hand down his face, Blaine looked at her. "That's not what I meant."

"I know what you meant. You have an opinion. I don't agree with it."

"I won't be able to see you until February."

"Probably not," she said. "Does that change things?"

"No. I'm going to be busy too. I wish we had more time together."

So did she. She wasn't going to waste time being angry. She did the crime. She got caught and she accepted the consequences of her actions. It had been worth it. Blaine was worth it.

"Well, let's not waste it." Selena held out her hand. "Let's go up to your room."

Blaine slung his arm around her. "I don't care who sees us."

"No one will care if they do."

"I miss my private elevator," Blaine muttered as they waited for the elevator to come to the lobby.

She rested her head on his shoulder. "I'd understand if you don't want to start anything until after the expo."

"It's already started," he said. "And I'm not ending it."

"So is this an exclusive thing?" she asked.

"Damn right it is."

Finally the doors opened, and they got in. Then it was another eternity before they got to his room. She was shaking by the time he opened the door to his room for her. It wasn't the penthouse, but it had a big bed.

"Are you sure you're up to this?" she asked.

"Sex is a great stress reliever." Blaine cupped her face in his hands. "I think I love you."

Her breath caught, but before she could say anything, he kissed her. Selena lost track of time after that. They stood just inside the doorway kissing. Then, her back was against the door and their clothes were half off. His tongue swept hers in long, slow kisses. Then, Blaine was putting on a condom while she gasped for breath. More kissing and when he slid inside her, she came. Gripping his shoulders, Selena arched against him, needing him closer. She came again while he pounded into her. Still kissing, he dragged her to the bed. After tossing aside the rest of their clothes and the condom, Blaine joined her on the bed.

"Let's take this slower this time," he panted.

There wasn't any time for talking. Just for this. "Please," she said, rubbing up and down the hard length of his body. His fingers dove between them. Selena sprawled on top of him and let him play with her until that crescendo of pleasure built again. Tangling her fingers in his hair, she rode his fingers to another orgasm.

Limp and panting, she let him flip her on her stomach. Blaine put on another condom and pulled her hips up, so she was on her hands and knees. Rubbing himself up and down her pussy, he muttered, "How am I going to go two months without you? Without this?"

"Sexting and FaceTime," she muttered into the pillow, loving the feel of him dragging his hot cock over her sensitive folds.

When he thrust in, she groaned at his desperate pace. Blaine was thick and he was relentless in his deep, hard strokes. Shivering, she clamped down around him. "Yes," she cried out, holding on to the sheets.

Her breathing matched his as he steadily, thoroughly rocked into her with quick, satisfying pumps. The bed shook and she missed the hard rap of the bed frame against the wall as his strokes grew harder and faster.

"Blaine," she whispered as she tumbled over the edge.

He held on to her hips, his fingers digging in. Deep grunts of pleasure left him as he slammed her back into him and came with a jerk and shudder. Collapsing next to her, he gathered her into his arms.

"Looks like you're going to appreciate the internet after all in the upcoming months."

She leaned over and bit his biceps.

The next morning when she woke up, Blaine was on the computer. Selena just shook her head.

"Come back to bed," she drawled, letting the sheet drift down over her breasts.

Blaine immediately left the desk and joined her back in bed. He cupped one of her breasts in his hand and rubbed his thumb over it. "I was letting you sleep."

"We don't have time to sleep." Selena ran her fingers through his hair.

He sucked one of her nipples in his mouth and her eyes half closed in bliss.

"Are you sure I can't convince you to come to Detroit for a week," he said, her nipple held gently between his teeth.

"Convince me," she moaned.

He gave a deep chuckle. "I thought you'd never ask."

Blaine played with her breasts, teasing and sucking on them. He kissed down her body and lifted her thighs on his shoulder. Then he buried his face between her legs and licked her up and down. He speared his tongue through her slick folds, causing her to shudder and moan. He circled deeper until he could tease her clit and when he started sucking on it, she would have promised him anything.

She went to Detroit with him for the week before Christmas.

CHAPTER TWENTY

February

BLAINE STARED DOWN at trade show from far above it, in the corporate box Stephens-Miller rented. He leaned his head against the glass. Had it been worth it? The code was pretty. They had no more malfunctions in the test drive. The camera worked like a charm every time. It cornered like a sports car and it hadn't run over any dogs or little old ladies. Blaine was cautiously optimistic. The Pilot Program was gaining a lot of interest, both domestic and foreign.

And yet here he was in Paris and all he could think about was if Selena could get away and see him. They hadn't seen each other since before Christmas and their daily phone calls had drifted to weekly. He was terrified that he was losing her, and the hell of it was he couldn't blame her. He had been a lousy boyfriend these past months.

"We did it," Mitchell said, slapping him on the back.

"Yeah, we did." But it didn't make him happy.

Not when the cost of this was that he lost Selena. He was such an idiot.

Paul came up alongside them. "It was almost worth getting socked in the jaw."

"Most people get a kick in the ass to get them moving. For you it was a punch in the mouth." Blaine held out his hand. "For what it's worth, I'm sorry I lost my temper. It won't happen again."

Paul shook it. "What's gotten into you?"

"He took those lessons he learned in Hawaii to heart," Mitchell said.

"That and a good therapist did wonders." And the love of a good woman, but he might have lost that. He tried calling Selena one more time, but it went to voice mail. They were finally in the same city and she wasn't answering her phone.

"Why the long face?" his mother said. The whole family was in town for the unveiling and Blaine never felt so alone. "I thought you'd be happy. All your dreams have come true. There she is."

Blaine's heart leaped and he stared where his mother pointed. But she wasn't talking about Selena. She was talking about the car.

"She's a viable alternative to all the other self-driving cars out there. You're going to be famous."

The blissful feeling of success that Blaine had worked so hard for felt anticlimactic. He found that even when he was working on his laptop at home or in the office, his mind drifted back to Selena.

"I don't know who they got to cater our corporate box," Paul said. "But the food is off the chain."

"Oh yeah?" Blaine said, not really interested in it.

"Got the card here," his mother said. "The name of the caterer is Chanterelle."

Blaine's head snapped up and he looked at his mother. He couldn't possibly have heard that right. Chanterelle was the restaurant chain that Selena was planning to open once she got her MBA. "What did you say?"

"Chanterelle, owned by Selena Thompson. She's doing catering part time."

Blaine took the card. "Are you kidding me? Where is she?"

"Probably getting the cake. I've got to find your father. I'll be back." She patted his cheek. "Don't mess this up."

"Did you know about this?" he asked Mitchell.

"Yeah, she contacted us. She gave us a really good deal."

"I still can't get her to run the cafeteria at Stephens-Miller," Paul said. "So this will have to do."

Selena had made just as big of an impression on his family as she did with him in the one short week she had been home with him.

Paul took a big bite out of a hot dog topped with peppers, onions, pickles, and a large squirt of mustard.

"I don't think that's a beef hot dog, Paul."

Paul took another big bite and chewed. "Pork?" He shrugged. "Who cares? It's delicious."

"I say it's probably a tofu dog, if I know the chef."

Paul looked over at the banquet table. "No kidding."

"Have you seen her?" Blaine asked.

"Yeah, she was looking for you when she dropped off the food, but you were on the showroom floor. She said she had to go back for the dessert anyway."

"Why didn't you call me?" Blaine was rethinking his stance on not punching Paul out again.

Mitchell looked down at the hot dog on his plate. "You sure this is tofu? It tastes good. When I hired her to cook for you in Maui, I really hit it out of the park, didn't I?"

"Yes, you're a friggin' rock star."

"It must be love, if she got him to eat tofu."

"She'd better be coming back," Blaine said. "I can't believe you didn't let me know she was here. I haven't seen her in months."

"She hasn't changed," Mitchell said. "And she'll be back."

Blaine helped himself to a hot dog. For the first time in a long time, he felt hungry. After he finished it, he was disappointed that Selena still hadn't come back with the dessert. Had she changed her mind? He opened the door and was about to go downstairs.

He almost ran into her as she was carrying a three-tiered cake. On top of the cake was a miniature version of his car. She looked gorgeous in her sexy chef jacket and with her hair pinned up under her chef's toque.

"Selena," he breathed and leaned in for a kiss.

"Don't let me drop this," she said.

Blaine helped her steady the cake and together they found an empty space on the banquet table for it. Once it was settled, he grabbed her in for a big hug.

"I'm so happy to see you. Why haven't you returned my calls?"

"Smooth," Mitchell coughed into his fist.

Selena raised her chin and stared at him defiantly. "You're not the only one who's busy." She softened her expression. "I knew I'd be seeing you today."

"It's a great surprise."

They stared at each other awkwardly. "Well, congratulations on the car," she said. "It's a big hit. Just from hearing the random conversations on the floor while I was bringing the food up, it's getting a lot of buzz. And this time, for the right reasons."

"Do you want to get out of here?" Blaine said with his hand on her elbow.

"Get out of here? This is what you've been working toward for the past five years. This is the whole reason you were blowing off surfing lessons and hanging around by the ocean in Maui. The whole reason these last few months have been so tough."

"Yeah, I was an idiot. Even more so because I think I hurt you."

"You didn't hurt me," she said, shaking her head.

"Like I said, I've been busy too and the time zones don't make it easy either."

Mitchell came over. "I'm sorry to interrupt, but the exposition chair wants to talk with us."

"You and Paul go without me. I've got something more important to take care of." Blaine shooed his brother away.

"It can wait," Selena said. "You should be with your company and your family right now."

Blaine shook his head. "I did what I had to do. They can take it from here." Blaine turned to his brother and Paul who stood in the doorway. "I mean it, guys. Go talk to the event coordinators and see what they want. Selena and I have a few things we need to discuss."

Mitchell tried to hide a smile, but Blaine saw it anyway. As soon as Mitchell and Paul left, Blaine locked the door behind them.

Selena raised her eyebrow. "I see that look in your eyes," she said. "You can forget it, mister. I'm not having sex with you in a trade show booth."

"It's an owner's box," he said. "No one can come because I just locked the door. And nobody can see in, unless they've got a huge ladder." Blaine took her by the elbow and walked her over to the window to show her the floor below.

"Still not having sex with you."

"What if I want more than sex?"

She crossed her arms over her chest. "I told you,

I'm not going to be your personal chef in Detroit, Michigan."

"How about being my fiancée then?"

Selena's jaw dropped. "Fiancée?"

"I don't even have a ring or anything. I thought I had blown it for good this time."

"You didn't blow it."

"I can have a one-track mind sometimes. I didn't mean to neglect you and our daily calls. It just happened."

"I know," Selena said. "It happened with me too. You were always in my thoughts, but sometimes there weren't enough hours in the day and on the days there were, I just wanted to sleep."

"I can arrange to stay in Paris for a while," he said. "If you think I wouldn't be too much of a distraction?"

"I'd like to be distracted," she said, hugging him. "I wanted to see you so bad, that I brought you guys real hot dogs, real beef hot dogs."

Blaine smirked. "I have the guys convinced they're tofu dogs."

She made a face. "They really don't taste the same."

"Now you tell me."

EPILOGUE

One year later

SELENA WAS GLAD to be back in Maui, lying on the bow of the sparkling new boat her friend Kelli Ann had bought with her rocker boyfriend Tyger Li to do snorkeling tours around the Molokini Crater. Selena had her sunglasses on, and her towel rolled up under her neck.

Blaine was idly drawing patterns up and down her thigh with his fingers. He propped his head up on his hand and smiled down on her.

"Congratulations on your MBA," he said. "I knew you could do it."

"There are a few times that I wasn't so sure." She lifted up to press a soft kiss across his mouth. He could kiss her forever and she would still feel this giddy excitement. And that was just what it was going to be, forever.

"I got us reservations tonight for dinner," he said. "But we don't have to go, if you don't want to."

"As long as I don't have to cook, I don't care where we go."

"I got us the chef table at Bolete Maui."

Selena's eyes went wide, and she almost choked on the laughter that bubbled up. She sat up, crossed her legs and leaned down over him. "Are you serious?"

"I can't believe you didn't even mention that he had opened up a restaurant here."

"That's because I didn't know," she said. "I stopped obsessively stalking him shortly after I met you." She admired the flashing diamond engagement ring on her hand. "I had better things to think about. And I was a little busy this year."

"I made the reservation just to be a smart-ass," he said. "We don't have to go if you don't want to. Or if it will bring up bad memories."

"No, I want to go. Hell, even if I didn't have my master's degree from Cordon Bleu, I'd go," Selena said. "He can't hurt me anymore. I no longer care what he thinks of me. The only people who have to like my cooking are you and my customers."

"Well, you have nothing to fear on my end," he said. "I love your cooking, even when you make me a peanut butter and jelly sandwich."

"That's cream of peanut with a grape-jelly reduction sauce on artisanal brioche bread."

"Do I get turnip chips with it or can I have the real stuff?"

"That depends on how good you are going to be tonight."

"So, I'm not allowed to spit out my food and say that I have tasted better food from a vending machine. Or say that this chicken is so tough, I handed over my wallet, no questions asked?"

Selena thought about it for a moment. "No. If you do that, I'll smother you with potato chips."

"Sounds kinky." He pulled her down for a sweet, long kiss. "I love you. I can't wait until our wedding."

"I love you too. But I am going to miss Paris when we move back to Michigan."

"Actually," he said. "I've been meaning to ask you about that."

"Oh?"

"Stephens-Miller got an offer to develop our cars in France. I'm thinking of taking over the Paris team. That would mean staying there for part of the year. If I take that job, would you stay with me?"

"That's kind of what married people do," she said.

"I just didn't want to make the choice without consulting you first," he said.

"I just have to figure out where to open Chanterelle. But until I do, I think I could get used to living in France for a few months, as long as we could spend a few months in Detroit and maybe a few months in Florida."

"I can arrange that," he said.

"I just don't want you falling back into your bad work habits."

"If I do, I'm sure you'll be able to put me back on the right track."

"Yeah, ukulele lessons until your attitude changes."

Blaine reached into his pack and pulled his ukulele out. He started strumming something that sounded like "Somewhere Over the Rainbow," if you really pretended hard. She let him play for a few minutes and then put her hand over the strings. "You need a lot of stress-relief practice, but I'm willing to help you through that. If you're willing to take the journey."

"Always," he said, and he put the ukulele away in favor of taking her into his arms.

* * * * *

COMING SOON!

We really hope you enjoyed reading this book.
If you're looking for more romance, be sure to
head to the shops when new books are
available on

Thursday 29th October

To see which titles are coming soon, please visit

millsandboon.co.uk/nextmonth

LET'S TALK
Romance

For exclusive extracts, competitions
and special offers, find us online:

f facebook.com/millsandboon

🐦 @MillsandBoon

📷 @MillsandBoonUK

Get in touch on 01413 063232

For all the latest titles coming soon, visit
millsandboon.co.uk/nextmonth

MILLS & BOON

THE HEART OF ROMANCE

A ROMANCE FOR EVERY KIND OF READER

MODERN

Prepare to be swept off your feet by sophisticated, sexy and seductive heroes, in some of the world's most glamourous and romantic locations, where power and passion collide.
8 stories per month.

HISTORICAL

Escape with historical heroes from time gone by. Whether your passion is for wicked Regency Rakes, muscled Vikings or rugged Highlanders, awaken the romance of the past.
6 stories per month.

MEDICAL

Set your pulse racing with dedicated, delectable doctors in the high-pressure world of medicine, where emotions run high and passion, comfort and love are the best medicine.
6 stories per month.

True Love

Celebrate true love with tender stories of heartfelt romance, from the rush of falling in love to the joy a new baby can bring, and a focus on the emotional heart of a relationship.
8 stories per month.

Desire

Indulge in secrets and scandal, intense drama and plenty of sizzling hot action with powerful and passionate heroes who have it all: wealth, status, good looks…everything but the right woman.
6 stories per month.

HEROES

Experience all the excitement of a gripping thriller, with an intense romance at its heart. Resourceful, true-to-life women and strong, fearless men face danger and desire - a killer combination!
8 stories per month.

DARE

Sensual love stories featuring smart, sassy heroines you'd want as a best friend, and compelling intense heroes who are worthy of them.
4 stories per month.

To see which titles are coming soon, please visit

millsandboon.co.uk/nextmonth

JOIN US ON SOCIAL MEDIA!

Stay up to date with our latest releases, author
news and gossip, special offers and discounts, and
all the behind-the-scenes action
from Mills & Boon...

 millsandboon

 millsandboonuk

 millsandboon

It might just be true love...